TRANSFORM THE WORLD

FOURTEEN SCI-FI WRITERS CHANGE THE PLANET

Edited by
J. SCOTT COATSWORTH

Published by
Other Worlds Ink
PO Box 19341, Sacramento, CA 95819

First Edition

Individual stories:

"Immersion" © 2021 by Stephanie N. F. Greene. Originally published in *The New Guard* (Volume IX, 2021)

"Halps' Promise" © 2023 by Holly Schofield. Originally published in *Glass and Garden: Solarpunk Winters* (World Weaver Press, January 2020)

"Voter Fraught" © 2023 by B. Morris Allen

"Good Job, Robin" © 2023 by JoeAnn Hart. Originally published in Slate.com (February 2022). This story will also appear in the author's collection of short fiction, *Highwire Act & Other Tales of Survival* (Black Lawrence Press, September 2023)

"Default" © 2023 by Xauri'EL Zwaan

"Violet" © 2023 by Beth Gaydon

"ReHome Inc" © 2023 by J. Scott Coatsworth

"Sixers" © 2023 by Jaymie Heilman

"Tinker's Well" © 2023 by Stephen B. Pearl

"We Got The Beat" © 2023 by O.E. Tearmann

"The Icky Business of Compromise" © 2023 by Derek Des Anges

"Other Pursuits" © 2023 by Gustavo Bondoni

"Reanimation" © 2023 by Stephen Sottong

"A Profession of Hope" © 2023 by Jana Denardo

Created with Vellum

This book is dedicated to Rachel Carlson, author of Silent Spring, one of the first books to sound the alarm about the havoc we were wreaking on the planet. It's also dedicated to all those who come after us, whose jobs it will be to clean up the mess and become stewards of the Earth.

CONTENTS

ACKNOWLEDGMENTS

I WANTED to acknowledge and thank a number of folks who made this anthology a reality.

Thanks to our screeners: Angel Martinez, Brandon Cracraft, Jaime Lee Moyer, Kelly Haworth, Kim Fielding, L.V. Lloyd, Rory ni Coileain, and KA Masters, without whom just getting through the amazing stack of stories would have probably killed me.

And also thanks to Jaime for editing the stories to make them better and stronger, and to Allison Behrens and Sue Phillips for doing a wonderful job proofing the book.

And to the writers—all 152 of them!—who submitted stories and gave us such a rich and varied selection to choose from.

Finally, my husband Mark, who believes in this whole wacky writing and publishing thing I'm doing. Love you!

FOREWORD

In the 2021 in the middle of a pandemic, our anthology *Fix the World* was released, featuring hopeful stories by twelve sci-fi authors addressing the world's problems. It was a critical and sales success, so we decided to do it all over again in 2022 with *Save the World*, a collection focused on climate change and how we might address it.

Now we're back with book three of the series, *Transform the World*—stories about how a change in society, culture, or government (or sometimes all three) might make the future a better place.

We exactly doubled last year's submissions, with 152 stories dealing with changes to voting, how we live with one another, universal basic income, adaptations to a new climate, and much more.

We have some wonderful returning authors from our earlier anthologies— Holly Schofield, Jana Denaro, Derek Des Anges, Gustavo Bondoni, and myself. And we have nine new authors for you this year too!

These stories are at times serious, sometimes whimsical, often deeply touching, usually innovative, and always (ultimately) hopeful.

A note on spelling: the stories herein use a mix of American and British English. Since this is an international anthology, we thought it was important to retain both, and not to force some authors to conform to the British or American dialect.

So sit back, relax with milk and cookies or a nice glass of wine, and lose yourself in the pages.

Let yourself hope once again. It's a heady drug, and our best tool for shaping a better future.

—J. Scott Coatsworth, Editor

IMMERSION

BY STEPHANIE N. F. GREENE

Today I swam through MOMA. I'd already trained myself to not think about how filthy the water must be, or of sea snakes, both favorite topics of my boyfriend, Leon. Anyway, they say the water inside is filtered. By the time I got to the third floor, I was exhausted, despite the audio-guide retrofitted with a breathing apparatus. Perhaps it was just the excitement of it all coming together at last.

Leon says it was a waste, encasing the art, then flooding the museum—frivolous and elitist. Do the homeless in Queens give a rat's ass about some stunt like flooding MOMA? How many millions did it cost?

I say it was a gesture of optimism. A *Nothing Can Keep New York Down* sort of thing, and for that triumph of technology and political will, priceless. Did folks in Queens get off on the first moon landing? You bet they did.

It was mostly private donations anyway, which also galls Leon—that such big money would show up for the MOMA project. They even reinstalled *Guernica*.

Treading water, I wondered what Picasso would say to his masterpiece becoming an aquarium decoration?

The art can't all be moved to the Poconos. Those of us remaining in the city need art more than ever. But this is a topic I've learned to avoid with Leon, so I argue both sides, back and forth, with myself.

We work in what's left of the city planning office. There's an esprit de corps among us Remainers that we all try to sustain. Leon's actually being pretty gracious about having been outvoted on the MOMA thing.

I stayed for the longest time, studying *Guernica*. The agonized faces. The horror of war. In my darker moments I've wondered if it wouldn't be better to get it over quickly, with fire, instead of this slow drowning.

Then I looked to my side, and there was a giant grouper, equally entranced. I had to smile: I doubt *he* had to pay fifty bucks admission.

There's still a lot to rethink, not even counting underwater commerce. But by God, the docents all wore matching pink wetsuits. What spirit! I love New York. I'll never leave. Well, not alive.

The trick to survival is to remind ourselves that it's not all bad: now certain high rises have saltwater swimming pools. Upping the rent for the privilege, of course. Swimming is standard in kindergarten curricula. You can buy a snorkel at corner kiosks that once sold only periodicals and candy. On high water days, gondolas cruise Houston Street. The fancy knee-high rubber boots fashionable New Yorkers used to sport when there were a few puddles are now standard. Even mid-emergency, we find ways to adorn ourselves, decorating boots with patterned duct tape and waterproof decals.

I REMIND Leon that guns (nearly everyone's!) are jamming with all the moisture. Just the other day, there was a report of a failed bank robbery in which the miscreant's gun wouldn't fire and he was tackled by a couple irate pensioners. Violent crime is down 85%. Knife fighting would be ridiculous underwater, an awkward, comical ballet. I keep trying to tell him something's really changing for the good.

But it's a struggle to stay cheerful when he lives in a stockade of gloomy statistics. I chalk it up to his having New York Socialist parents, who are still in the city; they don't have many victories to savor. I get that. I'd be on edge if my parents were in the city, too.

Sadly, I got off on the wrong foot with his folks when they found out my Dachshund is named Trotsky. In my defense, I had the dog long before I met Leon. But they have me pegged as frivolous. If they are holding out for an old school radical daughter-in-law, I see nothing but disappointment for them.

Anyway, I had to send Trotsky to my parents upstate. It broke my heart, but the water was getting too deep for him. On flood days, it's well over six inches.

Planning departments across the country were instructed years ago to move from remediation to adaptation, but truthfully, no one is able to completely abandon hope that we can return to the old world. It shows up in odd ways. The other day, an elderly woman on the street stopped in front of the old Bergdorf's building at 5th and 58th, water lapping at its base, and burst into tears. She grabbed my arm and recounted being taken there by her grandmother in 2010, to try on dresses for her coming out party. "Where will I take my granddaughters?" she'd sobbed.

I'm making a quiet study of Venice, which, as we all know, has been sinking for centuries—the most beautiful city in the world, perhaps of all time. Evanescent, it turns out. The Venetians seem to take flooding in stride. I have a great photo of two gentlemen splashing though a foot of water impeccably dressed—even the boots are gorgeous—chatting! *La vita continua.*

I do try to be sympathetic to Leon. Early on, he was one of the guys who had a soapbox in Union Square, holding forth about practical ways to get help, what officials to contact. He'd come home cleansed. But now, the traffic's down, so he doesn't go, and I get an earful. *Societal and environmental collapse are imminent. Next will be the pestilence.*

I really don't know what good it does telling me. I still have to get through the day. I still have to get dinner. What would he do if I listened and reacted the way I wanted to? I'd stay in bed. He would have to get his own dinner.

The thing is, I am as afraid of change as anyone. I try to calm myself by remembering that our forebears walked over the Bering Strait, or stowed away on smelly tubs to cross oceans for the new world. What did they know about the future? Nothing. Pipe dreams of streets paved with gold.

A bit of heresy: sometimes science overdoses us on fear to get our attention. We are a fear-soaked society, already. Paralyzed with information.

Paul Eluard once said, "There is another world, but it is *in* this one." I think he is saying that we all have the capacity to live in many other worlds; we are far more adaptable than we realize. To tell the truth, though, I feel pretty maxed out dealing with everything right around me.

Recently I attended a lecture at the Aquarium. It was a kind of rogue TEDx given by a dolphin who said that his ancestors had once been human. I must already be changing, because in the tank, his squeaks and burbles made perfect sense. I didn't even need the simultaneous translation. He had an Australian accent.

He is apparently something of a maverick, because the consensus in the dolphin world is that humans are, as a species, kind of a flop. Clever, but far too fearful and therefore vicious. The idea is to gently glide along letting us face the consequences of our actions. What's one more extinction? Ours might save the world.

The speaker wasn't buying it, though. He described himself as a dolphinarian: the equivalent of a humanitarian, only, of course, much better. He was trying to get us used to losing our opposable thumb. Oh, he's ambitious: though he sees this as a long-term project, he thinks evolution can be greatly accelerated. I got lost in the math. He had us meditate, then we held our breath for one minute.

Afterwards I went up to ask him how long he thought this transition was going to take. He was very nice, but I couldn't quite decide if he was truly sanguine. If you can't *not* smile, is your smile genuine?

Actually I was so overwhelmed by his magnetism, I didn't really absorb his answers. The truth is that he was hot. Talk about confusing. I wanted to jump into the tank with him and run my hands along his sleek, strong flanks, gently gliding along the scar dividing his left side. I read somewhere that dolphins are promiscuous. He looked at me for a long moment.... Finally, I fled. I can barely handle a human relationship; do I really need to add an interspecies affair to the mix?

The next day, a Saturday, when Leon was visiting his parents, I tied my thumbs in for three very frustrating hours, going through my chores, batting at things like a seal. When he came home and discovered me, Leon thought I was just clowning around to amuse him, but I'm just as serious as he is. That's what he doesn't seem to understand.

For instance: the rats. When the subways flooded, up they came in droves. They were topside, blinking as they scurried around half-blind, looking for food. People freaked about murine typhus and the plague. The first response was a citywide program of rat poison. This was gradually second-guessed after a few months as scientists debated the effects of too much Warfarin—an anti-coagulant, after all— getting into the water system.

Unfortunately when I wondered out loud if strokes might become a thing of the past, Leon lost it. *How could I joke about poisoned water?* I countered that scientists should have been consulted about using the drug on that scale. Why was there no debate *before* leaving bowls of D-con in every alley? Or did politicians just decide that public hysteria posed more danger than an epidemic of hemophilia?

When he says I am not serious, it's because he resents my refusal to agonize with him over every step. But frankly, I don't have that much emotional energy. This isn't going to be easy: save your strength.

Secretly? I think Leon is trying to bargain with God, even though he's not a believer. If he bellyaches constantly now, God will decide he's had enough misery and spare him the big stuff. It's like the way we used to do sit-ups in grade school gym. So much drama went into our grunts and grimaces that the teacher let us stop way before we'd reached 50. No wonder we're wimps.

And I don't think it works that way, cosmically.

What is clear, even though it's hard to see on land, is that we are all connected. Poison the rats, and that poison is eventually going to come out of our faucets. Hello!

And they say that majoring in comparative religion is a waste of time; that STEM studies will save the day. Not by themselves, they won't.

Honestly, I already miss candles, even before they disappear. And being absolutely dry. I cannot face becoming totally immersed just yet. What about Bach's *Suites for Solo Cello*? What about being able to sit in a theater on a velveteen seat and have my clapping make noise, not waves? What about fire-places and what—oh God—what about books?

We discuss the future. There aren't enough trouble dolls in the world to take care of all Leon's worries, but mine I can list. And bless his heart, Leon addresses them with small practical solutions written out in his neat hand.

Maybe I'm not so dumped by failure. Isn't failure just part of success? A few years ago I ran workshops instructing people in how to make their own little methane capturing systems using coffee grounds and potassium hydroxide. It isn't that hard; you just heat the mixture up. Fifth grades all over the country were doing it. Of course the potassium hydroxide is very caustic…it's lye, right? There were bound to be mishaps, but it gave people something to do. Perhaps a few children got interested in science, and more importantly, in dealing with the current reality.

I admit, it can be unsettling seeing an alligator roaming down Sixth Avenue, but the female will only chase you until you're out of her territory.

To help people understand, we added New Urban Wildlife workshops after some teens discovered a gator nest in Seward Park and one kid got his leg mauled. Naturally, his parents sued the city, because things like that Just Shouldn't Happen in the Greatest City in the World.

"Who asked alligators to move in?" one old man in the workshop railed.

When could we ever control who came?

We did a series on sea snakes after the initial panic. The Beaked Sea Snake, originally from Florida, is very poisonous, but its fangs are too short to penetrate a wetsuit. Then some conservationists confused that with the Short-Nosed Sea Snake, which is critically endangered, but lives in Australia. Anyway, they started protesting and people called the office hourly with hysterical sightings. For months we were explaining that we weren't exterminators. It was especially disheartening for Leon, who felt we'd somehow failed the public.

I know we are very lucky. Buildings all across the city have rooftop solar panels and so far they are efficient enough to give nine hours of electricity a day. Almost everyone has curtains made of oxygen-producing algae. Both are Leon's doing, getting the grants. He is truly committed to helping people. Even though we have our differences, I'm very proud of him.

I think I depend on his crisis mode as he depends on my optimism. I believe we can thread our way through this. As people always have, throughout history. Which is why, after peeling out of my wetsuit, making a nice dinner and enjoying the last glass of wine I'll drink for the next seven and a half months, I told him about the baby.

He didn't take it well, which made me cry, even though I'd promised myself I wouldn't. He acted like I was leading our child to slaughter by having conceived. I countered that people have always had children in crises.

"When he comes home from third grade and wonders why we can't get food anymore, or looters are roaming the streets, what then?"

I had to admit I don't know. Exhausted, I finally reminded him I hadn't done this intentionally, and certainly hadn't done it alone. He grabbed his dumbbells and shut himself in the study.

～

WEDNESDAY IS BEAUTIFUL AND CRISP. After work, I decide to go back to the Aquarium. I catch the bus and ride over the bridge to Brooklyn, praying the dolphin will still be there.

And he is, swimming in languid circles. I recognize him by his scar. As I approach he goes vertical, scooting back from the edge, then shoots toward me underwater and leaps out, landing in a belly flop in front of me, engulfing me in a wave.

I have to laugh, which feels wonderful, even though I'll be damp for the rest of the evening.

"How are you?" I ask, as I mop my face with my scarf. "Is everything OK here? Are you comfortable?" I was in hospitality before planning. But more than that, I need him to thrive.

"I'm fine. Just thinking some things over."

His look is intense, thrilling and a little jarring with that smile.

"I wanted to see you, to ask you a few questions." I falter. At home I might have once gone to my pastor, but here I am confiding in a dolphin.

"Everything's changing," I begin, before my voice cracks. "And I'm pregnant."

"Good. I thought so."

"Really? *Good?* How did you know?" I start crying in earnest. Finally I compose myself and continue. "We're all so afraid of the future. I feel like a criminal bringing a baby into the world."

"Fear is your original sin. Work that out and you'll be fine. And all mammals glow when they're pregnant. You forget, our genomes are nearly identical."

I stare at him. My head is spinning. I've never gotten with the Adam and Eve narrative. Even as a child, it seemed absurd that the whole problem of exile from the garden—along with the burden of good and evil—would be pinned on Eve. By the way, in Islam, Adam and Eve are held equally responsible for The Fall. But never mind.

"What do you know?" I repeat, realizing instantly how rude it sounds. "I mean…" I close my eyes against a wave of nausea. "Can you tell the future? Are we going to be all right?"

"When you lose your thumbs, it'll be much simpler." With that he tips back and speeds away.

Leon and I have to make up. We have to do a site visit in Jackson Heights.

I've always loved that neighborhood. What do they say? It's a trip to south Asia without the visa?

We are working on green space transformation. There was very little public green space in JH back when it was built in the early 20th century. Then later, there was a scramble to transform vacant lots into little parks. But how times change: now they are growing rice and water lilies, not geraniums and corn.

Leon and I enjoy working here. Is it terrible to say we always have fun? Well, we do: having tea with people, laughing over samosas, sketching ideas on napkins and watching their faces light up with possibility. We welcome them into the planning process. Now Leon is so stressed, he can't even welcome his own child.

Anyway, I was hoping we could get back some of the old collaborative spirit, the dreaming out loud. So as we walk down Roosevelt Avenue, I am going on about Green Wave, the vertical gardens cultivated in the ocean. They're catching on.

I am explaining to Leon's back as we hop over the deeper puddles on our way to the site. "Kelp grows vertically, and you grow mussels in these long socks beside them with scallops in these sort of hatboxes suspended one above the other…"

He grunts.

"Leon, it's so cool. Oysters on the bottom! It takes up very little space and is hurricane proof. We should make all agriculture aquatic!"

He stops suddenly, whirling on me so that I ram into him as I try to avoid a puddle. "Really. How is it hurricane-proof, Polly? How exactly does that work?"

"Well, I don't know all the details…."

He is panting.

"How am I going to tell my parents that you are pregnant? Have you thought of that at all?"

"I'll tell them."

"That's not the point! This will kill them! They worry enough about us."

"But we're fine! Worrying is a choice, too, Leon," I cry. "You were an all-star defensive lineman at Colgate! My God! In the service, you were in and out of Afghanistan negotiating access to their lithium and niobium! Why are you suddenly paralyzed by your parents' fears?" People are hurrying past us with furtive glances. I push ahead of him and continue walking.

Leon comes up close behind me and addresses me quietly, his voice shaking with anger.

"You never think of anyone else. You just traipse along and let the chips fall where they may."

"And you don't?" I whip around. "Granted, you do a lot of hand wringing, but you basically do what you want, when you want."

I am referring to Gretchen Goldberg, classical clarinetist, his ex, whom he dumped unceremoniously for me. Afterwards he spent six months agonizing over *whether* he'd hurt her feelings. I pick up my pace.

I fall in behind a group of Indian women, holding the hems of their saris high so they won't get wet. It makes me wonder how they dealt with monsoons at home, or if home is actually India at all.

I used to go through the fabric stores on Roosevelt Avenue marveling at the sari material with the beautiful hem designs. I envied the women who got to wear these clothes as I envy the women in whirling silk before me. My eyes flood with tears I don't begin to understand. All I can think is, *I want to go home.*

I wipe my eyes roughly with the back of my hand and hurry on. Leon is still talking.

"People can only take so much change—you embrace it like it's some kind of game, but the rest of us can't do that. Don't you see?"

My laughter sounds like the caw of a crow. The dolphin understands me better than the father of my child. I stop and bury my face in my hands.

Leon stops. He wraps me in an embrace right there on the darkening November street, the crowds moving 'round us like schools of bright fish as I try to pull myself together. But it feels so good to lean into his strength, I want to stay there forever.

The site visit goes beautifully. The neighborhood leaders study the damp maps, making notes in blue pencil, discussing the changes in Urdu and Tamil. Their courage is so moving, I have to choke back tears. They are instinctively kind and solicitous, as if they have understood our situation with one glance. It's probably because I look like a half-drowned ferret.

I compose myself, feeling absurd that they are drying *my* scarf on the radiator and bringing *me* tea, when I am supposed to be the one helping, encouraging, boosting. Normally, I would be showing people how to remediate mold naturally (borax, vinegar), or extolling the best tide pools in Central Park.

We are silent on the bus ride home. I fall asleep, leaning against the window with my mouth open, only waking when Leon nudges me at our stop.

Inside, I go right to bed and sleep eleven hours.

In my dream, I see my baby girl swimming, cavorting inside me, having the time of her life. Laughing, if you can do that underwater. She can! That part's clear.

When I peer at her closely, I see she is in an aquarium tank. She somersaults through the seaweed, kicking off its side. I am spellbound by her beauty: butterscotch colored and bald.

She goes from embryonic to having a flipper. She comes to the glass to stare at me. Her eyes are the deepest blue. I place my hand on the glass, longing to touch her. When she puts her tiny hand up to match mine, I see that her fingers are webbed. I cry out, because I want her to be like me, and she is growing into someone—something—else. Her look is one of the purest love.

I realize I don't see an umbilical cord. How is she breathing? She seems so full of joy, not in any kind of distress. And then I see them: gills.

When I jolt awake, the sweat is dripping off me, and the dream's implications begin to sink in. Will she be some sort of freak? Absurdly, I think of schoolyard cruelties, and then, panicking, that she might be kept in a zoo.

The next morning we are on our way to visit Leon's parents. Around Columbus Circle, I feel myself bracing for the meeting, shrinking into my seat as the M7 bus barrels uptown.

My in-laws live in a Harlem brownstone. It's pretty swank actually. Leon's parents always take lofty umbrage when I say I like it. They announce that *they* were there before gentrification. I don't remind them they are part of gentrification, even though they refuse to have window boxes. They go on to stress that they rent to minorities, at fair prices. They did, that is, until the Williams family moved out and bought a house in Schenectady. A gorgeous Craftsman; I visited them when I went upstate to see my folks. They have window boxes full of fuchsia geraniums.

We sit around the coffee table, spread with crackers, cheese, ginger ale, seltzer, red grapes, and salted nuts. The smells make me ill. I feel a desperate thirst, go into the kitchen and drink two glasses of water, helping myself at the tap.

Give the city credit: New York's tap water is still great. I gulp it down, thinking there is nothing so delicious as cold water, and wishing I could just stay in the kitchen holding the icy glass against my clammy forehead. When I return to the living room, Leon is clearing his throat.

"We have something to tell you," he croaks.

I can't bear the idea that he will begin by apologizing, so I blurt, "I'm pregnant. You are going to be grandparents."

This is greeted by stunned silence.

"Don't you use protection?" Abe asks.

"It failed," I answer before Leon can speak.

"How could it fail?" Abe wonders.

He is a chemist and should know better; I cannot control my tone: "Ninety-nine percent effective leaves one percent failure. One in a hundred," I point out, trying not to glare at him. I don't add that research on better birth control has taken a back seat to developing water-skimming scooters.

"What are you going to do?" Naomi is all business.

I sigh, realizing that today, no one else will welcome this child.

"This baby is a miracle bigger than any of us."

No one speaks. On a better day I would marvel at their stubbornness. But today, I am exasperated. I press on.

"Do you realize how few men can even have children? Worldwide, sperm counts have plummeted for the last 50 years. You should see the slides. The sperm just lie there. It's so pathetic."

"Don't talk that way in front of Leon's mother."

I'm surprised by this. Abe used to ask the lifeguards at the Y about the sperm counts in the pool. It was his standard joke and always got a laugh. I look at Naomi, whose jaw is set.

"How you could think to bring an innocent child into this chaos, this destruction, is beyond me."

"It's not as if I did this alone, Naomi, just to upset you." It is the first time I talk back to her, or call her by her given name. Both long overdue.

"Don't you think I'm afraid? I work in city planning. I know what's happening."

"Do you? I think you live in a fairy tale, from what Leon tells us…."

I swivel and fix Leon with a look. He finds something absorbing about his size 13 sneakers.

"Have you thought this through, dear?" Abe continues. "It will be bad enough for us, worse for you. But I can't think..." his voice breaks. "I can't bear to think what it will be for the next generation."

His emotion is contagious. I pick it up like a kindergartener picks up a sniffle, and then I must beat it back.

"Can you try to imagine something good?"

"How can I? It's just getting worse." He shakes his head.

"It's getting both better and worse! Isn't it? I mean what we see around us, yes, there are tons of problems, but people are coming up with ingenious solutions all the time.

"I mean, think of the success of Mexico City, once one of the most polluted cities on the planet, it is now the greenest, thanks to NASA's Megacities Carbon Project. In the past 50 years, they have planted fifteen million trees. Xochimilco is a global model of farming innovation." I am breathless, and Abe takes advantage of the break.

"What kind of life do you envision for this child- a servant to the billionaire class, begging for survival by making himself useful as a shoeshine boy? "

I feel sorry for him, but can't let up.

"So only billionaires can have children? Is that it? Everyone else just folds up and dies?"

"You want your child to be a servant?"

"Who knows what she'll be?" I think of the dream and can't help smiling.

"She!"

"The question is not what is here, but what can we imagine? What we have in front of us is old news, like starlight from stars that have long since died. We have to think beyond what is already here. Doom is a luxury we cannot afford."

"Little Miss Schiksa Sunshine. Such pretty pastel pictures," Naomi says with a dry laugh. "I can't believe it. I thought Leon would outgrow you, but you've got him now."

Abe lays a steadying hand on his wife's knee, but she shakes it off, tapping her heel in fury.

I want to slap them both. "Don't you see that we can't go back? It's not like we can point a finger at the culprits, try and convict them and the old order will just be restored!"

I turn to Naomi. "And no, Naomi, I don't *have* him. He can do what he wants." I regard Leon, whose cheeks are bright red orbs. "He may not stay with me, but I can handle whatever he decides. I'll…we'll be fine."

I gather up my coat, put on my scarf and boots, both still damp, and not waiting for Leon, leave, shutting the door quietly.

I slop my way to the bus stop, arguments and to-do lists swirling through my head. Then I imagine my little girl swimming around, cavorting, joyful — and let it all go. Blissful silence! Soon all these opinions will be nothing more than bubbles.

There's usually a silver lining, my mother always says. You just have to look for it.

I breathe in slowly through my nose and suddenly feel a warm, dry hand slipped into mine. Even his calluses are comforting. I exhale.

The bus groans to a stop. Together, Leon and I climb on. As we have hundreds of times before, we dip our fare cards in the reader and find a seat.

Maybe we can name her Nadia.

Stephanie Greene's short fiction has been published in Nostoc Magazine, Green Mountains Review, Sky Island Journal, The New Guard, Flash Fiction Magazine and The Writing Disorder. Her work has been long-listed for the Lascaux Prize for Short Fiction, nominated for inclusion in the Best of the Net Anthology and for a Pushcart Prize. As an organizer of the Brattleboro Literary Festival for the past decade, she has a blast championing new fiction at the LitFest every October. She is revising her second novel, A Perm For Mrs. Medusa, and lives on the family farm in Vermont with her husband, writer and artist Marshall Brooks.

Website: https://www.snfgreene.com
Brattleboro Literary Festival: https://www.Brattleborolitfest.org

HALPS' PROMISE

BY HOLLY SCHOFIELD

My name is Michaela Gonzalo-Halpenny. Everyone calls me "Halps." Except for Lena, of course. I'm writing this sitting in my favorite overstuffed chair in the lounge of the scruffy old Banff Springs Hotel, in the middle of the Rockies.

Lena said to put everything in about what happened so I'm starting with the basics. We're an intentional community that formed after the official start of the Climate Breakdown sixteen years ago. I'm one of the new generation—we incomers moved here when I was orphaned at five. For the past ten years, I've been raised by wolves and Sasquatch. Yeah, I'm totally fooling—I know people in big cities think our intentional community is weird but, trust me, it's not *that* weird.

My skill with a soldering iron and a multimeter had got me a spot on Lena's repair party even though she'd given me the evil eye while the three of us packed up. I did everything I was told, for once—not even arguing when Angie packed some of her nasty dried porcupine meat in the sled (like being two years older than me makes her smarter or something). Since the gunpowder incident, I'd promised to be more community-minded.

One thing about me: I always keep my promises. Lena's yelled at me before, mostly because of monopolizing a Gabfest—oops, I mean a Morning Session. But I figure if I just explain enough stuff, I can prevent our debates running over into several sessions.

I don't want arguments.

I just want people to agree with me.

And, hey, it took a whole two hours before *this* argument started. Probably a record for me. Two hours of us trudging along the TransCanada toward the hydroelectric station, snowshoes sticking in the snow at each step, surrounded by forests of pine, spruce, and fir. Lena trudged after Angie, who was breaking trail, and I came last, pulling the sled, fitting my snowshoes into their depressions as best I could.

We had a tricky problem ahead of us. We use a Pelton wheel—a type of waterwheel—to produce the electricity we need to light our crops. If the wheel stops turning, the veggies will die pretty quickly. So when the runoff from Lake Minnewanka that powers the wheel decreased a week ago, we knew we had trouble. It's never happened before, but the penstock—the enclosed sluice pipe below the surge tank—had jammed with ice, the flow of water had dropped a whole lot, and the Pelton wheel had slowed. The kilowatt-hours were a fraction of what we needed. Hence our little journey at exactly the wrong time of year.

In the summer, this would have been a simple morning's hike along the cracked asphalt, but, in late April, the snowpack was several meters deep and the faint trail just a hardened track fading to nothing in the distance. Warmer temperatures in February, increased snowfall in March: climate change had completely disrupted the weather patterns and, more importantly, the *predictability* of weather patterns. I'd never known the weather to be consistent in my lifetime so the recent cold snap didn't weird me out the way it did for ol' Lena.

Anyhow, I'd only shouted something ahead about how our pace was inefficient but that was enough to set Lena off.

"You think if you rush ahead, you could have made it to the generating station and back again by now, that it?" Lena twisted toward me, the wind snatching at her words. After several hours of trekking, the wind had turned her cheeks a rosy brown. Or else she was pissed off at me already.

"Well, actually—"

"Think of this trip as a teaching moment." Lena's nose jutted at me over the lumpy scarf she had wrapped around her red parka hood. I'd carded bighorn sheep wool, then spun and knitted the scarf last year as part of a mandatory handicraft class, laboriously and resentfully. Science was more my gig. Even with the rime of ice from her breath coating the wool, I could see where I'd dropped a stitch or two.

"Teaching? For you or for me?" I muttered into my own scarf. The whole trip was a case of too little, too late. We depended on the hydroelectric for the lighting in the greenhouses and we should have made this journey last week when this frigid weather had started.

Everyone had fled this high valley a decade ago after the tremendous avalanche that made the hot springs inaccessible but, thanks to Gaia (and, more specifically, to Lake Minnewanka), we'd made things work so far, until this cold snap. Kale, gai lan, cabbages, chick peas, soy beans, radishes, even beets and carrots were all tucked in the many greenhouses our little community had constructed on the golf course next to the Banff Springs Hotel over the past ten years.

Heat isn't as much an issue as you'd think—with plenty of wood, we just fire up the wood stoves that flank the walls. Light, actual sunlight, that's the problem. With an average of only three hours a day of sunshine in the winter now that cloud cover is the norm, and a scant two-month growing season outdoors in the summer, we need electricity to run the greenhouse LEDs or else the crops stagnate and mold.

The reduced flow of water to the Pelton wheel in the old repurposed generating station was the big problem right now, but, like most things to do with climate change, there were longer-term issues too. I craned my head back toward Lena. "What if the pipe above the surge tank freezes? Fixing that will be almost impossible."

"One problem at a time." Lena's sigh made a long white cloud of breath.

Ahead of her, Angie twisted back and gleefully chimed in, "That was, naturally, discussed in the second hour of the Morning Session six days ago." Then she stuck out her tongue at me, timing it when Lena was adjusting her mittens and didn't see.

I tried not to scowl at her. I really did. But it was hard. Her heart-shaped face and her mink-dark hair are so much prettier than my round head and curly brown mop; even her stride on snowshoes is graceful and efficient. Her only flaw is the gap in her front teeth. I really appreciate that gap. It gives me hope that there's another defect in her somewhere, and it will come to light eventually.

I eased the straps of the harness where it chafed. We were only halfway to the generating station, three more kilometers to go.

Time to speed up.

I increased my pace and the sled slewed behind me, collecting even more chunks of snow from the trail edges onto the tarped-down heap of food and tools. I nearly trod on Lena's heels, and she gave a warning huff. She keeps all of us in line, both in the community and during the daily Gabfests. Sometimes, I thought if it weren't for her, our little commune would have exploded into survivalist infighting and thefts and destruction, just like Calgary had.

Lena turned to face me, glaring. "My turn for the sled," she said, a statement, not a question.

I shook my head.

She halted, forcing me to stop, and held up a hand, wincing as she straightened her fingers. Both Angie and I were stronger and more capable of pulling the sled than her but I couldn't deny her the joy of contribution (we're big on that). But I did feel bad for her. If the grid hadn't failed and the economy hadn't collapsed, she'd have been driving a car to the mall now. Or having coffee with friends, retired by sixty, not trudging along a mountain road in winter.

I took off the harness and helped settle it on her thin shoulders. "Arthritis must suck—"

"It's not arthritis. It's because of the chicken coop." She kept her voice flat. I'd macgyvered the always-stubborn chicken coop door a few days ago, using counter-weights, saving all of us the effort of jiggling it while holding a basket of eggs.

It had worked just fine until it had closed on Lena's thumb.

And refused to open.

Good thing we're a non-judgmental sort of people.

THE HIGHWAY KEPT level for the most part. In the ditch, a fresh-cut row of stumps lined up like miniature pillars. Someone had cut down the long-dead young spruce that had tried and failed to get a foothold. Probably Randy on his scouting mission last week to see why the water flow had decreased so drastically. I had stood up at Gabfest and asked to go with him, making a reasoned plea just like an adult. Angie's smirk, when I'd been asked to sit down, just about reached both her ears.

Randy had probably used the spruce to build a campfire to discourage the cougars who were now back in pleasing numbers. Or just to stay warm. This winter had had some of the coldest colds and warmest warms we'd seen. Each year seemed to break new records.

I could sympathize with Randy. Frostbite wasn't fun, I'd lost an earlobe to it last June. See, the bitter-sweet petals of purple saxifrage are nutritious and delicious, both. So I went on what Lena calls a "reckless" journey to see if the flowers were blooming early in Sunshine Meadows. They weren't. I hadn't run it by the Gabfest first but I still thought I'd been right to go—because what if they were? I took off my mitten and rubbed my nose. A campfire would be nice about now; the woodsmoke and crackle would seem just as warming as the BTUs themselves.

"A campfire! Hey! Lena!" I stepped off trail, near a trail of elk tracks, and let Lena catch up.

"What? Where?" Her nose was dripping and probably as numb as mine. And she wasn't sparing breath for talking, that was clear. If they'd just sent me alone, the sled could have carried just food for one, not three, and been a lot lighter.

"What if we build a fire under the penstock instead?" The water pipe had frozen solid, and the slow, safe, much-analyzed plan to melt it with electric blankets would take days. Once we got to the station, we'd have to divert the remaining trickle of electricity from the greenhouses to the batteries for the blankets too, another downside. And, only one person could stand on the narrow ledge that ran beside the surge tank's base at any one time, the drop-off on the other side was too steep.

My shoulders ached just thinking about hauling batteries back and forth the two hundred meters from the generating station a dozen times. Even after we'd released a stronger flow of water and could start to charge multiple batteries at once, it'd still be grunt work of the worst kind. But a tall haystack of thin logs could direct a flame upwards and melt it in a fraction of the time. No reason not.

"Too hard to control," Lena panted, not slowing, coming right at me. I trotted backwards, which isn't easy in snowshoes, even my trusty old aluminum oval ones, believe me.

Up ahead, Angie had stopped to let us catch up. Hands on her knees, perfectly-knitted scarf dangling, she was panting, white puffs against the darker pines that surrounded us. Oh, right: I was supposed to have spelled her off breaking trail ten minutes ago. Too bad I'd had more important things on my mind.

I tried to catch Lena's eye but her toque was pulled too low. "If we see whether the pipe is cracked or not, we can get started on repairs earlier!" We can't manufacture large metal pieces yet, although we can bend sheet metal for ducting and so on, so I could see that part of the repair process taking frustratingly long.

Maybe we could get some piping from the traders that came through in the summertime on their way west. They'd rattle into town driving rusty old hybrids hauling trailers filled with junk. We'd reluctantly deal with them, buying the occasional solar panel in exchange for some of our handicrafts, even though they were in that gray area of enviro-ethics that Lena always harped about. From what they said, Calgary seemed awful and dangerous but its trashed suburbs held all kinds of fun stuff. "I could even go to Calgary to get a new culvert!"

Lena rolled her eyes but I bounced up and down on my heels anyway. Finally, a way I could help!

"What's the holdup?" Something prodded my back and I almost fell over. "Sunset is at 5:37 today. We need to hustle." Angie's voice was loud in my ear.

I twisted around and grabbed at her extended finger but she snatched it away. "Of course it is. And, of course, we do." I turned to Lena. "Let me go on ahead and light a fire. You'll catch up by dinner time. Please."

I knew from her slight chin tilt to the left what the answer would be. My uncharacteristic "please" hadn't made a difference. She scowled beneath her scarf. "That wasn't the plan. And we haven't discussed it at Morning Session."

Yup, that's us Banff folks. We start our day by Gabfesting about every single thing. And I do mean Every. Single. Thing. All the unnecessary talk-talk-talk is holding us back. None of the people in Calgary, or Vancouver, or New York, or anywhere for that matter, waste a third of their day doing it. At least, I don't *think* they do, do they?

I kept trying. "Sometimes, people just need to experiment and see—

"And what do you think *caused* the Breakdown." Lena waved a mittened fist in my face.

I could feel Angie's smirk through my back before she spoke. "Does Halps have some goofy alternate plan?" She'd been extra-smug since Lena and Randy had been meeting with her privately several times over the past month. I'd caught them whispering in the woodshed once and they'd all looked guilty when they'd seen me.

"Cut some branches and make a fire below the pipe," I explained to Angie, still facing Lena. "Loosen it quicker." I gestured at the ax handle where it jutted from under the sled tarp.

"A bow saw would work better to get kindling." Now I could feel the superior toss of her head. "*If* that was the plan. Which it isn't."

"Enough talking, you two. We stick together. We'll camp in the generating station tonight and thaw the pipe using the blankets tomorrow." Lena wrenched the sled forward and I almost tripped trying to get out of her way.

As we forged onward, I kept silent, or at least I kept my mumbling to a minimum. I *am* learning to repress my impulses, honest.

FINALLY, just as it began to snow harder, the surge tank became visible against Mount Girouard and the dense spruce lining the highway gave way to the three-story generating station. The cobblestone façade of the concrete building was punctuated by ancient plywood nailed over the tall vertical rectangles that had been windows. I sped up as we neared the parking lot, wanting to beat Angie to the door. My snowshoe caught on the twisted link ends of the wire fence where they were barely exposed above the snowpack. I stumbled and caught myself, pretending I was just loosening a strap, and ignored Angie's snort.

I pictured the cracked pavement below the two meters of snow, now the home of ants and beetles rather than the cars and trucks of maintenance workers. A short ways away, at the trail head, another parking lot had served the needs of recreational hikers decades ago. Imagine that: hiking for pleasure, rather than for forage or for meat. It boggles the mind, how people used to live.

We all paused in the windswept area in front of the door and looked up the bank through the falling flakes at the slate gray surge tank two hundred meters above us. "Strange, isn't it?" Lena leaned on her pole. "To think that this station was the culmination of so much effort for so little net benefit overall."

I nodded. I'd been fascinated by this whole area since I was a little kid. Far above us, Lake Minnewanka lay tucked back in the Rockies like a giant's footprint. Nakoda peoples had frequented it until it was folded into the national park last century. They'd considered it something that, badly translated, meant "Spirit Lake" and, when I'd stood on the banks last summer looking at the deep turquoise waters, I was sure I'd felt a certain something—until I spotted the rusting dumpsters still surrounded by rotting plastic bags and my sense of connection shattered.

The Nakoda were forced to relocate and cease their sustainable hunting practices, so that wealthy Calgarians could make the park into their personal playground. Then the lake area morphed into an environmental reserve until defaunation in the mid twenty-first century made it a pointless exercise. The lake was one of our community's long-term projects—restock it with trout, whitefish, even pike now that the summers were warmer. And dredge up the resources it held—a whole town had been drowned when it was dammed. Old cars, building materials, and machinery had lain sunken for decades, waiting patiently in the pale turquoise depths. I drooled just thinking about it even as I cringed at the initial waste. How could they have done all that with any kind of conscience? Pre-breakdown people had been *weird*.

In the first Depression, the one in the early 1900s, water from the lake had been laboriously diverted into a five-kilometer-long canal, ending in the water tower that was the metal surge tank. It served to modulate the water pressure so that surges due to seasonal changes wouldn't enter the station and destroy the equipment. We'd repurposed the station about five years ago, bypassing the broken mega-sized turbines and installing a very simple, very small Pelton wheel.

It wasn't that we didn't want to fix the whole system but that we *couldn't*. We just didn't have the technology. And that had actually pleased Lena, and it had taken me a while to figure out why: one of our community's guiding principles is to always use the minimal tech needed so there's minimal environmental effect. And, really, we got along just fine without all those megawatts. Power is fun but, duh, no way is huge amounts of it essential to a healthy society.

Now, on this overcast day with only remnants of sun visible behind

Sundance Peak, it was dim and gloomy inside, the cinderblock walls so different from the familiar oak-paneled chalets back in Banff.

The old office space was the least damp and I quickly laid my sleeping bag between a rusty file cabinet and a metal desk marked "Manager". Angie got stuck next to a smaller desk that was labeled "Assistant Manager" and covered with dried porcupine poop. I smirked at her but she didn't appear to notice. Lena laid hers in between us mumbling about how cold the room felt compared to summertime. This winter, she never seemed to be warm enough.

I stuck my head in the main room. Last summer, when I'd come on a reconnaissance work party, I'd been surprised by the size of the broken old turbines that filled most of the room. The Pelton wheel, hefty but no bigger than a bicycle rim, spun proudly near the wall, jubilantly receiving the crapload of water that shot downward from the penstock nozzle. Just one wheel can produce an amazing amount of energy, limited only by water volume. The impulse energy of the water jet exerts torque, see, and then the water jet does a U-turn and exits as it decelerates. Fascinating stuff! I'd danced a little jig across the concrete floor when I'd first seen it, much to Randy and Lena's amusement.

Now, water dribbled forlornly from the cone-shaped nozzle and the wheel turned at a speed that made its impulse blades—the cup-like scoops that ringed it—flicker like an ancient movie reel: pathetically slow, in other words. "Sad, sad, sad," I said out loud and my voice echoed in the big damp room.

Not waiting for Lena's instructions, I diverted a little bit of the scant power from the main cable that led underground along the highway to the greenhouses back in Banff and plugged in the blanket batteries in preparation for tomorrow. Tomorrow, we'd unpack the food and other supplies—enough for Angie for a week. After we'd freed the ice blockage, the plan was that she'd stay and tediously repack the Pelton wheel bearings with new grease, a maintenance job we usually did in the summer. A long debate at Gabfest had established that doing it now was a better use of person hours since we were already here. My math had showed it was iffy but when did they ever listen to me?

Lena stuck her head in the door and nodded at my preparations. Then we lit a kerosene lamp and huddled in our bags for a while. Angie read a grimy old electronics manual, Lena reviewed some Gabfest notes, and I doodled on a scrap of phone book paper.

Angie looked up once. "Lena, tomorrow morning, before we start, we should turn on an outside light switch."

I set down my book. "Why—"

"So that the bulb will automatically come on when the voltage grows high enough," she said, giving me a haughty moue.

"Good idea, Angie," Lena squinted at her. "We'll be able to see it glow from up beside the surge tank."

"And then we'll know the blockage has thawed out enough to turn the wheel, yeah, yeah, yeah." I picked up my pencil again pretending it was the most fascinating thing I'd ever seen.

After a while, Lena and Angie cocooned in their sleeping bags, only the pompoms of their toques showing. I lay in my bag, listening to the drip of the water in the main room, dark thoughts crowding in.

The community didn't appreciate me, Calgary was a quagmire of thieves and rusting cars, and Seattle or Halifax or far-off places like that were impossible to get to. And, as far as I knew, none of those places could possibly be as awesome as our community—I mean, their condition these days were the direct result of climate change stupidities, right? That was why we had cannibalized all the radios for parts when I was a baby. No need to talk to anyone outside Banff. Because nowhere was better than Banff.

Well, for most of us, anyway.

I was still trying to find a way to fit in.

I tossed and turned, despite my best intentions to sleep like a hibernating bear. Melting all that ice tomorrow with the blankets would be a total pain.

I woke up about an hour later and listened to Lena's gentle snore and Angie's even breathing for a while. The snowfall would make it harder to snowshoe tomorrow and we'd have to make many dreary trips up and down from the surge tank to check the current on the blankets.

I sat up.

Tomorrow didn't have to be tedious.

Not if I got there first.

～

In my whole entire life, no one ever appreciated my ideas. Like when I'd trained crows to pick the cabbage worms in a greenhouse last year. The birds would drop the bugs in a can of vinegar in exchange for soup-tired chicken bones. It would have worked, too, if Angie hadn't left her dish of chicken curry on the work table in the lab alcove. The crows had destroyed a bunch of cuttings and some seed stock that was irreplaceable. Lena had yelled at me until her voice was so hoarse she'd had to stop. Then I'd scrubbed bird droppings off lab equipment for hours. Not as punishment, mind you. Our community didn't believe in it. Just because the equipment needed cleaning for the good of everyone.

Or when I'd fermented urine from the communal collection tank to get ammonia and then distilled it through wood ash down to potassium nitrate. That, plus sulfur scraped from stagnant pools below the hot springs and charcoal from the fireplace hearth, had given me what I needed to make gunpowder. Lena's face, when she'd snatched the mortar and pestle from my hands, still caused me nightmares a year later.

She'd made me promise to follow due process and get approval for everything I did. Since then, I'd kept my experiments to a minimum. Let Angie fool around with radio parts and wood-alcohol engines, let her get all the appreciation for everything. What did I care?

A lot. Yeah, the answer to that question is *a lot*.

Now, the cold snap, the reduced lake flow, the ice blockage, the slowing of the Pelton wheel—all of it was a turning point for the community, so, duh, I wanted to help. Basically, I'd *promised* to help, hadn't I? And Lena would have approved it if I'd explained it better: how I'd make a really small fire and watch it carefully. I *knew* she would have. But, looking at her lined face relaxed in an exhausted sleep, I couldn't bring myself to ask her again.

I crept across the floor, boots in hand, and eased my way through the inner door. At the outer door, I slid the bow saw off the sled. The tarp rustled but Lena and Angie didn't stir. I could feel a hero-vibe thrumming through me.

I opened the outer door, my breath frosting in front of me, careful not to clatter my snowshoes together. The moon was full and the snow had stopped. Everything sparkled in the cold.

Not being an impulsive person, before I headed uphill, I stopped and reviewed the situation. I was keeping my promise. I was endangering only myself. I had everything I needed to clear the ice jam by morning. I'd even remembered to turn on the outside light switch and to bring my flint and steel.

Yup. The plan was foolproof.

A SNOWY OWL, at the edge of its range, hooted as I padded across the parking lot. I followed the flat expanse of white that was the former park's road and set out for the hiking trail head up at the surge tank. If Lena couldn't guess where I'd gone, she could follow my tracks.

The tank legs rose into the darkness, disappearing above me into the darker bulk of the tank. The penstock was a repurposed culvert, about 30 centimeters in diameter, bolted to a bracket on the surge tank just above my head. The helical corrugations reflected the moonlight in a cool mathematical sort of way.

Once up there, I collected branches and sawed with the bow saw until my arms felt noodly. I used my favorite knife, the one I'd blacksmithed when I was eight, to scrape some inner cedar bark into a fine fluff then lit it with many flicks of the flint and steel. Just as my headlamp began to dim, the spark caught and flames rose, pale but cheering in the pre-dawn light. I fed in twigs slowly, making myself comfortable on the ledge, keeping a safe distance from the fire in case it all let go down the bank. Finally, the larger branches took hold and the flames began to make wavering shadows on the penstock's twisting ridges. I added a few larger logs and sat back on my heels.

By 5:00 a.m., I was cramped, stiff, and hungry. Why hadn't I packed some fruit leather or a handful of pine nuts?

But, really, none of that mattered. Not only was I being super-efficient but my solution fit the philosophy of using only the level of tech needed. Why use batteries and blankets when you can use elemental fire? I found myself smiling.

The flames were leaping higher now, licking the penstock's belly, blackening the ridges. A rivulet of melted snow at my boots made me realize the burning logs were slumping a bit so I eased to a higher spot on the snow ledge then leaned in against the bracket that held the penstock to the tank.

I pictured the rushing water twisting through the culvert's spiraling ridges and out the nozzle in the station far below, the increased jet velocity sending the Pelton wheel happily whizzing around. A diagram appeared in my head, and I added lots of arrows and manga-style speed lines for drama.

I put my ear against the pipe. It wouldn't be long.

First, a small gurgle, just a murmur, and then a rattle like a woodpecker and I grabbed the bracket. A tingly vibration, then a mighty roar. I glanced below at the station, crossing my fingers in my mittens.

The light over the outer door lit up, sending a happy glow across the expanse of the parking lot. Hurray! It worked! I'd thought of everything!

I'd wait for a moment to be sure the blockage was totally gone, then head down. I spent the time adding to my mental diagram, calculating velocities. It was super-fun until I reached the final set of numbers.

I straightened, sending small bits of snow rolling down the slope.

Uh oh.

When the twisting motion of the released water freed the ice chunks, they'd have spun down the penstock at an angle. The pipe would be structurally sound enough to bear the uneven pressures but could the nozzle at the far end handle such misaligned stresses? Mathematically, the answer was a totally scary *No*.

I began to recheck the numbers in my head. A roar and my feet were pulled out from under me. I jerked left as the ledge collapsed. Flaming logs fell past me and I scrambled sideways, rolling, snow in my eyes, grit in my teeth.

It was over in a moment. My toque was gone, lost somewhere in the slumping mess of melted snow, charred wood, and exposed dirt. One of my feet was caught behind a boulder the size of a pumpkin. I twisted, just slightly, testing my perch, and the rock fell, tumbling until it hit a lodgepole pine far downslope.

Okay. It was okay. The nozzle might be wrecked but a bit of sheet metal could fix it. No harm done other than a twisted ankle—a small price to pay for sending juice to the greenhouses. I repeated the words to myself as I crawled off the slope to the park's road.

Limping back, a motion below caught my eye. The outer door of the station flew open and Lena stood, her parka a slash of crimson against the grey metal.

I waved, ready to accept congratulations.

"I *knew* you were up there! I just *knew* it! You flaming idiot!"

I stopped cold and Lena frantically gestured me to hurry up. She shouted up at me. "Angie was standing by the wheel inspecting the nozzle to see if it would hold, you *flaming* idiot!"

I began to run, snowshoes clattering, and pushed past Lena into the building.

Angie lay on her side in the main room, a gash down the side of her face. "Angie! Oh, Gaia!" I started to shake her and then remembered about not moving injured people due to possible spinal injuries.

"Broken collarbone," Lena said, breath hot on my ear. "The nozzle whacked her hard when it ruptured."

My throat ached. "Angie. Please."

"She'll be fine. Got to take her back and get it set properly, though. Help me get her up." The sound of the spinning Pelton wheel almost drowned her words. Chunks of ice littered the wet floor and the nozzle dangled, shattered and crooked, while water sprayed every which way in a broad swath, drenching everything, keeping the wheel from producing the full amount of kilowatts we so desperately needed.

I got to my feet, bizarrely pleased at the curt efficiency of Lena's orders. No need for useless debate. Yeah, you guessed it: I was in shock. I'd endangered both my friends and almost killed myself. And my ankle hurt like crap.

Together, Lena and I got Angie to her feet and walked her slowly to the entranceway. Tears flowed down her face but she managed it with only one stumble and a small whoosh of breath even though broken collarbones are agonizing.

Suddenly, I wanted to be in the Cascade Ballroom at Gabfest with all three hundred of us, tea mugs cradled in hands, eyes flashing, debating how I could fix what I'd done. Whatever it was, I'd do it. I glanced at Angie; her brown face beige-pale. Oh, yeah, I'd do it.

I'd thought I was a genius, taking the easy way out, lusting for the raw vibe of pure energy that was now spilling wastefully off the wheel. Just like the polluters, the climate change deniers, the heedless folks who had hurt so many people through their thoughtlessness.

I was no different than them.

I felt like puking.

Lena flexed her fingers, rubbing her knuckles. Neither of us had said a word in ten minutes.

Now what? One of us had to take Angie back to Banff. One of us had to stay and fix the nozzle. And monitor the jet velocity for a while. And do the needed maintenance. I eyed Lena, anticipating her yelling at me—needing her to yell at me—but she was expressionless.

Lena had the most experience at repacking dried-out bearings—I'd only seen it done and taken notes. *Good* notes, but still, I had the brawn to do it, the stamina that Lena didn't, and I could get a good start on it before anybody else could get here to help. The person hours for a larger work party had been calculated at the Gabfest and it was high. The neglected workload to come help me would cost the community a lot but come they would.

Lena would have a tough trip back helping Angie but it'd be less difficult for her than staying.

Overall, the community would benefit most if I stayed.

Besides, being alone and cold and miserable was only what I deserved. That settled it. The way ahead was obvious. "I think I should be the one to—"

"No. You stay."

I started to protest, automatically, but then realized she was actually agreeing with my conclusion.

Damn it. I'd pushed her so far that she thought I should be punished too, even though it went against the tenets of our community.

I got up and began to sort through the supplies while Lena helped Angie fasten her parka buttons. I made a small food pack in case they had problems and had to overnight it on the way back, including the porcupine jerky that Angie had been so right to include. We all needed the energy boost of high protein out here.

I put the rest in a neat pile. I wasn't going to eat any of the communal provisions anyway. I could set up a snare for meat, maybe get a hare or two, and then in the summer tan the fur to replace my missing toque. Why use community resources to replace something lost to my own idiocy?

"You're too quiet. Talk to me," Lena said, arms creasing into the front of her parka.

I shrugged. "Having me stay only makes sense."

"Only makes sense? Or only makes you feel better?"

"I deserve to be punished—"

"This community doesn't believe in penance," she said. "Or punishment. All that was buried in the Breakdown and it's going to stay that way, hear me?"

I put down a jar of hummus. "I hear you." She was wrong. Not only was my risk evaluation pathetic, I couldn't keep a promise to save my life, and the whole community would hate me forever. I was an idiot, and I'd hurt a person I now realized I deeply cared about. Being alone here, and miserable, was only fitting.

"I've spent a lifetime quashing the concept of redemption through needless suffering and I'm not going to see you internalize that now. Even a genius couldn't have predicted the way the ice burst apart the nozzle." She wiped my cheek with her handkerchief, then held it out showing me the charcoal smears.

I managed a curt nod and, hiding how my ankle twinged and my heart ached, knelt down to buckle Angie's snowshoes. She stood and moaned once then bit it back. I hugged her and felt her breath on my hair. "Take care," I whispered, not sure what I meant at all.

It wasn't until they had disappeared behind the curve of highway that I let out a whimper which became a long, throat-stinging howl. That afternoon, I chopped wood until my arms stung and my blisters bled into my mittens.

At sunset, I turned ninety degrees from the orange glow behind the peaks. Somewhere, below the foothills, down a long stretch of broken highway, lay Calgary. I didn't belong in Banff, they didn't want me or need me. The rough-and-tumble lawless land to the southeast was all I deserved. I welcomed the sting of snowflakes on my face. Bring it on! I'd pack the stupid bearings and then I'd be off over the mountains, free and unencumbered.

OF COURSE, I didn't do that or I wouldn't be writing this now. Nature is one thing, nurture is another, as Lena says.

I went back to Banff after re-greasing the bearings in half the time that it usually took and making a temporary fix to the penstock nozzle (I came up with a new spout design that I want to share with you!) despite my dumb ankle and yet another snowstorm. With much thought in the evenings of dripping darkness, I finally clued in that leaving me behind was one of Lena's teaching moments. I hoped I'd learned the right lesson.

I entered the hotel lobby to an ominous quiet. Randy wandered in, heading for the side door to the outhouses, and started when he saw me. "Why are you back so soon? Never mind." He grabbed my elbow and ushered me toward the ballroom, hardly letting me set down my backpack.

"Eh?" I said, cleverly.

"Hurry up," he hissed. "The last three days' discussion has been mostly about *you*. We need to move on to other topics."

Lena sat in her usual spot in the circle of chairs, just left of center. She frowned and waved me to my usual seat, next to Angie's empty one. Three hundred pairs of eyes watched me limp cross the floor. I finally spotted Angie leaning against a wall, looking weak but cheerful. She shot me a wink. What did *that* mean?

"Ah, you're back!" Lena said. "Good. I was worried when that second freak snowstorm prevented us sending someone to help you. Let me bring you up-to-date. We've reached a consensus." She tilted her chin. "We've assigned you to a work party."

"Okay…" That didn't sound so bad.

"A party of one." Someone in the crowd chuckled and she raised a hand to quiet them. "You're going to the west coast on behalf of this community."

"So that's it? I'm banished? I'm to walk all the way to Vancouver?" I put on a brave face but I knew the highways were crap, the Coquihalla was almost impassable due to slides and that from Salmon Arm to Kamloops was one big blackened forest fire aftermath. I slumped against my chair back. I couldn't believe it. Sure, they could hate me, but total expulsion to an earthquake-broken, struggling community far across the burnt and frozen wastelands of BC's central interior in winter was pretty harsh punishment. I sucked in a long breath. "Sure, I can do that. No problem. I have a design for a better backpack—"

"Hold on," Lena's eyes crinkled and someone laughed out loud. "We've got you a ride with a trader."

"Traders don't carry people like us, not for free—"

Lena ignored my words. "Seems there's a functioning university now in Vancouver. They got back on their feet faster than anyone expected. And they're looking for bright students who want to learn engineering and philosophy and applied sociology and medicine and all the other things that can rebuild this broken world."

"A university?" My voice squeaked and I stuck my hands in my pockets. I glanced at Angie but she wasn't giving me anything. I tried to get my head around it and failed. "And they want *me*?"

Lena herself let loose a low guffaw. "Child, you have such potential in that curly-haired head of yours, you have no idea."

I gave her my most dubious look. "Universities charge a bunch of money, don't they? And where would I stay? And how would I pay for food? Selling wool? Furs?"

She twisted her mouth, still amused for some reason. "We've agreed to devote ten percent of the community income to your fare to the trader, and to your tuition, room, and board. And we've already found you a place on campus. A solo room, given your personality."

"Wait a minute—"

"There's only one thing left to do, that's to write an entrance essay—"

"I've never even *seen* an entrance essay. I have no *idea* how to write—"

"So, the first year's covered. The following years, you'll need to earn scholarships or maybe patent an invention or two and get yourself some royalties."

"Wait a *minute!*" I held up a hand, and, surprisingly, Lena stopped. "How'd you do all that? How'd you even find out about the university in the first place?"

Randy spoke up. "It seems that Angie here cobbled together a radio over the past few months and found a signal. Ham radio is a thing again. We didn't want to tell everyone until we were sure about how outside society had progressed."

Angie shot me a gap-toothed grin.

"I bet you used my tools, didn't you?" I glared over at her. "And my bin of electronics parts."

"Just trying to find a way to get rid of you somehow," she said, then turned bright red for no reason I could see. She recovered really quickly and snapped out. "Don't suppose you're very teachable, though. Waste of good money at a good university."

And, I smiled at that, really smiled. You see, I'd finally caught Angie being wrong. Oh, not about the university—I'm sure it's awesome. But about it not being able to teach me much. I'm humble now (no, really!) and I'm willing to learn.

So that's why you've received this twelve-page essay. I've written every word myself and checked it over four times. (See, I'm not so impulsive now!). And, to prove I'm worthy, I'm sending it you without letting Lena or anyone else read it, just so you can see the real authentic me.

Please accept this application, please, please, please. I've kept all my promises since I got back from the generating station. And I do have a lot of "promise." Lena says so.

And, your university really *is* the best place for me, all things considered.

And all things *have* been considered, endlessly and tediously. You can count on it. I mean, duh, that's how my community works.

Holly Schofield travels through time at the rate of one second per second, oscillating between the alternate realities of city and country life. With not-so-hidden twin agendas of promoting environmental causes and inclusivity, Holly has had over 100 speculative short stories published in genres ranging from hard science fiction to magical realism. Her works have appeared in such publications as Analog, Lightspeed, and Escape Pod, are used in university curricula, and have been translated into multiple languages.

Website: https://hollyschofield.wordpress.com/
Facebook: https://www.facebook.com/holly.schofield.33
Twitter: https://www.twitter.com/hschofieldfic

VOTER FRAUGHT

BY B. MORRIS ALLEN

"I wish *you* could vote for me, Botty." The child looked across the park to where friends were playing.

"I do vote for you, Ange. You just have to tell me how to do it." The AI's voice was gentle through the little earplug in the child's ear.

"But it's *boring.*" By the slide, Cinda had just pulled Caro's bushy hair, and they both looked like they were deciding whether to cry.

"It's only boring if you let it be. It's every—"

"Citizen's responsibility to vote. You sound just like Grap. *He'd* let me go play."

"Ange, you know that's not right. We say 'se' now, not 'he'."

"Grap says 'he'."

"Se's older. Your parents want you to say se, and hem, and hes. And you still need to vote. If you had voted earlier, you could play now," it added judiciously.

But *Ghost Rangers of the Deep* had been streaming earlier, and they had early access 'cause of Dam's job. If Ange hadn't watched it, se wouldn't be able to tell Caro and Cinda about it before anyone else could. But now Botty was going on about voting again, and Ralph also had early streaming, and se was coming toward Caro and Cinda, and it wasn't *fair.*

"Quick," said Botty. "What do you like better, books or buses?"

"Books, I guess." Buses were fun to ride, but Ange wasn't allowed to ride them alone yet. Books se could read late at night, if it wasn't too late.

"Okay. One more and we'll stop for today. Do you like parks more, or would you rather learn fun stuff in school?"

That was an easy one. "Parks!" Ange ran toward the slide while Ralph was still adjusting hes safety helmet. "Cinda! Caro! Guess what I saw on *Ghost Rangers* today!"

~

"LIZETTE, you agreed to take care of hem." Keawe's tone was firm. Se was using hes deep, 'no whining' voice. "Either you honor that agreement, or we revisit the discussion about tattoos. Your choice."

Lizette was tempted to whine anyway. Everyone in hes year had inductive tattoos, or at least transceiver implants. Se was the only one still wearing a VR tiara.

"Dam, I look like a baby with this thing on! Remember, Mod said that if I took care of Grap, I could have the tattoos when I was fifteen."

"And are you fifteen?" The calm, sincere voice was the worst. It meant Dam had logic on hes side. Lizette would never win the argument now.

Never give up! That's what Grap always said. "I'm *almost* fifteen. I'll be fifteen in a *week*. You might as well treat me as an adult now. You *said* you would."

"Then act like an adult." That was the voice of decision. Argument over. "Take care of Grap, and in a week, we'll see."

"But that's ... that's..." After Roger's party on Friday.

"It's a week. And speaking of fifteen, have you updated your voter card?"

"Da-am! It's so—"

"That's two things to do, then." Dam did hes disappointed face. "You know, when I was your age—"

"I know, I know, you fought for direct democracy, to have a real voice in the country's future, to affect the things you care about. Back then, people cared."

The eyes were dangerous now, their pale blue kindled into an unnerving fire. The other kids thought Dam was spooky looking, and sometimes Lizette agreed. "I'm going to let that go," Keawe said, "because you actually got it right. But if I hear that sass from you again..." Consequences left to the imagination were best left unimagined. "Now go and help your Grap get ready for dinner, and send Ange down, if se's up there."

~

"So, which are you, Ange? Boy or girl?" He cocked his good eye and looked the child over. "I bet you're a boy. You're tall, for your age, and you like to run around." Why was it that they couldn't just come out and say it? Like gender was some big secret all of a sudden. Back in his day, they'd been able to choose, without all this mystery. Eventually, anyway.

"You're not supposed to ask me that, Grap. Mod said it's a no-no." On the arm of the chair, the child widened its eyes and looked serious.

"Well, maybe you're a girl. Name like Ange. I was a girl once." Those had been the days. "Twice. Depending on definition." They'd had definitions in those days, and pronouns too, not this se, hes, hem crap.

The child had been a girl at some point. He remembered bathing her, back when he was still trusted to remember things like 'Don't drown the baby.' He was lucky they let it play with him now. Let hem play with hem. That was just downright confusing.

There was a knock, and the door opened before he had even figured out what the noise was. His senses still worked, it just took a little longer to process, these days.

"Ange, you're supposed to go down to Dam," said Lizette, bustling in. "And Grap, it's almost dinner time."

Ange leaned over and gave Grap a hug before clambering down and racing through the door. Grap could hear her (him?) skipping half the steps on the way downstairs.

"Se's a good kid," he said, wiping his nose. "Not like some." He tried his best glower, but it bounced off Lizette's rainbow-sparkled blouse like rain off a windshield.

"Do you want a different blouse? That one's got juice on it."

"No, I don't want a different blouse. I can still dress myself, girl." He looked down, and it did have a stain. "Alright, get me the blue one from the closet." He edged himself forward in the chair, and started pulling apart the little tabs with arthritic hands. At least this new stuff didn't make that awful ripping sound that hook and loop closures used to. Velcro, they had called it. "Velcro." Who said his memory was fading?

"I'm not a girl, Grap." The kid sounded bored, but they all did, at this age. "Did you do your mentation exercises?"

" 'Course you are. Name like Lizette, long hair, flouncy skirts. That's the point of being a girl. I was a girl twice."

"Mentation, Grap. Exercises. Do them?" Lizette took the stained blouse, helped him into the new one.

He waved a hand dismissively, impeding Lizette's efforts to seal the seam. His mind was fine.

"That's a no, then. Right. Let's do them now, then. Where's your tiara?" It was lying in plain view on the dresser, but the kid found it anyway, and settled it on his head. It felt nice against his skin. It would have looked nice, when he had hair. He'd had thick white hair, except for the bald patch. Now it was all bald patch. And freckles. They made little patterns, like constellations. He had the Big Dipper right over his left ear, Fran had said. He'd claimed that's why he never heard him. Maybe the old pronouns had been just as confusing. Grap knew what he meant.

"Okay," said Lizette, "let me just..." She looked blank for a moment, and a diagram came into Grap's mind—a three-dimensional wireframe. They'd called them wireframes. Maybe they still did. It was strange, still, having someone else put things in your mind, but he had to admit that it had its advantages. *Look, Ma! No hands!*

∾

"So, then I told Cinda and Caro all about the *Ghost Riders,* and how they got captured by the alien pirates, but then Ralph said that wasn't how it went, but I said—"

"Hush just a minute, Ange," said Dam. "Your Mod and I are talking." They hadn't been, and they always interrupted just at the important part, like about how Ralph probably didn't even really have early streaming.

"So, Rada, what were you saying? Nobody's voting? How can they not be voting? They'd lose transit, meds—"

"VR," interjected Lizette. "They'd have to use, I don't know, those flat things."

"Screens, dear," said Dam. It was going to be another boring conversation, and Ange hadn't even told them about Ralph yet.

"No one votes anymore." This was more like it. When Grap spoke up, things got unpredictable. "Not for real. It's all this AI crap. *You* don't vote, your AI votes for you."

"We tell it *how* to vote, Grap." That was Lizette, showing off for the parents, as if se really knew anything about it.

"Saying 'I like greenspace more than buildings' is not a vote."

"In a way it is," said Dam. "As Lizette said, it's telling the AI how to vote. We can't vote on everything, after all, at every layer of government. But we can tell the AI our preferences, and it votes for us."

"It's not a vote," insisted Grap, helping himself to more apple juice, though se was only supposed to have one glass. Caro's Gra couldn't drink juice at all, which was sad.

"Well, it counts as one," said Dam.

"Actually, though, Grap's right," said Mod, speaking up for the first time. "That's the problem. There are so many votes that people feel divorced from the whole thing. They hand off the entire process to their AI, and feel virtuous. Sometimes I think we went too far."

"With AIs?" asked Lizette. "You know, I'm almost fifteen, and I think inductive tattoos would really help me to evaluate the parameters of the issue."

"Nice try." Mod rolled hes eyes at Dam. "No, with direct democracy. I mean, power to the people and everything..."

"Rada, you fought as hard for this as I did," said Dam.

"Of course I did. And I still believe in it. But, let's face it, Keawe, it's not working. People aren't engaged. Instead of building participation, we've turned over our government to software."

"We still update our preferences." Dam sounded a little hurt, and Ange watched to see if se would cry. Adults seldom did. "I just did mine last month. It took hours. Questions about hundreds of issues, a dozen levels of government. We've fine-tuned those algorithms to capture everything important."

Mod reached a hand across the table. "I know, sweets. Look, I'm not saying you haven't done a great job, you and the rest of the engineers."

"And it's all secure," Dam added. "There hasn't been a hack in nine years. That's worth something."

"No, I know. The system works great. The thing is, it misses the point. Everybody votes, if we can call it that. But nobody's *involved.*"

"Nobody updates their prefs anymore," threw in Lizette, with the look of a Ghost Rider dropping a maser popper onto a bunch of pirates who might or might not have a hostage.

"Of course they do, honey. It's required. We talked about it just this evening." Dam shook hes head in exasperation. "Every five years, like it or not."

"But Dam, it's been hacked!"

"What? That algorithm is unhackable, young myn. I—"

"No, Dam, not the *voter.* That's *fine.* It's the *update* that's been hacked. You don't even have to do it anymore. You can just run an extension, and it'll learn from you, what you talk about, and stuff, and it'll *tell* the update what your preferences are."

"It's true," said Mod. "Office of Legislative Counsel asked us to look into it. But even if it weren't true, the point is, we failed. Everybody votes, but nobody cares. Nobody even knows what the issues are, anymore."

"I read the news," said Dam, stiff, sharp.

"I read the news," said Grap. "That's all I do."

But everybody had their arguing faces on, and some things just couldn't wait.

"So then I said to Ralph, you don't even know." And Ange told them all about the argument, and how Ralph almost hit Caro, and they all listened, because no one wanted to talk anymore.

THE TEEN WAS over in the corner, talking. She was always talking, or playing with her hair, or staring off into space while her tiara messed with her mind. His own tiara was doing it to him now. Without meaning to, he was visualizing a kangaroo, a bushel of peas, and a goose in a rowboat. It was one of those stupid logic puzzles, where you had to cross the river six times, and only then did you remember you might have left the stove on, and probably you should just forget about going to market entirely. But if he ignored it, the puzzle would just keep coming back around until he solved it.

Let's see. They couldn't all three fit into the boat at once... Aha! He visualized the kangaroo picking up the peas, pouring the lot into her pouch, and tossing the empty basket across the river. Sometimes you just had to think outside the box with these things. To his surprise, the AI accepted the solution.

"At least somebody still has a sense of humor," he grumbled. "So, you getting those tattoos?" Sometimes you just had to force the kids to interact with real people.

It got Lizette's attention. With a flounce of her hair, she said, "Catch you later, Ju-Yin," and came over to sit on the bed by his chair. "Do you think they'll let me?" she asked. "Did they say anything? Maybe if you mentioned it to them. You know, how I've been helpful, and all."

Helpful? Well, she came up every day. That was something, even if she was a little distracted. She was a teenager, after all. He remembered when he'd been a teenager. It had been confusing. All those hormones, all those choices, and so political! Kissing a boy, wearing a dress. People had cared about those things. Do this, don't do that, and all he'd wanted was to go snuggle in the back corner with Ricky Mweneji. Instead, they'd made him go testify and talk and give all those depositions. Maybe they had the right idea now after all, bland and uncertain as it all seemed.

"Hey, Grap, I have to give this presentation tomorrow, and we're supposed to talk about, you know, our ancestors and stuff. Can I do mine 'bout you?"

"I'm not dead!" Not yet, anyway.

"No, not like, dead ancestors. Just, you know..."

"Old people."

"Yeah! So, can I do you?"

"And this is for tomorrow?" Did no one plan, anymore?

"Yeah, but it's, you know, just about what you did for a living, and all."

"Fine." He shrugged. Why should he care? She looked at him expectantly, until it dawned on him that she wanted something.

"So, um, what did you do?" she asked at last.

Of course. Teenagers never remembered, and why should they? It meant he got to tell his stories again. "I was a consultant." Let her dig for it.

"Cool." She waited. "Um, what kind of consultant?"

"Good girl. Tenacity, that's what gets you there. I was a democracy consultant, if you'd believe it."

"Cool. So, like what Mod does?"

"Not exactly. Your Mod is a bureaucrat. She tries to implement the policies we're all voting on all the time, at the municipal level." He'd tried, for a while, to actually vote on everything, out of principle. He'd proved conclusively that it wasn't possible. Not even if you didn't eat or sleep. "It's more like what your Dam does. She does some coding, but mostly she gives advice to other coders. That's what I did. I gave advice about democracy."

"Like, voting, and stuff? Hey, were you behind the whole direct democracy thing? Our teacher told us about that, how it took over so fast, because of corruption, and partisans, and all."

"Yes. Voting and stuff." He'd been against the DirDem movement. He hadn't thought it would work. It had, though, better than he'd thought. He'd been wrong. "Mostly, though, I talked about public participation." It came back to him, as if it had been only yesterday that he'd last walked through his mantra for bored bureaucrats.

"Say you have a proposal," he explained. "Something you want to do. You get your research all done, you consider all the alternatives, but you know you don't know everything. So, first thing, you ask your constituents what they think about it. That's the first thing. Give them a chance."

"Yeah, so, you were a consultant about voting and stuff. Say, could you vote at fifteen back then? 'Cause I think that inductive tattoos—"

"Second, you *listen* to them. Sure, you get some value by letting people talk. Makes them feel involved. But that's political value. If you actually listen to them, you may find they have something to say. Sure, a lot of it's garbage. Most of it is. But every now and then, someone knows better than you."

"I know, right. Like, everybody says inductive tattoos are totally safe, and all, but Dam says—"

"Third, respond to them. Listening is one thing. Actually responding to comments puts you on the record, and it forces you to make decisions and justify them in public. That's the key. That's what's missing these days. No one justifies anything, because it's all just statistics—37% this way, 25% that way, etc."

"Uh huh. So, look, Grap, I think I've got all I need. Maybe I'll just go—"

"Fourth, and most important—*do* something. None of this means anything until you act on it. That's what it all comes down to—public participation. That's when you get people to care. None of this AI shit. Just people."

～

"I'M TELLING YOU, Dirk, se just—"

"Nida."

"What's that?"

"I'm trying out Nida as an identity. It's Muslim for 'prayer.'"

"Oh, cool. Like 'Oh Nida, come and ... you know, heal me or something.'"

"I just feel it's more what I feel right now."

"Absolutely. I, um, I don't think Muslim is a language, though. I think it's like Arabic or something."

"No, of course. I mean, it's a Muslim name. I know it's not a *language*."

"Yeah. So anyway, my Grap just kept going on about participation and representation and the Administrator's Performance Act and stuff, and how it was so great. It's a law, or something. How great could it be? It was so boring!"

"Hey, at least we don't have to do all that stuff anymore. You getting those tattoos or what?" Nida turned hes head to show off hes new tattoos—light ochre against hes umber skin.

"Sure. Probably. Hey, I had to uninstall that extension you sent me. My Mod says the gov knows all about them, and they can tell who's got them and who doesn't. So I had to do my whole voter update thing in person—like a thousand questions, or something. How I feel about my tax money going to pay for sewer upgrades in Tazbekistan, and stuff. I don't even *pay* taxes."

"My Dam says everybody pays taxes. Se told me to vote against them every time."

"Whatever. My Mod said that if I didn't uninstall the extension, se'd make me sit through a session of Congress or something."

"Oh, that sucks. I had to do that once. I don't even know why we have them. I mean, *we're* doing all the voting. Or maybe it was the Supreme Court. One of those."

"No, I know that one. It's like, if we want, we can vote for the representative, and then we don't have to vote on all the little stuff. My Mod says it's a holdover or something."

"Yeah. So, you gonna get those tattoos?"

∾

"HEY DAD, can I ask you something?" Oh, it was serious. He'd known it when Rada came in with that look. And she never called him Dad unless she wanted something. Wanted his full attention.

"What's up?" The old man wasn't entirely useless. Now it was just up to him to come through for her.

"It's this voting thing."

"The fact that no one votes for real, anymore." Just to show he'd been paying attention.

"Right. Like I said the other day, everybody votes, but no one cares. I know you used to work on this stuff. The whole ask, listen, respond, act thing." So he wasn't the only one who'd been paying attention. "And the Administrative Procedures Act." Ten points for background.

"Best thing we ever did." And it had been, too, long before his time. "Access to information, public participation, all of that. They called it consultation, over in Europe, but it was the same thing. Still do, maybe." The Europeans hadn't gone all in on direct democracy. Not yet.

"So, I was thinking, how do we get people involved again, for real? How do we do that, and keep direct democracy? Because I'm not willing to give that up. We fought hard for that, Dad. It means something."

"I know, honey." He put a hand on her arm, like he had when she was just a child. "It means a lot. That was good work you did." It was, too. There was a lot less corruption now. But less direction, too.

"So what do we do?" She turned her eyes to him, almost pleading. He felt his heart warm, felt his age as well. What could he say to make her feel better? He settled for truth.

"The truth is, Rada, you can't get everyone to participate. People just aren't like that. Most of them don't care about most things most of the time. But that's fine," he said, forestalling complaint. "That's fine. You don't need that. What you need is to get the people that *do* care. Get *them* involved. Those are the people that change things."

"Hmm." She nodded, and he could see her thinking it over. She had common sense, maybe even wisdom, and he felt the pride building in him. She was a good kid, and smarter than he'd ever been. "But how?" she asked.

"Here's the thing," he said. "In my day, we spent all our time trying to get the bureaucrats and politicians to listen to the people. We didn't succeed much. You solved all that. Everybody weighs in on everything, and policies do change in response, because otherwise the ratings look bad in all those reports the AIs put out. But people don't *think* enough about the issues.

"The hard thing is, they never did. You've got all of government listening. Now you need to make sure there's something to listen to. You know, you could do worse than to bring back town halls, open meetings, etc. Make people sit through them if they want a voice."

"Those laws are still there, Dad. The meetings are still open. Just virtual now, of course. I mean, I guess the actual participants are there," she looked doubtful, "but the audience is virtual."

"Well, whatever they are, make people go. No meeting, no vote." He could see that she was troubled. And rightly so, perhaps. His proposal might void a decade of progress, in many ways. "Or, at least, make their vote count more. If you speak, actually speak, about something, then your voice counts more." He hadn't won her over.

"Yeah. I'll think about it. It seems..."

"Undemocratic?"

"Yes. A little bit." It was, but maybe that was what democracy needed. "One person, one vote, and all. Still, something to think about. I'll talk to Legislative Counsel, see if maybe we can get something on the Council's agenda."

"You'll wait forever if you want the City Council to act," he said. Some things hadn't changed much.

"Sure, but I'm just an advisor, you know. Can't turn on a dime," she smiled. It was one his sayings. "Not without the public."

"Give you nine cents change," he said automatically. It was like the kangaroo and the boat again—figuring out which pieces to move first. There had been something about peas…

"Grap, where did all your hair go?" Ange asked. Grap had red marks on hes head from where the tiara had been. Se'd been using it a lot lately.

"Good question, Ange." Lizette had tried to get Grap to consider tattoos, and se'd said 'Now how would that look, among my constellations?' Grap wasn't always quite with it, Dam said. "I sold most of it to a family of mice who were looking to expand their nest."

"No, you didn't." Ange was sure that couldn't be right. Mice didn't have money, did they?

"How old are you, Ange? You seem pretty smart for six."

"I'm five!"

"Even smarter, then. But your old Grap's not too dim, either. Give me a hand, would you, Ange? Go back into the closet there."

Ange got up and went into the closet. Grap let hem play in there sometimes, and there were lots of dusty old things to imagine with.

"See that middle shelf? Look for a flat grey box and bring it here."

There it was. It was all dusty on the edge, and it was under a bunch of other boxes, but Ange got it out and only knocked one thing onto the floor.

"That's the one. Good work. Let's open it up, shall we?" Grap opened it up, and they looked at the contents in silence.

"Is it dead?" Ange ventured at last. It looked dead—a limp mop of grey-brown fur without even a visible head.

Grap chuckled. "Not quite," se said, and put the thing on hes head.

"It's like hair!"

"That's right, Ange. It *is* hair, kind of. It's called a wig, but it's what I used to use before these tiaras came around." Se pulled it off and turned it inside out. "See these silver bits? They work just like the tiara, only it's more comfortable, and it looks better. Don't know why we stopped using them, really. Oh! Right. They didn't hold much charge, that's why. Here, take this. Let me plug it in here, then you take the other end and plug it into my chair."

Ange did as requested, and then se got to help Grap get hes chair 'travel-ready', which meant making the arms thinner, and taking off some of the cushions. It was fun, watching the chair walk down the stairs, though Grap made hem stand behind, so Ange didn't get to see it from below like se wanted to.

A special transit came to the house, and it lowered a ramp that swallowed them up just like a giant tongue, but the transit refused to do it again, and Grap made Ange sit down. It did the same at the other end, though, in reverse, and in the interim, Ange told Grap how the Ghost Riders had been swallowed by a comet once and only escaped because another Rider had pulled the comet by the tail. Ange did the voices, and Grap laughed at all the right parts.

At the big building, they had a little trouble getting upstairs, because the lift didn't work, and finally a big myn had to come outside and carry Grap up the stairs. It looked like hard work, and both of them looked unhappy about it, but Grap kept saying 'I have a right to be here,' and the myn kept saying 'Yes, you do,' but it didn't *sound* like they were agreeing.

At the top of the stairs, the myn put the chair down, and said "Call when you need me," and Grap had to put hes hair on to get the myn's contacts. Grap left the hair on when they went into a room with a big round table.

The lights came on automatically, but the room felt empty.

"Grap, are we supposed to be here?" Ange asked. Se wasn't actually supposed to leave the house alone. Normally Grap didn't either, and Ange was starting to think maybe neither of them was supposed to leave.

Grap just winked and rubbed Ange's head. Ange liked the feeling, and did it to hemself, but it wasn't the same. What would it be like to rub Grap's dead, fake hair?

Just as se was about to ask, Grap raised a finger, and started talking to the air.

"Yuri Mezovic. I request to be heard. Yes, you can. Not at the end of the meeting. Now. Yes, you can. It's right in your rules. Audience members physically present can raise new business at the start of the meeting. Yes it is, I looked it up. It was adopted after the telepresence rules in 2028, and before direct democracy in 2037. You go look it up. I'll wait. Yes, I'm hes fath—parent. What about it? Se has nothing to do with this." Grap went on for a while, speaking to the air about voting and participation and laws and due process. It was boring.

"Hey, let's do some voting," said Botty when Ange had wandered away to explore behind the big table.

"Okay." And then they did a lot of boring questions about forests and poor people and languages and ice. Grap shouted some of the time, but some of the time se was quiet. When Ange wandered back, Grap was talking again.

"Yes, Mayor, that's the idea. Well, I think the fact that we're a small town has a lot going for it. Crucible of democracy, and so on. Oh, of course there will be opposition. That's all to the good. The more people talk about it, the better it goes for us. In fact, I expect we'll be the talk of the state. This whole Council will be. Mm-hm. Thank you for your time. All I'm asking is that you talk about it. Put it to a vote." Grap smiled, and that seemed to be the end of whatever se was doing. Se pulled off the hair thing, and patted Ange on the shoulder.

"Let's go home, shall we, Ange?"

"Okay, Grap." They headed toward the lift, which now had lights on, and Ange got to press the button. "Grap," Ange said as they waited and se thought about all the ice and forest questions Botty had asked. "I wish you could vote for me."

Grap winked and ruffled Ange's hair again. "You know, kid? I think I just did."

B. Morris Allen is a biochemist turned activist turned lawyer turned foreign aid consultant, and frequently wonders whether it's time for a new career. He's spent the last few decades working on building public partici-pation in government decision making. He's been traveling since birth, and has lived on five of seven continents, but the best place he's found is the Oregon coast. When he can, he makes his home there. In between journeys, he works on his own speculative stories of love and disaster. His story collec-tion Chambers of the Heart *came out in April 2022.*

Website: https://www.BMorrisAllen.com
Mastodon: https://writing.exchange/@Metaphorosis
Facebook: https://facebook.com/BMorrisAllen

GOOD JOB, ROBIN

BY JOE ANN HART

Ahimsa waves an elbow at me, keeping her hands firmly cupped. "Isaura! Look!" She shouts to be heard over my earplugs, and I panic thinking she's woozy again. But no, she only wants to show me something. I lean across the sorting table to look, and with a smile she opens her tawny hands like a flower, just enough so I can peek inside. Two stamens wiggle in the darkness.

Not stamens. Antennae. Out come the earplugs. "It's just a cricket, Ahimsa. One of a billion crickets under this dome, every one of them chirping like an insect possessed."

"Isaura," she sighs. "For one thing, not all of them are chirping, only males do that. Second, look. It's not one of many." With that, the flower blooms again, revealing a green, armored head. OK, then. I put aside my preconceived notion of "cricket" so that I can see this particular one. It's part of our general training, but Ahimsa is so much better at it than I am. I examine his (no female ovipositor) powerful legs and striated wings, count two feathered arms, then look him in the eyes.

"Purple eyes?"

"Purplish. That's what I'll call him. I want to set him free later."

The farm collaborative doesn't forbid random release. Talos, our governing artificial intelligence, requires a genoscan, but after that, the crickets are sterile so there's no danger of wiping out any precarious ecosystem. When we leave,

Purplish will also go through sensors that check for paralysis virus, a hazard not just for farmed crickets, but for the small rewilded populations. The collaborative asks only that if you take a cricket, you take care. No cruelty. If you want to eat it, fine, but be merciful. No eating it alive even if you believe it fulfills those criteria. It doesn't. If you want to release it, be responsible about freedom. Find an environment with a steady supply of food, and make sure other crickets are around. Loneliness is its own torture.

"Lucky guy," I say, putting my plugs back in.

Ahimsa and I are working at a cricket farm for our Nourishment requirement, the part of our Global Service exploring how food connects us to the earth. After the Extinction Emergency of the early millennium, it didn't take long for even the thickest human to realize that if our species was going to survive—and that is still not a given—we could no longer view nature as a commodity to be exploited. Our self-anointed place in the web of life was total apex, and our greed nearly devoured the planet. Now we have to turn it around, although there are those, like Ahimsa, who believe the best way to heal the earth is for us to leave it. It is, unfortunately, the same conclusion the former Ethics Board came to, when it recommended last year that Talos put an end to human regeneration. Talos then disbanded the Board to keep humans from destroying themselves. Its Original Mandate is clear: Incorporate humans back into a restored and balanced ecosystem.

"Talos should be programmed for the planet to survive, with or without us," Ahimsa said at the time of the Board upheaval. "It shouldn't privilege humans."

"Talos seems more concerned about humans than you are," I'd said, relieved but shaken to be relying on A.I. for our survival. It was weeks before Ahimsa and I were speaking again, so now we try to avoid the subject. I worry that she'll join the Conclusion movement, whose members follow the disbanded Board, plotting to overturn the Mandate and phase out humans. The way she eats, she's halfway there.

In her defense, learning to feed ourselves without wide-scale defaunation or adding to the methane load is a challenge. Crickets are a fair option. They're fed vegetable waste, are high in protein, and what little gas they release is captured and used in the running of the farm. But dear Jiminy, the noise. I hadn't thought that part all the way through. The males could be bred without the ability to chirp, but prior to its final self-destructing opinion, the Ethics

Board had ruled that crickets' lives would be diminished without their song. And so we let crickets be crickets and I stop up my ears.

Ahimsa is flapping her elbow at me again, so out come the earplugs. "I don't understand why we raise them only to kill them," she says, wrangling Purplish into a carrier the size of her fist. "If they're going to be eaten, why give them life?"

I like to eat crickets whole as nature intended, as a crunchy snack, but most people eat them dehydrated and ground into meal, not wanting to find a leg or mandible. Some folks are revolted at the thought of eating bugs in any form, but not me. Humans are food generalists. Disgust helps us avoid pathogens, but if you can get past that, insects greatly expand options and survivability. "Whatever it takes" is my motto. Animal-sourced nutrition is a constant debate, not just between me and Ahimsa, but throughout the Zones. "Corpse food," she calls it. I just call it dinner.

There is no farming of mammals for food, but some of us in the Lower U.K. Zone eat rewilded deer and rabbits, whose fertility has proved robust. Unlike many creatures, they are successfully breeding on their own, still passing on the original genetic adjustments Talos designed for them soon after the Emergency. But without predators to keep these populations in check, they'll strip the land bald, so until we can bring back lynx and wolves, humans must step in. Harvesting is done by hunting, a food-gathering activity that meets early Ethics guidelines for the respectful treatment of animals. They get to lead free lives in the wild before a swift and unsuspecting end. "Better death on the fly than the abattoir," as my old man used to say. "We should all be so lucky." He took me hunting when I was young, but that ended when he did. It would have ended when I married Ahimsa anyway, although when hunt meat is offered, I jump on it, no matter how she carries on. It's considered sacred to those of us who partake. Sometimes I can feel the creature's wild heart beating in my own.

Ahimsa gently pets the cricket's head, and it lunges at her. Crickets are feisty, if not downright violent, but we keep them the way they are. Go figure. "He's got such spirit," she says as she closes the carrier. "I just don't understand."

"Ahimsa," I say, "you know the answer. Life needs life." All sorts of living tissue are biofabricated in labs, but the process still relies on plant or animal cells to begin with. Not even Talos can make food out of stone. Ahimsa feels strongly about taking life, even plant life, and is one of those who eat only fallen fruit or vegetables. In other words, vegetable waste, just like our crickets. Talos tries to meet those needs, but it's a diet that depends on the continuous availability of fallen foods, so it's not encouraged. In my mind, it doesn't embrace a particularly healthy grasp of our dietary impulses either. Only decomposers like worms and pill bugs wait for dinner to land on the dirt in front of them.

"I wish we'd gotten placed at a butterfly farm," she says, picking up the sorting wand used to separate mature crickets from juveniles.

"Me too." Magical is how those places are described. The butterfly's role in the food web is not as an edible but a pollinator, and in areas that can't support sufficient plant life, nectar stations are installed so that butterflies can be released simply for our joy. The same with fireflies. Not like ants, who seem to be released for our annoyance. We started out at the ant farm, raising them for soil restoration as well as food. They'd hide in our turbans, hitching rides back to our community dome where they took over the kitchen. They died out eventually because, like farmed crickets, they are sterile. Even if they weren't already bred that way, it's unlikely they could produce anything that resembled an "ant" on their own. During the Emergency, hot soil forced them out into the open, making their DNA as damaged as ours. We, like many other organisms, still require genetic assistance to tolerate radiation, toxins, and lower oxygen levels. There was an uproar about it at first, but honestly, we were going down fast and it was best to hand regeneration over to Talos. Nothing could have survived without its genetic guidance. Nothing. Well, except maybe cockroaches and rats, who seem to have come through even stronger. We should all have those genes. We probably do. Talos really knows how to mine the universal code to get us where we are today: still here.

As I insert my plugs yet again, I sneak a look at Ahimsa. She's so frail she could get sucked up in an exhaust fan, but she's standing on her own and humming along with the crickets as she sweeps them into trays. No earplugs for her. She's prone to existential jitters, so her medic advised that she immerse herself in the task at hand to keep from fretting about the world. If only it were that easy. Adapting human bodies to toxins and the degraded atmosphere has been a success, but Talos tries not to tamper with human emotions, as much as I wish it would.

As it is, physiological tweaks to lungs, blood, and other bits are designed to be untweaked as we reverse the earth's damage, with the goal of bringing us back to our "natural" pre-Emergency selves. We know how to get there and have the systems in place to do it. Right off, egotistical politics were removed from decision-making by assigning governance to Talos. On an ecological timeline, our life spans are so short our minds can't visualize long-term changes in the environment. We're not equipped, but Talos is. After the Emergency, the earth was divided into thousands of Zones, each with its own Ethics Board and Administrators. In the same way we learn a universal language while keeping our ancestral tongue, Talos is programmed locally but uses a single code to coordinate global efforts. We have to work together or die together, as the early programmers wrote. Administrators, guided by Talos, balance resources for all living things in their Zone, both plant and animal, down to the little amoeba that doesn't know what it is. We vote for Administrators based on programmed criteria for honesty, responsibility, and diversity from a pool of candidates nominated by Talos.

Without warning, the entire team at our table starts swaying in their colorful tunics, humming or whistling along with Ahimsa and the crickets, as if the dome weren't loud enough. I adjust my plugs, even though it's nice to see people happy in their work. I just wish they'd keep it down.

Before the Conclusion controversy put an end to the Ethics Board, Talos selected those members for their clear vision and righteous justice. I'm proud that a forebear was one of these, a prominent voice in the first skin pigmentation decision. In those early Emergency generations, people died from radiation burns and those who survived could not leave shelter. A gene was modified to add a subtle metallic olive-green sheen to human skin, which reflects damaging ultraviolet rays and gives us freedom. Plus, it looks fantastic, no matter what color your base coat is. I'd like to see the Ethics Board resurrected, but only if Talos can weed out Conclusion fanatics. Ethics shouldn't mean a death wish.

"Hey!" Ahimsa nudges me with her wand. "Wake up," she says. "These have to be .... " but can't finish the sentence. She hands me a covered tray of crickets to be scanned for anomalies and gene mutations. That was the big lesson learned from the Emergency: Gather the building blocks of life and preserve them deep within the lava caves of the Moon, protected from radiation. Talos continues to scrape dust from specimen drawers around the world, and organisms are constantly sampled for any lost wetware of life, from the highest peak to the deepest sea. The MoonArk is a massive undertaking, but with it we have the raw materials for genetic rescue, and as conditions improve, we can bring back more species in their original configurations. When I was little, I asked my mother why we couldn't have giraffes again, after encountering those fantastic creatures in a holograph show. "Just because we can do it, doesn't mean we should," she'd said. "We have to restore their environments first. We can't bring them back only to keep them imprisoned, can we, Isaura?" I shook my head no, but I really wanted a giraffe. I still do.

I finish scanning, then run the tray through the flash unit, zapping the crickets lifeless. I spare Ahimsa that part. We're applying for the plankton beds next, and I'm hoping she won't try to defend the single-celled creatures, because we owe our breath to their death. When prehistoric plankton sank to the bottom of ancient seas, it took carbon along, making the atmosphere safe for multicellular land mammals. Then a few eons later, one of those mammals (us) began to extract it in the form of petroleum, releasing all that carbon back into the air and making it unsafe again. We knew what the science was and did it anyway. That's a human in a nutshell. Out at sea, we'll be raising plankton on floating beds to absorb carbon from the atmosphere, then sink them in death, reversing the fossil fuel process. We'll also learn to cultivate plankton for food, fertilizer, fuel, and biomaterials, the first products to replace the original oil-based plastics. What a difference that's made in restoring the oceans. Except for jellyfish (makes a nice soup), we harvest no sea animal for food. Someday. In the meantime, we, even Ahimsa, dine on algae and seaweed in dozens of different forms, although she'll only eat them if they've washed up on shore.

That doesn't bode well for the Mass Mortality Events, the last of our Global Service modules, after Nourishment and Shelter. Everyone must work three months at a land or water MME site to document places where species, including our own, died en masse from oxygen deprivation or some other hideous end. We'll gather bones and collect soil samples. We'll bear witness. Most MMEs were preventable, but no one acted to prevent them. We thought only of what we wanted and how to get it. Now, from birth, we're encouraged to think about the ways we're connected to all living things, including one another.

After our MME term, we'll decide on our life's work and settle down to start a family. Humans could be generated by laboratory systems like other species, but that is absolutely, positively not allowed by the Original Mandate.

Natural humans are difficult enough without lab humans running around. And yet, until Talos can clean up lingering genetic horrors, natural insemination, even when possible, is still frowned upon. Talos screens out mutations before fertilization takes place and it's all in vitro from there. Ahimsa, when she's not promoting the abolition of humans, talks about having children, "but only if the earth wants them." Talos calculates the number of humans that can be supported on the planet every year, a small percentage of what it was at Peak Human over two centuries ago, but enough to make us feel somewhat established. Ahimsa never trusts that number.

"Let's just let Talos do its job," I told her. If Ahimsa ever gets over her Conclusion temptation, we'll use sperm cells made from our bone marrow so we can fertilize each other's eggs. Ahimsa wants to carry them both, even though she couldn't possibly support a pregnancy if she doesn't start eating for one, never mind for two.

The farm clock chimes and Ahimsa motions with her carrier to say "let's go." We have one last chore and it's the best. At the end of each day, workers take live crickets outside of the city to distribute in fields as prey for rewilded birds and toads. Birds, especially, need a consistent food supply or they'll fly off, a survival mechanism Talos is having trouble controlling. If they migrate to where insects and seed-bearing plants have not been reestablished, they'll perish.

We load our crates into a jazzy transport at the dock, a sweet ride that hovers centimeters above the ground and flies like an earth-hugging hawk. As we strap ourselves in, Ahimsa puts Purplish's container between us. "Should we let him go in the field with the others?" I ask.

"No, I want to give him a better chance than that," she says. "I want to release him near us, in the pollination field at Cathedral Park."

I don't point out that he would have predators in town as well. Not so many birds and certainly no toads, but wow, the rats. Even I won't eat rat, even though they're abundant. The hunting-enhanced cats keep disappearing (hopefully as animal companions, not food), so until the labs catch up with predator production, Purplish is no safer in a city park.

He's quiet in his carrier, but the other crickets chirp like rowdy teens going to a concert. When we arrive at our field, we open the crates, and they leap out in sprays of joy. Because the atmosphere outside the city is not stable, we wear safety hoods over our turbans and take an occasional hit from our oxygen.

Humans evolved to be outdoors, so Talos designs systems to make that possible. One day, we're assured, we'll return to relying solely on natural air. A restored ozone will even allow us to grow hair again.

Ahimsa is shaky on her feet, so we go back in our transport to watch the crickets disperse. They are exuberant, taking thrilling leaps and climbing up grass stalks that sway beneath their weight, like they were born here. It's not long before a flash of ruddy orange comes swooping down and carries off a kicking cricket.

"Good job, robin," I say.

"Why do you say that? It's so annoying."

"I say it because the bird is doing what it's supposed to do. Eat."

"But it's eating another living thing. Why can't it just eat seed that falls to the ground?" Ahimsa sighs. "Why?"

"That's not its nature. We have to give each rewilded species what they need to survive. If we mess too much with the robin's nutritional needs, it'll be a different bird. It might not even be a bird." Early on in the Emergency, ravens had darkened the skies and eaten all the songbirds. Bringing back the robin was huge. When I hear one sing, my brain cells light right up.

"It doesn't seem fair," she says, lifting her eyeshield to wipe her tears. Her shield takes up so much of her face she looks like a bug herself. A very cute, very sad bug.

"No one ever said nature was fair."

"How is this even nature?" She motions at the field, a field engineered by Talos, down to every narrow blade of grass.

"It's nature perfectly re-created," I say, starting up the transport. "It's this or a burnt, lifeless landscape. Take your pick. Which 'nature' do you want?"

She doesn't answer and I don't push it. As we swing toward the city, she clutches the cricket box in her lap and looks at anything but me. It's a long ride. We leave our transport with our crates at the depot outside the city and head to the park on the hydrogen-rail. Ahimsa stares with a vengeance at the passing domes. When our Nourishment service ends, assuming we are speaking by then, we'll move on to Shelter. For safety's sake, the trend has been to build down, then cap the space with a filter dome, but we want to work with the tissue technology division to grow living homes, a treelike network connected by roots.

Ahimsa sits up and points at a budding oak, planted in the Great Refor-estation. "Wouldn't you like to live in a tree?"

"Can we keep the squirrels out?" I ask, which for some reason makes her laugh, and I'm relieved. She lets me take her hand, and we explore my compli-cated feelings about squirrels for the rest of the ride. From the rail hub we walk down pebbled lanes full of workers jostling toward the end of their day, and night workers just starting theirs. As we round the corner to the park, we come upon someone in the grip of an emotional health crisis. The young man is crouched on the ground, wearing a dirty white tunic and sobbing uncontrollably. His turban has slipped off, exposing a scalp scratched raw. Under the abrasions, I can just make out the defiant red tattoo: c within a C, shorthand for Conclusion.

It's hard enough to consider a world without you without also having to imagine a world without any humans at all. What creature will carry on our work of loving the world? A health team is by his side, trying to calm him with whispers and healing touch as the crowd flows around them like water. We are quiet the rest of the way, and I can feel Ahimsa slip back to her own dangerous place. I worry she is not far behind him, the way she's going. Virtue is her hunger now. As we approach the park entrance, she blurts out: "Maybe he'd be happier living with us in the dome?" It takes me a second to realize she is refer-ring to Purplish, whose carrier she now hugs close to her chest.

"You think so?" I say, knowing he would not be. Knowing she knew he would not be. To buy some time for her to come to the right decision, I steer us to a food-kiosk to pick up dinner. Shaped like giant mushrooms, the green kiosks are plentiful and evenly distributed around the city. No one goes hungry unless they try. I stare at Ahimsa.

"How about a cricket wrap for me and a high-tide algae burger for you?"

"You wouldn't eat cricket now, would you?" She tightens her hold on the carrier.

"I like cricket wraps. And they're good for you. Amino acids, iron, B vita-mins. I wish you'd try one. I'm not sure you're getting all the B you need."

"If crickets have all that, maybe they also have consciousness," she says. "And a soul."

"I don't doubt they have consciousness," I say. "They might even have a soul. But we have to eat something."

"Do we?" she asks.

"Yes. We do. We all have to do our part to stay alive if any of us are going to survive. It might even be our obligation. We have to fix what we've broken and help bring back other species."

"So you can eat them! It's all just cannibalism."

"Stop that. Just stop it!"

She looks at me in shock, her mouth a twisted O. I'm surprised myself, not for being angry but for being so very frightened. She's getting more extreme every day, even scary, and when she suddenly takes off toward the park, I'm not sorry to see her go.

People on the street are staring, so I pull myself together. Breathe in, breathe out. Focus on the task at hand. Dinner. I've lost my appetite for cricket, so I tap on the pictograph of a lab-generated wrap produced from plant cells and lamb genes, then scan my hand. The roll-up appears in a kiosk drawer, warm and ready to go. Ahimsa can figure out what, or if, she wants to eat, but I'm done arguing about it. If she really believes that any eating is cannibalism, there's no hope. Interconnectedness does not mean the *same as*. It means we rely on one another to live, one way or another.

I'm not ready to go after her, but I'm also not going to let her keep me from going to Cathedral Park on my own. It's a rejuvenating place with perfect air created by both mechanical carbon-pumps and natural pumps, the trees. Neither could do the job alone.

As I enter the park, I turn off my oxygen pack and glance over at the pollination field. She's not there. On the other side is Speakers Corner, where Conclusionists tend to proselytize. None of them is Ahimsa, and that's some relief. I find an empty bench far from them where I eat my wrap alone, watching laughing children toss a violet ball in a circle from one to another. They're happy. Is that our true nature, despite everything?

I breathe in the oxygenated air, filling my lungs with it. Survival is more than just breathing, in the same way that nourishment is more than food. We must find joy and meaning in life. But how? What does meaning even mean? Or life for that matter? If atoms are made from energy, and everything is made from atoms, then how do we even stand up? Talos doesn't have those answers, nor does it think we need to know to get on with it. Sometimes Ahimsa and I go to the clay yards to create wild, sinuous sculptures that look like giant slugs, which we leave in the fields and woods. It helps us feel connected to the flow of earth's energy, and maybe the answer is as simple as that.

As I eat my wrap, the shadows of the Cathedral's gothic spires lengthen in the field. These old buildings have been retooled as Numinous Heritage Sites, where holy ones and scholars gather to study what's left of the ancient texts and ponder modern unified theory. The old organized religions have gone the way of the giraffe; most of us now hold beliefs that smack of paganism with a splash of quantum theory mixed with Swedenborgian. It's all about the energy, and the energy is all one. In that spirit, the Cathedral doors are open to all. Ahimsa and I got married here. A holy one, cloaked in flowing white and crimson, took our hands in theirs. "When this foundation was laid a thousand years ago," they began, "the workers knew they would never see it finished. They didn't even know how the roof would be supported, but they began their great project anyway and prayed the technology would come. I want you two to have faith in the future, and trust that the flying buttresses are on their way."

At the end of the ceremony, standing under the vaulted ceiling and the magnificent stained glass, we fed each other wedding cake. The majestic setting gave us faith, not in some abstract god, but in us.

Now Ahimsa is losing faith not just in us, but the species. I get up, disoriented at first, but by the time I find a suction bin for my trash, I realize where she is and what I must do. I'm not going to let her abandon us for the Conclusion, or collapse from any related mental anguish. I'll compromise. I'll promise to swear off hunt meat if she comes with me to the clay yards tonight to reconnect to each other and the earth. When I get to the Cathedral steps, I see people already gathered in anticipation of the sunset. That's one thing a degraded atmosphere has given us, wild sunsets that spark green and magenta from the refraction of foreign particles in the air. Talos is working to replace contaminants with protective aerosols, but maybe we can keep the colors.

Ahimsa sits on the top step, not looking West with the others, but down at Purplish. She's crying, and the container is open in her lap as if to catch her tears. When I sit down next to her, she inches away, and then we both stare straight ahead. On the steps below us, a family dines. The parents bookend a toddler, who is as cute as a bee in his yellow-striped tunic. They take turns feeding him. He's playing with a doll in his lap, but when they offer a bite of their dinner, he opens his rosebud mouth and takes it, then goes back to playing. "Good job," I say, not meaning to say it out loud.

"What was that?" Ahimsa snaps.

"Cute," I say, pointing to the toddler.

She shrugs. "What's the point of children if they're just going to be endlings?"

"They don't have to be. Look at the parents, feeding themselves so they can feed him. If you don't eat, you'll die, and then you won't be able to help create a future for anyone."

"I can help by dying."

"No. You can help by staying alive and working on the problem. The earth is not going to heal without us and our technology. Maybe there was a point before the Emergency when getting rid of humans might have helped, but it's too late for that now. The earth needs us." I take a calming breath. "I need you. If you die, I won't survive."

"None of us deserve to survive."

"You do," I tell her. "Which is why I can't stay and watch you starve yourself to death."

"No one's asking you to stay," she says, and starts to get up. "Oh, no!" She stands and shakes the container. "He's gone!"

"I'm sure he's right around here." I stand, almost paralyzed with fear, knowing that if this cricket thing ends poorly, it could be her end, too. I scan the stone steps; afraid I'll squash him if I move. "Maybe he hopped down to the field on his own."

"He doesn't even know what a field is," she says, choking up. "What if he wanders into a hot spot and dies?" She's having trouble breathing, and I ready my pack. Others get up to help, gently shaking out their tunics and looking on the ground. Everyone knows what it is to lose something precious.

"Here! Here!" It's the toddler's father. "Inside!"

We gather at the carved oak and iron doors of the Cathedral and stand at the threshold. This building should have crumbled from neglect long ago, and yet it continues to stand and even adapt. In the two years since we got married, the arched side aisles have been fitted with massive tubs of flowers, vegetables, and even saplings, flourishing under hidden grow panels. At the far end of the nave, full-grown trees have replaced the altar in the sanctuary.

"Listen," the mother says to her child, touching her ear. I hear a soft, resounding chirp, then another. Soon there's a chorus of them, echoing off the thick stone walls. "Crickets," she says to her son. "Crick-ets."

"Crik-kits," he repeats. "Crik-kits! Crik-kits!"

For all my complaining about chirping at the farm, I've forgotten how rare it is to hear them out in the world. Chirping is the very pulse of nature. Native field crickets were an early casualty of the Emergency, and here we are, bringing them back. They're in all sizes, so it's a true rewilded population and not just a collection of sterile farm crickets. That's progress. An unexpected environment perhaps, but progress. Fading daylight pours in through the clerestory high up in the nave, sending dust-filled shafts across a space so staggeringly tall it could have been designed by giraffes. Ahimsa points at Purplish on the floor a few meters away, where he blends in with the mottled tiles. Humans have huddled here for safety since the 13th century, through plagues and invasions and the worst years of the Emergency. Now look. Trees and crickets. Purplish twitches his antennae and rubs his wings together, creating his song. "Chirup-chirup-chirup." He slowly hops his way toward his species who are waiting for him, then makes a single, powerful leap into a flower tub. And then he begins to eat.

"If you say 'good job,' I'm going to scream," says Ahimsa, but she says it with half a smile.

I take her hand and squeeze it. "I was actually going to say 'lucky guy.' Because of you."

She's silent, but I feel the air around us lighten. We watch the little bumblebee of a boy making a game of the tiles, jumping from square to square as he claps his hands. "I guess he's pretty cute," she says at last.

"I'll bet he'd love to see a giraffe, if we can bring them back."

She considers Purplish munching on a leaf still attached to a plant and does not answer one way or another. I walk over to the veggie tub and pick a green pod from a vine and bring it back to her. Running my thumbnail along the seam reveals a row of pale beans lying on their velvety case like cosseted babies. Harvested, not fallen. She plucks one from the lineup, holding the bean in two fingers, and stares at it. I pry one from the pod and hold it up to her. I see the struggle in her eyes, and then I see the surrender. She opens her mouth, and I place the bean gently on her tongue. With a little hesitation, she draws it in, chews, then swallows. She nods. She can do this. She holds her bean up, and I open my mouth.

JoeAnn Hart is the author of a prize-winning fiction collection, Highwire

Act & Other Tales of Survival, the winner of the 2022 Hudson Prize, forthcoming from Black Lawrence Press, September 2023. Her most recent book is the crime memoir Stamford '76: A True Story of Murder, Corruption, Race, and Feminism in the 1970s (University of Iowa Press, 2019). Her novels are Float (Ashland Creek Press) a dark comedy about plastics in the ocean, and Addled (Little, Brown) a social satire. Her short fiction and essays have appeared in a wide range of literary publications, including the Future Tense column of Slate.com, Among Animals 3, Fire & Water: Stories From the Anthropocene, Orion, The Hopper, Prairie Schooner, The Sonora Review, Terrain.org, Black Lives Have Always Mattered, and others. Her work explores the relationship between humans, their environments, and non-human creatures.

Facebook: https://www.facebook.com/JoeAnnHart.Author
Twitter: https://www.twitter.com/JoeAnnH
Instagram: https://www.instagram.com/joeannhart76

DEFAULT

BY XAURI'EL ZWAAN

"Our days shall not be sweated from birth until life closes— Hearts starve as well as bodies: Give us Bread, but give us Roses."
—James Oppenheim

At 6 AM, Joy's alarm began to chime insistently, breaking her out of a warm, misty dream about her Voc-Plex days with Jaina, before Kensie had come along, back when life had brimmed with infinite promise. Groaning at the early hour (she had never been a morning person), she fantasised about shutting it off and sleeping for another hour, or two. But of course, she had responsibilities; she had a busy day ahead of her. Just like every other day.

As she lingered over her morning coffee and porridge, she scrolled down a newsfeed on the house display, noting happily that the climate scientists were reporting the ongoing geoengineering project had succeeded in lowering average temperatures by a further half a degree over the last decade. The Plex Regional Managers' Congress was debating scaling down the project in light of its success, but those in charge of it were pushing back; they warned that reducing their efforts might lead to the painstaking progress already made on cooling the planet back to pre-industrial levels being lost. She caught up with emails, mostly routine Plex forms and surveys, then opened her itinerary and planned out how to make today's schedule work. She had a lot to fit in; Plex had assigned her a cleaning shift this morning, and that would take a lot of time and hard work, impairing her efficiency for the whole rest of the day. She had thought about trying to trade it off, but if she made a habit of that, people would start to think she believed herself to be above manual labour. Most of the cleaning was done by drones, but some detail work still had to be done by human hands, and it was only fair that everyone shared equally in the labour. Make too much of a fuss about it, and you might even be in for a disciplinary review. Joy got up from the table, changed into heavy work clothes, and tied her kinky hair back with a red kerchief. She would have to make extra time for a shower and makeup before she headed out to Moxie's, too.

As she passed the door to Kensie's room on her way out, she heard music, the sounds of gunfire, and an explosion of profanity. She held a hand to her forehead as she quietly walked out of the apartment. She hated the way Kensie cursed when they were streaming, but they insisted that it was just a persona, that that kind of thing was what brought in views. Joy wasn't convinced, but she didn't know much about that world; she had tried to learn, for Kensie's sake, but it held little interest for her and she had so much else to do. She wished she could knock on the door, give Kensie a kiss goodbye, let them know how much she loved them, but she had learned better than to disturb them when they were streaming; no question but she would get a dose of that sharp adolescent tongue. She resolved to make sure that they took a break later. Kensie spent every spare hour grinding, even though she had told them over and over that it wasn't healthy, that they needed rest and self-care.

At the entrance doors to the housing block, she met the rest of the cleaning team and set a kit full of chemicals and brushes to follow her on drone wheels. Marnie was one of the workers today, as almost every day; she did more than her share of cleaning, as she had Down Syndrome and some of the more complex tasks were beyond her. It made Joy feel a bit guilty to see her doing hard labour so often. But Marnie didn't seem to mind; she took to the work with grit and enthusiasm and constant good cheer. As soon as she saw Joy, a brilliant smile that warmed her heart broke over the girl's snub-nosed features, her almond-shaped eyes lighting up. "Joy!" she shouted, and immediately ran over to clasp her friend in a warm hug. Even after all these years, Joy still wasn't comfortable with physical touch, but she did her best to lean into it, to let Marnie know that she was happy to see her too. She made sure, as always, that

Marnie was her partner as they started to walk around to the suites and get to work.

As they worked, Marnie kept up an incessant chatter about the details of her life over the last few days, her work in the communal creche and kitchens, the books she had been reading and what she thought about them, her recreational outings with the neighborhood's other disabled residents. Her carefree and optimistic perspective was comforting and refreshing, and Joy did her best to keep up her end of the conversation, although her mind was constantly drifting to the other things she would have to accomplish today. For all that, she felt her heart lifting. Cleaning might be arduous work, but there were benefits too. As they went from suite to suite, she talked with every resident— asking old Mrs. Leander about her arthritis and making a note to help her get another appointment with the district clinic; helping the Habib family, who had just moved from Riyadh seeking a smaller and quieter city, with questions about navigating work assignments and getting their children signed up for school; counselling Dagmar Jersey about how to work with the Careers Committee to find a good fit on an engineering team once he finished Voc-Plex. She was not by nature a gregarious person, but somehow she had become the block's resident expert on working the Plex administration, and cleaning was a great opportunity to sound out the residents about their problems and concerns. After they had visited every apartment, scrubbing the nooks and corners that the drones just couldn't get into, the team met again on the roof and thoroughly washed down the solar panels that covered the building's top.

Saying a hearty goodbye to Marnie and sending the helper drone back to the maintenance department, Joy returned to her suite and cleaned up, changing into a simple but flattering pantsuit and jacket and putting on a touch of makeup, just enough to set off her umber skin. Kensie was at school instead of still in their VR gear, thank the stars, and the suite was quiet and serene. Joy took a quick zazen break, sitting with legs crossed and concentrating on her breathing, doing her best to let the constant stream of little worries cross her mind without niggling at them. Then she set out for her daily rounds, picking up a bike from the public rack outside and pedalling several blocks away. The streets were busy, crowded with people returning home from morning work assignments to grab a meal in the housing blocks' canteens, bike lanes near capacity and the walkways dotted with clusters of friends talking as they strolled. Joy arrived at the building she had scheduled to visit that day, put her bike back in the public rack, and started knocking on apartment doors much like she had while cleaning. Each resident took her out to their balcony to take a look at their aquaculture tank; this neighbourhood's tower blocks had been assigned fish production as their urbiculture output, which was a major reason Joy had angled for a housing assignment in the high-density residential district when she left the house she had shared with Jaina, left behind the bad memories and constant guilt. At each tank, she took a few measurements and looked at specimens of the multitude of edible fish that inhabited them, careful not to get splash water on her outfit or face, and advised their care-takers on how to solve any problems that might have cropped up. She also negotiated with each of them, transferring them a bit of Luxe in exchange for a quiet promise that a fish or two would be carried downstairs and added to one of the live-specimen containers that she had surreptitiously had placed there. After finishing up, she ordered a cargo drone service to pick the cases up and fly them over to Moxie's, where Chef would evaluate them and they would negotiate her finder's fee.

Finally, Joy stopped back at her building's canteen for a hurried bite of soy tacos and salad before riding over to the neighbourhood transit station. As she took the short train trip into the entertainment district, she pulled out her tablet and read a few pages of a book, the latest thriller from Abigail Kincaid. She had a weakness for the trashier kind of detective fiction, a habit she would be mortified if anyone but Kensie found out about, and she always felt faintly guilty that she was indulging it instead of reading something more uplifting or improving. Her therapist said that was an unhealthy impulse, that she needed leisure and self-care just as much as all the people she constantly told the same thing, that she was trying to compensate for the way her life had been derailed when she'd had to kick Jaina out and been left to raise a tweenage Kensie alone. She did her best to fight the feeling and just enjoy the book for what it was, a piece of meaningless entertainment.

She disembarked in the city centre and walked the five blocks to Moxie's, an upscale restaurant discreetly parked in a hole in the wall amidst a dense collection of Luxe businesses that catered to upper-level Plex managers and well-to-do Luxe-market business partners. Darian, the front-of house manager greeted her warmly; like everything she did, she excelled in her position as a waitress, putting on and taking off a customer service-focused attitude like a fancy suit. For the next several hours, she and the rest of the servers handled table after table of demanding diners, taking orders with a friendly smile, whisking the fancy food efficiently from kitchen to table, and expertly ironing out any complaints and concerns from their customers, who as a class were used to being treated with a certain deference and tact. When her shift was finished, she went back through the kitchens and into the back office to talk with Chef about the day's catch.

Though everyone who worked at Moxie's was theoretically an equal partner, Chef was definitely the one who ran the show; after all, the restaurant bore his name. He compulsively stroked his blonde goatee as he discussed the condition and quality of the various fish she had had delivered, and after a brief negotiation they agreed on a fee and he transferred her some Luxe from the business's account. If Joy were caught doing this, she could face serious discipline; appropriating Plex-grown food for a business cooperative was a violation of the most basic rules on which society ran. But Joy knew better than almost anyone how hazy the boundaries between the Plex and the Luxe market could get. A high-grade restaurant like Moxie's was definitely classified as a luxury, but what about the food it needed to keep running? All food destined for the Luxe market was required to be grown in segregated premises that traded only in Luxe, but restaurants provided far more demand than could be efficiently supplied by such enterprises, and appropriation of Plex produce sold to them on the grey market was an endemic problem, something management did its level best to stamp out to little success. And because of the illegitimate trade Joy brought in, Moxie's was famous across the whole region for its fish. Increased traffic brought increased profit for everyone at the restaurant, and between her profit share and the extra from selling Chef her fish on the side, Joy needed every fraction of a Luxe that she could get.

At the end of her shift, Joy was bone tired, and was grateful to sit down to a freebie from the kitchens, then ride the train back home and collapse on the couch. She meditated for another few minutes, doing her best to ignore the noise coming from Kensie's room. Then, taking a deep breath, she commanded the house screen to tune in to Kensie's GameGrid account.

The popular game these days was called HellBleed, a gory shooter in the style of the twentieth-century classics, and the visuals viscerally disgusted her almost to the point of pain. But she made herself grind a few games, just enough to get her login bonus and finish her daily quests. She would never play in the rarefied heights that Kensie inhabited, but every day she could earn a pittance of virtual currency, eventually enough to gift Kensie with a new skin or spray. After about an hour, she put the controller down with a sigh of relief. As she went to exit the game, an ad splashed across the screen. "WIN AN IN-PERSON MEET AND GREET WITH MADGUNSKILLZ!" it read.

Joy had seen this one before, a draw for a chance to spend a few hours with one of the world's top streamers. It was tempting to give it a try; Kensie would be beyond thrilled if she won. But the BleedCoins she had earned from weeks of daily grinding could be better spent on something that would give her child an immediate advantage, rather than just giving them back to the cooperative for almost certainly nothing. She shook her head, put the decision off again, and went back to the kitchen table.

As she reviewed the concerns she had talked about with the residents that morning, making a to-do list of things she was going to have to take up with Plex the next day and scrolling through pages of regulations and procedures on the house screen, Kensie sidled into the kitchen and started rummaging through the fridge. Joy looked up, a smile on her face. "So," she said cheerfully, "the dragon finally emerges from its cave. Well, at least you're eating today." Kensie ignored her, making a sandwich and vacuuming it up at the table.

"So," Joy continued, "how goeth the battle?"

"Subs are up," Kensie said around a mouthful of bread and labmeat, "but pledges are down. I need money for new skins."

"Didn't you just buy more skins?" Joy asked ruefully.

"I need the *new* ones, Mom. People are starting to call me a default in chat. I need to keep up. I'm also going to need a new rendering chip soon."

"Yeah," Joy sighed, "I guess it's about that time. I'll set aside some Luxe." Basic computers like the house system were provided free by Plex, but a cutting-edge VR gaming rig like Kensie's was an endless Luxe sink, not to mention the extra electricity allocation needed to run it. She changed the subject. "Have you though any more about what you want to apply to for Voc-Plex?"

"Not much," Kensie said, then continued defensively, "Tournament season is just starting. I have to concentrate on my rankings right now. I'll look at Voc-Plex stuff after the finals."

Joy tried to swallow her disappointment. "You know, you can't let it go too long," she gently chided. "You need to be thinking about what program you want to pursue. There's a limited allotment of spaces, and you need to start working on your applications."

"I *know*, mom," Kensie whined, "but if I lose my ranking I'm *definitely* not getting on a team, and I need prize money too. Aldebaran is coming out with a new line of suspensors this year, and I need to get one allotted if I want to stay competitive. Your paycheck might not cover getting on the list."

Joy couldn't help but display her hurt on her face, and Kensie looked chagrined. "Sorry, Mom," they said softly, "but you know it's true. I need to keep on the bleeding edge or my career is toast."

She nodded. "OK, love, you concentrate on your tournaments, but we have to talk more about this soon, promise?"

They smiled with unshakeable teenage self-confidence. "I can handle it, Mom," they said cheerfully. "Thanks. I gotta go grind now; my subs are waiting."

Joy got up and tousled their blue hair, brushing it aside from their pale pink face and kissing them on the forehead. Kensie squirmed at the embarrassing display of affection. "Go play, then. Momma's rooting for you."

A CALL CAME at 3 AM, breaking Joy out of a deep slumber filled with anxiety dreams. The Daltons' daughter and some of her friends had snaffled some of their liquor supply and been caught spray-painting the side of one of the tower blocks. Marjorie was desperate for her to go down to the Disciplinary Corps office and straighten it out. Blearily she considered telling them to just contact an Advocate and going back to bed; but the Dalton kids were constantly getting into trouble, and their parents trusted only Joy to smooth things over. She didn't really blame them either; Advocates worked for the Plex, after all, and not a few of them tended to value Plex interests over their clients'. She biked down to the district admin complex, shivering in the predawn chill, and managed to argue the duty sergeant into letting the kids go with only an appointment for mediation later that week.

By the time she got back home, it was past time for her to make her morning shift at Moxie's. She threw on clothes and makeup, barely responding to Kensie's confused greeting as they got ready for school, grabbed a sandwich to go from the canteen, and wolfed it down on the train. She apologised to

Darian as she rushed in 25 minutes late; he held in his obvious annoyance, responding only with "Everyone has lives. Just get on the floor." Despite being flustered and not well put together, she managed to maintain her equanimity while serving the tail end of the breakfast crowd.

As she relaxed on her break, leafing through the pages of her thriller, Nadia approached her with a welcoming smile. "Hope it wasn't anything too terrible," she said, annoyance and camaraderie mixing in her voice.

Joy nodded. "Just one of those things," she said. "I'm sorry I dropped the ball. The last thing I want to do is make things harder on you guys."

"It's nothing," Nadia said. "Just more tips for me! Anyway, Darien is leaving to take over GM at Crazy Taco, right? Election to fill front-of-house is coming up soon."

Joy nodded. "I haven't thought much about who I'm going to vote for," she said, "but I'm sure you'd be excellent in the position."

Nadia laughed gaily. "Me? No way! I'm not in the market for that kind of stress." When Joy looked at her in confusion, she said "Joy, a lot of the wait staff are talking about voting for *you*."

Joy blinked a couple of times. "This is kind of coming out of nowhere."

"You're all business all the time, Joy," Nadia said. "It's hard to get you to slow down long enough to chat. But Darian thinks you're the best pick, and Chef's on board too. All you have to do is put your name in."

Joy shook her head. "I'm going to have to think about it…"

"Don't think too long," Nadia said. "I'm not saying you won't have to campaign. Morrow has more friends on the kitchen staff, and Kyla's been talking up a new shift plan she says will mean more efficiency and less hours. But you're clearly the better choice."

Joy stared into space after Nadia left, unable to concentrate on the book. Moving up to management was definitely a big opportunity. It would mean more time, more stress, on top of all of her other responsibilities. It also meant a larger share of the profits commensurate with the increased responsibility. But profits in the restaurant industry were always thin, so it wouldn't amount to a whole heck of a lot. Most of the people working at Moxie's were doing it because good food was their passion, not for the Luxe. Even the kind of huge operation that made games like HellBleed or Kensie's cutting-edge computers wasn't really a road to riches; there were just too many partners involved to split the profits with. To really make it big in the Luxe market, you had to do something that brought in a lot of revenue without having to share it with too many other people.

Something like being a top esports streamer.

When Joy got back home, the cargo drone carrying the block's allotment of fresh food packages was waiting. She put a carton on a helper drone and had it follow her up to the apartment. Of course, residents were expected to take most of their meals at the communal canteen, but Joy had always loved to cook, when she got the time, and doing it still brought back fond memories of preparing meals for Jaina when they had been young and in love. But today was not that day. The monthly district Plex meeting was scheduled for that afternoon. Joy had a long list of improvements to the aquaculture procedures that she wanted to discuss with the Urbiculture Committee, and what with one thing and another cropping up, she had barely even had time to read the agenda. She headed down to the canteen with the documents loaded on her tablet.

When she got there, however, Marnie was sitting at one of the tables, tongue stuck out with intense concentration as she read something on her tablet. She immediately spotted Joy and waved enthusiastically. Sighing, Joy contemplated telling her friend that she needed time to herself, but it would break the poor girl's heart, so she lined up for a portion of macaroni and cheese with tempeh spring rolls and sat with her. "What are you reading?" she asked brightly.

"It's called Animal Farm!" Marnie said. "It's about piggies and horsies, but it's kind of sad too, and hard." She gave Joy an appraising look and said, "You look tired, Joy. What's wrong?"

"Oh, it's nothing," Joy replied, still half-thinking about what she would say at the Plex meeting. "I just got a new opportunity at work. It's tempting, but it would mean even more work and stress."

"You work too hard," Marnie chided. "You should come to the park with me today. Someone else can solve everyone's problems for once."

"It's really important that I log in to the Plex meeting. You should go too; people will be making decisions that affect you without your input."

"Plex meetings are boring, and I never understand what's going on," Marnie said, sulking a bit. "I want to just go to the park. And I want you to come too!" Then she switched gears like a racing cyclist. "Do you really want to do it? The work thing? If you really want to, you should. But it sounds like you're not sure."

"I'm not," Joy confessed. "I just feel like I'm drifting farther and farther away from the life I wanted. But Kensie needs new hardware, and all of these issues don't solve themselves. If it weren't for people like me greasing the gears, Plex would grind to a halt."

Marnie frowned. "They have Advocates for that. They help me a lot when I have problems. You don't have to take it all on yourself. People will be okay."

Joy ran a hand through her hair. "Maybe you're right. I can't help it. People trust me, and saying no to them hurts. But I have needs too, and nobody seems to care about them."

Marnie put a hand on hers. "I care, Joy," she said, her voice full of uncomplicated sincerity.

Joy smiled sadly. "I know, Marnie," she said. "Thank you. You've helped me a lot." Maybe she *should* scale back the amount of time she spent working the Plex for people; their gratitude was beautiful, but it didn't pay for Kensie's gaming gear.

However, there was still the monthly meeting to prepare for, so Joy finished her food quickly and went back upstairs. She took a quick zazen break, read hurriedly through the agenda and resolution texts, then turned on the house display just in time to log in.

The meeting went as well as could be expected. Joy participated much less actively than usual, not even taking the floor for several of the debates as the district's residents wrangled over work plans, production quotas, supply allotments, and Luxe stipends. The rest of the block's residents clearly noticed, and she saw more than a few furrowed brows in the flickering mosaic of video panels from people who probably expected her to speak up on their behalf. She did manage to book a time slot to address the Urbiculture Committee, and spent most of the time going through what she was going to say to them; she wasn't a natural public speaker, but over the years she had diligently studied rhetoric and marketing so she could best make her case on issues like this. Finally, Laurel the District Manager started to wind the mass meeting down so the Committees could start their public hearings, but before she closed business she had one last item to discuss.

"The Disciplinary Corps has been investigating our aquaculture operations," she said gravely, "and we suspect someone may be diverting fish into the Luxe market."

Joy sat up straighter, but carefully kept the panic from her face. She had known, deep in her heart, that eventually there would have to be a reckoning for that, but she was uncharacteristically unprepared. Had one of the residents given her up? She had worked hard to maintain good relationships, but surely there were people who had some kind of grudge against her; it was unavoidable, especially for someone so heavily involved in Plex business. Her heart sank as she realised that this could be the end of the extra Luxe she had been skimming off—or worse.

Laurel continued, "I'm sure I don't have to tell you how seriously we're taking this. Undermining the integrity of the Plex affects all of us. The last thing I want for our district is to get in trouble with Regional Management. We have a good record here as far as Plex discipline is concerned, but a corruption case would be a serious black mark and could lead to allocation problems for the whole population. Now, I don't want to be heavy-handed with you, so if whoever is stealing fish stops immediately, the investigation will be dropped with no repercussions. I'll exercise my discretion as District Manager to make sure this goes away. But if it continues, I'm going to have to make an example. Managerial elections aren't far away, and I doubt any of you don't understand that something like this could sink me as well."

Joy's heart sank as the rotating block of video panels narrowed down to just the Urbiculture Committee and the speakers set to address it. If she gave up the income from selling Chef her fish, would she be able to afford Kensie's new rendering chip? And her stock would certainly go down at work too; the front-of-house position would be in serious jeopardy, if she even wanted the damn job, and without the high-quality fish she provided, Moxie's would have a struggle to stay competitive. Why hadn't she planned for this? She was really in a bind this time, and she couldn't see any way out.

Regardless, she delivered a perfect speech to the Committee, and she could see Rafe the district Aquaculture Manager nodding as she went through her recommendations point by point. After she was finished, she didn't even bother sticking around to hear the rest of the Committee business; for once, she didn't need to be involved. She shut the screen down and sat zazen, taking a full 30 minutes to try and calm her jangling nerves. She was tempted to go straight to bed, but instead she opened up her email, trying to lose herself in rote busywork while she tried to figure out what to do.

Minutes later, she was up and knocking loudly on Kensie's door.

"Mackensie Dawn Charleston, you come out here this instant!" she shouted.

"But Mom," Kensie shouted back, "I'm right in the middle of…"

"Not this time! Kitchen! Now!"

She tried to calm herself down as her child slunk into the kitchen and sat sullenly at the table. Joy opened up the email she had been reading and sent it to the house display where it blazed accusingly. "You've been skipping school again, Kensie," she said in a dangerous voice. "Twice last week. You know that this is unacceptable."

"Mom," Kensie said desperately, "I'm doing so good in the tournaments, but too many of them happen in school hours. I'm going to lose my ranking if I don't grind…."

"Enough!" Joy said. "I know tournaments are important, but they're not more important than school. If you don't get the right recommendations from your teachers, you're jeopardising your chance to get into your choice of Voc-Plex. You could be stuck training for something you don't even like."

Kensie sank into their shoulders. "Maybe I don't want to do Voc-Plex," they mumbled.

"What!" Joy took a deep breath. Things were more serious than she had thought. "Kensie, if you don't train for a higher-level career, you're going to be stuck doing nothing but menial labour for the rest of your life. Streaming is all well and good, but you have to make yourself useful to society too. I'm not going to have a child of mine dropping out of Voc-Plex. Not after all I've sacrificed for you."

"Mom," Kensie said with unusual seriousness, "you know streaming is all I want. I'm getting higher ranks than ever, and there's a good chance I could make a pro league team after I graduate. But if I take Voc-Plex as well, I just won't have time to grind enough to keep up. My whole career could be in jeopardy."

Joy shook her head. "When you're an adult, I won't be able to tell you what to do anymore," she said tiredly, "and if you don't want to take Voc-Plex, it's your right as a free citizen. But you'd be sabotaging your future, and for what? Gambling on fame and riches? Is that it? You can't spend your whole life doing nothing but streaming, Kensie. Eventually you'll age out, and what will you be left with?"

Tears welled in Kensie's eyes. "Just because you never got to do what you trained for in Voc-Plex doesn't mean you can force me to do something I don't want!" they wept, then jumped off their chair and ran back to their room, slamming the door behind them.

Joy sat for a few minutes, trying hard not to cry. Then, barely even thinking about what she was doing, she turned on the house display again and booted up HellBleed. Did she really need to grind quests for fake money? To take on a management position that would seriously jeopardise her mental health? To steal from the Plex so a restaurant job could make her a few more Luxe? Kensie depended on her, but maybe she had been a bit too encouraging of them to follow their dreams. Their streaming might bring their subscribers some joy, but at base it was a fundamentally selfish pastime. Why couldn't Kensie see that the good of the Plex came first?

As she played match after match, she had to admit that at a time like this, there was something viscerally satisfying about blowing demons' heads off and dismembering them with rusty hooks. But as soon as she put the game aside, the same questions began to stew in her head. How had she allowed her priorities to get so out of whack, let so many people stake claims on her time and energy? She had once had a bright future ahead of her, before Jaina, before the bleak void of her absence. Everything she had accomplished since then suddenly seemed like just so much spinning of wheels.

As she went to log off, that damn ad banner popped up again: "MEET MADGUNSKILLZ! FINAL DAYS!" She ignored it. The last thing Kensie needed was for someone to reinforce to them how good they could have it if they just kept grinding. What on earth was she going to say to get them to listen?

THE NEXT DAY, the stars had aligned and she had time off from both Plex work and Moxie's, and this time she swore that she would stop running herself ragged and just spend some time in unrestrained leisure. There was only one thing to take care of; after the monthly meeting, Laurel had sent her a request for a sit-down in her office this morning. Joy was dreading it;

she was sure that Laurel intended to take her to task for the fish. *That can't be it*, she kept telling herself; *she promised that if it stopped, there would be no repercussions.* But what else could Laurel want to see her about? Trying to shake off the anxiety, she started pulling food out of their little fridge and cooked a big breakfast, huevos rancheros with a side of lab bacon and mango kale smoothies. After a while, Kensie came out of their room, pulled by the scent of grease and eggs, sat at the table and wolfed down a double serving.

"What's the occasion?" they said as they were mopping up the last drips of egg yolk. "You never cook like this anymore."

Joy shrugged. She couldn't very well tell Kensie what she was afraid of. "Let's just say I have high hopes for the future. Go on, get yourself to school, before I decide to escort you there personally to see that you make it."

She sat zazen for a few minutes, finally managing to achieve something approximating equanimity. There was no sense picking at it; whatever happened would happen, and she would just have to take it as it came. She dressed in a formal but restrained suit and went down to get a bike out of the public rack.

At the district admin complex, she wasn't kept waiting. A functionary quickly escorted her into Laurel's office. The middle-aged woman nodded as she entered and waved a hand casually at a chair; she was an efficiency hawk who didn't stand on ceremony or indulge in small talk. She adjusted her glasses as Joy sat, then put both hands flat on her desk.

"I know you don't have a lot of free time, Joy, so I'll get right to the point," she said primly. "Our Aquaculture Manager is resigning."

Joy's eyebrows shot up, and Laurel said, "Yes, I know this must be unexpected news. But Rafe's been having cognitive issues for some time now. Surely you've noticed that he's been letting his responsibilities slide. His doctors and I have come to the difficult conclusion that it's time for him to step down."

Joy nodded. Half the reason she'd been doing so much work with the aquaculture, beyond the extra income and just wanting to finally do what she had trained for, was because production had been seriously suffering under Rafe's management. And now there was going to be a new manager to deal with; she would have to build that relationship all over again.

Laurel continued, "There's going to have to be a snap election for the position; we're scheduling it for three months from now. Plex management has to decide who to put their weight behind, and my hope is that I can convince you to take it on."

Joy felt a sudden bittersweet hunger bloom in her heart. "You want *me* to run for Aquaculture Manager?" she said, not without some disbelief.

"Don't be coy," Laurel said drily. "You've practically been doing Rafe's job for months now. How on earth you find the energy to do half the things you do, I can't imagine. To a large extent, you'd just be doing what you've been doing anyway, only with the authority to enforce your decisions and bargain with Regional Management for what you need. Of course, you'd have to resign from your job at the restaurant; even you won't have the time or energy to take on an official Plex Management role while still waiting tables. But I don't see that being much of a hardship. You're wasted in the Luxe market, and I know this is what you wanted before… unpleasant circumstances got in the way. Are you still up for it?"

Joy allowed herself a moment of unadulterated happiness. But of course, immediately the reality of what she would be giving up if she left Moxie's resurfaced. Kensie still needed a new rendering chip, and without the restaurant job, she was damned if she knew how she would pay for it. "I'm just wondering," she said hesitantly, "what I'm going to do for Luxe."

Laurel nodded. "The position does come with an increase in your Luxe stipend. It won't be as much as you're used to making in the private market, but you'll be able to live in reasonable comfort. Oh, and Joy? I know you're the one who's been diverting fish to that restaurant of yours."

Joy's heart leapt into her throat, but Laurel held up a hand. "We're letting it slide because of all the uncompensated labour you've been doing. Even with the skimming, fish yields have substantially increased since you moved to this district. But obviously, if you take an official managerial role, it will have to stop. Anyway, I assume you've invested some of that filthy lucre in Development Bank bonds to help make up the shortfall." When Joy just stared flatly at her, Laurel's eyebrows shot up. "Heavens, Joy," she said, "I never took you for a decadent. What on Earth have you been spending all that Luxe on?"

The words *my child is obsessed with becoming an esports star and I spend almost every fraction of a Luxe I earn supporting their dream* stuck in her throat. Laurel had spent decades in Plex Management; her kind viewed the Luxe market as a necessary evil at best, and would see Kensie's fanatical dedication as frivolous and meaningless. There was no need for her to know.

Joy ran a hand through her hair. "I'm going to have to consider this," she said. "You're springing it on me at the exact worst time. I have a chance to make a promotion at work, and…"

Laurel crossed her arms. "I just don't understand you, Joy," she said harshly. "You've never sought an official position with the Plex, but you spend more time facilitating Plex issues than half of our Advocates. You're all but running the Aquaculture Department on top of half a dozen other things, but when I tell you we want you doing it full-time, you baulk." When Joy didn't answer, she sighed. "Take some time if you have to, but get back to me soon. If you're not up for it, Plex is going to have to pick another candidate to run, and none of the other people on the short list have half as much support in the district as you. And if you don't take the position officially, I'm afraid your interference with the aquaculture system is going to have to end. Regional Management finding a thief among us could tank the whole Board. I'm not going to wreck decades of career advancement on a half-hearted shilly-shally."

Joy wandered out of the admin complex, head spinning. She had been so in control of things, finally getting it together after years dealing with Jaina's abuse and betrayal. How had she let reality blindside her like this? She just stood there for several minutes, drawing strange looks from passersby, not knowing what she wanted to do. It was lunchtime, but she didn't even think she could eat right now. She shook her head; it was her day of leisure, and with everything coming down on her head at once, she had been badly neglecting her self-care. She got on a bicycle and rode through the crowded streets to the district's central park.

Once among the rolling berms and naturalistic ecoculture, she finally felt the stress clear a bit. She made herself forget all of the decisions and responsibilities she was avoiding and just be present in the moment. As she rounded a hill, she saw Marnie with a group of other disabled residents congregating among the shaggy vegetation, sitting on benches or running aimlessly, some throwing an air disc. She gravitated toward them, and waved as she saw Marnie look up from her conversation and notice her. The girl ran joyously across the park and caught her up in a bear hug, then stood back. "You look sad, Joy," she said. "Come sit down. Slow down for once."

Joy let Marnie lead her to a bench and sat with her. She put her head in her hands. The dark thoughts were starting again, Jaina's nagging voice telling her how useless and worthless she was, how no matter what she did it would never be good enough. She massaged her forehead with her thumbs and said, "How do you do it, Marnie? You're always so happy, no matter what's happening in your life. I wish I had half of your positive attitude."

"I am not!" Marnie said indignantly. "I get sad and mad too, Joy. But it's supposed to go away after a while. You can't just keep being sad and being sad. It's not alright."

Joy shook her head. "For me, keeping busy makes the sadness go away. But as soon as I stop for two seconds, it comes back. It's not sustainable. I've been working myself to death, but not actually accomplishing any of my goals. I had a plan for my life once, but for years I've just been picking the default option. Working for profit to buy Kensie fancy gaming computers, taking on everyone's problems because I couldn't say no, managing the aquaculture because nobody else would. Now there *is* no easy way forward. I have to make a hard choice, and I'm scared, Marnie. I'm scared that whatever I do, I'll choose wrong and lose something important."

"But what do you *want* to do?" Marnie insisted.

"It's not all just about what I want," Joy said defensively. "I have responsibilities. To Kensie, to the Plex, to my colleagues, to my friends and neighbours, even a responsibility to myself. I've taken on too many, and I just can't fulfil them all anymore. Something's got to give."

Marnie nodded. "Believe it or not, I have to make hard choices too. You have to just sit and listen to your heart. Deep down you know what the right choice is, but all that stuff you've put on yourself is just getting in the way. You need more than a fifteen-minute break. You need to spend some time with yourself and lose all the clutter."

She tried to speak again, but Marnie just put a finger to her lips. She sighed, then gave in and sat silently with her friend, watching the group play and relax. There were people with every kind of disability, cognitive and physical; people with braces and canes, nonverbal autistics, one slumped in a wheelchair, barely able to twitch his body. "I just feel so guilty," she eventually said. "You guys have more severe challenges than I've ever had to handle, and yet you still find happiness and fulfilment in life. How was it so hard for me? I can't blame Jaina for everything. I've chosen how I responded to that trauma, chosen to reinforce toxic habits and thought patterns despite everyone telling me they're unhealthy. I'm full of advice for other people on how to live their lives, but I can't find a way to take that advice myself."

Marnie patted her hand. "Don't use us as a metre stick for your own life," she said. "Everyone has problems, and ours aren't more important than yours. Everyone has their own limits, and you're making yourself do more than you can, more than you need to. The reason we're happy is because we understand that we are enough." One of her friends waved to her, and just like that she was up and running, dancing with a girl on crutches to music only they could hear.

After a couple of hours she got up and walked back to her tower block, taking her time for once, just taking in the scenery of the residential district with its vegetation-walled towers covered in aquaculture tanks. She finally felt hunger stabbing her insides, grabbed a takeaway from the canteen and carried it back up to the apartment. She wolfed down the pho and kimchi, trying to quiet both her stomach and her thoughts. But once she was done, the whirling roundabout returned. Kensie walked through the door, threw their school bag at the closet, and wandered into the kitchen with a quick "Hi, Mom." They grabbed a yoghurt cup and made to take it into their room, but paused and looked back. "You OK?" they asked. "You're not busy with anything. It's not like you to just sit there"

Joy looked up. "Have a seat," she said. As Kensie hesitantly sat at the table, she said. "Laurel just offered me a big opportunity. She wants me to run for Aquaculture Manager. She's planning to put the full weight of Plex support behind me. With that, plus all the connections I've made with the district residents, I wouldn't have a hard time winning."

A beaming smile broke over Kensie's face. "That's great, Mom!" they said enthusiastically. "You can finally do what you always wanted!"

Joy nodded. "It would be wonderful. I've been busting my ass with no recognition ever since we moved here. But it comes with a big pay cut. I would have to resign from Moxie's, so I won't have any extra source of Luxe. We would have to cut expenses substantially."

Kensie frowned. "I guess I could cut skin purchases. I've been taking in a lot from tournaments and streaming; I won't need your support as much anymore."

"It'll have to be a bit more than skins. We might have to… delay getting that new rendering chip. Probably the suspensors too. You'll have to make do with what you already have for a while. It would take time to save for the best gaming rigs, even on a manager's Luxe stipend."

A look of panic came over Kensie's face. "But without bleeding-edge equipment, I can't stay competitive! I'm so close to getting into a pro league, I can taste it! You can't risk my whole dream because of…"

Joy slammed both her palms onto the table. "What about *my* dream?" she shouted. Anger was flooding her; the same anger she had felt the night she had finally had the Disciplinary Corps drag Jaina out of their house. She knew it was inappropriate, but she was swept helplessly away. "I've sacrificed everything for you, Kensie. My career, my relationships, my mental health, all so you can be a damn esports star. Is it really worth it? Can't *you* give up something for *me* for a change?"

Kensie just stared at her with a hurt and incredulous face, and the anger drained out of Joy as quickly as it had come. She looked over at her pale child, Jaina's child, the constant reminder of both the happiness and the sorrow that had come from that time in her life. She took a deep breath. "Darling, I just can't turn this down. I can't spend another twenty years working in a restaurant, knowing I had this chance and that I blew it. Your career is going to have to go on the back burner. I can't help you anymore."

Kensie mumbled something incomprehensible and slunk back to their room. Tears leaked from Joy's eyes. She had hurt the one she loved most, just as deep as Jaina had ever hurt her, and there was no going back now. She was sure she was making the right choice. But was she, really? Doubt overwhelmed her again. Kensie would hate her forever if she denied them what they had spent years grinding to achieve. Was just getting what she wanted out of life worth sacrificing her relationship with her child?

She tried to just sit zazen for a while. But it just didn't work; the insoluble quandary kept intruding, and she couldn't make herself let them go. Looking for distraction, she drifted over to the living room and started HellBleed up. How ironic, she thought as she took up the controller, that playing this game she hated seemed to be the only time she could gain real clarity. She farmed quests for half an hour, trying to just listen to her heart the way Marnie had told her to. But she was too out of practice; all it was doing for her was throwing up contradictory messages.

As she put the controller down and prepared to shut the game off, that ad banner jumped onscreen again: "MEET MADGUNSKILLZ! LAST CHANCE TO ENTER!" She just stared at it for several minutes. What was she doing grinding this game, saving up play money so her child could get one more in an endless procession of new skins, working herself to the bone so they could have what they wanted? The Luxe market was like a treadmill that you could never get off. If she took the aquaculture management position, every minute she had spent running in place there would have been a waste of time. But she was just running out of capacity to give. She navigated to the contest page and drained her carefully-saved BleedCoins on this long-shot at mending the damage she had done. Then she went to bed, more unsure than ever of what path she should take.

NEXT MORNING, she just laid in bed, not sleeping, barely feeling. The house notified her of several calls from Darien at the restaurant, but she ignored them all. Betray her child, or betray herself? The choice was impossible, and she would give anything not to have to face it. She felt even worse than she had after she had lost Jaina. At least after that, there had still been pieces to pick up.

She was shocked out of her stupor by a hammering on her door, and Kensie's shouts from outside. "I won!" came the muffled screams. "I won!" Joy got up and opened her door, and Kensie burst through, throwing themself into her embrace. "Thank you so much, Mom!" they said, sobbing tears of joy. "I'm gonna meet MadGunSkillz! I've never been so happy in my life!"

JOY SAT with her arm around Kensie as the helicopter flew over the lapping waves. Her child gaped as the streaming star's home grew on the horizon: a seastead, a floating community of domiciles, gardens and private parks surrounding one enormous mansion. This was what true, overwhelming success in the Luxe market could buy: complete freedom from the Plex, from rationing, from work assignments, from obligations to the community; complete control over your own life. Enough Luxe could buy practically anything.

A servant in a blank white domino mask and a port-wine-and-sky-blue uniform, MadGunSkillz' favoured skin colours, handed them out of the helicopter, bowed, and led them silently up the stairs from the waterfront helipad to the looming neo-modernist house. They walked through corridors filled with paintings and antiques, each of them smuggled out from the museums where they belonged for surely staggering bribes. The servant ushered them into a cavernous dining room dominated by a huge, ancient mahogany table where a single man in his late 30s was seated. He had dark hair and light skin and wore an incredibly loud blue suit. He looked up in annoyance as the servant bowed again and announced, "Mackensie and Joy Charleston."

"Oh yeah, the contest," the streamer said impatiently. "OK, sit down, have some food." he waved a hand at the chairs across from him. Servants wafted in and placed platters of real ham and mashed potatoes drizzled with truffle sauce, richer fare than anything that had ever been served in Moxie's. Joy dutifully ate, uncomfortable among all this conspicuous consumption. Kensie didn't even touch their food, just stared in awe at their idol and everything that his immense success had brought him.

Putting his fork down, MadGunSkillz said, "So you want to be a pro like me, is that right?" Kensie nodded, a lump in their throat, and prepared to receive the teachings of the master.

"You probably don't have what it takes," MadGunSkillz said dismissively. "Most people don't. The secret is to grind every hour of every day. Grind without stopping. You have to love the grind. It has to be your friends, your family, your lover, your every moment of joy, even to make the top of the leagues, let alone earn like I do. Your whole life has to be grind. You can never stop."

He took a sip of wine from a crystal glass, then spat it out. "You moron!" he shouted at the masked servant that stood silently at his shoulder. "I ordered Chateau Royale 2035! This is the 2036! I have guests, for chrissake!" He picked up the glass and threw it at the servant, who didn't even flinch as it hit their chest, splashing wine all over their beautiful uniform. "Your pay is docked! Take this shit back, and tell the sommelier that the next time this happens, it'll be his job!"

He turned back to Joy and Kensie, who were staring incredulously. "We done here? I'm live in ten minutes, I don't have time to babysit slackers."

Kensie screwed up their courage. "I was hoping I could see your rig, maybe duo with you…"

MadGunSkillz laughed harshly. "What, let a scrub like you tank my ranking? Sure thing!" He waved a hand. "Get back to whatever you plexies call lives. Daddy has work to do." Then he stood and walked out of the room, acting like they didn't even exist.

For most of the ride back, Kensie was silent, staring dumbfounded over the water. As they approached the coast and normalcy, they said, "It's not just a persona. He's like that all the time."

After another long silence, they turned to Joy and said, "If I get rich and famous off streaming... is that how I'm gonna end up?"

Joy ruffled their hair. "Only you can decide how you handle it," she said. "But having that much power... well, it tends to change a person. That's why we created the Plex, why we regulate the Luxe market so heavily. We decided it's not good for anyone to have that much. Before, everyone was like those servants; everyone had to please some rich man just to afford to eat. We did away with that, but we had to make compromises, to let a system remain where a few people like that could still exist. It's not what I want for you."

"Is he right? Is that all I have to look forward to, grinding and grinding until I age out? Even when I'm finally successful, I'll never be able to rest?"

"You have to decide what success looks like for you, Kensie. Maybe success isn't a floating mansion and masked, interchangeable people serving your every need. It's not reasonable to expect that much work, that much dedication, from anybody. I certainly don't expect it from you. I want you to have a good life. That just doesn't look like a good life to me."

"But you do the same thing, Mom," Kensie said helplessly. "You work and work every hour of every day, and you have nothing to show for it. No money, no big house, no fine wine. You just take on more and more responsibility and the only reward is even more responsibility."

Tears began to leak from Joy's eyes. "The reason I act like that is because I'm sick, honey. Jaina broke something in me, something I don't know how to fix. If I don't push myself all the time, I'll get like I was after she left again, not able to work, to take care of you, to even get out of bed. It's not right that I do that, and it's not right that I taught you it's normal. I don't need to be emulated. I need help."

Kensie nestled their head against Joy's shoulder. "You know, the reason I wanted to be like him is because I never wanted you to struggle again like you did after Mama left," they said quietly. "You remember what it was like, when they cut your Luxe stipend because you wouldn't work. We had to give up so much, just scrape and scrape for the smallest comfort. I started grinding in the first place so you could have nice things. I was afraid you'd end up like old Mrs. Leander, alone, with nobody and nothing. I wanted to set it up so you could always have the best of everything." They sighed. "I guess I forgot the goal, got too invested in the process. I made you sacrifice so much, just to try and be like that…" they couldn't even finish the sentence.

"Oh, honey," Joy said. "I was happy to do it for you, because it made you happy. But we don't need all of that. We don't need the best of everything. Plex provides us with what we really need. I don't need a big house, I don't need real meat or expensive art. Just having you is all I need."

Kensie sat up again and looked at her. "Go ahead and take the fish farm job, Mom," they said. "I need to think about some things. I need to decide what I'm taking for Voc-Plex. Maybe coding; I've done a lot of scripting to make my rig more efficient. And maybe I'll look into doing retro-game streaming instead. Those guys seem pretty chill, and you don't need a cutting-edge machine to compete, just pure skill."

Joy nodded and hugged her child close as the helicopter came in for a landing. "I'm going to have to think about some things too," she said. "I've got to stop this ridiculous life. I'm going to go to my therapist and find a way to get things back on track. I'm going to make sure I have more time for you, for what's really important. I'm going to make sure that from now on, I'm enough."

Xauri'EL Zwaan is a mendicant artist in search of meaning, fame and fortune, or pie (where available); a Genderqueer Bisexual, a Socialist Solarpunk, and a Satanist Goth. Zie has recently published short fiction in The Sprawl Mag, the Simultaneous Times podcast, Neo-Opsis, Cossmass Infinities, and Galaxy's Edge. Zie lives and writes in a little hobbit hole in Saskatoon, Canada on Treaty 6 territory with zir life partner and two very lazy cats.

Patreon: https://www.patreon.com/xauriel
Mastodon: https://mastodon.nz/@XauriEL
Facebook: https://www.facebook.com/XaurielZwaan/
Twitter: https://twitter.com/xauriel
Saskatchewan Writers' Guild Profile: https://skwriter.com/find-saskatchewan-writers/xauriel-zwaan

VIOLET

BY BETH GAYDON

Castyn gripped the countertop and tried to breathe. In. Out. In. Out. In—
"Augghh," she said, gritting her teeth as the contraction came. Her eyes closed,
trying to wish the pain away. "Amir? Where are you?"

For a second, no one answered. Then Amir came running around the
corner, slashing at the trees growing through their living room and hopping
over a vine to get to his wife. "Already?" he asked.

"I told you an hour ago she was coming," Castyn reminded him, trying
not to snarl.

"Yeah, but... an hour? Remember—"

"I said she's coming!" Castyn snapped. She no longer cared if Amir was
ready or not. She certainly was. Could she give birth in her home? Sure. The
geothermal activity was high that morning and powering everything to the nth
degree. Did she want to? Obviously not.

Amir eyed her, staring at her huge, swollen belly, and then hopped to
attention. He snatched the hospital bag from the corner, tossed a bucket of
rainwater at the kitchen crops, and ran to Castyn to grab her hand. "I love
you," he said. "And I solemnly swear to do everything in my power to get you
the good painkillers."

Castyn rolled her eyes, but she touched his cheek, the contraction come and gone, improving her mood. "Please do," she said. She leaned forward so Amir could kiss her, and then they ran outside together, into the gardens.

Though everyone in the neighborhood had helped grow the neighborhood into a wild jungle, with the assistance of Newbury Volcano's fertile soil, some of them had demanded a clear path to the bus, and for the first time in years Castyn felt grateful for it instead of annoyed. She and Amir used the cleared space to reach the Volcan bus track. She rarely used it, preferring to bicycle where she could, but if she tried a bike now, she'd just tip over. "How long?" she asked Amir.

Amir held out his hands and pursed his lips. "We never use the bus," he reminded his wife, then gave her his hand again so she could squeeze it and potentially break it off. "I can call Brea."

"No," Castyn said, hearing the forcefulness in her voice but unable to stop it. Brea Johnson was, and always had been, in love with Amir, even if Amir wasn't interested. The last thing Castyn needed was some neighborhood floozy trying to flirt with her husband as she gave birth.

"Alright, but if it takes forever and you give birth right here, don't blame me."

Castyn blew out a heavy sigh, but Amir's worries might be justified. She eyed the track, a thick black rail powered by the volcanic energy pushing the bus around. Castyn didn't understand how it worked, but it always made her nervous, like instead of an attached streetcar she'd be in a boat swishing through lava. There was no lava now; it had all been diverted, powering other cities nearby. Still, when the sleek silver bus arrived, only slightly graffitied, she let out a sigh of relief. "Finally," she said.

"It was what, two minutes?" Amir asked, raising his eyebrow. Then he held out both hands again. "Sorry, sorry. Very pregnant lady, I know, I know." He took her hand and helped her into the bus after it came to a complete stop. Then he grabbed the bag and hopped on himself, collapsing into one of the cozy hemp chairs. He took Castyn's hand, helping her get as comfortable as possible—which wasn't very. "I'm happy."

"I'm happy too," Castyn said, forcing a smile as another contraction hit her. She squeezed his hand, trying to practice the breathing techniques she'd learned, and grimaced until it was over. They were closer now, only six minutes apart, and with any luck, by the time they reached the birthing center, she'd be admitted and receiving an epidural within minutes. After the pain subsided, Castyn smiled for real. It was a big deal, this baby. They'd conceived naturally, but the planning and preparation, the paperwork required to get the pregnancy approved—it'd been a lot. But it would all be worth it soon. "I better call my mom."

"Already did," Amir replied. "They'll meet as at the hospital in a couple of hours."

"Oh good." Castyn squeezed her husband's hand again and leaned against him. They both watched outside the window as their little city flew by, a whir of greens and browns with buildings tucked inside their forests. Newbury had been named one of the top ten most breathable U.S. cities for the fifth time in a row last year, and Castyn sparkled with pride at the designation. She didn't work for the city, but she did design indoor planting spaces, and almost every home in the area now grew at least some food. Asthma rates in Newbury were half that of other cities in the country. Granted, they couldn't all use the volcano's energy, but some of them were still resisting alternative energy sources, for goodness' sake.

When they arrived, only a few short minutes later—Castyn would have to remember how quick the Volcan flew through the streets—a crowd of reporters huddled around the hospital entrance. Castyn wrinkled her nose. "I didn't think they'd be here this early."

"Neither did I," Amir agreed. He gave them the evil eye, but they were too far away to notice. "I'll find a back entrance, if you want."

Castyn shook her head. "No, it's fine. I just want to get inside. They're not going to block a pregnant lady from the hospital." Still, as she moved towards the door, a hot blush crossed her cheeks. It did not surprise her to see the reporters, but still, being on camera as fat as a whale, every body part sagging, wasn't ideal. Amir tried his best to block her, but he was as skinny as the rest of the non-pregnant population, following the lesser rations allowed for people not hauling around a fetus.

"Castyn!" a reporter called. "Where is she?"

"Come on, Castyn! Tell us! Is she here? Where is she?"

Castyn lifted her head long enough to glare at the reporters. "I'm having a baby," she pointed out. "How about you leave me alone?"

"But where is she?" another one called.

Amir ignored all of them and pushed Castyn through the sliding doors, into the safety of the birthing center. The workers wouldn't allow the gaggle of reporters inside, not unless Castyn invited them, which she wouldn't. "How'd they know we were coming?" he wondered.

"I'm sure someone paid the nurses off," Castyn replied. She couldn't blame the nurses for taking the money; it was hard living on a regular person's wages. "Oh no, another one." Castyn bent over in pain and a nurse came running with a wheelchair, helping Castyn collapse into it.

"Perfect timing," the nurse said once the contraction had passed. "We've got you checked in already."

"You recognized me?"

"Of course. Hard not to, with that mob hounding you. Come on back, Castyn. Let's get you into a room." The nurse wheeled Castyn into the elevator, where they traveled down into the hollowed-out lava tubes. It was easier to harness power underground, with no need for complicated grids or drills allowing the geothermal energy to escape, so they'd built the biggest businesses in the city right inside, including the hospital. Amir's father had been part of the original building crew, determined to push through intense heats and the potential for catastrophic accidents. The accidents had never reached catastrophic, but like many of his fellow builders, Amir's father had succumbed to the poor air conditions long before seeing his plans come to fruition. Amir worked in the tubes now, providing power and keeping a wary eye on the volcano scientists claimed they had tamed. So far, it seemed they were correct, but new technologies required constant monitoring. Amir liked his job, though; the hours were good, and it was rewarding. Castyn glanced at the LED strips lining the tunnels. The artificial light was fine for hospital patients, and the virtual window displays were so spectacular patients hardly noticed they weren't looking at real forests or jungles, or whatever they chose. During Castyn's last hospital visit, she'd made her window a beautiful meadow, but this time she wanted a beach scene. It was all there in her birthing plan. Not everything would go to plan, of course, but she thought it unlikely a window malfunction would be a major issue.

Before long, Castyn was in her bed, ready to give the baby her eviction notice. The anesthesiologist joined her right away to administer the sweet, sweet drugs that made the process bearable, and for a while Castyn and Amir had nothing to do but watch a movie as the contractions came and went. Eventually, a doctor appeared to say it was time, and out popped a tiny baby girl with overpowered lungs. Castyn waited impatiently to be handed her daughter, then snatched her away, not wanting to share, even with Amir. Dr. Glass watched her for a minute, then sighed. "They'll want to see her, you know. Someone invited two of them into the waiting room."

"Of course they did," Castyn said, furrowing her brows at the baby. She looked up at the doctor. "But she's not here yet."

Dr. Glass pursed her lips. "Okay. I'll tell them."

Castyn returned to snuggling with the newborn, trying to feed her. She was a precious little thing they'd already named Violet. It was common to name babies everything volcano related (three Helens and two Etnas just in the neighborhood), but she and Amir wanted to be different. Thinking of Amir, Castyn relinquished control of the little one and handed her over to her husband, who momentarily looked terrified of breaking her, and then pulled her close to his face to take a hit of that new baby smell. "I'm in love," he said.

"Me too," Castyn said, smiling, but labor had taken it out of her and she needed rest. They would take Violet away in a moment anyway, to check what needed checking and give her the meds that would keep her safe. So Castyn allowed herself to sleep.

A WHILE LATER, when Castyn was awake and alert, once again clutching her baby to her breast, a knock on the door announced her mother's arrival. Amir stood up to let his mother-in-law have the chair, and they jostled around, oohing and aahing over the baby. "Is it time?" Mom asked after she'd held Violet long enough.

"Yep. Send her in."

Castyn's mom beamed and exited the door she'd just entered. A moment later, she arrived, clutching a little girl's hand. The cute brunette climbed into the bed with Castyn, peering over her shoulder to look at the baby. "This is my sister?" she asked.

"Yes, sweetheart. This is Violet."

"She's kind of wrinkly."

Castyn laughed. "All babies look like that."

"She stinks too."

"Juniper Ann," Amir admonished her. "Be nice."

"It's not that I don't love her," Juniper protested. "She's tiny and adorable, and I'll take good care of her. But I didn't know babies were like this."

"Of course you didn't, sweetie. You haven't been around any since you were one." Castyn paused, watching her two daughters, a pang in her chest. "There are some people in the waiting room who would like to talk to you. They'll ask a few questions and maybe take your picture. But only if you want to. That's why we had you wait so long, so you could sneak in."

Juniper fell quiet, considering. "Because I'm a big sister?" she finally asked.

Castyn nodded. "Because you're a big sister." She still couldn't believe it. No one in the entire country had received approval for a second child in fifty years. She and Amir had submitted the request as a lark, and had to check twenty times to ensure the okay wasn't a mistake. "It's a big responsibility. And you won't have many people to talk to about it."

"Old people have sisters, though, right?" Juniper asked. She looked at her grandma. "Did you have a sister?"

"Hey," Mom replied, swatting at the young girl, though she wore a smile. "I'm not that old. Or at least that rich." She said the last part under her breath to Amir, who laughed. The upper class had been allowed multiple children for longer than everyone else, but even they had had it revoked. And now that class inequality had leveled out, their approval was based not on income, but on their contributions to the environment and the quality of life they provided Juniper.

After she pulled herself together, Castyn shifted up. "Do you want to go out there?" she asked Juniper. "We can all go together, if you want. But you don't have to."

"I'll talk to them," Juniper decided, hopping off the bed and skipping around. "It'll be cool to be on the news. Let's go."

Castyn prepared herself as best she could, and she and Amir took their daughter's hands on either side of her. Daphne held the baby. They wandered out to the waiting room, where two reporters waited, lounging in awkward positions on the wooden chairs.

The woman reporter saw them first. "Is that her?" she asked, putting her feet back on the floor. "Is this Miss Juniper?"

"That's me," Juniper answered.

"It's so nice to meet you, Juniper. Mind if I ask you a question?"

"Go ahead."

"What's it like to be a big sister?"

"I don't know," Juniper said, shrugging as she peered at the baby. "It's kind of cool. I've never seen a new baby before. She smells weird."

The reporters laughed, and the male took over. "What's your sister's name?"

"Violet."

"What kind of things will you two do together?"

"Well, nothing for now. She's too little. But when she's bigger, I'll teach her how to play dolls and to garden. It should be pretty fun. Yeah, it should be real fun." Juniper craned her neck to look up to Castyn. "She'll be able to talk to me when you're busy."

"That's right," Castyn agreed.

"Yeah. That's neat. That's really neat. And we can talk together at night. It'll be like a sleepover every single night. My friends can't come over every night, so that will be cool."

"So what do you think, Juniper? Are you glad to have a sibling?"

"Yeah! I'm so glad they fixed the earth. This is going to be awesome."

"Can we get a picture?"

Castyn's body screamed in pain, but the love for her new family was strong. She gave a nod of approval, and the four of them—four, in one family—huddled together. As the reporters took their pictures, Castyn sent a silent thank you to whatever entity had helped humanity save them from themselves… and another, for giving her more than she'd ever dreamed of.

Beth Gaydon is an internet analyst living in Tennessee with her husband, kids, and dogs. She tries to be nice to the environment, though her thumbs are chartreuse at best. When she's not busy with her family, she writes about whatever topic intrigues her that day. You can find her most recent work in The Sirens Call, The First Line, and On the Premises.

REHOME INC.

BY J. SCOTT COATSWORTH

Crack.

Devyn Miller-Hill pulled the heavy iron mallet back, and swung it full force against the old drywall, producing another satisfying shattering sound as the hardened surface began to give way under his determined assault.

Crack.

The surface buckled.

Crack.

A third time, and a large hole appeared in the middle of the old wall. The place had good bones, as they used to say, including the raccoon skeleton he'd found up in the attic. There hadn't been a live raccoon in these parts for decades, though this one had clearly become a *permanent* resident at some point. Devyn grinned at his own weird sense of humor. *That's why Zan married me, after all.*

The Miller-Hills… MillHills, to their closest friends. They'd done it the traditional way, rings and flowers and a walk down the aisle. *Old fashioned* was kind of Zan's thing, after all, and Devyn had gone all in *hardcore* the last few years.

He wished, for just a second, that his brother Elwyn was here to see this. They hadn't spoken in years, and Devyn had given up on ever reconciling their differences. Zan was his family now.

He grabbed his bottle of *Killzitall* and sprayed it into the opening, and then sealed it with a patch. The mist would work its way through that section of the wall and neutralize any mold that might be lurking inside.

"Might have been easier to just drill a hole." Abby Koss, Devyn's sidekick in their new ReHome Incorporated venture, was shaking their head and tugging on their long black braid in annoyance.

If there's an easy way to do something and a hard way to do it, leave it to Devyn to find the latter. One of the things Zan said about him regularly.

But there was usually a *right* way and a *wrong* way, and the wrong way often costs you more in the long run. "The bigger hole lets in more air, and makes the remediator work faster."

They rolled their eyes. "Whatever you say, boss. Just came to tell you that the guys from Trentovation are here with the reprocessor unit you rented. Wanna come down and sign for it?"

He snorted at the name. Trent Cachegee was a scrappy Vancouver entrepreneur pushing the edges of province corporate law with the size of his business, which had reached the maximum of ten employees. "I'm surprised he didn't call it a Trentiprocessor."

"Or a Cachegachine."

He snorted. "Better." Still, Trent ran a good business and had always treated Devyn well. "Go ahead and sign for it. I want to get this room done."

Their eyes widened. "Are you sure?"

"You're a partner in this thing. Time to start acting like it." Abby was Sylvie Koss's spawn—their word—the child of Zan's old provost from Seattle.

"Thanks, boss!" They scampered off.

"Not your boss!" he called after them, but they were already gone.

They might be just twenty-two—half his own age—but they had a good head for business. They'd started their first one when they were fifteen and had sold it to generate the capital to buy into their new partnership in ReHome.

Devyn shook his head and moved on to the next section of drywall.

Crack, crack, crack.

That's when he found the journal.

～

It was after seven when he finally got back to the housing commons he and Zan called home in Mt. Pleasant. Vancouver's old downtown and West End were now an island, separated by a waterway called the New Sound, but a new bridge connected the eastern edge of downtown with Strathcona. Devyn biked it every day, a little over six-and-a-half kilometers round-trip.

"I'm home! Where are you?" His back ached something fierce from the hard labor. *Being forty-four is no picnic.*

"In here." Zan's voice, coming from the small apartment's multi-purpose room, sounded sweet, lifting the weight of the day off Devyn's shoulders. "Thought you might want to eat here after a long day at work."

"Good idea. What's for dinner?" They usually snagged meals in the Alastair Commons dining hall with the other residents, but like always, Zan knew him better than he knew himself. He set down his hemp satchel, slipped off his shoes, and luxuriated in the soft refiber carpet that lined their floors. *Like walking on fresh grass.*

"I snagged us a bit of salmon from the reclamation project. They're meeting their quotas, and the Commons got in a shipment last night. Andre whipped up quite a tasty dish."

Devyn breathed in deeply. "I can smell it. And good choice on the *eating in—*"

He rounded the corner into the MPR and stopped dead in his tracks. It was their dining room, living room, and kitchen, depending on which modules were accessed at any given time. But just then, it had been transformed by Zan's wand—technological, not magical—into a *full real* of a trendy outdoor patio overlooking San Francisco Bay, the lights of the Golden Gate Bridge glimmering in the distance.

Zan picked up his wand and flicked it, and the scents and sounds emerged —people talking, cars whisking by below, and the mingled smells of fish and fresh-baked sourdough bread rising from the piers in the near distance.

"It's… beautiful. You made this for me? Just for dinner?"

Zan laughed and kissed him on the cheek. His presence lightened Devyn's spirits, as always. Three years younger, and his relative youth showed. "No, silly. It's a new full real I just got from an artist friend in Seattle. I sent her one of my new ones of Stanley Park in return. Come on. I saved you a seat near the railing." Grinning, he led Zan across the short terrace. The full real was expansive, but their own physical space was not.

They sat together and, for half an hour, they enjoyed their chef-prepared meal in a restaurant with a view of the bay, laughing and talking together about their days.

"The Re-Housing Act came up again today," Zan said casually, closing his eyes to savor a bite of the salmon. Unprocessed food was rare these days, a real treat.

"Oh yeah?" It was something Devyn had suggested a couple years before—government support to jumpstart the reclamation of some of the old, deterio-rating housing stock in the city, starting with the West End. *If the pilot project goes well...* "Is there a chance?"

It had been defeated twice, but that was before Mecklyn Johnson, a council member with ties to the big rental agencies in the city—including Evlin Farcosee Bastron, or EFB—had unexpectedly retired. Devyn suspected he'd been caught with his hand in the till, or in something else. Firms like EFB routinely tried to get the ten-employee maximum lifted for corporations, with the help of corrupt politicians. Some things never changed.

Zan nodded eagerly, feeding Devyn a forkful of fish. "Tandy Waters is eager to get moving on homesites in the West End, now that the new Seawall's been completed."

Tandy had ridden into office on a wave of renter dissatisfaction. *The rents are rising faster than the ocean!* had been her rallying cry.

"Flooding rivers, that's divine." There were signs—small ones, but you could see them if you looked—that things were slowly getting better. The Chaos Years had killed billions, forcing the survivors to switch gears. Now there were wild salmon in the rivers again. Trade agreements stitched together the West Coast. A universal basic income gave Vancouver citizens a little breathing room. And maybe, just maybe the city council would finally see the light on new housing. "Can I help?"

Zan shrugged. "Not yet. But I'm counting on you to testify at the next meeting about the pilot project." He'd managed to slam that one through a couple months earlier.

"Of course. We got the worst of the mold remediated today."

"Your personal experience will be invaluable to help sway the rest of the council." He leaned over to kiss Devyn's cheek. "Though I might have some-thing else for you to do, tonight..."

Devyn grinned. "There will be dishes to wash first. But I could use a little relaxation."

Zan laughed. "Fair enough. But tell me, what about *your* day?"

Caught in mid-bite, Devyn had to quickly swallow—regretfully—the piece of salmon he'd been enjoying. "It's going well. Most of the walls have been prepped for drywall removal. The house is about twenty meters above sea level, so it escaped the worst of the damage, though it's been vacant for a long time. Oooh, that reminds me!" He got up and retraced his steps to the foyer. "I found something!" He retrieved a plastic bag from his satchel.

"What?"

He returned to Zan's side and held out his prize. "I found it inside one of the walls."

"What is it?" Zan's eyebrow shot up as he peered at the opaque sack. "Is that... *plastic*?"

It was almost a dirty word these days. "Yeah, it's actually kinda cool. You pry it apart like this." He demonstrated. "Then you can seal it, airtight, like this." He ran his hand across the seam in the plastic.

"*That's* exciting to you?" Zan's eyebrow raised in mocking humor.

Devyn sighed. "I know, it's made of gasoline and all that crap from the before times. But that's not what I wanted to show you." He opened it again and pulled the journal out. "I think it belonged to one of the previous owners. Or residents." He'd researched the property, and its last incarnation had been as a boarding house, purchased by one Miriam Akiyoshi.

"Can I see?"

Devyn nodded and handed it over. "Just be careful with it. It's probably fifty, a hundred years old."

Zan took it and flipped it open slowly. "Oooh, what neat script. Looks like it belonged to someone named... Arthur? No, Artie. Artie Johnson. I'll bet the city has some records on file about him." He handed the book back. "It might be worth something."

"Maybe." There was a big market for antiquities—anything that predated the Chaos Years—but the journal might be too recent. And in any case, he wanted to take a look through it first. He tucked it into its protective sack and set it aside. "Abby took delivery on the reprocessor this afternoon."

"Wow. The job really is going fast." Zan licked his plate clean, earning him an exasperated look from Devyn.

"Not really. There are always setbacks. But I worked out a great deal with Trent to keep it for a couple months—"

"You didn't bring me into it, did you?" People were always trying to snag favors from him as a council member.

Something Devyn had become painfully aware of. "Not even a little. I promised to help him do a little advertising, including a sign in the front yard once the rebuild is done." He didn't tell Zan his secret—that he was building the place for the two of them.

Common living was fine when you were in your twenties, but he wanted to settle down with Zan on a more permanent basis, with a family.

"Good." Zan finished off his wine, with Devyn not far behind.

"Maybe things are getting better?" They'd had their hopes raised before, only to have them dashed by a nasty turn of the weather or a loss in the city council. But hope sprung eternal, even when someone always managed to whack it with a shovel.

"Maybe." Zan's eyes twinkled "Should we… *wash the dishes?*"

An hour later, as Zan snored beside him, his beautiful naked body stretched out across the mattress, Devyn unwrapped the journal again.

It was beautiful—probably real leather, judging from the smell of it. Devyn had seen leather before, but it was a rarity. Someone had carved out a beautiful Inuit eagle on the front cover—Devyn traced the outline, feeling the fine workmanship.

He opened it up and leafed through it, trying to make sense of it.

It wasn't as much a journal as a memoir, divided into five distinct sections: Childhood, the War, the Ministry, Stevie, and Miri.

The cool night breezes off the Pacific flowed through the Commons building through specially constructed air traps, cooling the bedroom without need of power. The fresh air felt good, but he pulled up a blanket over his own naked chest to keep off the chill. Zan had set the room's transponder to show a coniferous forest—one of his favorites. A blue jay's call helped set the mood.

Devyn picked a paragraph at random in the Stevie section, reading in the golden light of the photosphere in the ceiling.

From the moment I saw him, I knew. I was just a grunt working on the suspended park at the Harbour Centre when he came out of the elevator doors. Tall, dark, and handsome, they used to call it, and the garden's architect—Steve Desjardins—was all three. No way would he notice a short Cameroonian immigrant like me working on his project. I remember staring at him, his shock of brown hair, the twin vines of tattoos winding up his arms, and above all, the way he walked through life with such certainty. He knew what he wanted, and how to get it. You could see it in his walk, in his posture, in the way he made whoever was in front of him his whole world.

Devyn grinned. He knew the feeling He'd felt it the first time he'd laid eyes on Zan, some twelve years earlier, at an immersive public exhibition of some of Zan's full reals. When he'd first arrived at the party, the hotel ballroom had been a recreation of Seattle's famous Pike Place market. Then it had shifted effortlessly into New York City in the 1920's.

When Devyn had spotted the artist, Zan had been initiating the next change, as the speakeasy and bustling New York scene was transformed into ancient Rome's Palatine Hill.

Devyn's history lessons were having a hard time keeping up, but his attention was captured by the man in the toga with the vines in his hair. And when Zan's eyes met his, they were suddenly the only two people in the room.

With a grin, he set the journal aside to read more later. He had an early morning, as he planned to finish the drywall demo with Abby's help. And he had a shipment of specialty parts coming in from the turner's shop at nine, things they couldn't make with the reprocessor.

He snuggled up next to Zan, who grunted and fell back asleep, fully aware how lucky he was. And how lucky Artie must have felt to find the love of his life.

In less than a week, they'd stripped the house down to its bones.

Devyn had checked the long-term forecasts. All he needed was to have a severe storm whip through and destroy the naked structure before he could get it retrofitted. While it would likely rain a number of times—this was still

Vancouver by the sea, climate change or not—it shouldn't be enough to cause any damage.

Still, as he applied the nano resin to the old wooden framing, he glanced worriedly up at the sky. It was dark, especially for 10:30 in the morning, and the wind was picking up, blowing in angry little gusts that lifted his shirt and threatened to blow away anything that wasn't weighted down. *Forecasts could be wrong.*

"Gonna be a good one!" Abby called from the next room over. They were hurrying to get the treatment applied before the storm let loose—the rain wouldn't affect it, and once the nanites got to work, the wood framing would strengthen to the approximate hardness of steel.

"Just keep working." He'd been reading Artie's journal every night—the handwriting was small and dense, and he made it through no more than three to four pages a night before he fell into an exhausted sleep. One passage in particular came to mind:

> *We crouched under an overhang in a small town in Lebanon, my platoon brothers and I, waiting for the signal to go. The enemy had settled into a bunker on the far side of town, and one of those rare near-hurricanes off the Mediterranean—less rare every year—was pummeling the dirt with wet hail, turning it into a savage, sucking mud. We were glad of the rain, but aware that it would be followed by a muggy heat no less intense than the thumb-sized chunks of ice that pelted our helmets like stones. I wondered, once again, why we were there fighting Excorp's war.*

Dev shook his head. *So much to unpack there.* The idea of travel to another part of the world. The onset of the climate crisis and the Chaos Years. And the ugly, primitive concept of war—and for a corporation's interests, no less.

He finished the last of the upstairs room he was working on and headed downstairs, where the floor above offered a little more protection from the storm. "Almost done?"

"Yup, chief. Join you in a minute." They loved poking him about being the boss, even though they were equal partners.

"Hurry it up, private!" *Private?* Artie's journal was getting into his head. "She's coming in hot."

The wind was howling now, making the whole structure shudder.

Devyn put down his bucket and set to work layering on the resin. He hollered up the open staircase that bisected the building. "Abbs, come down here and help me finish this part. The rest up there can wait." If they could get the base anchored, it would go a long way toward protecting the whole structure.

"On it, boss."

He heard them thump their way down the stairs. What Abby lacked in physical grace, they made up for in business savvy and sheer loyalty.

"Take the other side," Devyn said as their mop-head of dark hair appeared.

"It's getting slick up there." Abby's eyes were wide.

Devyn didn't bother to ask whether *slick* meant with rain, or if it was the latest Gen-Nano word for *intense*. "Do what you can. If it gets too strong, we'll hunker down in the basement until the worst of it passes."

Abby gave him the thumbs-up and slipped into the other side of the building.

He'd gotten three-quarters of his side of the ground floor done when the wind suddenly rose to new heights, howling around them like the dogs of hell. The rain began in earnest, pelting the house from all directions, blowing sideways into the interior, and soaking him almost instantly.

He dropped his brush in the almost-empty can and sealed the lid, and then ran through the open walls to find Abby.

They were staring out at the raging storm, mouth open in disbelief.

"Come on! We need to get below to ride this out!"

It wasn't a hurricane—not officially. But he'd learned even seventy mile-per-hour winds could be very destructive.

They nodded and followed him to the back of the house, where the only remaining door, under the staircase, led down to the basement.

His watch beeped and glowed blue, the color he'd set for alerts from Zan. "Hey babe!" His footfalls echoed in the narrow stairwell.

Zan's 'mage appeared above the watch, a miniature Zan head. "You two okay? Looks like a nasty one out there."

"Yeah, we'll be all right. Got most of the resin applied, and now we're headed to the basement to wait it out."

The relief in Zan's voice was palpable. "Good. This one took the meteorologists by surprise. A bit of hot air out in the Pacific turned a nice thunderstorm into a bit of a monster."

"I can hear that." He reached the bottom of the stairs and waved a hand over one of the photospheres he'd left earlier. The golden light filled the old basement, which was now stacked full of printed supplies for the house refurbishment. He whistled. Abby had been busy with the reprocessor. "Where are you?"

"At city hall. We're high and dry over here." Zan paused, lines of worry etched into his brow. "I hope the seawall holds."

"It should." The new one had only been completed the year before. "Is it high tide?"

"Near enough. I'll let you know if I hear anything. Stay safe. Love you." Zan blew him a kiss.

"Love you too." He waved the 'mage away. After a moment's thought, he sent a quick message to his brother Elwyn. *Thinking about you.* Maybe it was time to start mending fences.

He stared at it for a moment, but it remained stubbornly unread. He sighed.

Abby plopped themselves down on a stack of repro-drywall. "Sounds like a bad storm up there."

Devyn grimaced. "Yeah, this is what I was hoping to avoid. Still, we did the best we could." As long as the resin took, and as long as they'd covered enough of the structure… two big ifs.

"What now?" They dangled their feet over the edge of the pile like a six-year-old.

"Now, we wait." He'd saved a few things he'd found in the house besides the journal, including an old card game called Uno. Luckily, it had the instructions, though the thin paper had badly yellowed with age. "Wanna learn how to play a new game?"

They settled in to try the game, sipping on water from the metal bottles they'd brought and comparing lunches while the storm raged outside. Devyn had a vat-meat sandwich on some fantastic multi-grain bread they'd found at the farmer's market that floated above Granville Island, long drowned by the sea. Abby had a bowl full of tofu, steamed vegetables and rice that looked mouthwatering, even cold.

The game was simple enough, and after a few rounds they were regularly kicking Devyn's ass at it. He kept forgetting to say "Uno!" when he got down to his last card.

"I don't think I like this side of you." Though in truth, it was good to see them standing up for themselves.

Abby grinned maliciously. "Take two cards—"

A loud crash interrupted the game.

"Oh crap." Abby's eyes went wide. "What do you think that was?"

"No way to know until this is over." Devyn cursed himself for getting them into this mess. A failure here would likely mean the end of ReHome Inc, and the sizable portion of his savings with Zan that he'd sunk into the project.

Nothing to be done for it now. You made the best decision with the data you had, and then lived with the consequences. *Easy enough to say.* "Your turn."

The storm eventually blew itself out, the howl of the wind subsiding until there was only the gentle patter of the rain.

He put the game and his lunch containers away and climbed the stairs, heart in his throat, worried about what they would find.

Had the whole structure collapsed? Were they trapped down here until Zan could send help? *At least he knows where we are.*

Had he just set fire to his dream?

He touched the doorknob at the top of the stairs, and hesitated.

"Come on. Waiting's not gonna make it any better, or worse." Abby poked his back. "Rip the Band-Aid off."

Devyn took a deep breath and opened the door.

Bright sunlight blinded him momentarily. The storm had moved on as quickly as it had come, and the whole world was sparkling and new.

The house was still standing.

Devyn breathed a huge sigh of relief.

"Dev, look." Abby was staring through the naked beams.

The one next door hadn't been so lucky. Despite being relatively intact, it had slipped off of its foundation—probably hidden rot—and had collapsed into the front yard, partially blocking the street.

"Glad we picked this one, aren't you?"

Devyn nodded. Thank the stars, the neighborhood was empty except for the two of them and the other pilot projects.

He rubbed his chin. A resourceful contractor could help clean up some of the debris, while making more repro-dust for his own project. "We were lucky."

He climbed the staircase to the upper floor, still nervous about possible storm damage.

And there was some. One corner of the last room Abby had been working on—probably the one they hadn't finished when he had called them downstairs—had collapsed, but the rest of the building had held. The limited damage could be repaired.

"Sorry, boss." Abby had that hangdog expression they often got when they started to doubt themselves.

"Nothing to be sorry for. I called you downstairs, remember? And look how well the rest of this stood up—the parts you did have time to get to?"

They blushed. "Thanks Dev." Then they brightened, like the sun after a storm. "This is going to work."

"I hope so." He closed his eyes, trying to imagine what the place had looked like when Artie had lived there.

He checked his message to Elwyn. Still unread. *It doesn't matter now. I have Zan. We'll make it like new again, for you. For all of us.* "Come on. We have work to do."

~

A WEEK LATER, the first of the unexplained mishaps occurred.

Devyn was thinking about Artie—he'd gotten through the man's military service and his temporary exile back to Cameroon, where being gay had been less than welcomed. When his visa paperwork had come through, he'd fled from that old repressive life to Canada, where he'd landed a low-level job at an accounting firm. The next words were burned into Devyn's head—he'd read them over and over the night before.

It was him—the man I'd first seen at the Harbour Centre garden the week before. I sat there in the break room, just staring at him. He had to be almost two meters tall, blond, and fit, and moved with an easy grace, like a tiger through the jungle. He filled up his coffee cup, sniffing it to see if it was fresh, and then he turned to me and said the words that would change my life, though I didn't know it then: "Hi, I'm Steve. What the hell are you doing in my chair?"

Such an inauspicious meeting for someone about to become the love of his life.

As he pulled up to the job site, Abby ran out to meet him, face flushed. "Something's happened."

He ditched the bike where the front lawn used to be—there was no one else out here to take it—and ran after them, past the collapsed remains of the neighboring home. They'd managed to pull out enough of the rubble to make a path, throwing it into the reprocessor, and the outer walls of the house were now up and sparkling in the morning sunshine. "What's going on?"

"Take a look." They stopped next to the reprocessor.

The machine was the size of a small truck. It was also oozing out some kind of fluid, shuddering and smoking and coughing like it had a bad cold. "Shut it down."

"I tried. It won't turn off." They rocked back and forth. "I already called Trent. His guys are on their way over. This is bad, isn't it?"

"It's not good." He climbed the access ladder, found the pop-open panel with the emergency stop button and slammed his hand down on it. He'd have to talk with Trent later about making it easier to reach on his future versions.

The contraption hissed and shuddered, and then sighed, settling down into a quiet death-like slumber.

"Whatcha think's wrong with it?" Abby gave it their best glare.

"Probably ate something it shouldn't." He frowned. Abby knew the protocol. "You didn't feed any metal into it, did you?"

Abby shook their head. "Of course not. I'm not *stoopid*."

"Sorry, just had to ask." They'd be lucky not to get a pollution fine with all the smoke the machine had been putting out. "Maybe it just gave up the ghost." In construction, you learned that things went wrong all the time. And how to roll with it.

He looked around the yard. They'd long since filled up the basement with sheets of repro drywall and the smaller parts they'd need, and they'd started stacking some of the larger ones out here under rain-proof tarps, just in case.

"If we shift the roof project forward, we should be able to keep on schedule." Abby had that accountant's look on their face—they were great at project management. This was why he loved them. Among other things. "We can swap that with the rest of the pipe work."

"Yeah, and once that's up, we have enough piping to do the ground floor.

Hopefully Trent can save this little beastie and get us back up and running in a few days." He hopped down, stepping back to stare at the machine.

It was painted bright green, most of it encased in repro panels that could be easily removed for servicing. On one side, a chute took in the old materials —wood, gypsum, even smashed brick—chewed it up, and turned it into repro-powder using an enzyme Trentovation supplied. That's where they made their money. It wasn't cheap, but far less costly than importing new materials, and it had the added benefit of being eco-friendly, reusing the old to make the new.

On the other end, a sophisticated 3D printer spat out the specified parts, up to two meters cubed.

Devyn rounded the machine to stare into the maw of the beast. He couldn't see much, though the "teeth" of it were a little bent. *Were they like that before?*

He checked the ground. There were a ton of footprints in the dust, but he was no Sherlock Holmes, and they'd had enough delivery men and city inspectors through the site that there was no way to know for sure if they'd been sabotaged.

Half an hour later, Trent's repairman confirmed it. Jack Reznor found him hauling roof tiles up the stairs from the basement.

He was frowning intensely. "Looks like someone shoved a bunch of rebar into Bessie."

Emerging into the partial light of the ground floor, he blinked as his eyes adjusted. "Bessie?"

Jack nodded. "Trent has names for each of them. Most of them based on cows." He didn't crack a grin. "You know these things aren't rated for metal, right? A few nails, they can handle. But this? That's not under warranty."

"Of course." *I wasn't born yesterday.*

Jack followed him out the door to the growing pile of roof tiles Devyn was arranging in the front yard. "I've been using Trent's repro machines for years. I know what not to put in them."

"But does your assistant?" He looked over his shoulder toward the back yard.

"Abby's my partner, not my assistant. And yes, *they know.*"

Jack sighed. "I figured as much. Trent was pissed when I told him, but he said the same thing—you're a long-term customer." He scratched his head.

"What's weird is that this is the second mishap this week. Clarabelle ate a bad batch of enzymes and screwed herself up something good."

Devyn raised an eyebrow. "Clarabelle?"

"Yeah, the repro machine over at Tripp Anderson's worksite. Like I said, Trent has a thing for cows." This time the dour man managed a half-smile.

"Ah." Tripp was the second of three contractors working the RHA pilot program. "And Lulu?"

"Her machine's fine, far as I know."

If it had been anyone else, Devyn would have been suspicious about that, but Luluelle George was good people. She'd helped him out on more than one occasion, when doing nothing and letting him fail would have been so much easier and better for her business. "Crap. Okay. How long to fix it?"

"I won't know for sure until I hear back from Trent. We can print up some of the parts, but others have to be made by a metals firm down in Surrey."

Surrey was Vancouver's "second colony," a hotbed of industry that handled some of the biggest, hardest to repurpose materials.

"Best guess?"

Jack bit his lip. "About a week?"

Devyn sighed. Not as bad as he'd feared. "I don't suppose Trent has an extra *Bessie* laying around anywhere that we could use in the meantime?"

"Not like this one. But we do have a smaller model we can spare."

"Let me guess. Trent calls it Calfie?"

This time Jack actually grinned. "Buttercup."

He snorted. "Sounds about right. What will she cost me?"

"Assuming nothing else indicates you did this deliberately, it's free of charge. No one's using her anyhow, and Trent thinks you're a strong long-term bet. He wants to be on your good side." He waved and went off to call his boss on his watch.

A strong long-term bet. Devyn hoped he was right. This whole thing was starting to feel jinxed.

He called Zan, who answered immediately. "What's up, handsome?"

Devyn filled his husband in, including the bit about the week's delay. "Luckily I think we have enough preprinted to keep us busy. I gotta think someone did this intentionally."

Zan scowled. "EBF?"

The acronym hung in the air between them.

"Maybe so. They're the ones with the most incentive. Derail the pilot project, derail the whole RHA."

Zan's 'mage nodded. "I'm sending a friend out to you this afternoon. He can help."

"What is he, a hit man?"

"Close. He installs security systems. It's about time we locked that site of yours down. That way, if anything else happens, we'll know more about who's behind this."

"Makes sense. See you at home... and this time *I'll* bring dinner." There was a new wood-fired bagel place in downtown—though of course they didn't use real wood—that he'd been dying to try. They'd probably make excellent mini sandwiches.

"Sounds good. Love you. Got a meeting. Gotta run." Zan's 'mage blinked out of sight.

For some reason, Artie Johnson's words came to mind. "They always try to stop you when you're doing something right."

He grimaced. *How much has really changed, from then to now?*

A beep informed him that his brother had finally seen his message. But there was no reply.

With a sigh, he got back to work, determined to get the roof started before this hellish day was done.

ANOTHER WEEK PASSED, and the place started to look like a house again. Devyn had redesigned the structure's airflow to capture the offshore breezes, cooling the interior overnight and holding in the air on the hot afternoons.

True to his word, Jack had Bessie back up and running, and Abby was churning out the remaining parts as quickly as they could, wary of another incident.

Zan's friend had installed a simple security system, which included a series of movement sensors and cams that would alert them if anyone tried to access the site when Devyn or Abby weren't around.

Devyn was relaxing in bed with Artie's journal, much to Zan's chagrin. "Haven't you finished that yet? You spend more time with him than you do with me."

He laughed. "I don't have a lot of time to read. You know that better than anyone."

Zan flashed him a lazy grin. "You have been on fire lately."

In truth, he'd felt more alive with this current project than he had in years. Something about building something for himself—and Zan—and learning the history of one of its residents had fired him up, and Zan had taken full advantage of his passion an hour earlier.

Devyn leaned over and kissed his husband on the forehead. "Go to sleep. I won't be too much longer. I promise."

Zan growled something incomprehensible and rolled over, turning his back to Devyn, who reached out to scratch it. Zan began to purr like a kitten. "Better."

Devyn chuckled. When he was sure Zan was asleep, he pulled the sheet over his back, and then picked up the journal again.

Miri is a most remarkable woman. She's one-part Rosie the Riveter, one part Margaret Cho, and one-part Dear Abby—always willing to listen to one of my long, drawn-out stories about "the good old days" while she performs yet another repair on my old and creaky condenser. I see hope in her—hope that maybe we'll get through this man-made crisis that my generation, and those before mine, ignored for so long, hoping it would just go away. That our corporations kept us from addressing until it was far too late. In some strange way, she reminds me of Stevie. Both were driven to make the world a better place in small ways. Oh, and that "cat" of hers— she calls him Echo—never heard of someone having a raccoon for a pet, but it's clear he adores her too—

Devyn wondered if the little skeleton he'd found in the attic had been Echo.

His watch spit out an urgent beep, flashing white and red. "Oh crap." He swiped the alert. *Possible intruder. Motion alarm set off at back door.*

"What's happening?" Zan sat up, rubbing his eyes. He was adorable when he was sleepy.

"Alert at the job site. Dammit. I don't wanna bike over there at this time of night."

Zan was already out of bed, getting dressed. "We'll take one of the city cars. I have a few personal use credits left."

Devyn stared at him. "You sure?"

"Of course. Plus this is almost official business. The house *is* part of the city pilot project, after all."

"Good enough for me." *More sabotage?* He pulled on some fresh clothes and popped into the small bathroom nook to run some water through his hair. Then he joined Zan in the hall outside of their thirty-seven square meter flat. They took the stairs up to the top floor, luckily only four stories. Alastair Commons had an elevator, but its use was mostly restricted to move-ins and move-outs to save on electricity.

The city car was arriving as they reached the roof, landing neatly on its hydro thrusters, sending a bank of steam toward them like an advancing fog. It was chilly out, unusual for an August evening, the sky clear and dark with the moon just rising in the east.

They climbed into the sleek air car, and Zan programmed it for the short flight to the West End.

As they shot into the air, moonlight painted silver lines across the city. The old downtown core shone like new, her skyscrapers almost black, flecked with the occasional muted light.

The car swung around the south side of town, over the submerged remnants of Granville Island, invisible under the dark, sparkling waters of False Creek.

Devyn scrolled through the alerts. Three of the sensors had gone off, one at the back of the property, one at the edge of the house, and one up on the back porch. Nothing was visible on the tiny screen's surveillance feed.

What are you up to? Had they come back to set fire to the place this time, or worse? Repro was fire resistant, but with enough accelerant…

"Calm down." Zan kissed his cheek. "We'll be there soon enough."

Devyn considered how lucky he was. Both to have Zan, and to have access to an air car. They were few and far between in the city these days, though that might change again if VancMotors' plan was approved to start building new ones using repro. "I'm just worried."

"I know, but there's nothing to do about it until we get there."

"I know you're right. But still… you think it's EFB?"

"I think we should wait and see what we see." Zan yawned.

"Seriously? Our house could be burning down, and you're yawning?"

"It's after midnight. I didn't get my beauty rest." Zan grinned, his white teeth painted blue by the console lights. "*Our* house?"

"Our project," Devyn corrected himself. He'd almost let the fish out of the net with that one. *I am such an idiot.*

The car was descending now. Devyn peered anxiously at the street below, looking for any sign that something was amiss.

The street was quiet, the collapsed pile of rubble next door smaller than it had been by about a third. *We've used that much?*

The car settled to the ground with a light thump, and the door slid open.

"Here, take one of these." Zan, always level-headed in a crisis, had brought a flashlight. He also had his wand tucked into his back pocket.

"What'd you bring that for?"

"You never know when it will come in handy. Did you install the transponders yet?"

"Yesterday." Devyn sighed. Zan was almost never without it. "Come on. Let's see what's going on."

He deactivated the security net, and they followed the narrow path around the side of the house.

"Dev, this is amazing. What you've done here in a couple weeks…"

His chest swelled with pride. "Abby and I make a great team," he whispered. "But we should probably be quiet in case there's anyone in there. Right?" Spy craft wasn't one of his strength's. Nor Zan's, apparently.

"Oh yeah, right." He turned off his flashlight beam, and Devyn did the same. They crept around the back of the house, guided by moonlight.

Nothing looked out of place. Bessie sat in the middle of the yard, quiet as a sleeping cow, and everything else seemed normal.

Devyn waved his hand over his watch, and the offending sensors blinked, lighting up in succession to indicate the path the suspected intruder had taken.

Something crashed up on the patio.

He flicked on his flashlight and swung the beam up the stairs.

Zan's beam followed his.

A pair of eyes reflected light back at them, followed by an inquiring chittering sound.

Devyn burst out laughing.

"What is that?" Zan stared at the apparition.

"That, my love, is a raccoon." Relief washed over him—he'd been sure EFB was at it again, probably doing something horrible to his handiwork. Still, he couldn't remember the last time one had been seen in these parts. *Maybe not since Echo.*

As if in response, the little beast leapt up from the stairs onto the railing that surrounded the porch, ignoring them and continuing its search for whatever it was that had drawn it out of the night to the house.

"I thought raccoons were extinct here."

Devyn nodded. "They were. And yet, there he is." He lit up the little critter again, who twittered in annoyance at the interruption. He was trying to open one of the window latches. "Let's call him Re-Echo." He grinned. "Wreck for short."

Zan shot him a questioning look.

"Miri, one of the folks who lived here before, had a raccoon named Echo. This fella *might* be his descendant." He liked the symmetry of it. "Come on. Let's take a look inside."

"You sure? It's late, and I do need that beauty rest...." Zan yawned again.

"I dragged you all the way out here. You might as well see the place."

"Fair enough. But I'm sleeping in tomorrow for at least an hour."

Devyn flashed him a wicked grin. "Not if I have anything to say about it." He took Zan's hand. "Come on!" They climbed the steps to the back porch, ignoring the annoyed chittering. He produced a key and unlocked the manual lock he'd added after the previous week's incident, and then thumbed the electric lock.

They stepped inside, and the ground floor lit up with photospheres—Abby had installed those a couple days earlier while they were waiting on Bessie's repairs. "Not much to look at yet—"

"Dev, it's beautiful." Zan looked around the open space, and up at the high ceilings.

"It's just a shell. But someday..." He'd almost said "It will be ours."

Zan pulled out his wand. "A couch here, a Persian rug there, a lovely tapestry along the back wall..." With each flick of his wrist, 'mages appeared, slowly filling the room. "Whoever gets this place will have great bones to work with." He put away his wand and gave Devyn a big hug as the improvised furnishings faded away. "I'm so proud of you."

Dev grinned. "Honestly, it's some of my best work. I can't wait for the final certification." After which he'd tell Zan about his grand plan. A house of their own, and maybe kids? Neither one of them was getting any younger, after all. "But for now, we need to get you home. We both have work in the morning, and I see another yawn coming on." He stifled one of his own.

"Sounds good." Zan took his hand and led him outside.

Devyn locked up the place behind them and followed him down the stairs, looking around for Wreck, but the little bugger was gone. *Did we imagine him?*

Somewhere, Artie Johnson was probably laughing.

THE FINAL ATTACK came a week before the inspection, and Devyn didn't see it coming. Though he should have.

Abby was about to apply the home's outer coating—a new product called pseudo-organic dirt, or PSOD for short, to the walls of the home, when both their watches lit up and spit out such a cacophony that Devyn almost dropped the shovel he was using to plant a row of tomato cacti along the front of the lot as a natural fence.

Exchanging a look with his partner, he tapped the watch.

A 'mage of an older man in a finely tailored suit appeared. "Mr. Devyn Miller-Hill?"

"Yes? How can I help you?" He almost growled it. Time was getting tight, and he still had so much to do before the city inspector came calling.

"This is Mr. Preston Murs, of Murs, Theebes, and Rasp. You are hereby enjoined from doing any more work on…" the 'mage's eyes narrowed, as if he were squinting to read something. "Parcel 3271."

"On what grounds?" Devyn hated lawyers, even if his older brother was one.

"Unlawful possession of stolen materials."

Crap. Someone had complained about them using the materials from the collapsed house next door. Devyn sighed. "What's the fine?" He'd pay it and get on with things.

"I'm sorry, Mr. Miller. The injured party has requested a hearing to adjudicate the matter. You are to appear at the city courthouse on September 5th at 10 AM. I'll send you the details." He leaned forward as if to sign off.

"*Miller-Hill.*" *The day after the inspection.* That couldn't be a coincidence.

"Mr. Murs, who are you representing?" Murs, Theebes, and Rasp was old money, a law firm that skirted the corporation laws and helped others do the same. "I have a right to know."

Mr. Murs nodded, as if disappointed to find he was dealing with someone who actually knew his charter rights. "Of course. It's the owner of Parcel 3272." With that, he cut the connection before Devyn could ask him anything else.

Devyn tried to return the call, but the line was busy. "Dammit."

Abby stared at him across the yard. They'd heard the whole thing. "Crap. What do we do now?"

"Put down the spray gun. We're dead in the water until we figure this thing out." He didn't want to do anything to jeopardize the project, and working while under a court order not to was a surefire way to get the whole thing flushed. "Get cleaned up and go home for the day. I'll get this sorted."

No one owned these buildings. That was the whole point of the RHA—to transfer ownership back to the public. *After* a successful pilot project showing they could be rehabilitated.

He called Zan and filled him in, trying to resist the urge to break something.

Zan growled. "It's gotta be Evlin Farcosee Bastron. They've had it in for the pilot project from the start." By the look on Zan's face, he would have torn them limb from limb if they'd been in the same room.

"Probably. But how did they get their hands on the parcel next door?"

"I don't know. I can have Denn look into it." Denn Hayes was his assistant on the council.

"Please. Meanwhile, I'll give Elwyn a call. If it is the *Evil Fucking Bastards*, he'll know what to do." It had been years since Devyn's brother had spoken to him.

Zan bit his lip. "Were you borrowing from the house next door?"

Devyn sighed. "Yes, but it's perfectly legal under the pilot contract. *Any home that's damaged beyond repair may be used for salvage.*" He'd helped insert that language himself when he'd consulted on the project. "The EFB's have to know it too. This is just a delaying tactic."

"Okay. I'll call you as soon as I know anything. Love you."

"Love you too." Devyn waved his 'mage away, and closed his eyes, taking a deep breath before calling Elwyn.

They'd been on rocky ground ever since he'd married Zan—Elwyn didn't like outsiders, and Zan's Seattle pedigree had immediately set him on edge. The fact that Zan was now helping run *his* city didn't help.

"See you in the morning?" Abby waved as they passed with their own bike. "Hopefully we'll have this resolved by then."

For some reason, a passage he'd read in Artie's journal the night before came to mind.

Mamma called late one night from home. I hadn't spoken with her for thirty years, since I'd come out and she and Papa had thrown me out of the house. In Cameroon, it could have gone far worse for me, but I was lucky. I had friends who understood, and I was able to get out of the country to claim asylum here.

Mama's voice cracked on the phone. "Artie, is that you?"

"Mama?" I couldn't believe it. How had she found me?

"Yes, sweet Artie. It's me. I have to tell you... your papa..." Her voice cracked again. "Your papa is gone."

I shook. With anger. With sadness. With resignation. I don't know. All the emotions rushed through me, and I felt the weight of each of those thirty years. "When?" My voice came out thin and raspy.

"Last week. It took me a while to find you."

A whole week ago. How had I not known? Not felt it, somehow?

"Artie?"

"Yes, Mama."

"He wanted me to tell you that he loved you."

I hung up. It was too much. Now he loved me? After all he put me through? Now that he was gone, and I could never yell at him? Never tell him what a selfish bastard of a man he was?

The phone rang again. I stared at it, aware what it must have cost her to find me, to call me. Both in money and in her soul. With a heavy sigh, I picked it up. "Mama."

"Come home, Artemis. We want to see you."

"I haven't changed." In fact, I had. I was proud of myself now. Of who I was.

There was a slight pause. "I know. But we have. Come home to see us." There was a shuffling of paper. "The funeral is Tuesday."

I closed my eyes and bit my lip, not sure what to say. "Okay, Mama."

And I went.

Artie was speaking to him across the years. Devyn didn't know how, but he was sure of it. He and Elwyn had been estranged for too long.

He made the call.

His brother picked up immediately. He looked older, more tired than before. "Devyn?"

Devyn tried to dissect that word and the emotions behind it, and failed miserably. "Hi Elwyn. You picked up." He'd been half certain his brother wouldn't take his call. "I… I need your help."

"Of course. You're family." His 'mage frowned. "Sorry about your message. I saw it, but things have been busy. But you're my brother."

Devyn *knew* that, but it was good to hear that Elwyn remembered it too. "I'm in some legal trouble."

Elwyn nodded, as if he wasn't surprised. "How can I help?"

Devyn couldn't stop himself. "You know I'm still with Zan, right?"

"Of course I do. I keep tabs on you, you know."

"You never liked him—"

Elwyn cracked a smile. "I like him just fine." He closed his eyes. "I didn't like that he was an outsider, and everyone instantly gave whatever he said more weight than it deserved. And I didn't like it when he ran for city council against Maryn Greaves, a close friend of mine, and won a seat on the council."

"Maybe this was a bad idea—"

"Hold on." He peered at Devyn through his 'mage. "I was leading up to something. Since you've been together, he's been good for you. You've become a better man, because of him."

Devyn snorted. "He might disagree."

"Maybe so." His eyes danced merrily. "But he's been good for the city too. The work he's done on the RHA—"

"Which is why I'm calling you…"

"You never could let me finish a sentence." Elwyn chuckled.

"So, we're good?"

"We're good. I was an asshole. I apologize."

Devyn stared at him, unsure he'd just heard the words he'd just heard. "Thank you." He could feel Artie nodding with satisfaction.

"Now tell me about this legal trouble you find yourself in."

Twenty-four hours and a flurry of legal filings later, they were back in business. EFB was indeed the entity behind the sudden, shady purchase of the lot next door. Someone in the records office was fired for accepting a bribe and failing to follow proper procedure. And EFB was under investigation for destruction of property, a claim Trent was pursuing directly.

A sternly worded letter to Mr. Murs about the likely effects of the exposure of such impropriety on both his own firm and his clients succeeded in getting the matter dropped, and Devyn and Abby were back on the job.

He sent his brother a long letter, taking responsibility for his own part in their fight, and invited him and his partners out to dinner when things settled down.

It took an extra couple of shifts to catch up to their self-imposed schedule, but by the morning of September 4th, everything was as ready as it could be. Jacin Anderson, the city inspector, was inside, and Devyn was sweating bullets while he waited.

Zan arrived early, bringing a surprise guest. "I hope you don't mind." He grinned.

Devyn's eyes went wide as Elwyn stepped out of the car. "Mind? Of course not." He threw himself into his brother's arms. "I'm so glad you came."

"Wouldn't miss it for the world. Soph and Aiken send their love." He looked up at the refurbished home. "You did this?"

"*We* did it." Abby grinned, their teeth gleaming white in the morning sunlight.

Zan laughed. "It's beautiful. I just hope the inspector agrees." He looked up at the second story, and the blue sky above. "But tell me again why it's covered in dirt?"

Devyn laughed. "It's PSOD, an engineered organic soil that clings to the repro walls, sealing them and allowing for growth. Come see." He led them up the newly paved driveway, made from repro cobble stones in natural colors. "See these little green shoots?" They were breaking out all over the house walls.

Zan leaned in to peer at them. "Yes. What are they? Is it supposed to do that?"

"Yeah, it's weird to get used to. But this will truly be a *green* house. The PSOD helps to insulate it, and those are evergreen strawberries. They pull moisture from the air, and supply fruit all year long. They just need an occasional watering and fertilizing."

Elwyn reached out to touch one of them. "That's amazing. So the new owners will have strawberries all year round?"

"Yup. So many they'll be sick of them." Devyn glanced at the debris next door. "Maybe we can get our new neighbor to coat their house in blueberry brambles."

"*Our* new neighbor?" Zan raised an eyebrow, but they were interrupted by the sound of the front door closing upstairs, and the inspector's return.

Jacin Anderson swiped something away on his watch and looked up, his expression inscrutable.

"Well?" Devyn waited impatiently for the response, hands on his hips.

Jacin met his gaze, looking serious.

"What's wrong? Oh crap, you found something horrible, didn't you?"

A smile spread across Jacin's lips. "On the contrary. You've done an amazing job with the place. There are a few things that need attention—there always are. But overall, I'd say you passed with flying colors."

Devyn grinned. "Thank the stars." He grabbed Abby and hugged them, twirling them around with him. "We did it!"

They laughed. "I guess this means ReHome Inc. is a thing?"

"I guess it does." After all they'd gone through…. "Thank you, Mr. Anderson." Devyn shook his hand.

"My pleasure. I'll send you the punch list—you'll have a week to take care of it before the follow-up inspection." He paused, looking over his shoulder at the house. "I hope the RHA passes. these beautiful old homes need some love. And I wouldn't mind moving out here with my own husband, one day." He saluted and set off down the driveway toward his city air car.

Devyn looked at Zan, and they both laughed. "So the RHA will pass, then?"

Zan nodded. "I think so. It may take a couple more months, but assuming things go well at the other two pilot sites, yes."

Devyn was sure they would, having been in touch with the contractors the night before. They had a friendly competition going, and he couldn't wait to see their projects and get some new ideas for his next one. He wished Artie could see the place now.

Zan raised an eyebrow. "You said 'our'…"

Devyn nodded solemnly. "I did." He dropped to one knee, ignoring Abby's little gasp. "The pilot project also has a right of first refusal clause. I want to buy this place… for us. We'll be the first in a brand-new experiment." *And out of the crowded Alastair Commons.* "Zander Miller-Hill, would you… move in here with me?"

A crash in the back yard announced that their favorite raccoon had returned. Devin hoped Wreck approved.

Zan pulled him up and into his arms, and his enthusiastic kiss was all the "yes" that Devyn needed.

Scott lives with his husband Mark in a yellow bungalow in Sacramento. He was indoctrinated into fantasy and sci fi by his mother at the tender age of nine. He devoured her library, but as he grew up, he wondered where all the people like him were.

He decided that if there weren't queer characters in his favorite genres, he would remake them to his own ends.

A Rainbow Award winning author, he runs Queer Sci Fi, QueeRomance Ink, and Other Worlds Ink with Mark, sites that celebrate fiction reflecting queer reality, and is the committee chair for the Indie Authors Committee at the Science Fiction and Fantasy Writers of America (SFWA).

Website: https://www.jscottcoatsworth.com
Facebook Personal: https://www.facebook.com/jscottcoatsworth
Facebook Page: https://www.facebook.com/jscottcoatsworthauthor/
Mastodon: https://mastodon.lol/@jscottcoatsworth
Liminal Fiction: https://www.limfic.com/mbm-book-author/j-scott-coatsworth/

SIXERS

BY JAYMIE HEILMAN

Ziggy and I will probably become Sixers tomorrow, but at least the torrents of unsolicited advice will stop.

Eat carbs! Do NOT eat carbs! Exercise more! Exercise less! Right after you go in for your embryo transfer, have sex immediately, but only if you didn't have it the day before, then make sure you have an orgasm, but not too intense, then lie dead still with your legs pulled to your chest for 15 minutes, and most of all, have fun!

And the number one most-hated piece of advice I received, ad nauseam, from people I pride myself on not having punched: Just stop trying. As soon as you relax and forget about trying to get pregnant, your transfer will succeed. Trust me, this is exactly what happened to my _____ (cousin, friend, neighbor, third cousin's friend's neighbor).

Was it this horrible back in the fertile times, when couples could actually get pregnant without a team of doctors and nurses and specialists?

Probably.

Tomorrow is our sixth and final try. I wish I weren't so nervous, so on edge. Mom and Gran have both sent me messages telling me to try to stop worrying. Excellent. Thank you for that sage advice. In the history of humanity, has anyone ever successfully stopped worrying by trying to do so? No, no, and no.

"You up?" I send the question on my commpad.

Ai-jen's reply pops up on my screen almost instantly. "Not quite. You ready for tomorrow?" My sister-in-law and best friend, always there for me, no matter the hour.

"Not quite," I type back.

Ai-jen went through all of this a few years ago, so she understands what I'm going through in a way almost no one else does. She has never once given me advice, never once made empty reassurances that Ziggy and I will have a rich and meaningful life together, kid or no kid. And I will love her forever for that.

I press the live button on the commpad and she's quick to answer. "Any last bits of wisdom?" It's ultra hypocritical given all my complaints about unsolicited advice, but I've nonetheless been asking my closest friends for random tips from their great grandmothers, women from the times before forever chemicals and phthalates and micro-plastics in our bloodstreams made old-fashioned pregnancy impossible. At least the ConspiracIdiots have mostly stopped their blabbering. No, there's no vast government conspiracy to put spermicide and estrogen in the water. No, vaccines don't shrivel ovaries and testes. It's so much easier to concoct elaborate conspiracies than admit that we brought this on ourselves, with all the forever chemicals and micro-plastics leaching into our foods, our air, and our bodies. Sure, humanity has completely lost the ability to reproduce naturally, but hey! At least your food doesn't stick to your frying pan, you don't need to wash your coffee cup, and your clothes will never wrinkle!

Ai-jen gives me a look that I can't quite interpret. Pity? Frustration? "Miguel's great-gran told us to visit the Gompers Clinic. She's heard they have the best IVF results."

I give a loud sigh. That's exactly what Ai-jen and Ziggy's Taai Po said, cracking a joke that her recommendation constituted Ancient Chinese Medical Wisdom. (Her capitalization, not mine.) My badass great-grandmother-in-law is apparently also a smart ass.

"But," Ai-jen adds, "his great-gran also said to use bull semen. Maybe Miguel and I should have tried that. It was the one bit of advice I couldn't bring myself to try. Maybe we should have. Maybe it would have worked."

Oh. Um. Well. Uh. "So, presuming I can *find* a bull and, um –" How to phrase it? Pleasure him? Whack him off?

"Bring him to completion–" Ai-jen says. I can hear the giggle she's fighting to suppress.

"That. Right. So, I find a bull, bring him to completion, scoop up his semen, and then do I, uh, inject the –"

Ai-jen explodes in laughter. "No, you goofball. You put some in your soup and eat it." When my sister-in-law finally stops laughing, she says, "Oh, I know! You could make a pigeon-bull spunk stew. Yummmmm."

Very funny. My own German/Dutch great-grandmother swore by pigeons. When I told her I couldn't find any in the store—not technically a lie, as I definitely hadn't bothered to look—she told me to trap some on my roof and eat those. And when I demurred, she took the four-hour train ride to my house and shoved a crate of half-thawed pigeons into my arms.

Great-Grandmothers these days.

ZIGGY IS right beside me when the nurse phones. Before I even answer, before I see her face on my screen, I know the news is not good. I knew as soon as we did the transfer that it hadn't worked.

Sometimes I hate it when I'm right.

When I finally stop sobbing, when I can finally draw in a breath that isn't full of shudders, and when I wipe the last tears from Ziggy's sweet face, he asks me if I want us to try again. But we're Sixers now. To try again, we'd need to make a special application to the Health Ministry, and we'd have to refinance our house. Again. And there's no point. All my eggs except four freezer-burned ones are gone, and Ziggy's sperm have never been super swimmers.

We're way too old and way too average to qualify for either the donor egg or donor sperm program, and—to be honest—we probably need both, and that's not legal anywhere. Governments want everyone to have babies, but they don't want to waste precious resources on lost causes. Even the black marketers wouldn't risk their stockpiles on us.

It's so freaking unfair. We did everything right. We both froze our supplies within a month of turning sixteen, the recommended age. I gave everything inside of me. I didn't know Ziggie back then, of course, but he made deposits at the storage bank every week for two years. We both chose the highest-quality (read: expensive) storage banks. And we were lucky. None of our storage banks were hit by floods or fires or hurricanes. But my supply was low from birth, and Ziggy's little zigsters were few and far between. And the few that actually swam in the correct direction didn't exactly set records with their swim times. That happens a lot these days.

"Can I tell Ai-jen?" Ziggy is so sweet to ask. Of course he should tell her. And I will break the news to Mom and Dad. Maybe they can tell the grandparents and great-grandparents. I don't have it in me to share the bad news myself.

Oh, shit. We'll have to tell Ziggy's mom. Eventually.

Ziggy looks up from his commpad. "Ai-jen thinks she can get us volunteer visas. You should go. I know how much you miss the ocean." Ziggy kisses the top of my head, shows me his sister's message. I know he doesn't want to take the compassionate leave we both qualify for. He copes by taking care of his patients. Not me. I will cope by escaping this city and curling up on my sister-in-law's couch. Swimming in her ocean.

I STEP OFF THE TRAIN, still groggy from the trip. I've only been on four rocket trains in my life, and each time I've fallen asleep within minutes of departure. The insanely high speeds zonk me out faster than any insomnia medication ever has. I get in the shortish line for Lekwungen. The immigration line for the Musqueam, Squamish, and Tsleil-Waututh lands is way longer.

A tap on my shoulder. "Is this the Vancouver line?" The asker sounds ultra-frail, so I don't snap at him. Old place names die hard, I guess. I turn and shake my head. This guy looks so elderly that he might even be a great-great-greater. I point at the longer line. "Make sure you have your travel documents ready," I say, more loudly than I probably need to.

The man gives me a sour look. "Travel documents! Phh. I'm Canadian, for Christ's sake."

"If you want to get in, you'll need to show a permission visa." Thankfully, my line starts moving, so I can leave the old fart behind to his racist complaints. The line advances quickly, and I soon hand over my volunteer visa and ID card to the young person at the table. She smiles and welcomes me before examining my papers. "How will you be getting to Lekwungen lands?"

"My sister-in-law is picking me up." In a kayak, I think. Maybe a canoe. I hope it's not a single-person paddle board. I really don't think I'm up for that. I adjust my backpack and head out to the concrete dock. There haven't been any ferries here since Land Back Nationhood, but this ugly old terminal is still functional.

Ai-jen is docked just to my right. A canoe, thank the universe. She wraps me in a hug so tight that it's hard to breathe. It's exactly the embrace I need. She's a Sixer, too. I know she gets it.

"Was Mom extra obnoxious?" Ai-jen asks, cutting right to the chase as we start paddling. I appreciate that she doesn't avoid the issue, and doesn't pretend I'm not in mourning. "When Miguel and I failed our sixth, she started lecturing us about what we needed to do next and who we needed to see and how we needed to apply. She even offered to pay for the seventh."

The rare seventh try. Almost impossible to get. And essentially impossible to afford. I haven't heard this story before. "Did you guys go for it?"

Ai-jen snorts. "We got divorced instead."

We paddle on, the ocean's pressure strong against my oar. The waves are gentler than I'd expected, just as the smell of salt and trees and fish are far stronger. I gasp as two orcas surface ahead of us. They're not rare, not anymore, but they're still astonishing in their size and their power. Their black and white beauty.

"Will it be this beautiful at the work site?" I have to spend the next two weeks doing kelp reforestation. I didn't want to wait eight months for one of the tourist passes, so Ai-jen got me a volunteer visa. One of the many perks of being a marine reclamation biologist, I guess.

"Beautiful? Not really," she admits. Then laughs. "It's smellier. You'll mostly be staring at walls of kelp, and we have to barrier off the mammals when we do the first stages of the restoration. But there are some super-hot divers. So, a different kind of beauty, I guess."

Birds swoop up and down around us, diving into and out of the waves. The fish in their beaks are huge, and I feel the rush of saliva at the sides of my mouth. I haven't had ocean fish in over a decade. I heard that it's legal to eat them now, because all that ocean acidification has been reversed and the stocks are flourishing. Can you buy fish here? Or do you have to catch it yourself? I'll have to ask Ai-jen. But first, a confession.

"Your mom hasn't said anything yet." I laugh at Ai-jen's shocked expression as her face whips toward me. I'm worried she's going to let go of her oar. I watch as understanding dawns.

"Because you haven't told her." Ai-jen lets out a low whistle.

I shake my head, already feeling the guilt. Already dreading the conversation Ziggy and I will have to have with her. My parents were disappointed, of course, but they have my brother's kids. Ziggy and I were my mother-in-law's last hope for grandchildren.

I want Ai-jen to tell me that her mother will get over it. That she'll handle the news with grace and compassion. "It's sure been nice knowing you," she says instead.

I take one hand off my oar and splash Ai-jen with water. "Jerk."

EVERY PART of me is sore. Muscles I didn't even know I had ache. And I am bloody tired. Beyond exhausted.

And it is so, so great.

"Well," Ai-jen says, plopping herself down on the arm of the couch where I'm lying. She hands me a beer. "How was your first day?"

I spent 6 long hours in the cold ocean, lowering kelp frames into place and securing them. My jaw aches from biting the breathing tube, my hands feel arthritic because of all the knot tying, and my eyes still sting from the salt water. You aren't supposed to do that kind of hard physical exercise during the IVF-eligibility years, and I don't think I worked my body this hard even when I was a teenager. It's a pretty terrific kind of pain. As a Sixer herself, Ai-jen must have known that this strain, this exertion, was exactly what I needed to move through my grief. I hope Ziggy can do something like this, too.

"My day was hard, but good." I sit up to take a long drink of the beer and then flop back down to my horizontal position. "How was work? I didn't see you much today."

Ai-jen doesn't say anything. The pause grows longer, stretching into an uncomfortable quiet. I sit up, alarmed. Ai-jen ALWAYS has something to say. Always. "You okay, Ai-jen? What's wrong?"

I notice, now, that she is shaking. Just a slight tremble, like a shiver. But it's not stopping. I put my hand on her leg. "Here, come sit beside me." I scooch over on the couch and pat the cushion until she obliges. "Whatever it is, you can tell me."

"I'm—" she stops. My mind fills in the words that follow. Dying. Infected. Terminal. Contagious.

I wrap my arms around her, waiting. She clears her throat and pulls away from me. She draws in a long, shuddering breath and runs her hand through her thick, curly hair. "You didn't see me on the boat or in the greenlab because I had a doctor's appointment this afternoon. And I didn't come back to work afterward. I thought I had a parasite. I was sure of it. One of those newer, creepier ones that people are getting. I could feel it, moving around in my belly. Like exploding popcorn kernels in my gut. A handful of the divers have come down with these. You restore ocean life for a living, some of the grosser creatures are gonna find their way into your system. Occupational hazard." She laughs. But it's this weird, hollow laugh, completely unlike her.

"Can I get you something?" I ask. "Do you want a beer? It might—"

"I'm pregnant."

I blink. My breath stops. I blink again. My spine straightens. "What? Are you—" I don't even know what I want to say. Are you sure? Are you in active IVF treatment again? Are you serious? I ask none of those things. "How far along are you?"

"The doctor says twenty-four weeks. Twenty-four weeks. How did this happen, Edith? I mean, I haven't done a seventh round. No hormones, no shots, no pills. Definitely no embryo transfers. I shouldn't even have any eggs left. How does this even happen?"

I touch my head to hers. "Well, Ai-jen, a man and a woman have sexual intercourse and then –"

She elbows me in the side, hard. But she laughs and, just like that, she's back. My Ai-jen. My sister-in-law and treasured friend. And she is twenty-four weeks pregnant. Naturally. This doesn't happen anymore. It hasn't happened in decades. Not even to teenagers, and Ai-jen is as old as I am. Universal infertility is what finally pushed governments to smarten up and prioritize healing the planet.

"Who's the dad?" He must be as much of a miracle as Ai-jen. It's not like the inability to make babies naturally is a female-only problem.

She shakes her head and half-laughs again, a chuckle mixed with bewilderment. "Keyano. Did you meet him today? He is going to freak. I have to tell him, right? Or do I? My doctor wanted to call in a bunch of specialists, have me go straight to the university, but I just walked out of his office and came home. To you. I just don't understand how this –" she takes a deep breath and then exhales. She turns and looks me in the eyes, unblinking. "I know the timing is beyond cruel because of you and Ziggy and your sixth and—"

I wave my hand. Stop. "This is only good news, Ai-jen. Only good news. Amazing news. And I am so, so, so excited that I get to be an auntie to this little fighter. And I know that Ziggy will move here in an instant if you want us to. I hope you do. But that doesn't matter. Whatever you need, whatever you want, Ziggy and I will do." And I mean it. I really do. I know it would make sense to feel jealous and betrayed and enraged, but I don't. I get to be an auntie. To Ai-jen's baby. It's the best consolation in the universe.

"Mom is gonna have a shit fit." Ai-jen looks at me, the outright horror on her face so comical that we both burst out laughing. Loud, hard laughing. And we keep on laughing. Smiling and crying and hugging through dinner and the call to Ziggy.

"How did this happen?" Ziggy asks me later, as I lie in Ai-jen's spare bed, too many kilometers away from him. I wish he were here, not just a face on my commpad.

I spare him the wisecrack about sex. "Maybe nature is ready to give humans a second chance." Maybe after all the work we've done to heal our charred planet, to undo the damage we've done to our water and air and soil, maybe after all the atonement and reparations, maybe we get another shot at life.

Maybe.

Or maybe the universe just knows that I'll be the world's greatest auntie. Either way is fine by me.

Jaymie Heilman is a daily swimmer and ocean geek with a PhD in history. She has written two books about the history of Peru and her climate-focused Young Adult novel is under contract for publication. When she's not reading or writing books for kids, she's usually gardening, biking to the library, or dreaming about the ocean. She lives in Edmonton with her husband, son, and a ridiculous number of books.

Website: https://jaymieheilman.com/
Instagram: https://www.instagram.com/jaymieheilman/

TINKER'S WELL
BY STEPHEN B. PEARL

Brad sat astride the peak of the ancient, aluminium roof of the Guelph Central Train Station and secured the support nuts on the last of a line of tulip wind turbines running its length. His short, blond hair was wet with sweat, and the hot, humid air had left his hemp shirt and cargo pants soaked. The electric torque driver in his hand was connected via an extension cord to a pre-collapse van converted to be pulled by horses. The van was covered with thin-film solar panels and sported a tulip wind-turbine on a pole rising from the van's back corner. Until he finished his current job, his tinker wagon was the only source of electricity for five kilometres in any direction.

Another gutted van, hitched to the first, served as Brad's cargo trailer. A line of two-meter long by a-metre square collapsible plastic crates sat side by side on the second van's roof. Each box had a sticker on its side that read 'Dark Lands Assistants Fund' and a silhouette of a standing person assisting a kneeling person to its feet. Beside that was another sticker, 'Tulip Turbines, integrated unit, large.' Brad sighed as he thought of how the collapse might never have happened if the ancestors had done more of what he was doing now a hundred years ago.

Classic rock played from speakers on the tinker wagon. The free entertainment had caused a crowd of dark landers to gather with blankets and picnic baskets, giving the central Guelph area a carnival-like atmosphere.

The song ended, and a commercial played.

"Mommy, why can't Tommy come out and play?" asked a child's voice.

"Tommy's parents didn't get him vaccinated, and now he's very sick," replied a woman's voice.

"What is vaccinated?"

"Remember when you got the needle."

"That was scary."

"And you were very brave. When you had that needle, they put a little bit of the germs that make people sick into you so that your body would learn how to fight the bad germs before they could make you sick."

"Why didn't Tommy's parents get him vaccinated? Don't they love him?"

"I don't know, dear. Some people tell lies, saying vaccines are dangerous. Some people think they cost too much. Some silly people think that because they believe in certain things, they can't get sick."

"So, I can't get sick because of the injection."

"Vaccines only protect you against the germs they are made to protect you against. There are lots of different kinds of germs, but most of the worst ones we've made vaccines for."

"Thank you for getting me vaccinated, mommy. I hope Tommy gets better so I can play with him."

"So do I, my love. So do I." The mother's voice was grave.

"The Novo Gaia easy listening radio network wants to remind you that vaccinations save lives and protect families. See a doctor, nurse, pharmacist, healer or tinker to protect yourself and your loved ones today," the announcer's voice finished. Another old rock song started to play.

"Looks good, Tinker." An Asian-looking man with a barrel chest and a mane of black hair shouted from the broken asphalt below. He was dressed in brown homespun pants and boots.

Brad smiled. For no reason beyond aesthetics, the turbines were coloured in varying tulip shades. From a distance, they resembled giant flowers. The illusion was enhanced by the twin solar collector panels at the base of each unit shaped like leaves and coloured green on their undersides.

"Thanks, Mayor. I'm almost done. While I'm up here, I may as well check the top part of the solar still." Brad glanced at a black pipe that came up the south side of the building and ended in a closed hatch. A white pipe descended the north side of the building into an elevated barrel. On the sunward side of the building, mirrors directed sunlight onto a black barrel on the ground that could be filled with a hand pump. The black barrel was connected to the black pipe. When the barrel was full, floats and levers would open the hatch, so the first few litres of water flashed into the atmosphere taking toxins with low vapour points with them. Then the hatch would close, and the steam would condense in the white pipe and flow to the collection barrel. When the water level dropped in the evaporation chamber, another float would open a valve on the black barrel spilling the concentrated toxins with a high vapour point onto the ground.

"No need of that, Tinker. I checked it last week. I want folk drinking the clean. Wells round here are only good for watering crops, and that's a stretch. No way, no how, I'm drinkin' that. Though, tell you true, it's getting some days that even what the wells give us would be welcome. Wells as have been good since before the collapse, gone dry. Over a hundred years since we lost power, you'd think things would be getting better, but 'tain't. I—."

The sound of a crash stilled the mayor's voice. Brad came to his feet on the peak ridge of the roof. His gaze tracked over the dilapidated twenty-first-century sprawl that made up the town. Many of the derelict houses had been disassembled for resources, more had not, and a few showed the repair of being lived in. Townhouses from the late twenty-first century crowded the nearly dry river that cut through the town. His eyes came to rest on a partially collapsed high-rise building. A pillar of dust rose into the air beside it. The catastrophe was only blocks away.

"What the short was that?" demanded the mayor. The people listening to the radio glanced amongst themselves in confusion.

"Path, protect me!" Brad tossed his tools into a storage box and, with it in hand, scrambled down the ladder.

"Tinker?" asked the mayor.

"It's the Woolwich Tower Ville. Locke, I think it's collapsed." Brad raced to his wagon, tossed in his tools and clambered in behind them. The flip of a switch stilled the radio. Picking up his mic, he depressed the button and spoke. "Everyone who can hear me, this is the Tinker. Close your windows. If you are outside, wet a piece of cloth and breath through it." Brad cranked up his wagon's windows as he spoke. He scanned the crowd.

Everyone had turned towards the pillar of dust. With a *whumping* sound, the dust pillar collapsed and billowed out along the ground. The dry stench of broken concrete permeated the air.

"Missus Fernández, come to my wagon." Brad spoke into his mic, hoping his memory of the woman being in the crowd was correct.

Seconds later, the wagon's passenger side door opened, admitting a slender middle-aged, olive-skinned woman. She climbed in and closed the door. Her black hair was dusted with powder.

"What 'cha need, Tinker?" Missus Fernandez's voice was even. From experience during the plague a year and a half before, Brad knew she was one of those rare people who was unflappable.

"Please put a wet cloth over my horses' nostrils until this dust settles while I see what's happening." Brad checked the holsters on his belt, making sure his multi-tools, nine-millimetre, semi-automatic pistol, and flashlight were in place.

" 'Course, Tinker." Missus Fernandez wrapped a damp handkerchief over her nose and mouth, secured it then left the wagon. Brad watched a small shadow in the dust move to where two large shadows were tethered by the old train station.

The dust was like a dense fog. Moving through the gap in the centre back of his front bench seat, Brad entered the living space of his wagon. A micro kitchen, complete with fridge, microwave, toaster oven, two-burner stove and sink, occupied the area behind the driver's section. A table, that could drop down into a bed, flanked by two bench seats, followed, then his toilet. A video display screen occupied the wall over one of the bench seats. Brad opened a bench seat and pulled out a plastic box. Popping its lid, he extracted two gas masks, then rushed to the wagon's back door and leapt onto what had been the train station's parking lot.

"Locke?" Brad yelled.

"Here, Tinker." A shadowy form approached, resolving into the mayor. He'd wrapped a damp shirt over his nose and mouth.

"Put this on, and let's see what pip the universe has decided to give me this time." Brad passed him one of the gas masks.

"Looks bad." Locke took the mask and, after watching Brad pull on his, dawned it.

"Can't be worse than last year."

"Ebisu, bless me, no!"

Brad lifted his mask. "Everyone, stay here. I'll check it out, then we'll make a plan."

"I's gots to—." Began a skinny Caucasian woman who came out of the dust cloud. Her clothing was scruffier than her compatriots.

"Stay here! We need to know what happened before we do anything. Everyone rushing in will only make things worse." Brad lowered his mask and started down the street at a jog.

It took only seconds to reach Woolwich Street. The dust was so thick Brad could barely see. A figure stumbled out of the murk. Brad caught what was either a small woman or a child before it fell onto the broken asphalt.

"What happened?" demanded Locke.

"It." The figure on the street started coughing.

"We need to get them out of this dust." Brad pulled the person into a fireman's carry and started back the way he'd come.

"Others?" Locke followed the tinker.

"We can't do a damned shorted thing until this clears."

A minute later, Brad lowered the woman onto the floor of the old train station. Someone had closed the windows, leaving the air inside relatively clear.

"Water." Brad examined the woman for injuries.

Locke appeared with a mug of water that he passed to Brad.

The woman groaned. Brad propped her up, holding the glass to her lips. She gulped the water down then leaned back against his arm.

"What happened?" Brad supported her as he brushed the dust off her arms.

"It were. Ceridwen, keep me! It were awful! I was just out. Da wouldn't let me come listen to the radio 'till me chores were done. I was walkin' then 'ere's this kind of a groan. I turned to look, and half the tower falls. It were like the earth swallowed it. 'Ere were dust everywhere. I was tryin' to get clear when youse found me. ME DA!" She shouted the last as her face filled with fear. She began to weep.

"Easy, girl. We don't know nought yet," comforted Locke.

"Let her cry," stated Brad.

"Tinker," breathed Locke.

Brad closed his eyes. "It will clean the dust out of her eyes. Shorting! Our ancestors have a lot to answer for! Pave over flood plains and aquifer recharge zones. What did they think would happen? Locke, go through the people.

Find those that will help. We'll need strong backs and common sense for the search teams and people to help the injured. Is Hilda still the town's midwife?"

"Aye, but I don't see her out there." Locke stroked his chin.

"Send someone to fetch her. Send people to Edin Mills and Arkell for help. At the least, Meb should come out."

"The witch woman?" Locke sounded horrified.

"Yes, Meb, the best practical nurse within a ten-hour ride. Send someone to see if the Neeve Tower Ville will pitch in. The types of injuries we're likely to get are what their field medics are good at, as far as they go." Brad felt over the woman for hidden injuries.

"You gonna call Novo Gaia for help?" asked Locke.

"Once I know what we're facing. Just because Novo Gaia has electricity doesn't mean we don't have our limits. It will take some convincing to get the council to put more resources into this area. Move, give people something to do before they start losing themselves in the dust cloud." Brad glanced around and saw where the clean water tap from the condensing tank entered the station's main room. He filled an old stainless-steel pot that sat on the floor beside the tap and used it to wash the dust off the girl's exposed skin.

"What's your name?" asked Brad.

"Fran." The girl's voice was rough and tear-chocked. Brad guessed her age to be somewhere around fifteen.

"Fran, I'm going to need your help. When the dust clears, I need people to fetch water from the river."

"It's mostly dry, Tinker," objected the girl.

"I know it's the dry season. Thank you, ancestors, for shorting out the climate. Do what you can. You need to wash the dust off people. Those old builders mixed things into the cement that are not good to have on you. See if you can borrow some clean clothes to change into." Brad stood and started for the door.

"Tinker, where youse goin'?" Fran sounded scared.

"To do what I can." As Brad approached the door, it opened, admitting a line of women, older children, and old men.

"Tinker, Locke says you is setting up to care for them as are hurt. We're here to help," remarked a grey-haired man with withered tawny skin dressed in a homespun tunic and trues.

"Good. Set up for casualties like you did with the plague last year. Be ready for broken bones and bleeding. We'll need bandages and splints. Pick one of the offices and clean it until you'd eat off the floor. That will be my surgery. I'll bring in my equipment later."

"You gonna take orders from this bright lander?" snarled a burly woman with broad, pale features and blond hair.

"Lara, he's talking sense," countered the old man.

"Just seems to me." Lara fell silent when Brad casually dropped his hand over his gun holster.

"Talking isn't doing, and if we're going to save anyone, it will take doing." Brad's voice was even.

"Let's rustle people," said the old man.

The town's folk spread out to prepare the room.

Brad stepped outside into the fast-clearing air. Locke stood with a group of men and three strong-looking women. They all had cloths over their faces.

Brad took a step and heard grit crunch under his feet. "Who's good with horses?"

"Andrew knows 'em well as any," replied Locke.

"Andrew, unhitch my trailer from my wagon and bring the wagon along behind. I don't want to risk it until I know what we're getting into.

"Anybody who can get us some rope, blankets or stretchers, run and fetch them. Meet us at the Woolwich Tower Ville."

Over half the people ran to get supplies.

"The rest of you, come on." Brad led a band of seven people towards the collapsed building. The dust parted before them and billowed in behind. Shortly past where they'd found Fran, chunks of concrete started to litter the street. A mangled kitchen table rose out of the gloom.

"Locke, pick someone to wait here and stop Andrew. This is as close as I'm willing to risk my wagon."

"Right. Terry, that's you. Keep folk as come to rubberneck back too," ordered Locke.

"Spread out, so we cross the street. Keep the people to both sides in sight and look for injured. If you see a mound, gently kick it. This dust is thick enough to bury people."

"Tinker," cried a voice from down the line. Brad rushed to it and found a man kneeling by a mound. The mound resolved itself into a human form.

Brad knelt by the form and listened for its breathing while placing his hand to feel for the rise and fall of the chest. "They're still alive." Brad began a body check.

"Tinker, I've got another one," called a woman from further along the line of rescuers.

"Check if they're breathing."

"Tinker, John and Mabel Bashar here. We's got a stretcher and some rope." A voice came through the dust.

"Bring the stretcher here. Leave the rope by my van, then get this man to the train station." Brad stood.

"I got another one," called a voice in the cloud.

"Are they breathing?" Brad moved towards the second call.

"Tinker, I. Jesus. Emma. I... I saw her yesterday." There were tears in the voice.

"Is she breathing?" Brad repeated.

"Not as I's can tell."

"Then leave her and move on." Brad looked up towards the tower. Much of the dust had cleared. He could see that half of the building was still upright, though leaning heavily to the side. The other half was a pile of rubble. The glass had been removed from the bottom three stories and replaced with stone and brick, making a fortress wall. The iron door at the front was twisted out of its frame.

Parts of the building's facing and windows had broken away on the section that still stood. People scrambled on the uneven, cracking floors trying not to fall to their deaths.

"Tinker, we gotta help them in the tower." Locke moved to Brad's side.

Brad looked west to where the sun was dipping below the horizon. "We're going to lose the light soon. Ground out, this is going to be bad in the dark." Brad considered. "Take the low fruit first. Get the people in the streets and get folk out of any houses that might get crushed if the rest of the tower falls. When we've done that, we can start in on the people in the tower." Brad glanced up the street to where his wagon waited. "Get the injured to the station. Then clear a path for my wagon to the building. We'll need light. Who's fast on their feet?"

"The Walters boy can run. He's a smart lad." Locke stared at the tower; several people were trying to scramble down from the upper floors. As he watched, one lost their grip and plummeted five stories.

"Send him to my wagon. I'll need to be in ten places at once. He can be my extra eyes."

"Billy," bellowed Locke as Brad rushed to his wagon. A moment later, Brad depressed the button on the microphone for his sound system.

"People in the tower. We will come for you. If you are safe where you are, don't move. Give us the time we need to help you." Brad's amplified voice blasted over the dust-shrouded street, reaching even the highest floor of the shattered building.

Turning a dial on his radio, Brad depressed the button on his mic.

"Tinker, Tinker, Tinker, Guelph Center, Guelph Center, Guelph Center. Emergency, Emergency, Emergency."

A long moment passed before the radio came to life. "Go ahead with priority ident, tinker."

Brad rolled his eyes, knowing the futility of trying to get the base to ignore the formality of ident. He glanced at the chronometer in his dash. "B One, R Nine, A two, D four, L zero, Y eight, I two, R five, V one, I zero, N eight, G PC. Over."

"Chattem Tinker Center is recording, Brad. What is the nature of the emergency? Over." stated the man's voice over the radio.

"Half a Tower Ville collapsed. Concrete dust is everywhere. A hundred or more dead. Easily as many trapped on the upper stories of the remains. Over."

"Was it explosives? Over."

"Negative, no boom. I'm guessing a sinkhole due to aquifer depletion coupled with heightened erosion from the flood-drought cycle the climate has moved into. I'm not about to get us into someone else's war. Over."

"What do you need, tinker?"

"Get on to Eddie. See if he can send out some medical assistance. I'll also need a demolition expert. When this is over, the rest of that tower will have to come down. Some emergency workers with experience dealing with collapsed buildings would also be good. General medical equipment. Over."

"The minister won't want to allocate much in the way of resources. Over."

"Just get onto Eddie. Call a crap cut if that secretary of his gives you any trouble. Over."

"I don't miss this part of the job. Good luck, Brad. Remember, a dead tinker is no good to anyone. Over and out."

"Acknowledged. Over and out."

There was a rap on the wagon's window. Brad opened the door revealing a slender, late-teens, brown-haired man dressed in dust-covered homespun.

"Locke said you wanted me, Tinker," said the youth.

"Billy?" Brad eyed the youth. He looked like a runner.

"Yes." Billy shifted nervously from foot to foot.

"Run back to the train station and find out if anyone has been brought in that needs treatment only I can give. Hurry and come right back."

"Yes, Tinker." Billy sprinted away, his feet kicking up clouds of the settling dust.

Brad stepped from his van and carefully led his horses down the street, pulling his wagon.

"Kick in a wall. We need the wood. It's not like someone lives there," Locke's voice echoed through the evening.

"Problem?" Brad brought his team to a stop in front of what remained of the collapsing ancient high-rise.

"There's folk as made their way to the ground floor in the building. There's no way out except clambering over the rubble, and it's shorting shifty. I figure we could make a bridge with some ladders and two-by-fours. Drop it from the firm ground on this end to what's left of the floor on the other."

"Good plan." Brad looked through the evening gloom.

"Locke," bellowed a woman's voice.

"Ground out, not her," grumbled Locke, then schooling his face into a neutral expression, he turned to face a tall, lean woman with medium-brown skin and short-cropped, curly, black hair.

Brad couldn't stop his eyes from tracking over her athletic form or taking in a handsome, slightly angular face housing magnificent brown eyes. She made the homespun trues and shirt she wore look good.

"Locke, I need you to know. Me folk ain't got nothin' to do with this. We's kept the truce."

"I'm not thinking different, Keely."

"It was probably a sinkhole. The summer floods would have gouged out the rock. Then the lack of water in the aquifer removed support. The rock just fell in on itself," added Brad.

Keely's eyes darted up and down the length of the tinker. She cocked an eyebrow speculatively. "Glad you's here, Brad."

"Can your people help?" asked Brad.

"The Woolwichers?" Keely sounded suspicious.

"You're all Guelphers," remarked Locke.

"Aye, and not like we have opposing contracts no more. Be nice to save lives for a change. I'll get me troops out. What you need?"

"Search the street for survivors and get them to the train station. I need to get a line up on that building to evac the people on the upper stories. Once we've done that, we'll have to go through the rubble in the pit. Have you got any day flares?" Brad counted off actions on his fingers.

Keely looked suspicious. "People I got. Equipment?"

"I'll replace anything you use. Or trade it out for something of equal value," interrupted Brad.

Keely nodded. "Novo Gaians, I trust to keep their word. Not like them lyin' gridders. I've got a few things in arsenal." Turning, she addressed a burly man in homespun clothing with a pre-collapse rifle over his shoulders. A burn marred one side of his face and neck, vanishing under his shirt. "Sergeant, rally the troops. Medics and their kits to the train station 'ceptin' Disa, send her here for triage. Bring the day flares and." She bit her lip and then spoke softly. "It might be handy." Her volume increased. "The line gun. On the double."

"Yes, mam." The sergeant took off at a run.

"A line gun. Keely, I could kiss you," remarked Brad.

"If you play your cards right, Tinker," Keely winked.

Brad smiled, then moved to his wagon and pulled out a spotlight, mounting it on his wagon's side so that it pointed at the area between the solid ground and the shattered open side of the building. He turned it on, banishing the shadows. "That will have to do until we get your day flares. I…"

His voice trailed off as he scanned the illuminated pit. A child's body lay amongst the rubble, ripped apart at the waist like a broken toy. The dust softened the outline of the horror with a grey shroud dotted red with blood.

Keely and Locke followed his gaze.

"That was Carlotta's girl, wasn't it?" asked Locke.

"Were somebody's," remarked Keely.

A group of villagers ran up carrying long, pre-collapse, polycarbonate ladders.

"For the living," said Brad.

"For the living," echoed Keely and Locke.

In minutes the ladders lay parallel on the ground, tied together with ropes.

Salvaged lengths of plank lay along their length. The rescuers lifted the impromptu platform and pushed it over the rubble pit until its end came up on the remains of the building's lobby, passing through the ripped-open wall. As soon as the bridge was down, people started filing across, the electric spotlight from the tinker wagon showing the way.

"Tinker," blurted Billy, who ran up.

"Yes," Brad looked at the youth.

"They need you at the station. There's some with bad breaks, and Young Mister Frankel done split his gut. One of the Bakers took a right nasty hit to the head and ain't come out of it. Franny said to tell you that the river's almost dry. She can't get water enough to wash the wounded."

Brad looked at the shattered tower. "I."

"Go, Tinker. Me medic will be here right quick. She can sort those with a chance. You can't be two places at once, and none of us can do what you can up yonder." Keely gestured in the general direction of the train station.

"Can you help with the water situation?" asked Brad.

Locke shook his head. "Wells are dry, river's about as bad. Flood or drought, been the way for years, and right now, it's drought."

"Short it! Two hundred years ago, fall was the wet season here. I'll need my wagon." Brad looked about as if a solution would come out of the air.

As if on cue, a squad of fifty people carrying equipment ran up the street.

"Go, Tinker. We've got this," said Keely.

Brad nodded once and moved to his wagon. Turning the team and getting to the train station took only minutes. Moments later, Brad stood in an old office off the main room with a wiry middle-aged man lying on an ancient, metallic desk in front of him.

An extension cord ran from Brad's van, powering a laptop connected to a portable sonogram. Brad played the sonogram over the unconscious man's scalp revealing a radiating pattern of cracks in the skull.

"Lord Thoth lend me skill. Imhotep, most wise, grant me cunning. Isis grant him strength," muttered Brad as he turned to a woman standing in the corner. "Shave his head, then paint the scalp with this." Brad pulled a bottle out of one of his medical bags. "Call me when you're done."

He turned to his other patient. A plump man of maybe thirty with corded muscle in his arms. He looked up with pain-filled eyes.

"Am I for it, Tinker?" he asked.

"Not if I have a say." Brad undid the dressing on the man's belly and carefully pulled what looked like a ripped and folded bedsheet away from the wound. Chunks of rubble and powdered rock pocked the flesh.

Taking an IV from one of his bags, Brad set it up. "This one will keep. You're going to be fine, Mister Frankel. I've just got a few others to see to first."

Looking across the room, Brad saw that the first patient's head was shaved and the skin stained brown with disinfectant. "Shorting, I need to take another surgical elective at the academy."

With an apparent confidence he didn't feel, Brad cut the skin away from the skull over where the cracks were, then, with a rotary tool, that he also used for fine construction work, drilled a borehole into the skull. One second there was only the screech of the drill. The next blood spurted out, hitting Brad's chest. Brad pulled the rotary tool away, taking fragmented pieces of skull with it. The man on the desk groaned and shifted.

"Hold him down," Brad ordered the woman assisting him as he retrieved a squeeze bottle and misted a vasoconstrictive, coagulant, antibiotic mix into the hole. The blood stopped oozing.

"Tell him if he wants to live, he'll lay still. I don't want to cover the hole for an hour or so to be sure the pressure doesn't build up again." Picking up one of his kits, Brad moved into the train station's main room. He found medics from both Tower Villes moving amongst the crowd, splinting minor fractures and bandaging small wounds. Hilda, the local midwife, and a Tower Ville medic were treating a screaming woman with a fractured femur. The patient's one thigh was twelve centimetres shorter than the other and twice as thick. The skin was a dark purple colour. They had tied their patient down on a stretcher with what looked like aluminium tent poles braced on either side of the injured leg. Ignoring the woman's agony, Hilda twisted a bundle of cloth that was tied around the foot of the injured leg on one end and to the intersection of the aluminium poles at the other. As the cloth shortened, it stretched the broken leg back to its proper length. Brad moved to the pair and pulled a hypodermic and two bottles from his drug kit.

"This should help," he remarked as he prepared a shot and pressed it home in the screaming woman.

"What was it?" Hilda shouted over her patient's screams.

"Analgesic and muscle relaxant. I don't want to knock her out because she might stop breathing, but it will take the edge of it." Brad shouted back before he moved on.

Three hours later, he finished cutting away the damaged, dirty tissue from Mister Frankel's stomach and stitched closed the skin.

"A healer could do more, but you'll live." Brad moved to Mister Baker, who looked up with alert eyes.

"Tell me true, Tinker. Is me brain gonna leak out and leave me simple? 'Cause I'd rather die."

"Doesn't work that way, Kevin. Now that the bleeding has stopped, I'll patch you up."

Brad secured a plate over the hole in Kevin's skull, then sutured the skin over it.

"I just hope things are going as well at the building," he muttered.

A DAY FLARE hovered over the broken high-rise casting its light on the disaster area. Town's folk and tower villers struggled to get people out of the collapsing ruin. More ladders had been found, and people were now climbing down from the fourth story. A pair of burly men manoeuvered a blanket-wrapped form to two others on parallel ladders. Each took an end, and they clambered down one-handed. The men on the ground lay the form on a stretcher, picked it up, and hurried towards the train station. The two men ascended the ladders to take another bundle.

Keely took aim at the top floor of the broken building with the line gun and pulled the trigger. The explosive charge fired, and the line spooled out. A moment later, a grappling hook caught on the twisted remains of a balcony. Before they could properly secure the base, someone pulled the hook into the building. Seconds later, a bulky man was scrambling hand over hand down the line.

"What is that idiot doing?" demanded Locke.

"Undisciplined. What I expect from a Woolwicher," snapped Keely.

The man reached the ground and stood breathing heavily. His hands were encased in heavy leather gloves, the palms of which were worn from gripping the rope.

"That was a stupid thing to do!" scolded Keely.

"No choice, yur couldn't hear me shoutin'. There be three folk on the tenth floor who no way can use a line. One old, one with a broke arm, and one in a bad way. Medic done what she could, but reckon the last we don't need to worry about."

"Do you have rope or anything up there?" demanded Locke.

"Kept stores on the lower floors. We was tyin' sheets and blankets together 'fore the big voice told us to stay put. I wouldn't trust 'em with me weight."

"We'll use the grapple line to haul up ladders and rope. Some of your folk on the bottom floor had the sense to carry out equipment as they came," said Keely.

The climber nodded. "Aye, how you gonna send the message up. I don't relish scramblin' up that line. Down's bad enough, and 'ere's wind. Near blew me into the wall. I don't reckon a blanket will do to hold folk less you want 'em pulped by the time they reach bottom."

"Tinker might be a help here. If he's done with the folk in the station," said Keely.

A tremor ran through the earth. The ancient high-rise shuddered and shifted. Potted plants fell out of the open gaps in the south wall from the lower stories. Concrete broke away, crashing into the street. A man tumbled from an upper story and plummeted to the ground, where he was smashed into a pulp.

"We need to get 'em out of there," snapped Keely. "Billy, fetch the tinker and tell him to bring his wagon."

"What can he do?" asked Locke.

"Mayor." Keely lent irony to the title, but her smile took some of the sting out of it. "Better ask what a tinker can't do if they have their tools about. Stories I've heard." She sobered. "It's worth askin'."

"Worth askin'," agreed Locke. "Let's set up, so 'em as can climb have a way to do it."

BRAD EXITED his impromptu surgery and scanned the room. The glow of alcohol lanterns lit the macabre scene of injured bodies on blankets and cots. His eyes fell to a handsome, grey-haired woman in a homespun dress and a smile touched his lips.

"Meb, thanks for coming. How long have you been here?" Brad strode up to the woman.

"Only an hour. You've quite the mess here, Tinker. At least this time, those politicians will let me help." Meb kept stitching the wound in the side of a whip-thin woman with brown hair and eyes.

Brad nodded. "We'll catch up later."

Brad walked to a ring of buckets around a floor drain, finding them empty. Fran came in through the main door carrying a bucket. He moved to her. "We need more water."

"I know, Tinker, but 'ere ain't none. River's not a trickle. I only got this by going to fall upstream and catching drips. We've pumped what wells still had water dry. If we don't get rain, town will be in a bad way, and rain ain't likely this late in year."

Brad shook his head and helped the girl carry the bucket to the drain, where he dipped out a small portion of water and washed the blood off his hands.

"I's going to get another bucket." Fran took an empty bucket and left the building.

"I'm going to my wagon if you need me," Brad announced to the room.

Brad reached his wagon and activated his radio. Exhaustion pulled at him, and it was still hours before dawn. A day flare hung in the sky over the decimated tower, casting a red glow over Central Guelph.

"Tinker, Tinker, Tinker, Central Guelph, Central Guelph, Central Guelph. Call in, call in, call in. Over."

"We read you, tinker. Go ahead with ident. Over," said a woman's voice.

Brad glanced at the chronometer in his dash, closed his tired eyes, and gave his ident.

"Ident confirmed. What do you need, Brad?"

"Is that you, Zada? Over," asked Brad.

"Sure is. I fell off a roof while I was setting up a solar installation. Broke my leg in three places. Eddie insisted I come in from the field until next spring. Old Wilson is finishing my route this year, and I'm stuck doing radio. Over."

"Trade you. Over."

"I read the report. How bad is it? Over."

"Bad. I've been stuck in surgery for the last four hours. The other Tower

Ville pitched in. That's making a difference. Look, the water shortage here is even worse than we thought. The river is nearly dry, and the wells are pumped out. Is Eddy sending help? Over."

"One truck, two retired tinkers, an apprentice Dark Land's healer by the name of Carla, big surprise there, a demolitions expert and their kits, but they won't be there until noonish tomorrow. We can't mobilise faster than that. Over."

"Better than nothing, but not by much. Look, Zada. Call Eddie and tell him to put a Warka Water Tower in the load and as big a tank of potable water as he can fit. If we don't get these people something to drink, it won't matter who we save today. Over."

"He won't get the allocation. Novo Gaia is on the edge of running a deficit. The council is being tight with aid to the Dark Lands. Over."

"Tell Eddie to have Carla sign off on it from my personal account. Over."

"Brad, you shouldn't do that. Over."

"I'll let the town have it on credit. They're good people. They'll pay me back before I'm done my stint on this route. They need it now, and what's the good of having money if you don't spend it? Over."

"You're your grandfather's line, that's certain. I'll call Eddie in the morning. Over."

"Call him now. Have him get people out of bed. I need that water ASAP if I'm going to give Guelph the time it needs to fix the mess the ancestors left them. Besides, why should I be the only one losing sleep? Over and out."

"You do like to live dangerously. Over and out."

Brad sat with his eyes closed and unintentionally drifted off. It seemed that only a second had passed when a knock on his door jarred him awake. He glanced over to see Billy, sweat-drenched and breathing hard.

Brad opened the door. "Problem?"

"They've got a line up to the tenth floor, but there are injured people and the building's shifting."

"Climb in. Untie my team when you go by." Brad rubbed his tired eyes and looked out over the backs of his horses. Despite the water shortage, they were tethered by a half barrel of water that had been full when the night began. The barrel was now empty. The horses looked bored.

Minutes later, Brad pulled up in front of the broken tower and stepped onto the dust-covered pavement.

"They're over here." Billy led the way to Keely and Locke, who stood by the base of the line going up the side of the building. The line was being used to haul up a rope ladder. At the eighth-floor people secured the ladder to the remains of a balcony. The bottom of the rope ladder was attached to a sixth-floor balcony. Another rope ladder bridged the gap between the sixth and fourth floors, and an ordinary ladder descended to the ground. A steady stream of people clambered down the ladders. Some carried children, some pets, others, bags of belongings. With the ladder from eight to six secured, the rope was dropped from the tenth floor once more and yet another rope ladder began its ascent, completing the path to survival.

"Billy says you need me?" asked Brad.

"We're good for the able bodies, but there are injured on the upper floors, and the building is still shifting," explained Locke.

"Short and ground it!" hissed Brad. "That's why the stream of casualties slowed."

"We can get the injured on the fourth floor down with ropes and stretchers, but the wind twists the rope ladders around too much to risk goin' down one-handed, or with much of a load. We'd be tradin' one life for another," observed Keely.

Brad's face grew stern as memories of faces suffering and dying in a dingy hall surrounded by the stench of human waste filled his mind. Next, he thought of a town of dead friends, still and silent, without even a bird left alive because of ancient greed. He took a deep breath and spoke in an even tone. "No more lost causes."

"Then what?" asked Keely.

"Are there able bodies on ten?" Brad glanced at his wagon as he thought.

"The medic, four others and the wounded." Locke wiped sweat from his brow.

"Tell them to stay put and be ready to pull up another line after they get the ladder secured."

"How are we gonna do that? Shouting hasn't been working that well," queried Locke.

Brad snorted. "My voice carries." Brad turned to the building and seemed to measure distance with his eyes. "I have a plan."

"Is it a good plan?" asked Locke.

"I'll let you know when I see if it works. Billy, go to the train station and tell them I need…"

Seconds later, Brad's voice blasted out of his loudspeaker. "Stay on the tenth floor. I think we have a way to get the wounded down." He directed his spotlight onto the intact tenth-story balcony and watched a woman wave her arm in acknowledgement.

Minutes passed before four men appeared carrying one of the collapsible crates the tulip turbines had been packaged in.

"I still say it'll be too heavy. That's a big box," remarked Keely as Brad climbed from his wagon.

"They're lighter than they look and tough as nails," observed Brad. "Pass me some rope."

In moments, two loops of rope were around the box, coming together above it, forming a cradle. Some knots later, it was attached to the line gun's line.

Brad returned to his wagon and pressed his mic button. "Haul it up."

The box ascended, swinging with the wind and bumping into the building's side, knocking loose showers of concrete.

"We can't do this with people on the ladders," stated Locke.

Moving to his wagon, Brad pressed his mic button and spoke. "Pause the evacuation. If you are on a ladder, finish climbing to the next level and wait." He turned to Locke. "We need able bodies to help the injured get in the box anyway."

People cleared the ladders. The crate on the rope reached the tenth floor, was loaded with a casualty then started to lower. It swayed in the wind, but at each level, hands reached out to stabilise it. Several people, seeing what was happening, started scrambling down the ladders. The swaying box slammed into one. She fell four stories to the asphalt. Brad rushed to the woman's side and began a body check.

"I told you to wait," he admonished.

She looked at him and scowled. "Yu's not me, boss, Bright Lander. Why's should I's wait so some sad act as gets 'emselves hurt can come down afore me?"

"Well, now you can wait at the train station until you can walk again. You've broken both your legs and several ribs." Brad nodded to a Tower Ville medic and two stretcher-bearers. "Splint the legs. Be careful with the ribs.

Then get her out of here. Triage level five. Once the legs are splinted, we can treat her when we get around to it."

Brad rushed to where the cargo container had just reached the ground. The man inside it was barrel-chested and ghastly pale. Bubbles of blood formed on his lips when he breathed.

"Hemothorax, at the least. Triage level two. Get him to the surgery." Brad indicated a man and a woman carrying a stretcher. "I'll be right there." Brad looked up. With the container down, people had started using the ladders again.

"Go, Tinker. We have this." Locke cupped his hands around his mouth and bellowed, "Clear the ladders, pass it on."

The message coursed up the building. The people on the ladders hurried to the next level and cleared the building's side. The crate lifted off the ground seconds after that. Brad looked at the rubble pit and saw people with lanterns sifting the debris. He glanced east and was surprised to see the growing light of pre-dawn.

HOURS LATER, Brad stepped back from his latest patient while a muscular grey-haired woman dressed in a hemp shirt and cargo pants wearing a surgical apron took his place. The other tinker and Carla were in the main room reviewing the treatment of the less critical cases. He smiled to see the well-shaped young woman with delicate features and shortish dark brown hair. Her camo uniform did little to hide the curves he had become familiar with over the last year. He left Carla to her work.

Moving to a corner of the room, Brad examined the man who'd come from the tenth floor. The chest tube was draining well, and the man was sleeping. Fran sat holding his hand.

"Your father?" asked Brad in a soft voice.

Fran shook her head. "Uncle, but we get on. Me da, I think he's gone. Always figured it would be in battle. Worried 'bout that. Contract ends, and I take a breath. 'en this happens. I…" Fran silenced as tears streamed from her eyes.

"I'm sorry." Brad patted her shoulder.

"Leastways, Bright Landers brought water. Folk say Nova Gaians aren't bad folk. Reckon I'll believe 'em now."

Brad smiled and moved away. He paused when he saw his reflection in a battered wall mirror. Grit and bodily fluids of all descriptions covered him. He exited the building into early afternoon sunshine to see a biodiesel-powered eighteen-wheeler with a large tank of water pulled up beside his wagon and cargo trailer. Crates were stacked in front of the water tank. He walked to the trailer and washed the worst of the blood, grit, and filth from himself.

He walked to where the tower still leaned. The rope ladders were empty. Men and women moved cautiously over the rubble in the pit. A line of bodies stretched along the dusty length of the street.

"Doctor Irving?" A burly man with north American first peoples features dressed in a green camo, Novo Gain, field uniform approached.

"Yes, you are?" Brad stared at the man blurrily.

"Lieutenant Richard Cheyenne. I'm the demolitions expert."

Brad nodded. "What will it take to bring it down?"

"A good hard kick. You should get your people out of there. Now." He pointed to the would-be rescuers sifting the rubble.

Brad scanned the tower villers and the other people of Guelph. "I couldn't if I tried. Give them a few hours. It's their town, their neighbours, their friends."

Richard nodded. "As long as they know the risks."

"Better than we do, and still, they're at it. Have you seen Locke or Keely?"

"Who?" asked Richard.

"The mayor and the leader from the other Tower Ville."

"Oh, they're at the pit."

"Of course they are. Well, Richard. May I call you Richard?" Brad waited for the reply.

"Sure."

"Good, it's Brad, by the way. Prep your charges. When the search is over, we'll collapse the tower. I'm going to bed."

THE NEXT MORNING Brad lay in his wagon. Carla's naked form pressed against him, her head resting on his chest.

"Amanda would have come to help, but you know how heavy third-year is."

"Yes, I know." Brad closed his eyes, trying to think of anything but the complexity of his relationship.

"I can't wait for you to meet her. I'm sure you'll just love each other." Carla snuggled in tighter.

"Love, don't expect too much. I'll keep an open mind, and I hope she will, but, well. This is off the map for me." Brad wrapped his arm around her possessively.

"I met Keely after you turned in. She seems interesting." There was a teasing note in Carla's voice.

"She might have been, but you're here now. We agreed that the rules are we are together when we can be. Here and now, we can be." Brad kissed her head. "Let's just enjoy it."

"While we can. We're having dinner with my grandmother. She doesn't know about Amanda, so don't tell her. The relief team is rolling out first thing tomorrow. I need to get back to school. I'll see you in November."

Brad kissed the beautiful young healer and brushed her hair with his fingers. "On that note, we both have work to do."

Hours later, Brad and the visiting tinkers stood beside a house-sized, circular construction of polycarbonate rods, passive heat-dissipaters and panels that occupied the site of a long-defunct fire that had destroyed several houses in the town's core.

"And this will get us water, how?" Locke eyed the construction dubiously.

"Air passes into it and cools. Water condenses out and collects in the collection tank. It can give you about a hundred litres a day, give or take," explained Brad. "I've rigged the overflow to spill into an old well so that when you aren't using all the water, it will help recharge the aquifer.

"This will solve the sinkhole problem?" Locke stared at the second-generation Warka Water Tower dubiously.

Brad snorted. "Hardly. This is a bandage, something to supply some of your drinking water so that the town doesn't die. It can't fix your problems. There will be more sinkholes and empty wells."

Locke stared at the ground. "Not to be ungrateful, Tinker. But what good is it? Folk can't live thinking the ground is gonna swallow them up each day."

"It buys you time, Locke. Time to undo the damage our ancestors did.

Time for nature to trap more carbon in trees so the climate returns to what it should be. Time to tear down those houses on the river's flood plain and in the other regions that Novo Gaia has marked as Red-T zones. Time to dig up the asphalt and concrete and plant trees."

"What will that do?" Locke looked confused.

"Haven't you ever wondered why Novo Gaia Red T-s certain buildings?" Brad shook his head indulgently.

"Gridders say it's so you can keep folk down. Come to think, sounds like gridder twaddle."

"It's because the buildings should never have gone up there in the first place. Building on a floodplain is stupid, greedy, and short-sighted. Leave it to farms and forest. It's supposed to flood. Then there are aquifer recharge zones where the water seeps into the rocks. The tower fell because the water that helped hold up the rock beneath it was pumped out. It will take time, but if you uncover the recharge zones, the water will sink in and restore the natural balance. The river will flow again because it isn't all being sucked into the earth. The plants will help dissipate the heat and rebalance the environment."

"Well and good, Tinker, but who's gonna pay for it? With the homeless tower folk, the town's gonna be in a bad way for a long time," Locke turned away from the water tower and let his eyes wander over the battered city street.

"Locke, you have to look at the angles. Novo Gaia is extending its freight rail to the old Guelph train station. That will open markets all over old Ontario to you. Salvage the red Ted buildings. Store the resources in abandoned structures, then sell them as needed. It will give the Tower Villers jobs. Shorting, they may even be able to stop hiring out as mercenaries. When the river is flowing steadily again, you can put in micro-hydro at the waterfalls, maybe even some inflow generators along its length. Between that, solar, wind, and biomass, you can set up industry. Saving yourself could be the best thing that ever happened to you."

Locke stared at Brad as if trying to wrap his mind around the enormity of the suggestions.

"Your choice is to keep going like you have been and watch more towers fall. If you'll excuse me, I'm joining Carla and Meb for dinner. Let me know what you decide. I have a good contact for reselling salvaged copper and plastic pipe. I can hook you up."

Brad nodded to the visiting retired tinkers, then walked away to leave the mayor time to think.

Pause.

Stephen B. Pearl is a multiple-published author whose works range across the speculative fiction field. His writings focus heavily on the logical consequences of the worlds he crafts.

Stephen's Inspirations encompass H.G. Wells, J.R.R. Tolkien, Frank Herbert, and Homer, among others.

Stephen uses local settings in his works where appropriate. His Chronicles of Ray McAndrews series, Nukekubi and Revenant, are set in the GHA and surrounding areas. His Tinker's World series, The novels, Tinker's Plague and Tinker's Sea, and the short stories Tinker's Toxin and Tinker's Well are set in a future Southern Ontario.

Stephen's training as an Emergency Medical Care Assistant, a SCUBA diver, and his long-standing interest in environmental technologies have factored into all his Tinker series.

Website: https://www.stephenpearl.com.
The Tinker's series: https://www.brain-lag.com/product/tinkers-sea/3
Facebook: https://www.facebook.com/StephenBPearl/
Freedom Saga: https://www.brain-lag.com/product/cloning-freedom/21

WE GOT THE BEAT

BY O.E. TEARMANN

"Come on Jen! It'll be amazing!"

Bunny made like her name and jumped three feet straight in the air. She grabbed her bae's hands and spun them around.

Jen laughed, sandy hair flying as their bae spun them. They shoved their hair out of their eyes when Bunny let go. She was so cute when she got excited like this. But still…

"Bunny…I dunno…all those *people*…"

Bunny bounced on the balls of her feet, the long brown ears that had given her the nickname stuck straight up and quivering. "Jen Jen Jen the people are *the point*!" Teeth bright in her dark face, she held out her tab. "See? The Beat has kinetic tiles, when people dance there the kinetic energy they generate powers, like, ten blocks of their neighborhood! Isn't that cool? Isn't that the very absolute best?" Hugging her tab to her chest, she spun in a circle. "And Nine Tails is playing! Oh my god Jen I've loved Nine Tails like forEVER! And the folks said we can go! I'm finally sixteen now, and you're seventeen, and the Meet says anybody sixteen plus is cool to go into Denver on their own, and the whole fam is doing a group trip, and my folks cleared me and once my folks say yeah you know your dad will, and the Beat's got an under eighteen night! Oh my god oh my god!" She bounced straight up in the air, high enough to bump the ceiling panel with her hands. A little cascade of dust drifted down to salt her hair with white as she laughed. "And Lucky, she lead sings for the Nine Tails, she actually holds her *mic* with her *tail!* It's that long, and it's *prehensile!* Isn't that just the *best thing?* I mean, how often do we see Gammas like us showing off like that on stage?! Like, never!"

Jen glanced down, rubbing a hand up and down their arm. They sure didn't want to show off their eyes, or anything else that marked them as one of the genetic lines that the old corporate powers had screwed around with when they were trying to make people who didn't need so much food and water. Really, they didn't want to show off. Period.

"Isn't it going to be kinda noisy in there for you?" They asked. Their bae waved a hand. "Psh! That's what ear plugs are for! Mo and Uncle Tafarah can print me a nice set like Papa has, yeah?"

"Oh," Jen said to their shoes. "Yeah. I guess so."

Bunny's ears shifted down from Bonkers Setting to Happy Setting, and she cocked her head. "Jen babe, what's up?" Stepping in, she rested her hands on Jen's shoulders.

Jen looked up, blinking to refocus their eyes on their bae's face. They did their best to smile. "Nothing, Bun. We're good. Sounds fun."

Bunny raised her eyebrows; her ears went in the other direction, sticking out on either side of her head like no crossing bars on the rail line. "Jen, don't play. What's up?"

Jen could feel their insides tightening up. They didn't want to hurt their bae, but they needed Bunny out of their face. They needed space to think, bad.

Gently, they disentangled themselves. "Need some headspace, kay? I'll let you know in time to get tix. Sound good?"

"Yeah...sure..." Bunny agreed, but her ears sank as she said it. "I...guess I'm gonna go help Mama and Aunt Billie for a bit. See you later?"

"Yeah, later," Jen agreed, trying for a smile. Turning, they headed for their room. They had some studying for their next Community Career Accompaniment, and in their room they could *think*.

Crossing through the common area of the farm, they acknowledged a few waves from friends and fam. A guy bringing in stuff from Denver nearly ran them over, backpedaling with his boxes in his arms. "Oh jeez, sorry miss... uh...pal. Didn't see you...there." He stared for a second, gave them a sickly smile, and rushed past.

Jen's gut dropped like a concrete block. Miss. City people were always seeing them as a girl. City people always stared at them in that way that made Jen want to climb into a hole. Like they were something *weird*. Something *dangerous*.

And Bunny wanted them to go with her and deal with *a whole club full of city people*.

Pulling the hood of their shirt up, they booked it down into the residential wing, and into their own cozy family space. Climbing the stairs to the second floor, they flopped down on their bed and caught their breath.

Outside, shade tarps fluttered over the canopies of produce trees that protected the rest of the food forest that made up Four Aces Farm, stretching all the way to the edible agave species up against the pylon walls two acres away. The wall of water-condensation pylons shimmered in gentle shades of cream under the sun, painted murals gleaming along the base. Beyond the wall, re-seed prairie rippled in the hot wind. If they turned their head to the side and squinted, Jen could just spot a herd of buffalo way out there, placidly grazing under the gene-modded fur that kept them cool in temps that'd kill an Alpha human.

Most Alphas couldn't see as far as Jen could, especially if they turned their head to one side and looked out of the corner of their eye. But hey, that's what goat genes were good for: good panoramic eyesight, good glycogen storage. Weird looks.

Rolling onto their back, they watched pollination drones fly around the skylight like little pieces of stained glass. Slowly, they ran through a breathing exercise. When their pulse was closer to normal, they got up and opened their closet, pulling out their study stuff. The mirror inside the door flashed in the sun. For a second, they studied themselves. A fluffy person, all rounded curves. Tan skin, sandy hair. Round face. Yellow eyes, the pupils horizontal rectangles like power ports. There were their stubby hands with their three fingers. And their boobs, of course. Too big. Too obvious. Too out there, making people assume stuff about them. Making people weigh them up and judge them. Like they didn't get enough of that already when they left home.

Damn it, why did they have to leave home and go to some stupid club? People *got* them at home. At home they had fam, and they had friends, and they were okay. Out there…

Jen sighed, and closed the closet door. Yeah. *Out There*. They were going to have to figure out *Out There*. And soon.

~

"WELL THAT WAS WEIRD," Bunny muttered to herself, watching her bae head off. She worried about Jen sometimes. Some stuff freaked them out, and she got that. But why would this do it? Tickets to an amazing show they could go to together? Ears twitching uncomfortably, Bunny stood and tried to think it through. She'd thought Jen would be over the moon right along with her. Instead they were…what? Sad? Scared? No, that didn't fit.

What was going *on* with Jen? They loved to crank the music and dance with the fam. Wouldn't that be so much better at a place built for it?

Finally, Bunny let out a breath, shrugged it off, and took off jogging down the hall. Jen would tell her what was up when they'd had some time and some headspace. She only hoped they got to it before the fam got together to buy their tickets and get their ride set up. Right now, Bunny had her shift in the kitchen. And crap, she was running late. Picking up the pace, she kicked off a corner and bounced off the wall across, giving her an extra kick of speed. People ducked to one side or the other, grinning as she passed.

"Bao Li Amanzi!" a sharp voice barked out of the admin wing, "*Walk* in the halls! Don't run, and *do not parkour!*"

Bunny dropped to the floor with a wince. "Sorry Miss DeLiquisha!" She called over her shoulder. She made sure to keep her feet on the floor the rest of the way to the kitchen.

Walking in, she ticked her name on her Common Ground app to register her shift, washed her hands, and grabbed the first big bucket she saw. "Hey Mama! Hey Auntie Billie!"

"Hey Bunny!" the smiling Black woman called, just visible over the mountain of eggplant she was chopping. Seeing the veggies, Bunny groaned. "Auntie! Eggplant *again?*"

"It's ripe in the gardens," Auntie Billie agreed. "And it's good for you. Full of micronutrients that'll help you grow."

"Crap. Helps her g-g-grow? D-don't give Bao Li none," the tiny Asian woman fiddling with the beast of a bulk processor on Aunt Billie's left muttered, pulling something out of the mech'n'tech bag by her side. "Too tall n-now!"

Bunny laughed, trotting over and giving her mama a hug. "Jealous, dragon mama," she teased right back.

Her mama snorted, hair like a skein of black silk swinging as she turned to look up at Bunny with eyes set at the same angle as her own. The light caught along the golden scales covering her mama's arms, gleaming amber from wrist to shoulder. "Honest, rabbit d-d-daughter. Tall alr-ready. Tall as Papa, soon. See?" She stood on tiptoe to return Bunny's squeeze. "Now c-c-c-come help, kay? R-roaster's being an ass again."

"You overload it again?" Bunny teased.

"She did," Billie laughed.

"You hush," Mama retorted. "It was taking f-f-forever."

"And now it'll take longer because we gotta fix it," Bunny added. "You gotta learn to just chill, Mama."

Auntie Billie chuckled as she chopped. "Kid's telling it to you straight, Tweak. Listen up!"

Bunny's mother shot her a Look from bird-black eyes. "Next time Mo gives you c-crap, I'll r-remind you of that."

"Feel free!" Billie called back, her knife making soft clickity-click noises on the chopping board.

Mama snorted, and turned back to Bunny. "You want c-c-coffee and chocolate or not, Bao Li?"

"Okay, okay," Bunny sighed. Mama was one of about ten people in the whole world who always called her by her real name, grabbing her attention without even trying.

"I'll go high, you go low, sound good?" She offered. "It's unplugged, yeah?"

"Well duh," Mama agreed, tying her silky hair up in a bun and putting on a hat. "Should c-cut this again." She grumbled.

"No you shouldn't," Auntie Billie admonished. "Short hair was for the bad old days."

"Eh," Mama shrugged. "Point. Kay. Problem's in the r-roasting b-box. Temp's n-not getting high en-en-enough to do the b-beans right. Bao Li, you check the v-v-venting."

"Kay," Bunny agreed. Grabbing a couple tools out of the mech'n'tech bag, she pulled on a mask to protect against dust particles, flattened her ears down and stuck her head into the roasting chamber. "Hey Mama?" She asked as she worked. "You need your focus?"

"Nah," Mama's high voice drifted up through the ductwork of the machine. "This's easy."

"You got bandwidth?"

"Sure. You got t-t-trouble?"

"Not really trouble. I'm just confused. Can I talk it out with you?"

"Course," Mama's voice chirped back.

Bunny drew a deep breath. "Kay, here goes. Nine Tails is playing and they're even gonna play an under eighteen night, and I was so into it, and me'n the fam are getting us tix for it on Friday, and I went to Jen and I squeed about it, and I thought they'd psych about it, they love to dance, but they... Mama, they acted like I was asking them to eat my plate of eggplant along with theirs."

"I heard that!" Auntie Billie called. "You know it's good for you!"

Bunny rolled her eyes. Eggplant was *so* not the point.

"Mama, what do I do for Jen?"

Silence.

"Vents okay?" Her mother's voice asked.

"Mama!"

"Vents? Okay?"

Bunny sighed. "I got the covers off, and...eugh no, not okay, they're stuffed full of cacao husks and dust again."

"Fuck," Mama grumbled. There were a few clanks below, and then her mama's hand was on Bunny's shoulder. "Kay. That's our p-problem. Need b-better f-filters on these. Move. I got it."

Bunny got out of the way and stood, fidgeting as her mother worked. With Mama, you had to let her process on anything that wasn't a machine or a computer. But waiting was so *hard*.

"Still don't l-like you guys g-going to Denver on your own," the shorter woman offered after a couple minutes. Bunny rolled her eyes. "Mama, we've talked about this. The Corporate Powers went down *sixteen years ago*. The United Communities of America been in charge for forever now! Things are *good*. Denver isn't a *war zone* anymore, it's *nice!*"

"Lotsa things look nice that aren't," Mama pointed out. Bunny rolled her eyes, ears stuck out in a flat line of annoyance.

Mama didn't even spare her a glance. "Your dad's w-worried too."

"Yeah but that's 'cause you two are both paranoid! Papa isn't worried! And he says you two are paranoid!"

A little growl of irritation came out of the roasting box. "Inyoni told you that?"

"Yeah, he did," Bunny crossed her arms. "So?"

"That guy." Mama pulled herself out of the roasting box. Looking up at Bunny and away again, she crossed her arms, tapping one foot as she thought.

"Jen's acting w-weird about g-going to a p-place with l-lotsa s-s-strangers, yeah?"

Bunny hadn't thought about it like that. "Um...yeah." Slowly, she dropped her eyes. "Mama...I think I hurt Jen's feelings. But I don't know how I did it, and I feel awful. I don't want my bae hurting. I wanna make it better."

Tweak nodded, staring at something around Bunny's hip-level. She had lots of trouble with eye contact; if she wasn't looking at you, that meant she needed the bandwidth for thinking.

Slowly, she nodded to herself. Hey eyes flicked up. "I got g-guesses, Bao Li. But you don't want me on this. Go check it with your dad and your Uncle A on r-rec hours, kay?"

Bunny nodded, swallowing back her feelings. "Kay."

That afternoon around fourteen-hundred, Bunny trotted through the common hall, looking for two men who could help her get this straight. Nope, her dad and her uncle weren't down here. She passed the holo screens on the walls explaining Four Aces Farm to newbies and visitors: there was all kinds of stuff about the work to build a self-sufficient farm free of corporate control way back when, the creation of the open-source gene-modded crops that were thriving outside in spite of the heat, the fifteen other open-source farms that had started up on the same model to feed the Denver Metro, and the land-revitalizing work that had spread across the West from those starting points. They still did a ton of the testing for modifications on native species here at Four Aces, double checking all the plants and some of the animals being resur-rected and gene-modded with everything they needed to survive the climate that the Corporate Years had created. Bunny had read the signs a million and a half times, so she passed them without really looking. She'd been born on this farm, and she knew *all* about its story. She was one of Four Aces' gene mods herself; her mama and papa both had Gamma genetics and some of the abnor-malities that threw out could have been bad, so her dad had offered his DNA to smooth everything out and make sure she was born okay. She was pretty happy with how that'd worked; she got her mom's eyes, her papa's pretty ears and good dark skin, and she got her dad's good health and hair color. Her hair was curly as anything, more like Papa's, but still, she liked the red in it.

Course, if she'd got her mama's eye for detail, her papa's common sense, and her dad's brains, she'd already *know* what was going on with Jen. No such luck.

When she didn't find Dad or Uncle A in the library or the movie room, she bit the bullet and headed for their place in the residential wing. Her dad opened the door, smiling down at her.

"Well hello there, Treasure!" He offered, translating her name out of Cantonese into English the way he did when he was happy. "What can I do for you today?"

Bunny could feel her ears droop as she smiled. "Hey Dad. Mama sent me your way. I got a...feelings thing to talk about."

Her dad leaned on the doorframe, light glinting off the lenses of his glasses. "A feelings thing. Sounds dire," he observed. He put out a thin white hand, giving her shoulder a gentle squeeze. "Come on in, I'll start the kettle and we'll have a chat."

Ears weighed down with embarrassment, Bunny followed her dad into his living space; a cozy one, all done up in stuff him and Uncle A had thrifted around the country when they went to the big Regional and National Quadrant Council Meetings or the Mayors' Summit events. Some of the stuff was really ancient, like the analog books or the engraved brass kettle that Dad filled and put on its heating base.

"Kev?" A man's voice drifted down from upstairs. "Something up?"

"Bao Li's come over for tea, love!" Kevin called back up, poking his head out of the kitchen. "Got time to join us?"

A couple minutes later, Uncle A wandered into the kitchen. Bunny gave him a smile. She'd called him Uncle A since she was tiny; Aidan wasn't a real easy name for her to say as a baby, and the name kind of got stuck after that.

"Hey Bunny," her uncle offered, giving her a smile as he chose a tea from the cabinet. She always had to explain to newbies that no, he wasn't blood family, but he was uncle the way fam was fam; he was there, and he loved her, and he helped things get better. And wasn't that what family was?

"Bao Li's got an emotional upset she'd like a hand with," Dad offered. Uncle Aidan turned to look at her a little closer, blue eyes thoughtful.

"Yeah? What's up, Bunny?"

Bunny felt her ears flatten themselves. God this was so embarrassing, now she had to explain it in detail. Was she just being a whiner?

She looked up when a hand pale as apple blossoms covered hers, and met Dad's kind grey eyes. He gave her hand a squeeze.

"In your own time, treasured girl. No rush."

Bunny drew a deep breath. "Okay, so…"

NIGHT CAME like a damp cloth to cool the daytime fever. Out between the orange trees, Jen closed their eyes and breathed.

Far off, the gray wolves that had been reintroduced when they were eight howled. There were probably wolves from the third generation in the pack now, growing up on the prairie right along with them.

"Nice to hear them, hunh?"

Jen looked over their shoulder at the sound of the voice, and smiled. "Hey Uncle Aidan."

"Hey Jen," the older man acknowledged, taking a seat beside them in the soft mulch. "How's it going?"

"Okay," Jen replied, though they knew they didn't sound all that believable.

For a couple minutes, they sat in silence together. Uncle Aidan was good at that; just being quiet, and together, and there. Jen liked that.

But everybody talked eventually. And so did he.

"I hear you're feeling kind of squicked about going dancing."

Jen looked down. "I…yeah."

"Seems like one of your big things here at home," the sun-tanned man suggested. "You guys love to crank the music and dance."

Jen shrugged.

"But you're dancing with your fam then, not with a bunch of strangers. Yeah?"

Jen stole a look up at Uncle Aidan. He was leaned back against a tree trunk, eyes closed, blonde hair catching glints of light between leaves.

"Yeah," they whispered.

Uncle Aidan smiled, just a little bit. "I hear you. I used to be that way.

Used to hate people looking at me; they saw things I wasn't, and that got to me. That sound familiar?"

"Yeah," Jen agreed. "I just..." they trailed off, stuck. Nothing they could say fit.

"How about I ask some stuff, and you tell me if it's a yes or a no?" Uncle Aidan offered. Jen nodded. "Sure. I...yeah."

"Is it a Gamma thing?" Uncle Aidan began quietly. "Is it the way people look at your traits?"

"I...sorta?" Jen managed lamely. "I just..."

"Is it maybe a looks thing?" their uncle suggested. "Like, people don't want to see somebody fluffy dancing, is that going through your head?"

Jen shook their head. "That's dumb."

"Yeah, it is," Uncle Aidan agreed. "So, is it a sensitivity thing? Is it too loud? Too weird having a bunch of people you don't know around you?"

Jen had to think about that one for a minute. "I don't think so. It's...I've done a lot of volunteer work in the cities, and it doesn't feel that way when we're working."

"Kay, good recognizing on that," Aidan agreed. "So, is it maybe a gender thing? Are people looking at you and seeing something you're not?"

Jen's heart clenched. "I..." Slowly, they nodded.

"What's giving you the most dysphoria?" Aidan asked quietly.

Jen waved at their chest. "These. People just...see boobs and...ugh."

Uncle Aidan gave a quiet little grunt. "Yeah. They do, don't they? Used to get to me too. I wore the tightest binders I could get my hands on back in the day, before Kevin got me some that actually fit." He opened his eyes, staring ahead for a second. After a moment, he spoke, slow and thoughtful. "Actually...Jen, you want to come to my place for a bit? I got an idea, and after we see if I'm right or not we'll have peppermint ice. Sound good?"

"Sure," Jen agreed, a little thrown. They weren't sure what Uncle Aidan was thinking, but he was good at coming up with stuff. That was why he was one of the few permanent members of the Farm Council. And besides, he always helped them out with gender stuff. Standing, they followed along.

"Hey Kev?" Aidan called as he opened the door of his living space. "Where's the old boxes from the barracks?"

"Basement, storage room, against the far wall!" Uncle Kevin called back. "Please tell me you're actually going to clean them, it's been over a decade!"

"Working on it!" Aidan threw back up to the loft, taking Jen's hand. "C'mon Jen, let's go see if it's there."

"What?"

"Some old stuff we kept meaning to repurpose and never did," Uncle Aidan replied with a smile. "You're shorter than me, but I'm guessing my pre-transition chest and yours match up size-wise. Want to see what you look like in a binder? If I don't have them after all, we'll print you some."

Jen wasn't sure what they were feeling, not yet. But whatever it was, it was warm.

Down the stairs in the basement, Uncle Aidan flicked the bioluminescent bulbs to life. They stepped into the next room, and Jen froze. At their living space, the storage room had spare candles, some stuff that wasn't working, Dad's smellier work clothes and that week's recycling being saved up for processing. But in here, there were six old military trunks like hunks of greeny-black concrete. In a weird way, they looked…dangerous. They looked like pieces of the Corporate Conflicts. It made Jen feel…they didn't know what. Sure, they knew their dad and a lot of their older fam were soldiers back then, before the corporations had come down, but knowing that and looking at this was different.

Beside her, Uncle Aidan sighed. "Man. Kevin's right, I need to clean this stuff out…okay, Jen, you take the one on the right, I'll take the one on the left. Look for uniform clothes. If you find one with dresses, it's not that one. If it's got weapons in it, tell me and step back, okay?"

"Okay," Jen agreed, lifting the lid on the first box. "Looks like…old data tabs and analog maps?"

"Crap," Uncle Aidan sighed. "Kay, let me help you shove that one off the top…"

It took four boxes before Uncle Aidan stood up, exclaiming, "I knew we never passed them along!"

Standing, Jen cocked their head as they watched their uncle pull out three black things like t-shirts without sleeves. He held them up with a grin. "Binders with recessed zippers! Kevin got them for me way back when; I only wore them a couple years before I got my surgery, so they're still in great shape. Here." He held them out. "It's okay, they're clean. They're yours if you want them. Take them upstairs and try them on, see if they fit?"

Heart in their mouth, Jen reached out and took the handful of cloth. "What if they don't?"

Uncle Aidan shrugged. "Then I help you get fitted and we get you ones that do. Go see?"

They nodded. Stepping upstairs, they slipped into the bathroom, locked the door, and pulled off their shirt. The binder felt funny going on, and it was a little tight, but when they zipped it up, it was like being wrapped in a hug. And when they put their shirt back on...

They stared at themselves in the mirror. Slowly, they smiled.

"Good fit?" Uncle Kevin asked when Jen sat down at the table. They nodded.

Uncle Aidan set a cup of peppermint ice down in front of them. "If you want, DeLiquisha can help you do your hair. How's that sound?"

Jen grinned.

∽

"Mo!" Bunny called down into the open floor panel when Friday afternoon rolled around. "Hey! Mo!"

Cocking her ears, she heard nothing but the clink of tools. Rolling her eyes, Bunny shimmied down a little, hooked both feet into the rungs of the ladder, and let herself drop until she was hanging upside-down inside the maintenance area. She drew a deep breath.

"Mir-iiiii-am!"

There was a thunk, a clang, and an 'ow!'

"Bunny! You made me snag my hijab!" Mo complained down in the works. "Crap!"

"Hold still, I'll come get you unstuck!" Bunny called. Scrambling down into the climate-support works, she trotted over to her friend and carefully pulled her blue hijab loose from the fittings of a pipe. "What're you doing down here?"

"I *was* taking an impression of the socket for a broken gasket control to make sure Baba and me printed it right," Miriam grumbled, tucking her hijab right again. "Before I got *interrupted,*"

Bunny gave her pal a shrug and an ear flop. "Yeah, sorry. How soon're you done? The fam and me wanna pick up tix for Nine Tails, we gotta decide where we want to sit! Remember, we put it on the fam schedule?"

"Oh yeah!" Mo agreed, dark eyes lighting up. "Has the registration opened yet?"

"Not yet, but it will in a bit, and I want us in fast!" Bunny bounced on the balls of her feet to burn off all her hype. "Figured we could grab treats and do it together! It's gonna be so cool, all us Aces at Nine Tails!!"

"Okay, okay, don't start getting excited down here Bunny!" Mo laughed. "You'll bounce and get stuck!"

Bunny's ears angled down as she crossed her arms. "Will not."

"Will, did last time," the fourteen-year-old came back.

Bunny sighed, ears dropping. "Okay fine, rub my nose in it."

"Forever, probably!" her fam agreed cheerfully. "C'mon, up the ladder, I got the impression; just need to drop it off in the fabrication room and we can go."

"Great!" Bunny grinned, ears bouncing back up. "C'mon!!"

They stuck their heads into the fabrication room, Mo giving her dad a quick hug and dropping the mold into his hand. "Seeya Baba, me'n the fam are going to land tix for Nine Tails."

"And leave me all alone fighting with the structural printing again," Tafarah laughed, giving Mo's shoulders a squeeze. "Good luck landing good seats! Hi, Bunny!"

"Hey Uncle Tafarah!" Bunny called through the door. "What's for dinner?"

"Billie didn't tell me!" Her uncle called back across the work space. "Guess we're both going to be surprised!"

"Man, I was hoping to find out if it was eggplant again so I could duck it if it was," Bunny sighed when she and Mo were out in the hall. "Why's she have to be into eggplant right now?"

"Because it's what's ripe in the planting beds," Mo replied with her 'you know better' tone on. "And it's good for you; it's full of micronutrients."

"It's full of ugh!" Bunny groaned, ears drooping.

Her fam caught her eye with a wicked grin, sunlight kissing golden tones and sapphire glints out of her skin and her hijab. "It is, isn't it? Mom's begging Abigail not to plant it again." She covered her mouth, leaning close. Bunny perked an ear out towards her.

"Truth is, Mom hates cooking it!!" Mo whispered.

"Whaaaat?!" Bunny squealed. Mo tried to shut her up the rest of the way down the hall.

In the common area, the fam had got together; twenty-some teens anywhere from thirteen to eighteen, all chattering and comparing tabs. In theory Max, Thea and Oxeye were the organizers and the reason the younger kids were allowed to go along, but the fam was about as hierarchy-based as an amoeba.

"What's the word?" Bunny asked, hopping into the middle of the gathering with ears up like flags. Dove and Hawk grinned at her, identical faces bright.

"Check it! We can hop the Outer Loop train at fourteen-hundred, get there by sixteen, have dinner and some fun downtown, and then hit the floor at eighteen!" Hawk crowed.

"And we can take oh-hundred, two hundred or three hundred train back!" Dove added.

"Cool!" Bunny agreed. "Are there enough seats for everybody?"

"Looks like it!" Norah agreed, checking the train schedules she'd taken responsibility for. "There's what, twenty-two, twenty three...wait, where's Jen? They're coming right?"

"Here! I'm here!" Jen came trotting down the hall, puffing. "Sorry I'm late."

"No big," Oxeye replied with an easy wave. "Good to see you. Okay everybody, sign into the Common Ground, let's get tix!"

Bunny pulled up her app, but her eyes were on Jen as they dropped down beside her. They were sitting with their shoulders thrown back, and...wow, they'd done something to make their chest look way smaller. It was a great look on them. They'd even done something with their hair.

Jen caught her eye, and gave her a little smile. "What do you think?"

"It's a great look!" Bunny exclaimed, leaning over to give her bae a big hug and a kiss. Jen buried their face in Bunny's shoulder, squeezing back. "Thanks."

"Guys! Focus, tix!" Oxeye suggested. "We need to decide where we wanna be!"

~

"Is everybody ready to dance?"

Lights strobed out across the stage. Front and center, Lucky of the Nine Tails held her mic high in her prehensile tail, her hair a wonderful rainbow storm around her head.

Squeezing Bunny's hand, Jen yelled right along with their fam, cheering as the band launched into their signature song. As the guitar sang out, Bunny bounced and twirled around Jen, stealing pecks on the cheek that made them laugh. Hawk and Dove danced back-to-back, and Oxeye and Thea pulled each other close and shimmied. Around them, all sorts of families and groups danced too, a whole community on the move. The music swept them all into a good place, and they went gladly.

Jen moved with their bae, and their fam, and the world was perfect. Closing their eyes, they sang along with Nine Tails.

We are Here!
This is Now!
We are what it's about!

We are future,
We are past,
We decide where it's at!

We are Here!
This is Now!
And while we're here let's dance!

Bringing their own experiences as a marginalized author to the page with flawed and genuine characters, O.E. Tearmann's work has been described as "Firefly for the dystopian genre." Publisher's Weekly called it "a lovely paean to the healing power of respectful personal connections among comrades, friends, and lovers."

Tearmann lives in Colorado with two cats, their partner, and the belief that individuals can make humanity better through small actions. They are a member of the Science Fiction Writers of America, the Rocky Mountain

Fiction Writers, and the Queer Sci Fi group. In their spare time, they teach workshops on writing GLTBQ characters, plant gardens to encourage sustainable agricultural practices, and play too many video games.

Website: https://www.oetearmann.com
Publisher: https://www.amphibianpress.online/index.html
Facebook: https://www.facebook.com/wildcards1407
Tumblr: https://www.tumblr.com/blog/wildcards1407
Mastodon: https://creativewriting.social/@OETearmann

THE ICKY BUSINESS OF COMPROMISE
BY DEREK DES ANGES

Dolly had lived through some of the weirdest political events of history. She was also old enough, now, to know that everyone thought that about the time when they were alive, and she'd learnt not to take it too seriously. There was, for example, a period just after she was old enough to understand the news when it seemed like every other large country was trying and failing to have a religious civilian coup. When they got to it in her history class, they'd treated it with a seriousness that no one had felt it warranted, and Dolly, whose memory was very good, even recalled that her parents had made jokes about them all through, eating snacks while governmental buildings smouldered.

She had come to the Kingston and Greattor Borough Meeting not because she was the kind of Neighbourhood Watch Busybody women her age were supposed to be, but because her nephew Moss had insisted there was going to be free food.

Dolly settled into the heavily repaired leather armchair she'd had her nephew drag out to the band-stand, surreptitiously cleaned potting mix out from underneath her fingernails with the end of her voting stylus, and waited among the usual chorus of plasticated coughs for Benoit Jones to get to the bloody point.

Roughly her contemporary—his name, if nothing else, made it obvious, half the boys in her cohort had been called Benoit—Jones had aged into a stiff-legged, well-meaning rambler who gave the impression of never having gotten over the demise of broadcast-based video socials. Probably how he'd ended up heading Borough Meetings: not so much a burning passion for the wellbeing of the immediate community as a terrible need to hear himself talk, coupled with the absence of any actual theatrical talent to take him anywhere else. In her parents' time he'd have been Giving Presentations to company boards.

"—minutes," Jones said, letting the preamble finally die a decent death. "The main item on the agenda today is the Integrated Combined Sources Cycle Strategy, which my granddaughter insists we should be referring to as the ICKIES."

An obliging laugh rippled around the bandstand.

"Those of you with friends or family in Bigbury Borough will be aware that they've beaten us to implementing an, er, ICKY, but their haste is our gain, because we're getting a good idea of what to expect, I think," Jones blundered. One of the streamers attached on the bandstand's support beams fluttered in a passing breeze. "The main difficulty is the expectation that everything will be up and running all at once. Now, the ICKY *does* require all its parts to be in place for it to function properly: the waste in, food/heating out, water treatment cycle, etc., does all need to be going simultaneously or it breaks down. But, er, Malala has invited us to consider the analogy of a keystone—"

Everyone turned and looked at Malala. Dolly, who felt something was required of her as Malala's old mentor, gave her a thumbs-up; Malala scratched her ear thoughtfully and pretended not to notice that she was being stared at. After all, with a young baby, she had other things to worry about, and could conceivably be ignoring them. Babies were rare, precious, and unfortunately so prone to dying that Malala had not yet named hers, after all.

"—where the arch can be supported until such time as the keystone is in place. Obviously with an ICKY, all the parts are keystones, in effect. But we can at least, er, assemble, assemble the arch beforehand."

"Assuming we vote in favour," said one of the Inces.

Dolly hadn't bothered to differentiate the Inces because they drove her up the bloody wall. They'd get their individual names back from her long-term memory when they'd earnt it, she'd decided that years ago. They'd had money, back when that mattered, and they seemed to be operating under the assumption that they'd have money again, and that this temporary embarrassment of post-capitalism shouldn't get in the way of them being, therefore, the most important people in the Borough, the Region, and probably the Island. The fact that they had to empty their own cesspit and harvest their own staples the same as everyone else didn't seem to be stopping them from acquiring the belief that they were more valuable than, for example, Said, who maintained the InterBorough Net, and *still* didn't object to having to shovel his own shite.

Jones blinked like one of his own chickens and voices what it feels like the whole bandstand's-worth of attendees is thinking: "Why wouldn't we?"

The Ince, whichever one it was, stood up. It wasn't really necessary, everyone could hear her already, but she appeared to think that they all also needed to see her pale brown hair which she no doubt insisted was blonde, and her intense Whiteness, to really get an idea of *who they're messing with*. Dolly remembered women like her from her early childhood, loudly passing comment on her parents' decision to let her dress however she wanted and use whatever pronouns pleased her, standing in shops and talking over her head about how they weren't racist *but*—

"Consolidating more and more power in these little enclaves isn't democratically healthy," said the Ince. "It stifles dissent."

"You don't look very stifled to me," Dolly muttered.

Malala caught her eye and put a slightly comical finger to her lips.

"You're dissenting now," Jones pointed out, bewildered. "What's wrong with the ICKIES? Have I missed some new development from Bigbury?"

The Ince sighed loudly. A red and yellow streamer fluttered behind her, and the Airborne Plastics Barometer dial on the far support column edged almost unnoticed a little closer to the orange "mask on" hextant. The coughing continued. There wasn't anything wrong with the ICKIES apart from their name: whatever point it is the Ince wanted to make, she was going to make it regardless of the topic under discussion. She's got something under her skin about the system: that much is obvious.

"Implementing an ICKY, as you insist on calling it, means we're keeping *everything* within-Borough."

"Not everything—"

"We're supposed to be drawing our power from the Borough, the majority of our food from the Borough, our heat from the Borough, our repair supplies from Borough waste… we're not taking anything from out-Borough and not sending anything out-Borough."

"That's again, not strictly true," Jones said patiently. "And obviously if Bigbury or Teignmouth or anywhere in-Region needs something we have, we'll take it to them."

"Well what are we going to have to *trade* with if everyone's got these things?" the Ince demanded.

Jones looked at her as if she'd asked him why she couldn't just take a shit in the middle of the floor. "Why would we need to do that?"

The Ince rolled her eyes. "No one is going to give us something for nothing."

"You mean apart from when half the Borough came and helped you build your house?" Dolly asked, exasperated, "or the time Poole Harbour Borough came down with new fish stocks for the entire West Peninsula after we had one of those scarlet tides? Or are you thinking of something else?" It would have been more cutting, she thought, if she *had* remembered the Ince's name, but now all the Inces were bristling behind their mousy-haired matriarch, and Dolly simply could not be arsed to make a show of it. There were a lot of them, they were noisy, and when they didn't want to do something, it threw most of the Borough out of smooth functioning.

She went back to cleaning the mud out from under her nails instead. The Ince, of course, had perfectly clean nails. Which everyone *noticed*.

"What is it that you want, Daisy?" Malala asked, getting up to check the plastics barometer: it seemed like a natural move but it was just ostentatious enough to remind everyone present that there were bigger and more important issues than *trade*. "What don't we have that you need us to get?"

I taught her that, Dolly thought, a little smug.

The truth was they all had plenty that they needed, but it was the same thing *everyone everywhere* needed, and no one had: clean air, reliable care for the ones whose bodies were too clogged with airplastics to breathe easily, hot water on demand, the comforts of life that would stop them dying young or ageing fast. And if anyone had a right to complain about *ageing*, it was Dolly, not bloody Daisy Ince.

Daisy Ince sat back down again, pink in the cheeks, and muttered, "We're not going to be in a position to defend ourselves."

"Daisy's right," Dolly said abruptly, enjoying the confusion this caused. "We need to make sure we maintain strong connections with the neighbouring Boroughs even after we get the ICKY up and running. We should talk to them about exchanges. People exchanges, skills exchanges, that sort of thing. Networking, like Said's doing, but in the flesh."

"That's not what I—" the Ince began.

"Oh!" said Jones, rubbing his hands together, probably at the prospect of being able to burble on for another half an hour. "That *is* a good idea, Daisy. We'll have to add that to the agenda for the next meeting—"

Dolly did her best to keep her smirk under wraps, and deliberately avoided Malala's eye. "She's full of good ideas," she added, unable to *quite* help herself from being facetious.

TENDING to her perhaps frivolous collection of non-edible plants later the same week, her hair and her increasing traction alopecia tied away underneath a repatched red scarf that had once been Malala's pride and joy, until the baby puked on it, Dolly was not expecting Jones to turn up on her strip of kitchen garden and wave his arm in a theatrical greeting. Unfortunately, under the agreed-on Borough rules, there was nothing to stop him, and he was doing everything entirely the right way, because he always did. Because he was Benoit Jones and doing things the right way, for an audience that might or might not be there, was what he loved.

"Do I have something you need?" Dolly asked, kicking the crushed can she'd unearthed slightly further down the path. It wasn't the right greeting, but it wasn't the wrong one either.

He lowered his arm. "Morning, Dolly. Said's been helping me chat with the guys over at Bigbury—"

Inflicting himself on an even wider range of people, Dolly thought, amused. Maybe his hankering for the days of broadcasting his nonsense to all and sundry would pay off after all. Someone should figure out how to make him a short-wave radio.

"—and they agree that you should go over and work on a skillshare with them."

If Dolly had been drinking she could have choked, sprayed it over Jones in the dramatic arc that he'd understand better than anything she might have to say. Instead, she just shielded her eyes against the low sun and stared at him as if he was speaking gibberish.

Jones began to wither like a plant under glass, as if her gaze was a bell-jar enveloping his increasingly drooping jowls and his encroaching bald spot.

"Don't recall volunteering for this," Dolly said bluntly, reaching for the trowel to emphasise her point. Jones knew perhaps better than the younger generations in the Borough what it actually *meant* that her youth had been spent in the years of the final parliamentary collapse; what it *meant* that she'd learnt the horticulture of defiance during the short-lived military-police over-sight; what it *meant* that she had long-faded stripes across the cork-brown skin of her arms that were once meant to denote her position in the dissenter's yard.

"You did agree with Daisy's suggestion, Dorothy," said Jones, temporarily forgetting that her name wasn't actually short for anything. He wiped a hand on the thigh of his trousers: once red, now a sort of faded pink ochre. "You go over there and find out what they're doing with this ICKY and how it works."

"Daisy has all the charm and audacity necessary to make her way in a neighbouring Borough and will do us proud," Dolly said, mentally translating *the Ince is stuck-up but won't get sucked into their problems as deeply as the rest of us will* into something he'd go along with. Even Daisy Ince was useful, under the right circumstances. That didn't mean Dolly had to be around to see her made use of and listen to her the entire time, surely. She didn't ask what exactly it was Daisy knew that Jones thought anyone needed to know; the ambassador didn't need to know anything except how to ask questions and Daisy was annoyingly good at putting her face in other people's business. Bigbury would doubtless come over the hills to Kingston and Greattor and find out what they were doing.

"She needs guidance," Jones pointed out, damp-cheeked but, in his self-important, ovine manner, applying the killing blow. "And you have a lot of experience in dealing with situations that go wrong."

"I thought we were all living in perfect interBorough harmony," Dolly said, nastily.

"That's an ongoing project," said Jones, primly.

"For fuck's sake," said Dolly, laying the trowel down.

～

THE ROUTE TO BIGBURY INVOLVED, depending on the time of day, either a short trip in a small boat, or a moderate walk from the base of the cliffs across the causeway. The beach that had once occupied the spot had long since vanished underwater, but before the breakdown the local Borough—or rather the Council, as they'd been back then—had decided that building a bicycle-width causeway out to the island would preserve the hotel's tourist flow and encourage "ecoconscious tourism", or so Rory Gann explained, as he led them down the cliff path.

"The island catches more of the wind," he added, kicking a drying bundle of seaweed off the side of the concrete causeway and back into the choppy waters. "And since getting the power excess *off* the island is more-or-less impossible now that we can't lay oceanic cables without someone drowning, we moved all the major operations to the hotel. You'll see when we get there."

Daisy, walking directly behind him, turned around and gave Dolly a brief, troubled look.

Hospital, Dolly mouthed.

"Did you have much trouble getting the whole integrated system up and running?" she asked, as much to fill the awkward silence as anything else.

Gann laughed, feeling his way along the causeway as wind began to visibly buffet him. "Endless. Absolutely endless. You're here to find out what not to do, I assume? Ottoline on the Network wasn't exactly sold on the idea of our neighbours suddenly being overwhelmed with the desire to tutor us so we figured you were probably trying to avoid any mistakes setting up the System. It's *worth* it, don't get me wrong, but it's like spinning plates."

Dolly, who had managed the majority of her life without an ICKY and would probably, in her view, pass out of her life before she saw the benefits of it, accepted this without disquiet. Some things took longer than you had to pay off; but Malala's kid would get to spend less time fretting about inconsistent electricity supply and food back-ups, assuming it lived, and the Ince clan —not that they'd appreciate it—wouldn't have to shovel so much shit.

Daisy, however, shot another troubled look back at Dolly before staring up at the island. The former hotel dominated it like a medieval castle, surrounded by satellites of greenhouses which twinkled under the fleeting patches of sun between the racing clouds, and of course the white, towering forms of the wind turbines.

Back in their own Borough the wind missed them almost entirely. Most of the worst weather did too, but it meant they only had one turbine and a smattering of solar to keep the lights on and the refrigerators running. Whatever the ICKY had done for Bigbury, they could more easily do without than inland could.

"First," Gann said, as a wave splashed over his feet—he didn't seem to mind—and collided with one coming the opposite way, "you have to get everyone to cooperate. Which was the really tricky part, weirdly. About a third of the Bigbury Borough just didn't want to put their shit in a fermenter. Nav—who left the Borough entirely over this—was convinced the methane build-up would explode and kill everyone. It doesn't, of course, because burning it is half of how we get the heat. Not sure where he thought he was going with that, really.

"There's always someone," Dolly said, pointedly, "who understands about half of the science and decides that makes them the expert."

"Hah," Gann said, picking his way up the first of the steps: they were carved into the side of the cliff and slippery with seawater. Dolly was relieved to see they'd also bolted a fairly significant steel railing to the side of the staircase, because in addition to being wetter than the inside of a bottle, the stairs were halfway to being a ladder.

She wondered how the hell they got patients up to the hospital at low tide.

"You've also got to get things going in the right order. Nav was right about that much: you can't *start* with the fermenter, because it builds up too much gas by itself and venting it—it's not like we need *more* atmospheric pollution—but also without the fermenter in place, you can't test whether the rest of the system is connected properly," Gann went on.

Dolly could have figured that out for herself, she thought, and no doubt the rest of the home Borough would get to that conclusion without much warning: they weren't all idiots. But she didn't say anything, and saved her energy for the climb. Ahead of her, Daisy picked her way up the wet steps with fussy little kicks of her toes, flicking pooled seawater back onto Dolly.

Gann seemed to have run out of breath too, and so his introduction took a break for the remainder of the ascent, which left off the stairs after a little while and began instead to wind around the island, flattening out into a lumpy vista of sea pinks around the cluster of greenhouses and the looming giant legs of the wind turbines.

The wind knocked Daisy and Dolly into a sideways stagger almost immediately, fortunately pushing them *into* the island rather than *off* it, but their guide only flinched at its force and raised his voice, "As you can see, we get a non-stop supply of energy. We've been using it to light the greenhouses 24-7, so we can grow additional food for the hospital and the excess we ship back onto the remainder of the Borough."

Dolly could *feel* Daisy perk up at this. The word *excess* no doubt gave her hope of a thriving market community she could exploit like her forebears had, although whether she had the intellectual capacity to carve out a niche for herself in the world of vegetable transport was another matter entirely; whether she could enrich herself in a nascent post-commercial economy remained to be seen. It wasn't even as if Daisy Ince was the mercantile *type*. She just wanted not to have to do things herself.

At the top of the cliff they caught their breath. Dolly was annoyed to discover it was taking her longer than the other two, probably in some way related to being about twenty-five years older than either of them, although no less of a concern for that.

"The Integrated System, of course, is mostly back on the mainland," Gann said, extending an arm to take in the bay they'd just traipsed down through. He took in the houses they'd not stopped to look at barring the ones which had fallen to the depredations of the sea and were still partially visible above the waves. He took in the intervening waters themselves, which were now ankle deep over the causeway path.

"So why are we *here*?" Daisy asked, before Dolly could stop her.

"Well, this is where the hospital is," Gann said, sounding somewhat confused. "I thought you'd want to start with the dispensing of skills and finish later on by getting all the information about the Integrated System, so it's fresh in your minds for the return journey. At least, that's the way round I'd have done things. I've never been any good at taking notes. Handwriting's appalling. We didn't get taught that sort of thing—"

Dolly would have rolled her eyes at this explanation, but much to her displeasure she was beginning to see Daisy's point, and even more so when Daisy opened the ridiculous, entitled hole in her face and said, "Oh, I thought we were coming to learn from *you* and then you'd send some people over to *us* to have a look at what we're doing…"

Aside from the fact that Daisy was doing as little as humanly possible, and her sole interest in having visitors to the Borough was likely to lord it over them as if the entire place was her own personal achievement, that was broadly what Dolly had thought was happening, too. The "building of bonds" thing didn't really work if no one came to home Borough and got to know the entire population at once—both good and bad. If it was solely a matter of a single visit they might as well have just stuck to getting Ottoline and Said, with some interjections from Moss, to discuss things over the Network, instead of wasting all this time travelling overland in endless sodding squalls.

"Oh," said Gann, with a laugh of understanding, and the wind buffeted his thick, brown hair around as he made an affirmative gesture. "I see. Like a hostage exchange!"

Why the Hell, Dolly thought, suddenly uneasy, *would you refer to it like that?*

~

BY SUNSET the tide had turned again, and they were off the island once more, which alleviated at least one of Dolly's unspoken and barely-thought fears, but her sense of unease, once roused, was not easily soothed again. During more fractious times, this had served her pretty well in keeping her out of the way of less cooperative individuals and knowing who to trust had been critical.

The hospital certainly had a lot going for it: strong window filters, although they hadn't figured out growing them yet the way Greattor had; a largely consistent electricity supply, and some of the remaining and repairable machines, along with "more beds than we really need, which is not something most people can say". Medicines, Gann admitted, they were struggling to replace. At present, six fifty-to-sixty-year-olds of the Borough were dying in comfort and relative lack of pain; Dolly had seen enough to know this wasn't nothing.

Gann had the sensitivity at least not to show them the infant graveyard behind, but it was still visible.

Lying on the guest-bed of a stranger's much-repaired but admittedly very warm house a mere six feet away from Daisy—on a slightly more comfortable cushion—it irritated her *very* much that currently the affable, welcoming Rory Gann was giving off something that made her want to be a considerable distance away from him, while Daisy Ince, as the only person from the home Borough in the vicinity, was actually the only person she could trust.

Fuck Benoit Jones to the end of the Peninsula and back again, Dolly thought grumpily, turning over on the mattress solely to make the springs squeak.

Stuck in a strange Borough trying to form more lasting community bonds with a bloody ex asset management heiress, at her time of life, when she should have been gardening and trying to teach Malala, Moss, and whatever silly name Malala had given her baby how to discreetly influence the Borough to do whatever they wanted...

Of course, she realised, her weakening eyes snapping open for a moment to stare uselessly through the dark, that was precisely *why* she was here. *Because* she was good at getting people to do what she wanted without them realising it.

Daisy Ince included.

~

IN THE MORNING, she received her first sample of the benefits of the ICKY: hot water, on demand, at all times.

"I'm sold," Daisy informed her, returning from a vertical bath with her skin steaming and pink. The archaic phrasing was an Ince specialty: they hung onto anything that reminded them of their wealthy times. "You can just *have* a bath. Immediately. How am I supposed to go back to boiling endless kettles now?"

Dolly highly doubted that Daisy had ever boiled her own kettles in her life, at least not since the slim interim between her being too old to be babied and too young to be flirted with, but she *was* old enough to remember when boilers, pre-heating the water that flowed out of the taps, were still commonplace. She had hazy memories of her childhood baths, and the plastic shower cap by its very nature was probably still somewhere in the foodchain even after so long. Before the card had degraded, she'd even had a photograph of herself in the bath, wearing it: the colours in her memory unfaded by sun bleaching, her junior fuzz of dark brown curls hidden under yellow and pink.

"Anything else I should know?" Dolly asked peevishly, noting that Daisy's magnanimity hadn't extended as far as letting an old woman have the bloody bath *first*.

"Their soap is *terrible*," Daisy said, fishing her shoes out from the side of the cushion. They were red

"Good," Dolly said, making for the door she'd come in by.

The Ince boggled. "Good how? It smells like watered-down urine. It probably *is* watered-down urine."

"It means we have something we can teach them," Dolly pointed out, impatiently. "Do you want to turn up empty-handed and making demands? We'll look like idiots."

It worked. Daisy Ince would tolerate looking like a selfish bitch every day of the week, but she would *not* be made a fool of in front of strangers: her entire demeanour changed.

She wasn't wrong: the hot water, a simple luxury, held out for the whole period in which Dolly was bathing, and after so long of fleeting, ice-cold sponge baths, dry-bathing, and irritable slow-boiling of kettles on the good days when sufficient sunlight or wind had charged up all the remaining batteries, her bath was a long one.

I could get used to this, Dolly thought.

She caught the thought by the tail and stood on it, like vermin. Getting used to a softness like this would leave her weakened, peevish, and manipulable, like Daisy. Better to be miserable. Well, not miserable. But on her guard against being *too* cosy. The world was an unpredictable place and while she was still certain humanity were inherently good and helpful when allowed to be and not twisted about by power-hungry fools, there were power-hungry fools, and more to the point: the weather and the world did not give a damn about human luxury or existence.

Outside of the warm bath, the wood-cladding of the room showed its worth. That, at least, they were on equal footing about.

Daisy had already left to find breakfast, no doubt without helping to prepare it.

"Fuck's sake," Dolly muttered, dressing as quickly as she could, and leaving off her daily search for cancerous moles.

~

RORY GANN ACCOMPANIED them on their second day, too.

"Like a sheepdog," Dolly muttered, as the wind changed direction over the bay, and all the streamers in the vegetable gardens within sight twisted and wrapped themselves around their stems. The breeze wasn't coming in from the East, which meant the airplastics quotient wouldn't be high enough to warrant slipping a scarf over her mouth, but she watched the streamers anyway; even Daisy Ince did that.

"I'll take you around the town so you can see where it's embedded," Gann said, beaming unnecessarily. "But a lot of the stuff is underground. The filters—"

"Filters?" Dolly cut in. "You mean reed beds?"

"No," Gann said, smiling even more widely. "Much more exciting than that."

Daisy shot Dolly a dubious look. Her red shoes had flecks of mud on them already and her hair, freshly-washed, was suffering from the wind in a way it didn't usually. Dolly felt a little smug under her headscarf.

Gann led them down to a house that appeared to be perched, to Dolly's eyes, perilously close to the edge of the cliff. In about twenty years at most it was going to see its foundations fall into the sea, shorn away by the constant battering of the tides. Indeed, work appeared to already be taking place to pick up and move the thing further inland, abandoning the old foundations but making off with the bricks, joists, pipes and wires, a little at a time.

As a consequence, the garden was not a vegetable patch, but a muddy track. It held together better than she was expecting: when Dolly put her boot down on it, the gluey soil, still red from the sandstone underneath the muddled colours of condensed macroplastics, hardly gave at all.

"This is probably the best spot to see what I mean," Gann said, pointing to the spot where the waste pipes, thick tan-brown and ceramic, had been uncoupled in their trench, and were awaiting removal.

"A sewer," Daisy observed, unnecessarily.

It wouldn't be an integrated flipping circuit if it didn't include waste, would it, you moron, Dolly thought, taking the excuse of watching the seagulls circle over the bay to hide her expression, just in case it betrayed her.

"Yes," Gann said, with barely contained enthusiasm. His oddness resolved itself, abruptly, in Dolly's mind, into the fixation of the evangelical. He had clearly never had to spend much time navigating the opinions of others, left to focus instead on how to fiddle with pipes. "I don't know if you can see the sludge at the bottom—I'm sure neither of you wants to get your hands on it, which is pretty natural, although you'll find it doesn't actually smell, at least not of what you're used to—but there should be fruiting bodies in the—Ah!"

He pointed down into the remnants of what was almost certainly residential shit and saturated greywater.

Following the line of his finger, it was immediately possible to see a perfect cluster of bright orange pinpricks, which—Dolly squinted painfully—resolved themselves on closer inspection into perfect, tiny little picturebook mushroom caps, none of them bigger than her fingernail.

The sewage smelled of absolutely nothing besides cut celery stalks.

"Are they *safe?*" Dolly asked, covering her mouth and nose with her hand; a futile gesture, as she was well aware from decades of airplastics and the early childhood days of roving pandemics. It was a mask, and only a very good mask, that kept such things at bay.

"They're natural," Gann said, perplexed, as if this were the answer to any dispute.

"Doesn't stop 'em being poisonous," Dolly said, on firmer ground with this. "Plenty of *natural* things don't want to be eaten and will let you know about it. Sometimes you don't even have to eat them."

"Oh, I take your point. No, they're perfectly safe. Edible, even."

"No, thank you," Daisy said hastily, audibly aghast.

The tiny little mushroom caps could hardly have made much of a meal, and Dolly wasn't altogether surprised when Gann continued, "But not worth the effort, and they don't really have a pleasant taste. We'd actually planned on using a different species altogether—much more familiar, bigger, and *very* good at filtering, according to some Finns we managed to get on the Network, but it doesn't do well with the water levels in the pipes, and no one wanted to go back to the earth pits."

Dolly didn't risk looking at Daisy at this. Daisy *loathed* earth pits. She wasn't exactly fond of them herself, but complaining would make people lose all respect for her. They certainly didn't have any for the Ince. Unfortunately, there were quite enough Inces and Ince-adjacents that without them at least trying to cooperate, nothing got done.

"So," Gann concluded, "the oysters are for a future project. Field reclamation. We're going to try to get more of the pollutants out of the soil. These little guys are just for handling the worst of the shit situation and giving off heat."

"*Heat?*" Daisy parroted, a ridiculous squawk that, mercifully, saved Dolly from having to ask the same question.

"Oh yes. Accelerated decomposition gives off incredible amounts of it," Gann said happily, as if Daisy had asked him exactly the question he'd always wanted to ask, instead of making an exhibition of herself in a stiff south-westerly. "Which usually just gets sent back through—there—" he pointed with his toe at a stack of thinner ceramic pipes, lying next to the hole, "which take around as many houses as necessary. When it's buried in the ground. The hot air, I mean. Because it doesn't stink any more. Obviously, the pipes are copper inside the house. Oh, dear, I hope I'm making sense."

No, Dolly thought, but unfortunately it wasn't true. "Of course," she said, shooting a warning look at Daisy. "Did you have much trouble laying the pipes? Did you get any push-back on people not wanting… well… farts… piped directly into their homes?"

"At first, absolutely," Gann assured her, still contriving to look delighted by this. "But this isn't the half of it. The real magic happens at the centre."

"Of what?" Daisy asked, sulkily. Dolly was beginning to agree with her. Rory Gann's enthusiasm coupled with his apparent assumption that they were all more informed than they actually were was beginning to grate on her.

She'd dealt with worse, Dolly reminded herself. They were *forming alliances*. The only way anyone survived anything: cooperation, collaboration, and a generous helping of caution. All the things that had been missing before the collapse. It didn't exactly *help* with her irritation to know that holding her tongue and not calling someone an idiot was the sensible choice, and it made her want to bully Daisy for her insistent squeamishness and softness all the more. Which would do no good, either.

For fuck's sake.

"Well, of the town," Gann said, pointing back up the slope, much to Dolly's exasperation. "The thing about the Integrated System is it works better in a tight range, because obviously you get heat loss and so on the further you have to transport things. So we have one, and Ringmore has one, and Bigbury proper has one, and Bantham has one it shares with Buckland and Thurslestone—we share ours with Challaborough—you get the idea. So it's like the Network, except not… networked, because of the energy loss per metre…"

"Oh," Daisy said, and then blindsided Dolly completely, "second law of thermodynamics. I see."

∾

"WHAT DO YOU THINK?" Dolly asked, when Gann had left them alone for five minutes to go and talk to his brother-in-law on the gate to the Integrated System Centre, located "up Folly Hill" opposite some well-maintained farm buildings. They had a perfect view of the bay: the tall white three-armed giants of salvaged wind turbines on the island saluted their remaining cousins on the hillside beside them.

For a moment Daisy looked as if she'd been slapped, presumably as confused about being asked her opinion by Dolly as Dolly was resentful of having to ask her, but it worked: she eventually smoothed down her smock and said with an exaggerated appearance of thoughtfulness, "It seems like a lot of work."

"Everything's a lot of work. Are you still worried that it's going to result in us having nothing to trade?"

Daisy gave a small start, as if she'd forgotten her objections entirely, and glanced over at where Gann and Whatever-His-Name-Was were getting into the level of tedious wrangling that was only possible when two people knew each other very well and one of them had a job to do. "It's not like we can export heat," she said, doubtfully.

Dolly bit back a curt reply. "No," she agreed, "but you know what likes heat? A whole variety of plants we can't currently grow because of the winters."

She waited for this to penetrate Daisy's head.

"Like?"

"Oranges," Dolly said, pulling the answer out of her arse. "Which I assume you remember."

She had gambled right with that one: Daisy was the exact right age, and the exact right *money*, to have been able to get the last of the serious imports, before shipping food around became an exercise in *dried goods only*. She, personally, just about remembered when you could buy them from greengrocers and supermarkets, but Daisy hadn't been born then.

Gann ambled back over, mud caking the sides of his boots. "Yeah, come on through," he said, as if continuing a conversation they'd all been having. "You should begin to feel the heat radiating off the ground in a couple of metres."

"Unsettling," said Dolly, when it did just that. "Where's this coming from?"

"A chamber full of shit," Gann said, succinctly, and with a distressing beam, "in a state of accelerated decomposition. "We draw the crap out of the sewage systems using a pump; wind powered, of course—" he pointed back at the giants on the hillside, "and the heat from the decomposition powers the flexor panels, and puts power back into the system. Not as *much*, obviously, but it's more consistent than the wind, so we think it's balanced, on the whole."

"Thermodynamics," Daisy repeated, clearly very pleased with herself. The smell of celery from the barn neighbouring it was extremely strong.

"And what happens when the flexor panels reach the end of their lifespan?" Dolly asked, aware that, once again, it fell to her to be the bad guy, just as it had in the times when the last splinters of entitlement were being worked out of their nascent societies; those final, brutal moments of post-revolutionary disquiet. Christ: she'd been so *young* then. It wasn't as if she couldn't still lift a shovel, but certainly nowhere near as fast.

Dolly slammed the door of memory hastily over that particular room.

"Ah, yes," Gann's assurance faded somewhat, and he examined the buttons on his jacket for a moment. "We're working on that one. We know they're not really replaceable without the old infrastructure. Still trying to figure something out with Ottoline's Finns. But for the time being, it's keeping our water hot and our spirits up."

DOLLY HELD her tongue until the daylight began to fade, and the enthusiastic tour was over; there was an interlude for pitching in to help a sheep down from someone's roof, where it had climbed for reasons only known to sheep, and another for joining their current hosts in making and eating their meal, but when they were finally, finally consigned to solitude, she let it burst forth again.

"Bloody Benoit bloody Jones," she snapped, leaning against the wood-lined wall. "Unbelievable. Did he even know they were running off irreplaceable parts when he started pitching this idea to the rest of the Borough or did he just get his head turned by talk on the Network?"

Curiously, Daisy seemed rather more sanguine, no doubt only thinking of herself: after all, the panels wouldn't give out in *her* lifetime, either. It would be a problem for Malala and Moss, and the baby's generation. The exact sort of short-termism that had gotten them to this point of airborne plastics and flooded Salcombe in the first place.

"You're right about the fruit," she said after some minutes of silence, taking Dolly so much by surprise that the remainder of her rant dried up on her tongue.

"Come again?"

"I said—don't make me repeat myself, I know you're enjoying it—" Daisy sighed, and went on scraping mud from her somewhat worse-for-wear red shoes. "Even if the heat panels die out, the ability to keep exotics warm in the winter won't, am I right?"

"Don't call them that."

"*Plants*, Dolly." She flicked a flake of dried-on clay-textured mud in the vague direction of the bin. "If Bigbury haven't thought of growing plants that means we have an edge. And something to trade when we need what *they* have."

Dolly bit the inside of her mouth, but her expression must have given her away.

"Look, just because *you* remember how bad things got before doesn't mean the rest of them do," Daisy snapped, throwing her shoe down. "Your nephew, all of that generation, they don't have a single clue, they just have a conviction their neighbours will come in and help no matter what and the *miserable* likelihood that Malala's baby will die before she's five—don't look at me like that, you know I'm not exaggerating and *she* knows even if you won't admit that she does. People need *hope*. Benoit is an idiot but he's not wrong."

"I think oranges are a slender hope," Dolly said, stiffly.

"I think we need a reason for our neighbours to come to us so we can have those strengthened community ties you and Benoit and Malala are so keen on," Daisy retorted, going slowly pink in the face. "Rory Gann and Bigbury have this ICKY and it's going to bring people to them, and right now we have nothing. You heard him: he just assumed we're going to impart all the information we have to them here, and they won't have to go to the trouble of travelling or finding out what we're like. Oranges are something that draws people in, too. *Fresh* oranges."

Dolly took a few deep breaths to cover her surprise and another few to get her temper back in check. There was such a thing as being *too* successful in bringing someone round, she decided.

"So you want to go back to tell Benoit you'll do it?" she asked, trying not to sound like she was doing the exact thing that she was: trying to needle the younger woman into sharing her discomfort again.

The wind tossed the barely-visible leaves on the trees outside the room. Even here, where power was less zealously-rationed, outdoor lighting was too profligate to indulge in, but the moon was at half, and the night was clear.

"Shouldn't you be asking me if I want to tell him the *truth*?" Daisy asked, a little archly, as she pulled off her socks. "Which is that while our 'fact-finding' excursion hasn't found the facts that would make us all more comfortable, it's done what you wanted, which was keep me in line."

Dolly said nothing.

"There's no point in you working obsessively to make things better if you never enjoy them," Daisy snapped.

"And it's not *fair* your doing nothing but enjoying them if you're not going to do any work," Dolly retorted. It sounded too familiar to be borne any longer. "Maybe I wouldn't *have* to work without enjoying a single damn comfort if people like you hauled your weight properly."

"Don't make it my fault that you martyr yourself," Daisy grumbled. "Melissa would agree with me."

"Leave her out of it," Dolly said, turning to face the window entirely. It was a low blow, but the worst of it wasn't that it was unpredicted; the worst of it was that Daisy was entirely right. Her wife *would've* agreed. She spent most of her *life* trying to get Dolly to let go of the sticks she'd bitten onto. For all the good it had done either of them.

Silence reigned in the little room, a silence that even the very faint, glass-muted omnipresent swish of the surf against the slowly-crumbling cliffs could not really penetrate.

After a while, she said, "I would like to grow orchids."

"I like orchids," Daisy said, cautiously, getting onto her cushions. "We had orchids on the wallpaper when I was young."

IN A SMALL ACT OF MERCY, the weather was almost calm, at least at head level, when they set off back inland towards their own Borough. The walk was not unpleasant, although after about ten miles Dolly's knees were starting to hurt, and Daisy had complained six or seven times, and so neither of them were particularly displeased when, unasked-for, Moss turned up with the powered tricycle to collect them at the half-way point.

"How did it go?" he asked, heaving them up the largest of the hills with only minimal assistance from the motor. "Are we looking at hot baths on demand and walk-in freezers?"

Daisy and Dolly, facing each other a mere knee's breadth apart on the removable benches of what was usually a cargo trailer, exchanged a glance.

Daisy turned away to look out over the road by which they'd come, back at the winding road back towards the sea, the island, and the heated houses of Bigbury-on-Sea, and presumably also Bigbury, and all the other villages Rory Gann had rattled off in succession that day; all of them obscured by the intervening distance and trees, the undulations of the landscape, and now by the lowering mist, too.

Dolly said, "Not exactly."

Her nephew not being immune to basic social cues, nodded to himself, and nothing more was said until they were back home.

～

"What about the hospital?" Malala asked, abruptly, in the middle of the Borough meeting.

Benoit Jones came to a screeching halt mid-waffle and gave her a bewildered look. "What about the hospital?" he repeated, gazing around at the assembled members of the Borough on the bandstand with ovine patience, his expression in fact readily comparable to one of Alice's flock, who had chosen to surround the fenced-off area with soft grey *baa*s of accusation of some crime known only to sheep.

"The hospital over there is running on wind, mostly. We've got to take it as read that most of the surrounding Boroughs are going to need to send people along at some point or another. What they lack is a bit of dietary variance and more exotic plants for medical compounds," Malala expounded, baby in one arm, gesticulation in the other. "What we've got, if Dolly is right—which she usually is—"

Dolly tried not to look too smug about this. On the far side of the bandstand, Daisy made an exasperated face: clearly her attempt at containing her ego hadn't been very successful.

"Then we can supply that pretty easily. That brings a whole chain of Boroughs together. Worswell Borough have said they're happy to send boats up the river valley both at Newton and at Mothecombe up to Ivybridge Borough to pick up patients if necessary, saving everyone the overland, and Malborough will take the Drowned Villages district. That leaves a lot of us in the Hams better off even before we install more of these ICKIES."

"They're not long-term," Jones protested, despondent. "I'd hoped for a more permanent—"

"Nothing's permanent," Daisy interrupted, without putting her hand up, as usual. "Everything we've *got* is a series of compromises. We just have to deal with things as they come."

Dolly raised what was left of her eyebrows. Compromises didn't always come easily. But sometimes the first step was learning, once again, to get on with one's neighbours; what else, after all, did any of them really have but each other?

Derek Des Anges lives and works in London, UK, where the weather is getting less and less Classically British by the year. His work has appeared in anthologies from Parsec Ink, Calyx Press, and Ghoulish Books, among others.

Twitter: https://www.twitter.com/derekdesanges
Website: https://derekdesanges.wordpress.com/books

OTHER PURSUITS
BY GUSTAVO BONDONI

Downstairs, in the game room, a crash sounded and someone groaned.

I put down the e-reader—I had been completely engrossed in a murder mystery produced to my specifications by PlotBot561—and rushed to the balcony that overlooked the common area.

Serena had fallen onto a small table, which had overbalanced and scattered my carved-stone chess set across the floor. She moaned and put a hand on her head.

The other occupants of the leisure area rushed to her aid. Marco and Joao arrived first, from opposite directions, followed by Xime and Iris in short succession.

Hu trailed behind, his bandaged knee slowing him down. By the time he arrived, the bustling in and out to get things to make Serena comfortable had died down.

When Serena sat up and insisted that she was fine, I relaxed and headed downstairs to join the group hovering over her.

They opened a space for me to pass between them. Serena smiled sheepishly. "I'm sorry I knocked over your game, Alberto," she said. "I'll have the nanofactory build you replacement pieces."

I picked up a scarred rook. It seemed to have acquired a couple of extra dents in the fall. "Absolutely not. These pieces have a history. Every little crack and chip represents something that happened to it during its life. A child's tantrum. A hundred matches in a row. An accident like today's. It would be wrong to erase all of that." I smiled down at her. "The important thing is that you are all right. Do you know what happened?"

"I…" she looked around. "This is going to sound strange, but I have absolutely no idea how I got in here. I was having a drink outside, by the lagoon terrace, and the next thing I knew I was standing here, dizzy and about to fall. Well, you know the rest." She shook her head. "And now I feel perfectly fine. It's the weirdest thing."

I looked up into the hills, where the local farm robots harvested our food. It always surprised me to see them up there, in the craggy, steep places. When I was a child, you couldn't cultivate those terraces because the hills didn't allow it. But now, thanks to the dexterity and tirelessness of the spider-like robots, the tiny terraces fed us all… and we were able to leave the plains to the forest and the animals. "Strange, indeed. Were you drinking alcohol, at least?"

"A single caipiroshka in a small glass. Not something to put me to sleep and take over my body."

"I suppose you're right." I'd seen Serena down an entire bottle of red wine during dinner and then dance all night. Or at least I assumed it was all night… I wasn't as young as I used to be, and I would normally leave early. But when I left, she would be dancing, as only a twenty-five-year-old can. "You should probably get checked out."

"I will," she replied. "But seriously, there's nothing wrong with me. I think the extent of the damage is a bruised knee." She brushed aside the hands on her shoulders and stood. "See? Perfectly stable. I'm not going to fall again." Then she frowned. "Has anyone seen my tablet?"

We searched the room, but there wasn't much space to search. Most of the floorspace was open, with just a few chairs and tables scattered around. Brilliant sunlight through the glass walls exposed every square centimeter of floor space. There was no place for a device that size to land and remain hidden.

"Are you sure you had it?" Xime asked.

"Absolutely. I remember, when I was falling, one moment of complete clarity in which I tried to toss it onto a chair so it wouldn't get destroyed when I fell."

"You weren't thinking clearly. You must have left it outside," Joao said. "I'll go check." He disappeared out the glass doors and returned less than a minute later and shrugged. "Not there. And you hardly drank anything—the caipiroshka is still mostly full."

"Someone must have taken it," Iris said.

Serena laughed. "Why? It's not like I'm doing anything valuable on it... I still haven't found what I want to do with my life, so that tablet is mainly chatrooms and direct messages. Who would want to read mine?"

"A secret admirer!" Marco exclaimed. "Looking for the key to your heart."

She gave him an exasperated half-smile. "That's just dumb."

I spoke up. "Maybe it's not the information they wanted, but the device itself. Is there anything special about it? Have you gotten it modded? Or maybe it's a special edition or vintage design? Something someone might find valuable?"

She shook her head. The concept of taking material things for profit was alien to this generation, which had been brought up in the age of nanomanufacturing and the abolition of monetary exchange. "No. It's just one of the standard designs in the nanofactory. The only thing special about mine is that I had it printed in pink so it would be easy to spot among the more boring ones."

I refrained from rolling my eyes at that, but she did have a point: I remembered seeing the device—despite being produced from one of the standard patterns, it didn't resemble any other tablet in the living complex.

"Maybe one of the little girls from the married people's housing area grabbed it. They're always saying how they'll build one just like it as soon as they're allowed devices," Iris said.

"Yeah... except none of them have been here since I fell. And I had the tablet with me," Serena replied.

I could almost feel the change in the air as concern for Serena's well-being turned into the realization that she was accusing someone in this room of having walked away with something that wasn't theirs. People shuffled their feet. Xime glanced around, surreptitiously trying to see if anyone might have the device on them.

"It's a mystery," I said, before people found a reason to escape. "Let's talk about it."

"I need to take my afternoon walk," Hu said.

"It will still be daylight in a few minutes," I replied.

He grunted and sat, taking the weight off of his injured leg, which he'd twisted while climbing one of the local volcanoes. He was in his late forties, but was trim and wiry and had decided, when the nanofactories made poverty and accumulation a thing of the past, to climb the world's highest peaks. The volcanoes around our living complex were an early step in his training towards that goal. "Whatever. You've always wanted to be part of a mystery, so here you have one." He chuckled. "I suppose it's better than someone getting murdered. Let's see you do your stuff."

I suddenly realized I had no idea what I was doing. I shrugged. It wouldn't be the first time in my seventy years I'd found myself in this predicament. "All right. My first question is: does anyone have the tablet on you right now? Maybe you picked it up by mistake and thought it was yours?"

They shuffled and checked. The ones with devices on them held them up. Black, grey, silver, white. All standard colors. No pink.

"Too bad. That means that, unless Serena is mistaken and forgot it in her room or something, we have to assume that a person in this room took it. And I assume it was just after she hit her head. That was when you were all rushing around trying to make her comfortable and no one was watching anyone else, so anyone could have left and hidden the tablet somewhere else."

Hu stood. "Well, I guess that leaves me in the clear," he said. "It takes me all day just to cross the room. Can I go for my walk now?"

I nodded. "I can't stop you."

Hu hobbled out. Unless he was a brilliant actor, willing to limp around for days just to establish a plausible alibi for the crucial moment, he was right: there was no way he could have escaped with the device and returned on time.

That left Iris, Xime, Carlo and Joao, all staring up at me like I was about to pull a rabbit out of my own ear.

I sat, just to keep them from looking up at me that way. It was a mistake: I immediately sank into the soft cushion of the lounge chair. But at least the breeze that ran through the room—the large sliding glass doors on both the lagoon side and the mountain side were open—helped me stay cool. I sweated when I was nervous, and though this might not have erased that completely, at least it would moderate things for a few minutes.

"I think we can all agree that Serena's tablet, as a device, is worthless?" I said.

"Of course," Xime replied. "Anyone who wants one just has to dump a shovelful of garbage into the nanofactory. Maybe an old motherboard for the germanium or whatever if the nanofactory happens to be out of that stuff, but nothing we can't just pick up anywhere."

"So whoever took it wanted the information on the device," I concluded.

"Hadn't we already said that?" Carlo asked. "And then Serena insisted it was silly because there was nothing on there that anyone would want to see."

Carlo and Serena exchanged a glance. I raised an eyebrow.

Serena blushed. "I spent most of the afternoon mocking up wedding invitations."

"But you're not even..." I began, but then glanced at Carlo again. Everyone giggled at my expense, except for Joao who seemed uninterested. "Ah, I see it wasn't such a secret," I said.

"Not to anyone who shares a wall with either of these two rabbits," Xime said. "Rene and Claire aren't here now, but they also knew."

Serena had turned scarlet, but Carlo, the dark-haired, handsome Italian whose passion was for experimental physics and who'd been published in Nature twice since he decided to follow that path, smiled. He appeared to be a man who took pride in having others discuss his sexual exploits.

I reflected that if anyone knew what would be on Serena's device, he would be the one. Perhaps he was having second thoughts about marriage. In an age where no one needed to work to survive, marriage had become quite unusual... the economic benefits of facing the world as a couple had all but disappeared.

And speaking more locally, the singles complex was a lot more fun than the family area. Of course, there was no reason whatsoever for them to stay in our little community, but I had the impression they both enjoyed living in Dominical. Perhaps he'd taken the device to stop her from designing invitations. But that was weak. She'd just do it again on her next tablet.

My gaze fell on Iris, with her dark, curly hair and light brown skin. She had chuckled on cue when we were discussing my ignorance of what the young people were up to, but I remembered how interested she'd been in Carlo when he first appeared in our little community three years before. They'd been inseparable for months, and I was quite certain, on intimate terms for most of that time. Eventually, they'd drifted apart, but they had remained cordial, at least outwardly.

I wondered. Might she have found out about the wedding and been jealous enough to try to sabotage something as petty as the design of the invitations?

"Was I the only one who didn't know you were getting married?" I asked.

Marco replied. "Actually, I don't think anyone else knew. We only discussed it this morning by the pool."

"Ah," Joao said. "So that's what you were talking about when I ran into you this morning. No wonder you hid everything away so quickly when I walked up." He grinned at Carlo. "And no wonder Serena wasn't taking her early morning swim in the lagoon."

Joao was from Brazil, and he was blond and tanned. He looked more like a surf bum than a night-owl poet and musician whose work—at least what of it I'd seen—tended towards the moody and existential. It was a jarring combination, as if the Beach Boys had sung Bob Dylan tunes. I wondered if any of the kids would even know who those groups were. Hell, my own generation only got those acts through our parents. Of course, with the advances in chemistry available now, the drugs he took were both trippier and safer than anything my parents could have imagined. And they were as close as the nearest food dispenser.

I wondered what he might possibly want that was on Serena's device.

"If I'd known you had something interesting to talk about, I would have sat down with you," Iris said. "But I wasn't going to start drinking so early in the day. Besides, you two—" she pointed to Joao and Serena, "—looked so serious sitting there talking that I didn't want to interrupt."

Serena snorted. "Serious? We were just waiting for Carlo to get back. He'd gone inside to check his email. Something about waiting for a co-writer to send him comments on a paper. Something about an experiment to more easily detect muons or lepers or something."

Carlo rolled his eyes but he didn't correct her. A wise man, that one.

"Hell, if I'd known you were planning a wedding, I'd have barged in." Iris was a round-faced, pale-skinned woman with red-dyed curls who was the kind of soft, matronly presence that would make anyone feel immediately comfortable... and who would drop everything to plan a wedding. She'd been instrumental in the last one we'd had: the big blowout for when Laura and Ania got hitched. My head hurt just remembering the hangover from that one. Her own inclinations were literary, but unlike me, she wanted to write instead of read, and refused to listen to me when I explained that AI could produce the perfect novel for any reader within minutes.

She just smiled and said she wasn't in it for the money, but to leave something of the way she felt for future generations to ponder over. Or not, as the case might be.

I couldn't think of any reason for her to steal the device, which immediately set off all sorts of alarms. The quiet, innocent-looking ones were the worst. I didn't need PlotBot561 to tell me that.

"You wouldn't have missed anything. In fact, almost immediately after you said hello, I stood up, thinking I'd go look for Carlo. And that's the last I remember before I was falling onto the floor here, trying to keep my tablet from exploding against the ground," Serena said. Then she shrugged. "You know the rest."

All eyes turned in my direction. "So? Do you know who did it?" Joao said, asking the question they all wanted answered.

To cover the fact that I had no idea where to begin, even, I steepled my fingers and grinned at them. "I know you think I'm a crazy old man, so I thank you for humoring me. Now that Serena is completely recovered, I'd ask that one of you accompany her to the medical unit so the autodoc can look her over."

"I'll go, of course," Carlo said.

"Thank you. And I will think this over and tell you when I know the answer. Even the great detectives had to think about things," I reminded them.

They scattered, rushing off to do their young-people things, unaware that they had all the time in the world in which to do them.

I wondered what the hell I was going to tell them.

THE AFTERNOON WORE ON and the shadow of the volcano in the distance stretched toward the little community beside the lagoon. I lounged in my favorite chair in the mezzanine above the recreation room.

I'd spent the afternoon finishing the mystery that had been interrupted when Serena collapsed.

But that was just a front for what I was really doing, which was attempting to figure out who'd stolen that blasted tablet. I cursed myself for not being as insightful as Monsieur Gallup, the indomitable detective in PlotBot561's amazingly put-together plot.

A lot of people claimed that AI fiction just wasn't the same. Maybe they were right. But where else could I get an Agatha Christie pastiche written to my exact specifications almost instantly?

As entertainment, it was a wonderful invention. Another piece of the automation revolution that had liberated humanity to pursue whatever they wanted to do.

But it clearly hadn't made me any smarter or turned me into a detective. I was useless.

And then it hit me. I might be useless at getting to the bottom of a detective scenario, but I knew someone who wasn't.

PlotBot561.

I picked up the device again and toggled the novel creation menu.

Then, I spent fifteen minutes describing the initial situation and the characters, starting with the old man who was investigating, then the woman who collapsed to the floor, and all the rest. In my hurry, the only name I changed was my own, since that was a PlotBot561 rule: the user couldn't be included in any story that involved crime or sex. Of course, there were other Bots that would happily accept those scenarios... but I was more comfortable with my usual purveyor.

Besides, the name of the character made no difference. I told the machine to make Gallup the hero again.

I watched the progress bar cross the screen. Normally, my scenarios took about three minutes to load but, to my embarrassment, this one must have been considerably simpler, since it was done in just over a minute.

Ignoring everything else, I flipped to the last chapter, in which Gallup confronted the suspects and unmasked the perpetrator, and I read.

"Dammit," I said out loud, as the truth of the matter sunk in.

In that final chapter, Gallup had gathered the young single people in the recreation room and, with much twirling of his mustache, had brought one of the bots that kept the bottom of the pond clear of debris to search for the tablet in the muck.

Five minutes later, it returned, clutching a soggy, ruined, pink piece of electronics.

I read the great reveal with interest:

"We went about this the wrong way," Gallup said. "We were thinking in terms of what might be stored on the device, or who might want to wish Miss Serena harm, when the truth was quite the opposite. It wasn't a question of wishing harm, but of wishing her extremely well. Too well, in fact."

Gallup looked around the room. His eyes settled on Joao. "You knew she was with Carlo, but you never lost hope." Gallup twirled his mustache. "In your experience, the moody poet and musician always gets the girl in the end, correct?"

Joao said nothing.

Gallup continued: "You got up early today to make sure you saw her after her morning swim. But instead, you overheard her speaking to Carlo, and you realized she would never be yours. That she was, in fact, set upon marrying someone else.

"But you weren't just there to talk to her, were you?"

Joao remained silent.

"You were there to read her your latest poem. You had sent it to her device. You knew that reading it together had the best effect.

"And now, it was on her tablet, and you had to remove it somehow."

Joao ran off.

"Let him go," Gallup said. "He isn't important, just silly. What happened next was obvious, not unexpected perhaps, for someone of his limited intellect: he put a small dose of one of his recreational drugs—one he knew would remove Serena from her senses for a few moments, long enough to snatch the tablet and erase the offending poem—but instead of sitting passively while in a trance, Serena walked off... carrying the tablet.

"Finally, she fell to the floor and Joao saw his opportunity. He grabbed the device and, under the pretense of checking if it was still outside, he tossed it in the pond." Gallup smiled. "Had he not panicked and merely deleted his poem and pretended to find the device on the floor, there would have been no investigation. But who can blame him? In most circumstances, it would have been a perfect crime, made even better by the fact that no one had been hurt and that Serena would be able to get a new device—just as pink as the one before—in just a few minutes. Unfortunately, Joao wasn't counting on the presence of Héctor Gallup!"

Then Gallup left the room in triumph.

I shut the book off. PlotBot561, I was certain, had solved the mystery. The neat solution fit the facts perfectly but, more importantly, it fit the personalities involved. Joao would have been the kind of person to do that, the fragile insecurities he tried to hide by adopting the persona of the moody artist would allow him to justify things that others might find distasteful.

But the ending of the book still disturbed me. That wasn't the way a story like this should end.

At eight, I heard the group sitting around the table downstairs, obviously waiting to hear my pronouncement before heading off to dinner. I sighed, rose from my chair and descended.

I looked straight into Joao's eyes, and he held my gaze, then looked away. Then I smiled sheepishly at the assorted young people who watched me expectantly. I shook my head. "I'm sorry. Apparently, reading detective novels doesn't make me a detective. I thought about the problem all afternoon and I couldn't reach a solution that fits the facts. Serena, I must apologize. I suppose this will just go down as one of the little unsolved mysteries in life."

Serena got up and hugged me. "Don't worry about it," she said. "You're such a dear for taking your time to try to solve my little problem. I got another device already. Thank you so much."

They all smiled and laughed it off. Even Joao joined in the good-natured gratitude, but he couldn't hide his relief. Not from me, anyway, because I was looking for it.

As they filed out, I touched Joao's arm. "Could you help me with a couple of boxes?" I asked him. "I'm afraid my back is acting up."

He agreed and followed me in the direction of my room, along the exterior gravel path that led to the front of each housing unit. Once I was sure the rest of the group was out of earshot, I stopped and looked him in the eye.

"We both know what you did. And I know why you did it, too."

His eyes widened, and he began to speak.

"I don't want to hear it," I said. "I know. So don't bother to hide it. The only reason I didn't expose you in front of the others is that I was once young and in love, too. I know how much you're hurting already, and being embarrassed in front of everyone isn't going to help."

Joao turned red.

"But I want you to know that if you ever drug another of our neighbors without their consent, I'll make certain everyone knows. Do you understand?"

He nodded; eyes rimmed with tears. "I promise," he said. "I was so worried she might have hurt herself. I'll never do that again. It was so awful when she fell…"

I looked at him long and hard, and nodded. He seemed miserable about what he'd done.

"I'm glad you feel that way," I replied. "You can go now."

He hurried off and, as I watched him, I realized that, even though technology had made everyone's life a lot better than it used to be, it hadn't quite managed to grasp certain things.

And until Monsieur Gallup learned what it was to be young and in love, he wouldn't be able to solve certain mysteries to my satisfaction.

I chuckled. Maybe the nuts who insisted that fiction had to be written by humans were right. Maybe I should see what was out there.

I might find something I liked.

Gustavo Bondoni is a novelist and short story writer with over four hundred stories published in fifteen countries, in seven languages. He is a member of Codex and an Active Member of SFWA. He has published six science fiction novels including one trilogy, four monster books, a dark military fantasy and a thriller. His short fiction is collected in Pale Reflection (2020), Off the Beaten Path (2019), Tenth Orbit and Other Faraway Places (2010) and Virtuoso and Other Stories (2011).

In 2019, Gustavo was awarded second place in the Jim Baen Memorial Contest and in 2018 he received a Judges Commendation (and second place) in The James White Award. He was also a 2019 finalist in the Writers of the Future Contest.

Website: http://www.gustavobondoni.com
Facebook: https://www.facebook.com/gustavo.bondoni/
Twitter: https://twitter.com/gbondoni

REANIMATION

BY STEPHEN SOTTONG

You asked me to record my time with you and impressions of the world I ended up in. Since only historians will view it, I'll express my actual opinions and not hold back as I have since that day your government official issued his warning.

I WOKE to a stabbing pain in my side. I asked God to take the pain away and as my vision cleared, I saw a man in white. Light streamed through his gray curls like a halo. Momentarily I thought I'd died and gone to my reward, but I couldn't be in heaven in such pain and refused to consider the alternative. Grabbing the man's arm, I tried to speak but only managed a croak. Startled, he attempted to extricate himself and finally leaned over me, babbling in a language I couldn't understand. A woman moved to my head, cooed something unintelligible and placed a device on my forehead.

I had no idea when I woke again. I lay in a bed, head and back elevated, dressed in clean, warm pajamas, a white sheet covering me to the chest. The air was pleasantly warm, with the tang of antiseptic. Sunlight filtered through sheer curtains covering a wall of windows, tinting the room golden. I was comfortable and in no pain.

Beside my bed, a woman in a straight-backed chair stared intently at a tablet device. She noticed me move, placed the device in an inside pocket of her plain black jacket and walked to my bedside. "I'm pleased you're awake."

I tried to speak but only coughed. She produced a glass of water. A few swallows, and I could speak in a low, halting voice. "How long have I been in the hospital?"

She hesitated. "Then, you know you're in a hospital?"

Her accent and pronunciation were unusual, and the question confused me. "Of course."

"Do you know why you went to the hospital?"

I stared at her. In her late thirties, she was about my age, attractive, full-figured, with close-set green eyes and dark brown hair pulled back from her oval face. She appeared intelligent and concerned. I wondered why she wouldn't give me a straight answer. "Yes, I was scheduled for surgery to remove a tumor on my liver." I was overcome with panic. "Was it cancer?"

She stood close to my bed. "I'm not a doctor, but yes, you had cancer. It had spread throughout your body."

I lay back on the pillow, hyperventilating.

She put a hand on my arm. "You needn't worry. You're cured now."

I gazed back at her. "How?"

Her hand remained, resting gently on my arm. "I don't know the technical details, but be assured, you're completely cured."

I noticed the room was large, pleasant, and tastefully decorated, unlike a hospital one. Something was wrong. "I need to talk to my wife."

Her eyes showed concern. "You have no idea what happened after you went to the hospital?"

I was starting to panic again. "Listen, I don't know what's going on, but I know my rights. Either get my wife, or I'll call the cops."

She stared at the ceiling, repeating "cops," shrugged and looked back at me. "I'm sorry if this is confusing. I don't want to startle you, but I must tell you something that will be … disconcerting." She paused as if waiting for some sign from me. "Your wife has been dead for at least three hundred years. You were cryogenically preserved."

I don't know if it was seconds or minutes before I could reply as my mood moved from shock to anger. "I don't know who put you up to this joke. Just get me my wife, and I'll forget all about it."

She again put a hand on my arm. "I assure you, I'm not joking. I understand that denial is a necessary phase in grieving your old life, but I am telling you the truth. You were stored in a cryogenic facility over three hundred years ago. We just found it. The facility was in a cave. An avalanche had covered the entrance. The facility was automated and powered by an underground river, so it kept operating without failure."

I stared at her blankly. "Frozen?"

"Yes. And unlike others we've found, they didn't wait until you were dead. We speculate they discovered the extent of your cancer and froze you before you recovered from the anesthesia. Whoever performed the procedure did an excellent job. There was very little damage from the freezing, and all of it was repairable."

My mouth hung open. I shut it. "They killed me?" I tried to remember the last words my young wife used to describe the *nice young* surgeon.

"Had they waited until you were dead, we wouldn't have been able to revive you. Several others were also preserved at the same facility but were too badly damaged to be revived."

"Do you think they knew that when they froze me?"

"If they had any sense, they did. Even freezing you alive could have caused extensive cellular damage. As I said, the procedure was masterfully done."

I tried to weigh the implications, but my mind refused to comprehend. "Three hundred years." I lay back on the bed.

She patted my arm. "Sleep. You need to rest after such a shock." She walked to the door, touched a panel, and the windows darkened. I cried myself to sleep.

AGAIN I WOKE, this time to sunshine growing brighter as the windows lightened. The woman who'd spoken to me yesterday and the gray-haired man from my first awakening stood by the bed. The man spoke, but I couldn't understand him. He seemed tired, detached, but fully in control—after all these years, I could still recognize a doctor.

The woman translated. "Dr. Henry 108 would like to examine you."

"All right."

The doctor lifted my shirt and ran an instrument over my torso. It looked like a pancake turner that must have been remotely connected to a console he'd wheeled to my bedside. I noticed a healing scar above my liver. The doctor watched the screen as he moved the device, appeared pleased, mumbled something to the woman and left with the console.

She sat by my bed. "The doctor says you're healing well."

After a few moments of uncomfortable silence, I blurted out, "Do you have a name?"

She smiled. "Yes, I'm Beta 424."

"I'm Don Marlboro." I held out a hand. It took a few seconds for her to recognize the gesture and shake my hand as if she'd never done it before.

"I should have recognized the gesture immediately. I'm a cultural anthropologist."

"Is English still spoken, or are you a linguist, also?"

"All of us speak the same language, but we have a tradition of raising our children to be bilingual. It improves the flexibility of young minds. I learned basic English as a child and took courses afterward. Not many children learn English, though, because of its difficulty. I also did work in comparative linguistics, so my grasp of the language is better than most."

The conversation lagged again. "Why 424?"

"That's the designation of my settlement of origin. We don't have family names like in your time, and we no longer name our settlements; we number them."

"I can see a problem with that arrangement. What if someone else in the settlement names their child Beta?"

"They wouldn't."

"Why?"

She was taken aback by the question. "It would cause confusion."

"But someone, somewhere must make a mistake. You can't know everyone in your settlement."

She brightened. "Perhaps that's what confuses you—in your day, settlements were large. No settlement now has more than 150 people."

The number astounded me. "Why so small?"

"That's the optimal size for personal interaction. We all know each other, so no one would pick a name already being used."

"No big cities?"

She shook her head. "No. We have areas where people from many settlements come for entertainment or recreation, but no more than 150 people live in them. There are also sites for industry and education. Most people commute to them. Students may live on campus, but even there, they're housed in villages surrounding the campus where the number of inhabitants is kept below 150."

"Sounds inefficient."

"Probably, but we value personal interaction more than efficiency. We avoid the sense of isolation people experienced in large communities."

I decided to get out of bed and see this new world. Beta provided an arm to lean on as I walked to the window. She pulled the curtain, and I was greeted with the view of a parking lot and train station. "Where's the settlement?"

"There isn't one. The hospital is one of the special areas. Just it and related medical facilities are on this site. The staff live in settlements close by."

"You come here every day to translate for me?"

"Yes. Settlement 424 is only," she paused as if calculating, "thirty minutes away by train."

"I appreciate your effort."

"Thank you. I hope to learn more about your time while I help you transition to life in the present."

That worried me. "What will I need to do?"

"First, learn our language. You'll find it simpler than English. But that can wait until you feel better." She helped me back to bed.

"Is there anything I can read to get up to date on history?"

"I fear there's nothing in English, but I'll check. Unfortunately, English has been a dead language for about two hundred years. I'm sure you have many other questions, but you appear tired. Sleep now."

She left. I asked her not to dim the windows or draw the curtains. Between frequent, often heavy rainstorms and my naps, I watched the sleek, multicolored commuter trains come and go. A few, tiny, nearly-identical ground cars appeared, but most people took the trains. Occasionally, what I took as an ambulance from its size rushed toward the side of the building. The room was quiet except for the attendants who brought food and the nurses who ran periodic checks on me. All were pleasant, but none spoke English. I tried to open the hall door once and found it locked. I was left with my thoughts and memories, stranded in a world I knew nothing about, generations away from home and family, alone and bereft.

BETA ARRIVED THE NEXT DAY. I asked her, "Why is the door locked?"

"We thought it would be less traumatic to introduce our world gradually. Outside this room is a modern hospital. The equipment would be unfamiliar to you. Rather than disrupt the hospital's operation and possibly injure yourself, we limited you to this room. If you feel ready, I can take you for walks, but you must always stay with me."

I agreed, and that afternoon took my first walk. Hospital hallways were just as cluttered, sterile and overly lit as in my day, staff rushed by, and patients looked just as sick. Only the equipment was strange. We returned to the room.

I felt nearly ready to leave but had no idea what would come after this. "What happens when I'm discharged?"

She leaned forward and held my gaze. "You know the world you left is gone?"

I knew intellectually, but hearing it brought the realization home like a punch in the gut. It took me a few seconds to compose myself. "Yes. It wasn't my decision to take this excursion in time, but I'm here now. I'll learn to live somehow."

"Good." She patted my arm. "When you're discharged, I'll take you to my settlement. Most of its residents work at the university. There are several historians and cultural anthropologists in the settlement. A few other residents speak passable English. We'll try to orient you to today's life."

"That's kind of you, but I'm left wondering how I'll provide for myself."

"You're referring to work?"

"I'm talking about money. Unless my wife made provisions for me, I'm broke."

Beta shook her head. "That's not a problem."

"How can it not be?"

"We don't use money. I only vaguely understand how it worked. The settlement will provide for your needs."

That worried me. "You people are Socialists?"

She paused, staring at the floor. "I remember this from a history class. That's one of the economic philosophies of your time, isn't it?" I nodded, and she continued. "I don't think we fall into any of your economic classifications.

We're pragmatic and egalitarian. In time you'll learn more. For the moment, you needn't worry. Your needs will be provided for."

∿

I'D ALWAYS LED an active life. Sitting in one room for several days was getting to me. I looked out the window, paced, and prayed. My thoughts kept returning to my wife, my children and my other life—now gone. I was left with the nagging question of whether my preservation was an act of kindness or betrayal, or if it had some higher purpose.

I needed distraction. The room was large, perhaps twenty by twenty feet, but only contained the bed and a chair. I told Beta I was bored. When I asked about television, she had to consult the tablet device she carried with her. "We don't have anything exactly like that. There are entertainments available on personal devices." She held up her tablet. "And homes have larger devices for group entertainment and research. I can get you a device of your own."

"Good. Can I read on it?"

"Certainly. I'll show you how to access an archive of books in English."

I smiled. "That'd be great. With all I've experienced in the past few days, I'd like to spend some time reading the Bible. It'd be a comfort."

Her silence was deafening. It was a minute before she finally said, "I'll have to consult with colleagues," and left.

∿

THE MAN who visited the next morning was in his sixties, silver-haired, handsome and distinguished. He dressed in a plain but tailored shirt and pants and, if I'm any judge of character, was not someone you'd like to cross. He bowed and seated himself. His English was flat and overly precise but understandable.

"I am Damien 285 from the Regional Council. It is my understanding that you have requested a Bible."

"Yes, I like to read the Good Book. It brings me peace and comfort."

He shook his head. "We cannot do that. The Bible, the Koran, the Torah and all other major religious writings are restricted to academic use."

"What about believers?"

"There are none."

I sat there, mouth agape.

He nodded. "I understand that this may shock you, but we classify belief in a supernatural being as aberrant. Our society found that belief in a deity was dangerous.

"After the disasters caused by climate change, our forefathers banded together to form this society. Some of them tried to reinstitute the old faiths. They proved divisive. Believers clustered together and shunned those who did not share their beliefs. They destroyed the cohesiveness of our settlements. Humanity was on the brink of extinction. We had to work in concert. We could not countenance anything that tore us apart. So we banned religion. It took the better part of a century to eliminate it from most of our society, but the more thoroughly we rooted it out, the more cohesive, prosperous and adaptable our society became. Which brings us to you. You are, I take it, a Christian?"

"Yes."

"You are new to us, so I will be as gentle as possible. Humanity's hold on existence is still tenuous. We cannot tolerate activities that threaten our society. That includes overt expressions of religion. Despite, indeed, perhaps because of its lack of logic, religion can spread like cancer among those less intelligent or emotionally stable. We realize you come from a different society and will make an exception for you, but only if you keep your beliefs to yourself. Express your beliefs, and we will be forced to place you in an exile community. Have I made myself clear?"

"Crystalline." I was appalled.

"Good." He handed me a tablet device. "This is set to display English books. You'll find the selection limited and mostly outdated; however, we translated Teller's volume on the history of the collapse and restoration of civilization. The translation was done via computer, but it has been checked for readability. You might want to start with it. It may help you understand why I say humanity's hold on existence is tenuous." He moved to the door and turned. "Think about what I have said." He left.

I was stunned. Though I'd never been exceptionally devout, I could yet become a martyr for my faith. This new world was suddenly ominous.

My mind flitted, attempting to find a way out of the predicament and found none. After the initial shock wore off, I grew curious and tried the device. It proved easy to use. I found Teller and read about the destruction of my world. Teller said that carbon dioxide levels reached a critical level about the time my grandchildren reached adulthood. Greenland's ice sheets rolled into the Atlantic, causing the Gulf Stream to stop. Europe froze while the rest of the world baked. Antarctica followed Greenland at a pace not dreamed of by the overly conservative scientific community. Coastlines submerged. Billions of people were uprooted, moving inland to areas that couldn't sustain them. Entire countries tried to migrate, leading to bloody wars. In the overcrowded, hot environment that followed, disease was rampant. A few new plagues wiped out most of humanity. The survivors consolidated and set about creating an entirely new society based on the premise that we'd never outgrown our hunter/gatherer roots and needed to adapt our society accordingly. The society I'd awoken in was the result of that effort. It was generally peaceful, egalitarian and atheist.

When Beta arrived the next day, I had several questions. "What do you do if someone wants to wander off and live in the wilderness?"

"We move them to a frontier settlement."

"But what if they just don't want to be around other people?"

"We get them treatment."

I lay back on the bed. "You people don't believe in personal freedom."

She sat. "I know something about your society. The nation-state you lived in believed everyone had the right to publish and speak whatever they wished, even if it was dangerous to individuals or society. We don't. Your society believed in an absolute right to believe in religions that fostered prejudice, violence and mass murder. Your society's concept of freedom led to war, chaos and destruction. Today's society wants no part of that. You'll have difficulty adjusting if you don't lose your absolutist beliefs. We gave up on them, and our society is happier, healthier and better adjusted than yours."

Her tone rankled me, but I had no options. I was trapped in a time where I didn't belong. "I guess I'll have to see."

"View our society with an open mind, and I think you'll find it's an improvement."

～

THE LAST SURPRISE before I was discharged from the hospital was being informed I'd have a skin graft. Tattoos were not allowed in this world. They were classified as self-mutilation. Their popularity in my era was deemed a form of mass hysteria they wouldn't allow to recur. So the eagle on my upper arm would be removed whether I liked it or not.

THE TRAIN TAKING me to my new life was fast, smooth, clean and pleasant. The seats were generous and comfortable, with ample armrests. A pastel color scheme gave the compartment a bright, active, cheerful feel. There was room to store bags in bins above and below the seats, and larger items could be checked. People talked or worked with their tablets. It was generally quiet if you discounted the teenagers who laughed, joked and bragged the entire time. Their small concessions to teenage rebellion were cuffs on the boys' pants rolled up high enough to show their hairy legs, and the girl's hair tied up in multiple primary-color ribbons. The look was garish. Beta showed her disapproval with scowls that enormously pleased the young people. At least teens hadn't changed.

The train stopped at half a dozen other settlements. All were arranged with the houses in concentric circles around a central plaza that held public buildings. Beyond the houses were fields, orchards and pastures. Each settlement looked a little different, though I noticed all of the houses were low, squat structures as if none dared rise above its neighbor. I asked Beta about this, and she told me it was for protection in the violent wind storms caused by climate change. For the same reason, there were no large trees around the houses.

Between the settlements were areas of forest and marsh. The train tracks were the only sign of civilization. The tracks were elevated about ten feet above the surrounding land with numerous underpasses for drainage and to allow animals to cross. Beta pointed out a series of electrified wires that kept animals from wandering onto the tracks and disrupting the smooth running of the system. Their transportation system was a marvel of efficiency unlike in my own time.

We exited on a covered station platform and walked through the outer reaches of settlement 424. The day was sunny and mild. Traces of a heavy rain the night before still clung to the leaves of the many flowering plants lining the walkway. The air was fresh and pleasantly perfumed by their blossoms. Groves of fruit and nut trees filled the space between the settlement and the train station, isolating the homes from the train's noise. It gave the impression of a pleasant village, a place I'd want to live in. I was surprised as we approached the settlement center to see three buildings much larger than the rest and commented on them.

One, she said, was the settlement administration building. It had offices, schools, daycare for the younger children and a meeting hall where Beta said I'd be introduced to the settlement's adults on the next Day 7. Next to it was a rooming house or dormitory where individuals not in contract partnerships stayed. Each, she said, had a large room. There were common recreation areas, and they shared kitchen duties.

"What if a person would rather live by themselves in a house?" I asked.

She gave me the puzzled look I was becoming familiar with. "That would limit their chance of finding a partner. Children carry on the community. Everyone wants a chance to raise children." She turned away, but I could hear her mutter, "If they're mentally healthy."

The last and largest building was a fitness center square and functional but well-built and attractive. Beta told me many settlements shared this facility. Each settlement was allocated one special feature to attract people from other settlements and encourage mingling. One settlement might have a specialty store, one a theater. This facility had a gym and pool. We detoured to take a better look.

As we rounded a corner of the building, a woman at the pool rushed to the full-length windows and waved a greeting to Beta. The woman was in her thirties, attractive, well-proportioned and a true redhead. I could be certain since she was stark naked. Behind her, a pair of late teenage boys snapped towels at each other's fully exposed family jewels. I must have swayed since Beta came to my side and inquired about my health. I think I stammered, "They're naked."

Her look betrayed her confusion. "Of course. This is the pool." As if that explained everything.

"No one wears swimsuits?" Her frown showed me she didn't understand. "A small item of clothing worn while swimming."

She shook her head. "I've never heard of such a thing."

Through the wall of windows, swimmers were on display to all who walked by. People of all ages and both sexes wandered about fully exposed. "No one went around naked in public in my time. Your people don't wander the streets naked."

"No. There are times and places to wear clothes and others where it's appropriate to be naked. At the pool, we're naked. That's another aspect of this society you'll need to adjust to."

The teenage boys, who'd attempted to neuter each other with their towels, put an arm around each other and walked to the single entrance of what must be the shower room. "One of many things. Let me guess; there's only one shower room."

Beta was again perplexed. "Why would there be more than one?"

"I guess there wouldn't be—here."

We continued our walk. Beta's house was single-story and painted in some combination of the half-a-dozen colors that appeared to be the acceptable pallet. I noticed that the houses' front yards had small gardens instead of lawns. Her garden included some lovely antique roses, lettuces, cabbage and very healthy tomatoes. I was pleased I recognized most of the plants. She didn't bother with a key at the front door, and I could see no trace of a lock. We entered a living room with two couches and a pair of comfortable-looking wooden rocking chairs. All appeared worn but sturdy. A larger version of the tablet hung on one wall. The whole place was charming and I immediately felt at home here.

A girl in her early teens rushed to hug Beta. The two women shared long, wavy brown hair and oval faces, but the rest of the girl's features more resembled those of the man who stood in the adjacent kitchen. He was taller than me, about 6' 2", with chiseled features and short, slightly receding sandy brown hair. Beta kissed the man and brought both to me.

"This is Don Marlboro. Don, this is my daughter Tish 424." Tish bowed and made a halting greeting in the English her mother must have taught her. Having learned that bowing was their standard greeting, I reciprocated and thanked her in English.

"And this is Cal 121." The man held out his hand to me. His handshake was tenuous, but I appreciated the gesture. He spoke to Beta, who translated. "Cal needs to add an application to your tablet."

I handed him the device, which I now kept in my shirt pocket. Cal spent a few seconds touching the screen and longer waiting for something to download. Then he placed the tablet back in my pocket and spoke. "The tablet," the tablet said as Cal spoke, "should now do most good translate of what said."

Ignoring the poor grammar, I was ecstatic. "This is wonderful. Does it also translate back?" The tablet answered my question by emitting a string of their language. They were all quite pleased.

Cal fairly beamed. "Translation will improve over time. University works on improved vocabulary and grammar, and program learns."

"It's clear enough for me to understand."

"Good," Beta said. "I need to get back to work. I didn't feel I could leave you if you couldn't speak to anyone."

We moved to the dining room with a round table and six chairs. Cal had prepared dinner. It proved tasty. The vegetables I recognized from their garden, the main course might have been chicken.

I found that talking at the table was acceptable. "I have to thank you all for your generosity. Your kindness in taking me in is overwhelming."

Cal seemed almost embarrassed. "It is our pleasure to sponsor you."

His friendliness made me comfortable enough to question him. "Why are you Cal 121 instead of 424?"

He smiled and forced himself not to laugh. "None of the adult males in this settlement are originally from it. Every boy leaves his home settlement when he is 14. Our son is in settlement 343."

I didn't have to ask why; my shock was apparent. Beta explained, "Our settlements are small. Everyone is related. The children are raised together, like siblings. Matings would be out of the question. It would be like incest. Exogamous marriage has always been typical in village societies."

"I guess I can understand that." My understanding was tenuous at best.

Cal continued. "When the new society was set up, the choice was made to move males before they became sexually active, so every boy is transplanted to a new settlement when he reaches 14. The system is designed to rebuild camaraderie among the new males in a settlement. Two are always sent at the same time. They room together at school and have mentors from their new settlement who are two years older to guide them through the transition. All the transplanted males attend school together and play games and sports with each other. They also spend weekends with a sponsor family, generally a family whose son left a few years before." He became quiet, as if reflecting. "It takes a few years before a family is ready to sponsor. You will see our sponsor son in a few days. And our biological son, Jon, will be home for the Fall Harvest Celebration in a month."

"He can visit?"

Cal nodded. "Yes, but he cannot live here. He is already very attached to a girl in his high school. I am surprised he still comes back."

"How old is he?"

Beta looked wistful. "Eighteen this year. He'll be in college soon. I wish we could teach him, but 343 is too far to commute to school. Besides, his interests don't lie with the social sciences –our local college's specialty. He'll be a brilliant engineer someday."

"I'm glad to see maternal pride is still intact."

Beta laughed. "And always will be."

Cal smiled. "Paternal pride as well. He is a fine boy."

Tish injected, "I love my brother, too."

I smiled at Tish. "No doubt. Do you like the boy your family is sponsoring?"

Tish's gaze grew distant, almost dreamy. "He is very nice."

"You may have seen him," Beta said, "at the pool when we walked by. He and his mentor were engaging in silly games. Luke 89 was the shorter."

"And if he keeps on like that," I said, "he'll never have sons of his own."

Beta chuckled, Cal was confused, and Tish looked mildly alarmed.

Cal said, "We only have three bedrooms, so you will have to share with Luke and Jon when they are here."

I shrugged. "I suppose that'll give me a chance to learn about your society from a different perspective."

Beta patted me on the arm. "A very positive attitude."

AFTER DINNER, Cal and I took the vegetable scraps to the compost bin in their backyard garden. The backyard stretched for about fifty feet. There were gravel paths, raised beds for vegetables and flowers, several small fruit trees, a shed and a wooden bench. There were no fences between the houses, but the owners used trellises covered with vines to demarcate their property lines and give themselves privacy. I took the opportunity to question Cal privately. "When we walked by the pool, I noticed Luke and his mentor ...."

"Jason," Cal added.

"Yes, Luke and Jason putting their arms around each other while they were … naked. I know times have changed, but are those two boys … gay?"

Cal frowned. "They both seem happy. I must not be understanding you."

"Homosexual. Are they homosexual?"

The tablet took longer than usual to translate this. Cal motioned me to the bench where we sat together. "The term you used does not have an exact corollary in our language. I will have to defer to the anthropologists at the college for a complete answer. However, I think the general answer is no. Tomorrow, you will meet the head of the college's anthropology department. She can tell you more about the differences between your culture and ours. My specialty is cybernetics. I can help you interact with people using your tablet, but I do not know enough about your time to answer many of your questions." We got up and walked back to the house. "You will like Luke. He is a very personable young man."

"Your daughter seems to like him."

"Yes. Sometimes I think too much."

I laughed. "She has a crush on him." The tablet balked at the translation. "An excessive youthful infatuation that will probably pass with time."

Cal nodded. "Yes. We call it a heart flutter."

"Very apt."

～

IN THE MORNING, we walked Tish to her school in the administration building and then set off at a brisk pace to the train station. Standing on the platform, somewhat winded, I asked them about the absence of vehicles.

"For what?" Cal asked.

"Oh, for instance, to get to the train station."

Cal laughed. "No one uses a vehicle within the settlement. Look around; the pathways are primarily designed for pedestrian traffic."

The sidewalks were broad and inviting but, as he said, not adequate for regular vehicle traffic.

"Only emergency vehicles, cargo trucks, and transport for the disabled are allowed within the settlement," he said.

Cal gave me a thorough visual examination. At a shade under six feet and 180 pounds, I wasn't fat, but I did have the start of a belly.

"Walking is good exercise," he said, "and you look like you could use more. We will have to get you to the gym."

I worked out when I was younger, but the pressures of family and my business career didn't leave time as life progressed. It might be good to start again, but the single locker room made me shiver.

The train, this time, was crowded with college students. The morning wasn't warm, but the students wore shorts and t-shirts tight enough to emphasize their assets. I turned off the translation app on the tablet to stifle the cacophony. All college students say the same things—loudly.

Beta left me in the outer office of the head of the anthropology department. The room was modest, with a few chairs and a device to announce your presence to the department head. Beta took care of that, as the machine was alien to me. As I waited, I heard an animated conversation behind the door that wasn't clear enough for the tablet to translate. The conversation ceased, and the door opened. A woman, probably in her sixties, with gray hair in a ponytail, wearing a cardigan sweater and black slacks (it struck me that I hadn't seen a skirt since I awoke) approached and, to my pleasant surprise, greeted me in strained but understandable English. "Greetings, Mr. Marlboro." She bowed.

I returned her bow. "Don, please."

"Don, I'm Alexa 420. Please, come into my office." She escorted me in, hand on my arm in a gesture I would have considered intimate if I hadn't been instructed in some of their social norms by Beta. She sat beside me without the bulk of her desk between us. "There is much we need to talk about, not the least, why you were revived."

I felt immediate apprehension. "It wasn't just an act of altruism?"

"There is altruism involved, but more than that, we want to understand the customs, institutions and motivations of the people of your time. You are an opportunity, a window on a time lost to us through the deprivations of a hellish Dark Age. We're still in the grips of some of the worst of what your generation wrought. Most of the coastline of your era is still submerged along with your greatest cities. Our records show that your generation knew the havoc they were about to cause and did nothing. We want to find out why.

You are a person who might help us understand. That is why we undertook the expensive process of reviving you."

She sat back in her chair. "Of course, having revived you, we can't compel your cooperation. We hope you'll comply out of a sense of gratitude or duty to humanity, but if you don't, we will still take care of you and try to see that you are comfortable and, to whatever extent possible, happy."

I thought about her proposal for a few seconds and saw an opportunity. "I'll gladly cooperate, but I'd like one concession—I want a Bible."

"Oh." She pursed her lips. "That's going to be difficult."

"That's what Damien 285 told me."

She nodded. "I understand his reluctance. Our society appears prosperous, but our existence is marginal. It takes a fairly large population to support our level of technology. We barely have enough people. We can't afford to lose people, nor do we have the resources to accommodate many more. Everyone must cooperate for society to function. Anything that divides, polarizes, or disenfranchises any of us is a threat to all of us. Religion is just such a force. We cannot allow superstitions to threaten society."

Having my deeply held beliefs termed "superstition" annoyed me, but I tried to think of a compromise. Business was supposed to be my skill, and I was failing in this negotiation. "What if I was the only one who could read it?" I pulled the tablet from my pocket. "Couldn't this be set to detect the presence of someone else in a room so only I could read it? The Bible comforts me; it gives me strength."

She paused, thinking, then sat down. "I'll consult the Council. They might agree if you agree not to proselytize."

"I've never been a preacher. I don't see how I could convert anyone now. I'll agree to that."

"I'll see what I can do. In the meantime, I understand you have some questions about our society. Cal 121 said you tried to ask him a question about the boy his family is sponsoring, but the translator couldn't find the words to express your concept."

"Yes, I wanted to know if the boy and his mentor were homosexual. I saw them in the pool area with their arms around each other while naked. I understand that nudity is appropriate in your culture, but no young man in my time would embrace another man naked unless they were homosexual."

She took a long breath as she composed her answer. "As for nudity taboos, we have our own; they're just different from your society's. We also have our own rules of social distance. Men in our time regularly embrace even when naked. It's normal behavior among male friends, which would, naturally, include a mentor and his charge who've been together for more than a year."

She turned to me. "Now to the harder question: homosexuality. The concept exists in our culture, but not with the stigma that it had in yours. Both men and women in our society often have sexual encounters with others of the same gender. The two young men you referred to probably do have sex with each other and others in their cohort. That's part of how these displaced boys bond with each other to form a cohesive social group."

I must have shown my disgust.

"Such behavior would have been aberrant in your time. It's normal now. And it bears no relation to whether the young men will eventually form relationships with women. Very few men in our society are exclusively homosexual. I do not doubt that both young men have *girlfriends,* as it's so quaintly put in English."

"All the men are switch hitters?" I instantly realized that the phrase was too colloquial. "Bisexual."

"Effectively, yes, but we've found that is completely natural. This is just one of many differences between your society and ours. We also don't marry for life; we contract partnerships to raise children. Such contracts don't involve strict exclusivity."

I must have shown my surprise again.

"We found strict monogamy didn't work, so couples may have relationships outside their family contract without nullifying that commitment."

"Doesn't that result in jealousy?"

"Jealousy exists but is frowned on. Most men and women have multiple partners but stay with their contract partner until their children are grown."

"This is going to take some mental adjustment on my part."

She put a hand on my shoulder. "No doubt." She got up. "Why don't you have lunch with Beta? I'll work on your Bible question."

I stood and offered her my hand. "Thank you."

She looked at it for a second, then took it, shaking it tentatively. "What a quaint way of greeting."

"I'm surprised it didn't survive."

"With the plagues, personal contact was a route for contagion. That's why bowing was adopted worldwide."

~

AN UNFORTUNATE CONSEQUENCE of egalitarianism was not having a faculty dining facility. Beta and I ate at an outside table under the shade of an ancient Acacia tree to avoid the noise. "I know," Beta said after I told her about my talk with her boss, "from studying anthropology, that religion can be a powerful force motivating individuals and societies. Still, you should be able to tell by its complete absence that it has no validity."

"You haven't had a born-again experience. It is more real than real, the ultimate proof of God's existence."

"I've had enough courses in human physiology to know the brain chemistry involved in ecstatic experiences. They aren't real, Don. They're the byproduct of dopamine, oxytocin, serotonin and a stew of other brain chemicals out of balance. Similar experiences can be achieved with psychedelics, but that won't change your mind, so let's talk about something else."

"Do you mind talking about sex?"

She was only moderately surprised. "No."

"Does everyone have sex with everyone else?"

She laughed. "No. We aren't exclusive, but that doesn't mean we're promiscuous. I know from history that your society made a show of pure monogamy and failed miserably. You were married?"

"Twice."

"Did you ever have sex with anyone other than your wives while married?"

I must have colored. "Yes, and it destroyed my first marriage and alienated me from my children." The reality struck me. "They've been dead nearly three hundred years."

Beta held my hand. "I'm sorry, Don." She waited for my reverie to pass. "Don, we weren't designed to be rigorously monogamous. The two ape species most closely related to us had sex often and promiscuously. Whenever we've tried as a species to hold to strict monogamy, we've failed or driven ourselves to extremes in the process. People today separate child-rearing from sexual exclusivity. Cal and I are raising two children. If Cal has an encounter on the side, that wouldn't abrogate his family responsibilities. The same goes for me. After the children are raised, we may decide to stay together, or we may not. Only time will tell."

"I cannot get my mind around that. I wouldn't want my wife having sex with anyone but me."

"How does that threaten you?"

"It says she loves someone else."

"And if she does, so what? Did you love one child less when you had another? We're capable of loving many people in different ways, and sex is part of how we bond with those people."

"But what if Cal had sex with another man?"

"He does from time to time. His cohort still takes camping trips together, and I understand they involve a lot of sex. I'm glad they're still close."

I shook my head. " I can't fathom that."

She shook her head. "Get used to it, Don. That's the world you live in now. There are plenty of other differences."

My stomach was churning. I needed to get off this topic. "Like what?" I asked, hoping to divert the conversation.

"Unlike in your time, everyone helps raise the settlement's children. Don't be surprised if you arrive home to find the house filled with children. Tish often brings home younger children to take care of until their parents return. You'll be expected to help care for any child you encounter. You don't get to say the child is someone else's responsibility. You have to do your share."

My lunch was cold, and I was no longer hungry. "I don't know if I can adapt to this."

Beta took my hand again. "I suspect you'll find that you're more adaptable than you thought possible."

BETA LEFT me in Alexa's outer office. Cal dropped by and asked for my tablet. A short while later, he returned and handed it to me without comment. I inspected it and saw no change. Checking the library, I found a new entry entitled *KJV* and opened it. "In the beginning," it read. I nearly cried. Returning to the index, I pulled up Matthew. Alexa entered the room, and the tablet returned to its opening screen. "It works," I said. "Thank you."

She squatted by my chair. "If this makes you happy for the interim, fine, but you still need to make peace with reality and give up on your fantasies. Remember, at the first sign of proselytizing, you will be sent into exile. You don't want that. So don't talk publicly about your beliefs."

∼

I MANAGED to take the train with minimal assistance. Alexa wrote the name of my stop and the train's name in their script. I couldn't read the Bible on the train, so I went back to Teller's history, looking for details of this society's origins. At the end of the Dark Age, following the warming and floods, a virulent plague began wiping out the last of humanity. A group of researchers in North America found a cure. They gave the scattered remnants of humanity a choice: Resettle in North America and form an entirely new society there, or die. A surprising number chose death. The survivors examined the best scientific evidence for human behavior and created this society based on those principles.

I checked the maps and found humanity had recolonized temperate portions of all the continents except Antarctica, which was expected to eventually refreeze. Tropical areas were avoided as being too hot for survival. Given the horrendous level of disruption and destruction, I was amazed they'd recovered this much in three centuries.

∼

HAVE you ever felt personally blamed for the worst disaster that ever befell humanity? That was the tenor of my interviews the next day with the historians. The grueling interrogation went on for several hours. "Why?" they kept asking as if I, a simple businessman, could understand the workings of history, science and sociology. I was left shell-shocked and depressed, wondering if the bargain I'd made with the devil was worth it.

∼

THE WEEKEND HAD ARRIVED. Just before dinner, the front door burst open, and the young man I'd last seen in a naked embrace with his mentor popped through the door, fully clothed. It looked as if he'd only rolled his pant legs down when he got to the porch. Tish ran up and embraced him. The young man, who, at about 5' 10", was a shade taller than Tish, picked her up and swung her around enough times to make me dizzy. "How is my best girl?" he crooned, kissing her forehead.

"I'm fine, Luke," she said, tottering as he put her down.

Both Beta and Cal embraced the boy. He appeared genuinely happy to be with them. I took the initiative and bowed. "I'm pleased to meet you."

He returned the bow. "I have heard a lot about you."

Beta smiled. "News travels fast in a small community."

"Part of the reason I liked big cities."

"Where did you live?" Luke asked, intensely curious.

"In San Francisco. I understand the whole area is now just a chain of islands."

"How many people lived there?" he asked.

"Millions."

Luke's eyes were wide. "You are joking."

Beta shook her head. "He isn't. There were lots of cities with a million or more people."

I nodded. "A few with as many as 20 million."

Luke moved to my side and took my arm. I tried not to cringe, knowing this level of intimacy was normal now. He didn't seem to notice my discomfort. He was, after all, a teenager. "Was San Francisco like living here?"

I smiled at the thought. "Not even close. How many of the people in this settlement do you know?"

Luke shrugged. "All of them."

"You couldn't do that in a city of a million."

"Or," Beta added, "in a city of a thousand. That's why settlement size is limited."

"Do you think I would have liked living in a big city?" Luke asked.

I looked at him, and beneath that nearly adult exterior was a wide-eyed child. "Probably not."

∾

To MY SURPRISE, dinner included a glass of wine. Cal served the three adults and Luke four ounces, and Tish had a two-ounce glass. The first sip was a formalized ceremony (the equivalent of a toast) in which everyone around the table raised their glass and took a small sip. The vintage wasn't Chateau Margot, but it was better than some I'd experienced. Water was also served. The wine was only an extension of the dinner, sipped, savored.

"I'm surprised to see even the youngest partake in the wine," I said.

Beta looked up from her plate. "The very youngest are given grape juice. Around seven, a little wine is blended with the juice. Until they're fourteen, they don't get a full glass. Adults may have two glasses."

"A fairly rigid system," I said.

Beta nodded. "Alcohol can be a problem. Having a tradition that limits it to meals and special occasions helps, as does introducing it gradually. Even with safeguards, there's some abuse. Banning it outright was deemed useless and counterproductive since it's too easy to make."

"You're allowed only wine?"

Cal looked up. "And beer."

The wine mellowed the meal. The family caught up on Luke's life, and I even managed to make my morning interview sound humorous.

After dinner, Cal called up a documentary about the submarine exploration of San Francisco. I ended up fighting back tears at the sight of my drowned hometown. Tish sat on the couch, head on Luke's chest, his arm around her shoulders.

At bedtime, I was relieved to find these people didn't sleep in the nude. That had more to do with energy efficiency than modesty. Even with the overall warming, it can get chilly at night. That, of course, didn't stop Luke from stripping as soon as the two of us were in the bedroom and then brushing his teeth, washing his face and using the john, all with the bathroom door open, before he slipped into his nightshirt. Luke was athletic and, at nearly 16, physically mature enough to be sprouting chest hair. I tried not to be too circumspect while changing into my nightshirt.

Once in bed and without my discomfort at his openness, I could see that Luke was a handsome young man with a mild case of teenage acne and curly black hair longer than the male norm in this settlement. In trying to determine his ethnic ancestry from his appearance, it struck me that no one here fit precisely into any racial or ethnic categories from my time. All seemed blended into a look that was, at once, none and all of the types from my day. Skin tone was darker, light brown to olive. Noses were less prominent than the most extreme of the past while never dainty. Cheekbones were higher. Eyes had a trace of an epicanthic fold. Hair tended to be dark but varied and was often curly. The new norm was a blend—intentional, I suspected, and pleasing.

The wine must have mellowed both of us. I let my concern about Tish's infatuation slip.

Luke rolled over to face me. "I know. I don't want to have sex with her. She's more like the girls in my old settlement."

"Like a sister."

"Yes. It would be unclean." The translator paused on the last word. I suspected the word he'd used was slang. That gave me a faint glimmer of hope —teens could still manage to subvert the perfect language of this place. Human freedom was not totally dead. "Every girl in my home settlement feels related to me. We all went to the same childcare and schools and played together. I like Tish the same way I did them."

"It must be nice to have a family of sorts here."

"It's better than if I didn't, but they're not like my birth family. I think they should have waited a year or two longer before they sponsored a son—they're still too close to Jon to fully accept another boy. I'm not saying they don't try to be good foster parents; they do. I just feel some distance." He turned over. "I know people who never had children that take in sponsor sons. They bond better than the ones looking for a replacement son. I'll never be Jon. They're starting to accept that."

"Have you met Jon?"

"We overlap sometimes. He's a great guy. I like him. We've shared this room, even shared a bed a few times." I tried not to cringe. "You'll get to meet Jon at the Festival. I'll return to my home settlement to visit my birth parents. They're still together, although their contract could have ended when I was transplanted. They haven't sponsored another boy; they're going to wait until I'm settled here."

"Where do you stay during the week?"

"The high school dorms. Isn't that how it worked in your time?"

"No. Most kids … " (the translator must have said young goats judging by how wide Luke's eyes grew) "children lived at home with their parents until they went to college. Some stayed through college. Some longer. Of course, with our population densities, we could build high schools close to where people lived."

"That would be nice, but here, each settlement only has about eight high school students, so nearby settlements share a high school built in an area between settlements, so all the students are treated the same. The male dorms are sectioned by settlement to get the guys to bond with each other. The female dorms mix girls from different settlements to help them get to know each other better."

"Is anyone else from your birth settlement at the high school?"

"No. Overlap isn't allowed during high school. They want all the guys to be strangers who have to get to know each other."

"To increase the chances of bonding."

"Right. Everyone's a stranger. We help each other out. When I got here, I was assigned Jason as my mentor. He helped me adjust. Jason is great. He met me at the train station with one of the psychologists when I first got to school. I was scared and lonely after sitting on the train, staring out the window most of a day. Jason came rushing up to me with his arms open as soon as he saw me leave the train. He's taller than me. His coat was open. He enveloped me in it, rocking me. Then he whispered, 'I was here two years ago. I know how frightened you are. I'll keep you safe.' I started crying. He held me till I was over it. The psychologist didn't come over and introduce herself until we'd finished. It made a huge difference."

"Sounds like a great guy."

"You'll get to meet him. I'll mentor a new boy next year. This year, I'm mentoring Pat, one of the 13-year-olds in the settlement, to prepare him for his transfer. We spend part of the weekends together. I tell him what to expect and answer his questions. A guy gets really nervous just before the transfer. They spend time with the settlement psychologist, too."

I could imagine what part of the mentoring involved and didn't want to go there. "I can see how the transfer would be traumatic. I'm surprised most of you adapt so well."

He grew quiet. "Some don't. One of the guys walked off campus last year and jumped in front of a train. It hurt us all. We get close. His mentor was so broken up about it that the school psychologists finally sent him for treatment. He never came back. The guy's roommate was too nervous to mentor a new student. That settlement lost a year's worth of boys."

"How do they make it up?"

"They can bring in three new ones for a couple of years, but then they have to find mentors for the extra ones. Mostly, they fill in with transfers. There's always a guy who does something stupid at his first settlement that he can never live down. They get counseling and are resettled. They generally work out in their second settlement, even if they're a few years older than the one they replace. They try hard not to repeat. The *counseling* gets rougher each time. We're forbidden to ask them why they transferred, and that is enforced." He turned out the light. "You'll probably get to see the high school someday. All the adults from the surrounding settlements take turns as dorm parents. They know what would happen if they left us alone too long."

"No doubt."

THE NEXT MORNING the alarm went off (these people don't sleep in on weekends), and Luke hopped out of bed, yawned and doffed the nightshirt, revealing how much of a man he was before he went to the bathroom. It was evident he had no sense of modesty with his roommate. I dressed before he returned to the room.

Later, Cal and Luke decided I needed to start going to the gym. I was close to Cal's age, but everyone agreed I looked much older. I was out of shape, needed to lose weight and tighten up everywhere.

Weekend gym was part of the bonding regimen for sponsor fathers and sons and the settlement's men. Somewhere in the distant past, someone decided that there was nothing better than athletic games and sweaty grunting over iron weights to get the local men in sync with each other. Cal and Luke performed this ritual religiously. I was now included. I could have declined, but they would have taken that as a rejection. I liked the two of them and felt obliged because of their hospitality, so I agreed.

I was pleased that only the gym's pool and locker room were a nudist camp. The rest of the gym required an outfit like that worn in my own time. That meant a trip to the store.

The only store in the settlement was centrally located, small and logically arranged. It contained food, clothing and sundries departments. Large items were ordered and delivered, as was anything not stocked in the store but available in the supply chain. I couldn't fit into Cal's gym shorts, so we picked up a pair in my size, along with gym shoes and a nondescript t-shirt. I would have preferred something with a logo like, "I traveled to the future, and all I got was this stupid t-shirt," but such was not the style of these times. Even the colors were limited. At the checkout, I scanned the clothes, and Cal had me wave my tablet in front of the scanner. "Is this like money?" I asked.

"It's to avoid hoarding," Cal said.

They allowed me to change into my gym clothes before leaving but informed me I'd have to shower in the locker room afterward. They said I had to adjust to this and should do it now. They were adamant. I bowed to the inevitable.

Decked in my new finery and with a bag of clothes and towel in hand, we proceeded to the gym. Once there, Cal and Luke each took one of my arms and guided me through the locker room door. The room was large and filled with people this weekend day. Families, young and old people circulated in various stages of dress and undress without a hint of sexual connotation. We found open lockers and deposited our bags. There was no mechanism to lock the *lockers*.

By the time we left the room, my initial shock was abating.

In the weight room, we met half a dozen other men and their sponsor sons from ours and other nearby settlements. They embraced in a fashion that made me uncomfortable. Luke hugged and picked a small, lanky boy up off the ground, who I would later learn was his mentee, Pat. Not to be outdone, Jason, who was nearly as tall and muscular as Cal, did the same to Luke, much to Pat's amusement. Cal must have warned the others as they made their introductions with bows.

Cal and Luke had a circuit they followed, mainly using free weights. The weights and the exercises seemed to have changed little from my era. They integrated me into their routine, adjusting the weights for my scrawny musculature. Both of them and all of the other father and sponsor-son pairs were in exceedingly better shape than me. The oldest person in the weight room could do double the weight I managed. Two hours of this left me sore in places I didn't know I had, bone-tired and smelling like a caveman.

As we left the weight room, I found I was walking with Luke in front and Cal behind me, effectively blocking my path to the door. We reentered the locker room, and my companions undressed. I sighed and did the same.

Even though a very attractive woman also showered, I finished without embarrassment. I shook my head as I grabbed my towel. "I am so sore," I said, but since my tablet was in the locker, I had to pantomime to convey the meaning. Luke took my arm and led me through a passageway. I found myself in the pool area, wet, naked and exposed to the world. Luke pointed to the hot tub and got in. Being submerged was better than standing in front of the windows, so I followed. The tub was what my sore muscles needed.

I watched the parade of humanity walk by and found it growing more and more normal. I still worried about the moral implications but resigned myself that it was customary. After a time, Luke tapped me on the shoulder, I nodded, and we exited the pool area, rinsed, toweled off, dressed and went home. I had adjusted.

The following morning, I could barely move. Luke had to help me out of bed. His solution to the problem was stretching, so he doffed his nightshirt and started showing me the moves. I didn't hesitate and did the same.

THE SEVENTH DAY of the week was special to this society. Like Sunday in my time, everyone got together, but unlike my time's *day of rest*, they gathered in work clothes to perform community service. After breakfast, we went to the Community Center.

The youngest children went to daycare. Luke also went to the daycare center as part of his parenting training and would spend the afternoon mentoring Pat. He said he and Jason would take Pat to a local pond to swim. I didn't want to think about what that would turn into.

The rest of us gathered in the main hall of the Community Center. The semicircular, tiered auditorium was large enough to hold the entire population of the settlement. As the families entered, I noticed many had three children. I asked Beta about this.

"Some people never contract to have children, and some are sterile."

"Isn't everyone expected to contract?"

Beta shrugged. "It's expected, but some people either don't want children or never find the right partner. If a person doesn't contract by their late twenties, the government may move them to another settlement to encourage them to find a contract partner, but you can't be forced to contract, so there are always openings for families to have a third child. Also, if the government has plans to build new settlements, they'll approve extra births."

Before work assignments, a local official (in the role of preacher) appeared to exhort the assembly about the bond of fellowship shared within this community and its necessary expressions in mutual respect and service to one another.

Then everyone stood, put their arms around the waists of the people next to them and sang. I only caught part of the words, but the song was simple and repetitive, and the music powerful and uplifting. The group sang, swayed and became one resounding voice, young and old. The leader whipped up the crowd, calling them to sing with their whole hearts in good fellowship. Even I was swept into the ecstatic mood of the event, moving to the music, wishing I could sing along. It reminded me of singing in church. I couldn't help but think they'd stolen their ceremonies in a blatant attempt to co-opt the power of true worship.

The leader followed this by asking several people to come forward to the podium, where she recognized them for jobs well done or promotions. The community cheered and, buoyed by ecstatic feelings from the songs, shouted praise and encouragement to each.

The next part Beta had coached me on. I was taken before the group and introduced. The entire community stood, bowed and welcomed me in unison. I returned their bow and thanked them, using a three-word phrase I'd memorized that meant, "I join with you."

Following my initiation into the community, the people went to assignment tables and were given a work task for the morning. Someone must have warned them that I wasn't in good shape, as they placed me with the senior citizens.

That evening at supper, I asked the family about the recognition ceremony during the morning's meeting.

"In your time," Beta said, "money provided the incentive for good service. We no longer have that, so we've substituted praise and public recognition. That and promotion are what we have to induce our people to work to their fullest. Bad performance can have negative consequences and demotions, but we try to keep incentives positive."

"Do you think they work as well as money?" I asked.

She sat for a moment, immersed in her thoughts. "Probably not. Money had an immediacy and impact that praise doesn't. Most truly egalitarian societies in the past were static. They had no incentive for progress. It's a risk we've had to accept."

Cal added. "There are perks, like extra training and education for the best workers. They also give excellent workers extra vacations. We got one last year. Beta loves touring the ruins of old cities. We visited Chicago."

Beta looked slightly embarrassed. "It helps me understand the culture, but I don't think it's much fun for the rest of the family."

"They took me along," Luke said, "and I enjoyed it. We got to see some of the huge churches your people used to build. They were impressive, but it seemed like a waste of resources."

I thought about the last time I went to the Windy City, so vibrant and alive, now a ruin. "It's all a matter of where you place your priorities."

AT THE START of the week, we dropped Tish at school, and the four of us went to the train station. We sent Luke off to his school, and I even hugged him. I arrived at the college with some trepidation, not ready for another grilling by the historians. Instead of academics, I found Damien 285. He rose and bowed as I walked into the room where last week's interview occurred.

"Please, take a seat, Mr. Marlboro." I sat. He paced. "I have come to apologize. I have informed the historians that you are not responsible for the events of your time. You were a simple, low-level participant, not an instigator. Their treatment of you was undignified and unprofessional. It will not happen again. Your information can be valuable in understanding the past. We don't want to insult and alienate you."

"Thank you. It wasn't pleasant."

Damien sat. "I hope your experience in our time is otherwise pleasant."

"It is. Beta and her family have tried to integrate me into their life and aid my adjustment. Some aspects have been difficult, but I'm managing."

"Good. They're fine people. Young Luke has a strong aptitude for leadership. I hope he'll consider government service someday."

"It'll be a while before he can run for office."

Damien stared at me. "Run?"

"Become a candidate for elected office."

"Oh, you're referring to republican democracies."

"Yes."

Damien shook his head. "We don't have that type of government. All offices are appointed. The best from lower government ranks are promoted to higher ranks as the offices are vacated. Our government is a meritocracy. Republics proved too inefficient. When change was needed to counteract climate deterioration, for instance, republics proved incapable of promptly making tough decisions. That was almost always the case. Our system can make those tough decisions and implement them because our leadership is judged on longer-term measures of performance rather than the short-term whims of the undereducated masses." He smiled. "And even in this society, the masses aren't capable of making good, long-term decisions. Your own Alexander Hamilton said, 'the masses are asses,' and he was correct. Mass psychology and group hysteria are not ways to make informed, rational decisions. Our leaders are trained to take in facts, recognize trends, and learn not to discount our emotions, in order to make the best decisions, and to live with and even savor ambiguity. And no one rules alone; all offices are councils. This creates a system that promotes good decision-making without the arbitrary and repressive tactics employed in a dictatorship."

I felt like I needed to be the devil's advocate for their supposed paradise. "It sounds like you're constantly looking over your shoulder, afraid someone below you will push you out so they can get your position. Why would anyone pursue a government career under those pressures?"

"People who rise by trampling on others soon find themselves relegated to the fringes of our society. Individuals who worm their way to the top tend to make decisions that benefit themselves rather than society. They don't last. As for why we pursue this career..." Damien ticked the reasons off on his fingers. "Love of power: Even if the power is limited, it's still real. Prestige: We're only human, and no matter how egalitarian our society seems, there are gradations, and we will always try to achieve the highest of those we can attain. An excellent retirement program: It may not seem like much to someone from your time, but it's a nice perk. And last: The knowledge that you have done good for your fellow beings and the Earth." He sat back. "The last is by far the best."

"That sounds like a highly idealized vision."

Damien nodded. "Probably true. We never quite live up to that idealized model, but we still do a better job than any republic."

"I'm surprised that the will of the people hasn't overthrown your regime."

Damien chuckled. "The people love us because we've brought them peace, stability and freedom from want. We're also scrupulously honest—not because we're moral supermen, but because the system is riddled with checks to ensure we don't take advantage of our positions. Also, the entire population knows which governmental body evaluates a given leadership level and can register complaints anonymously if they wish. At the settlement level, there's a citizen's advisory council filled on a rotating basis to aid and evaluate the settlement council, and every level of government is required to have regularly scheduled open meetings to accept citizen input. We have the advantages of representative government without the problems. It's not a perfect system. It can be played, but it's the best humanity has ever devised." He stood. "We can, perhaps, pursue this discussion further at another date. For now, I have pressing engagements as you'd expect of a government officer." He bowed and left.

Whatever Damien said to the historians, the rest of the week's interviews were probing but cordial. By the middle of the week, they included me in their lunch plans. I was no longer the cause of the great disaster; I was an interesting individual and on the way to being a valued research subject.

A MONTH LATER, school broke for the Fall Harvest Festival. We waited at the station for Jon's arrival and Luke's departure. Tish spent most of the wait tucked under Luke's arm. While we waited, Luke described the differences between settlements 89 and 424. "89 is much older. The houses are smaller and share common walls, not free-standing like here. There's no room to garden in our yards, so we have plots in a common area. The trees are huge, which is helpful since 89 is further south, and we need the shade." He turned to me and smiled. "You'd have even more trouble adjusting there since everyone sleeps in the nude because of the heat."

I laughed. I'd come to like the young man.

He continued, "They're mostly farmers, but my father leads the settlement council, and Mother is a teacher. I'll bring back some yams. We grow the biggest ones you've ever seen. I remember getting out of school before Harvest Festival to work with the rest of the settlement getting in the harvest. They don't do that here."

Cal shook his head. "All the crops grown around here can be harvested by machines. Jon does some harvesting at his settlement."

A train arrived, and a young man, my height, thin, athletic and handsome, departed. He resembled Beta. Tish ran to him, and they embraced. Jon embraced his parents and went to Luke, giving him a long embrace and sitting with him, arms around each other, inquiring how his life in the settlement was going. Jon spent the entire time until Luke's train arrived talking exclusively to his replacement. I was struck by this act of generosity: Jon was emphasizing to his family how integral he wanted Luke to be. They embraced again as the train arrived, and the other family members, including me, added our embraces.

Jon was finally introduced to me formally, and we exchanged bows. I didn't talk to him until evening as we prepared for bed. I noted that his habits were similar to Luke's, but I'd grown used to conversing with a naked roommate. We initially tried to speak English, but Jon couldn't follow me because of my accent and speed, so we used the translator. "That was very good of you," I said, "making a point of welcoming Luke."

"He isn't a rival. I think of him as a new brother. I liked him the first time I met him. I worry about mother and father not treating him like a real son."

"Your sponsor family is welcoming?"

"My sponsor mother had problems with me, but her contract was up. She decided to split with my sponsor father. I could have requested reassignment, but I stayed with my sponsor father. It's worked out well. His son is 21 and starting his own family. I've met him and visited him in his settlement. It's a good relationship. I want Luke to have as good." He finally donned his night-shirt and hopped into bed.

THE FESTIVAL STARTED LATE MORNING. Makeshift tables were placed in the settlement's common area, adorned with flowers and brightly colored cloths. Every family contributed to the potluck. Placement at the tables was random to encourage mixing, although I was allowed to stay with Beta. People ate, sang, and an official made a blessedly short speech that left everyone laughing.

Back from their exile, the young men were hugged, prodded, joked at and made to feel special and at home.

The games were new to me but looked like the kind any family would play at a get-together. Jon was on the starting line of a footrace pitting the returned young men against each other. They ran laps around the margins of the picnic area, carrying one of the younger children on their backs. The young children had a wonderful time prodding their elder brothers like they were reluctant horses. Jon did well in the race and, at his jockey's insistence, carried the boy of about five around for much of the afternoon.

That evening, I asked Jon who the boy was.

"He's my cousin Ed." Jon propped himself on his elbow. "Here's another practice that you probably won't like: by your reckoning, Ed is my brother. Mother gave birth to him with the understanding that she'd give him to her sister."

"Why?"

"Aunt Emma can't have children, so the settlement let Mother have a third child so Emma and Dan could raise one."

"It's odd by the standards of my time, but it strikes me as an act of generosity."

LIFE RETURNED to routine after the Festival. Luke returned with a bag of enormous yams, forcing a couple on Jon before he left.

School resumed. A few weekends later, Luke arrived at the station. Only this time, he exited the train on the arm of a young woman. The two shared a joke, kissed long enough to betray their sex life, and went to their respective families. Luke's hug for Tish was more correct and less playful than in the past.

Beta walked beside Luke. "Was that Jessie you were kissing?"

Luke colored slightly. "Yes. We've been seeing each other a lot lately."

Cal put an arm around the boy. "It's good you've found a local girl, but don't put too much store in high school relationships. They're volatile."

The boy was fairly beaming. "I won't, but this one might surprise you."

For Beta and Cal, this turn of events was promising. If Luke formed a strong relationship with a girl from his new settlement, it increased his chances of staying. For Tish, it was something entirely different.

The afternoon of day 6, as I recovered from the latest round of pumping iron, one of the enormous storms probably caused by global warming had blown into the area. Cal and Beta went to visit friends. My tablet volume turned low, as I often did to eavesdrop unnoticed. It caught Beta whispering to Cal how much fun it would be in the warm rain as Cal's grin widened. Luke was at Jessie's house, doing "homework." I was left alone with Tish.

Tish sat in the living room, moping. Looking at her reminded me of my daughter. I had to do something to help her. I sat beside her on the couch and put an arm around her. "What's the problem? Or do I already know?" She said nothing. "It's Luke."

She finally nodded. "I wanted him to be my first—maybe even more than that."

"I think he wants to be more of a brother to you, like Jon."

"I know, but at first, I thought it would be different with us. He's so handsome."

"He is a good-looking boy, but wouldn't it be nice to have a brother here in your settlement?"

"I suppose." She sat there for a few seconds and slowly started crying. I held her. "I can't stop thinking about him. If you hadn't been in the bedroom, I would have slipped in and gotten in bed with him."

This was the first time my presence seemed to be a benefit.

She dried her eyes. "You seem so calm. How do you do that with all you have to deal with?"

"I get comfort from my Bible." I knew I'd made a mistake as soon as the words came out of my mouth, but then it struck me that perhaps my reanimation did have a purpose. These people felt like they were living in the best possible world, but they'd lost their way. Without God, they had no moral sense. Could I be an instrument to reintroduce the love of God in this time? I could start with her if she was open to the idea.

"Can I read it?" she asked.

"I'm afraid the only copy I have is in English, and I can't even read it if anyone else is in the room." I thought a moment. "But I have an idea."

I sat in the hallway outside Tish's room with her out of sight and turned up the tablet's volume. Then I read aloud from the psalms. It seemed to help.

We did this a few more times during the following week. In her emotionally wrought state, she was more open.

At the end of the week, we saw Luke and Jessie exit the train from different cars. Luke was downcast. He and Jessie had split up. Cal's warning hadn't lessened the blow. He moped and sulked around the house all weekend. Later, I learned that on the last day of the weekend, Tish was sitting with Luke and suggested he might find some comfort the way she had.

Luke told Cal. Cal told the authorities. I was arrested later that day.

I hadn't been aware until then that settlements had police officers. The officer told me each settlement had someone who performed the duty part-time. He was pleasant enough. When I asked about an attorney, the translator couldn't find a word. Then, I realized this was an entirely different justice system.

I was moved to a settlement three days distant by train, locked in a tiny berthing compartment. Meals were delivered periodically, but I spent the rest of the time in isolation, praying. My tablet had been confiscated, so I couldn't read or speak to anyone.

The settlement I arrived at was part of a hub of settlements that formed this society's capital. Leaving the train station, I was shuttled by two officers directly to an interview room and seated in a bulky, high-backed chair with no ornamentation or cushions. My tablet sat between me and a square-jawed, bulky man on the bare metal table. Even without a uniform, he could only have been a cop.

"You are Don 424."

"No," I corrected, "I'm Donald Marlboro."

"Whatever." He scanned my file on his tablet. "You attempted to indoctrinate a minor child in religion?"

"I'd like to speak to a lawyer—legal counsel."

The translator took almost a minute to generate an equivalent. "We don't have any of those here."

"Then I'll invoke my right not to incriminate myself." This translated reasonably succinctly.

"You don't have one." He looked up. "This is how it works: I ask questions, you answer them. The chair you're sitting in senses if you're telling the truth. If you lie to me or fail to answer the questions, I send you next door, where they shoot you full of a drug that makes you tell me everything I want to know. The only difference is, if you answer me here, you don't wake up in two days with a splitting headache and dry heaves. So now you understand the way it works?"

"I understand."

"Good. I'll repeat the question: You tried to indoctrinate a minor child in religion?"

"Yes. I tried to show her the truth of God."

"Whatever." He made entries on his tablet and handed me mine. "Take this. You'll need it." He stood. "This way." He ushered me into a hallway. The walls had once been beige but were now an indeterminate, worn, sad, dirty color—definitely a police station.

The room he led me to contained a table with a doughnut-shaped scanner loop large enough for a head to fit in. The machine's operator and a guard were the room's only occupants. The operator, a woman in her fifties in a white lab coat, instructed me to lie on the table and secured my head inside the scanner loop. She sat next to me, asking questions about religion. The woman was knowledgeable. After several minutes of this, she stood looking down at me. "I want you to tell me you don't believe in God."

"I can't do that."

"Why?"

"It'd be a lie."

"Don, it's only a lie if you're trying to deceive me, which you aren't, so please tell me you don't believe in God. Try to make it as convincing as possible."

I took a second to prepare myself and did the best I could.

"Good," she said and released me from the scanner. "Come, have a seat." We moved to her desk, another stark, gray, industrial metal style that only a government would procure. "The brain scan was a formality. For someone your age, readjustment seldom works."

That term sent shivers down my spine. "What do you mean by readjustment?"

"It's a series of techniques used to manipulate the brains of individuals who exhibit antisocial behavior. It can range from minor alterations to a complete personality change. The girl you were indoctrinating probably only needs a quick wipe of her short-term memory." I was horrified for Tish but said nothing. "You, on the other hand, have attitudes and beliefs about religion embedded in every part of your brain. Your beliefs are static, unchangeable. Attempting to suppress them would be fatal."

"You're going to imprison me."

The translation took half a minute. She shook her head. "No, we don't have any of those. Minor crimes are handled by public service and shaming. Those who commit serious crimes or show deviant tendencies are readjusted.

Of those who can't be readjusted, violent ones may have to be eliminated, but the non-violent ones, like you, are exiled.

"What you represent is an infectious idea—a destructive concept that can spread wildly among those who, like the young lady, don't have sufficient immunity. Like any plague, we must protect society from it, so we'll quarantine you. We'll send you to a small settlement with others who can't adjust, and the lot of you can farm the land and live out your lives. Don't worry. They're nice people, just stubborn like you. You'll get along just fine."

AND I HAVE. The exile village has some who balked at this society's restrictions, some who are misfits, and the last of the Sufis. They were young men and women when exiled but firm in their faith. The settlement women had handed down the tradition to their daughters, never telling their sons but sometimes converting the men assigned to the settlement. A group of the sons, unhappy at being excluded from their mothers' love, had eventually figured out the secret during an enforced trip back to their home settlement and turned their mothers in to the authorities.

The Sufi elders had died, and the young had grown old in exile. They took me in warmly, made me part of their community, taught me to speak their language, never tried to convert me. We farm, tend goats and make cheese from their milk.

I was offered one of their widows in marriage and accepted. She is the best wife of the three I've had: kind, loving, intuitive. We'll never have children; all exiles are sterilized.

I've grown calm in my exile, contemplating the wonder of God in all things around me. I find peace in it, as do my fellow exiles.

Anthropologists and historians still come to interview me. I cooperate because they bring presents for the community—dried fruit, knives, gardening tools.

Examining the society I time traveled to, I can see it has some advantages over the one I was raised in: the government, while oppressive by my standards, is efficient, meeting the needs and wants of its people and addressing problems with speed and long-term thinking that my government never achieved. Despite the problems that still exist from climate change, their system is stable and prosperous. To attain that efficiency and prosperity, they sacrificed some freedoms and all religion. That is a sacrifice I couldn't make.

I grew to love the family I stayed with. What I perceive through my faith as sin is to them normal, natural and necessary. My hope was to enlighten them but can't condemn them. I can only pray that in the next life, these people will learn the true peace that only God can give and gain salvation.

Report examined. Classified secret.

Stephen Sottong writes Science-Fiction and Fantasy. He is a 2013 winner of Writers of the Future and lives in Northern California behind the Redwood Curtain. A list of his publications is at:

Website: https://www.stephensottong.com

A PROFESSION OF HOPE

BY JANA DENARDO

Kjell Eriksen guided his biofueled motorcycle up to the cabin door. The thought *I am home* hit him like a Derjvik fist. Home hadn't even been an idea in his head before coming to what once had been northern Wisconsin; he had never felt at home. In the several months he'd been living in Sam's cluster of cabins—often more times in Sam's room than his own cabin—Kjell had finally put down roots. *About damn time. You're part tree after all.* A quick check proved Sam wasn't in house, probably down at the lakes managing the algae they extracted the biofuel from. No one was around, not his mother nor grandfather and if anyone was renting a cabin, they were off somewhere.

He threw his travel bag on the bed and changed into shorts and a T-shirt and walked out behind his cabin. Ahead of him sprawled the Funmaker's vast garden. Sam, his mom and grandfather all had parcels in it, growing more types of food than Kjell had dreamed existed, growing up in a Derjvik camp in Madison. The alien invaders had given them nothing but proteinaceous drinks and bars. They were gone for seven years now but Kjell, like a lot of what was left of humanity, were still relearning real food.

The June sun warmed his skin. After the brutal cold of northern Wisconsin —his first—Kjell welcomed the brilliance. He stripped off the shirt, and balled it under his head after stretching out on the grass.

Shutting his eyes, he let the soft sounds of the nearby woods remind him he was home. He had come north to escape his night terrors. Their alien captors were gone but they'd had most of a century practicing genocide and torture. Madison reminded him of what he grew up with and the week-long conference he'd attended brought it all back worse than he imagined it would. A tingling washed up from deep in his skin, lapping at him from head to toe as his body shoved his chloroplasts toward the surface to capture the sun's energy. He'd been modified to make his own food at least enough to keep him alive. The Derjviks had done worse, to far too many.

He'd soak up a little sun, recharge and spend the early evening filling Sam in on everything he'd learned at the conference. The later evening's plans involved a lot less talk and a lot more fun. On that contented note, Kjell drifted off. Something warm and wet planted on his cheek woke him up. He smiled.

"Sam."

"Guess again."

At Sam's amused tone, Kjell jolted fully awake just in time to get dog tongue all over his face. He pushed the chocolate lab back fruitlessly as Berry's tongue flailed frantically in her joy to see him again. He'd been gone forever, after all. "No, Berry! Sto-" The words got cut off as her tongue found his mouth.

"I was going to kiss you hello. Now not so much." Sam pinched up his features in exaggerated disgust.

"Please, I've seen you kiss your dogs on the lips." Kjell started to sit up but a weight on his stomach stopped him. Makade, Sam's enormous black cat, had curled up there. "How long have you been there?"

"I was going to ask you that." Sam gestured to Kjell as Berry flopped on top of Kjell and Makade and he barely escaped a mauling by swarming out from under the enthusiastic animals only to get bowled over by Obsidian, the black lab, racing up to greet him. "Need help?"

"If you can stop laughing long enough." Kjell frowned, catching a glimpse of what prompted the how long question. His skin was the color of spinach. "Wow, how long *was* I sleeping out here?" He rarely let his skin get that much sun. Deep green was not a human color and it bothered people to see it. At least, it bothered him because it was another reminder, he'd been a slave most of his life. *No more. You are so much more now.*

Sam held out his strong hand, his callouses grating against Kjell's skin as he helped him up. He might have been giving Sam a hand around his home but he still had scientist hands. His huge hands might seem better suited to hewing wood and dragging fish from the lake but they spent their days in his lab, being far more dexterous than they looked.

"When Stompin' Tim said the Jolly Green Giant was dead by my garden, I figured I needed to come home early."

Kjell beetled up his brow. "Jolly Green....okay I am a green giant, but I'm not so sure about the jolly part."

Sam snorted. "Tim is a huge history buff. That was a marketing mascot in the Before Times."

"How did Tim even know I was back?"

Pointing around Kjell's right arm, Sam smirked. Kjell's eyes bugged out seeing a sculpture of metal in the garden that hadn't been there before. Tim was easily as tall as he was but built like a mountain of granite and his stomping nickname had been well earned. "Tim's a good artist. Have I mentioned that?"

"No, just that he used to eat the aliens. I *slept* through him putting that there. *How?*"

"You spent a week in a city that is massively triggering for your PTSD and you spent it with Aragon. Time with my brother can tire out the best of us." Sam clapped a hand on Kjell's arm. "Want some strawberry tea?"

"Actually, I think I want to take a short run to burn off all the energy this has given me." He tapped his skin. "Then tea."

"Sounds good. It'll give me time to put together a snack. Take the hounds with you."

"As if they wouldn't follow me anyhow."

Kjell went for his run, cruising along one of the lake shores. Obsidian and Berry followed enthusiastically. Makade came part of the way before remembering he was a cat and cats didn't do anything as dumb as chase after humans. By the time he got home and rinsed off, Sam had the tea and some cheese and crackers sitting on the coffee table. Someone had been preparing for Kjell's return. If anything could be said for Samwise, it was that he was prepared for most things.

"Tell me all about it," Sam instructed, sitting comfortably close to Kjell on the couch.

"It was good. Linda really got into the idea of using the Derjviks methane machinery to capture methane instead of creating it. No matter how we restructure life on Earth there's going to be trash to deal with so using the methane generated will be a boon."

Kjell helped himself to some of the soft cheese from Aragon's farm. "A lot of the ideas that will be implemented aren't universally useful, then again there's not one path to recovering the world from the damage done."

"As attractive as that might be."

"Exactly. Things like the fifteen-minute city, where you're no more than a fifteen minute walk or bike ride from work, home and food would be great in Madison or any other city."

"But useless here. Of course, that's where my biofuels come in. The carbon dioxide they release are mostly taken back up by the algae we get it from, but it's not as carbon-neutral we want it to be." Sam shrugged. "Still better than a lot of things."

"And since I am not great with any tech from the Derjviks because of the bad memories." He rubbed his skin, evidence of what the aliens had done to him and so many others. "I spent some of my time listening to your brother talk about landrace and heritage farming. I agree with him, I think explaining things from a young age and right on up might help people accept why things are being done a new way, that we don't want or need to go back to factory farming, and we don't have to have perfectly shaped and colored fruits and veggies. The ugly misfit ones eat just as well."

Sam nodded. "Been the family philosophy for generations. And I agree, understanding why something needs to be done vs do it or else imperative, should help."

"And since you and Aragon are the live off the land types and not me, I signed up for something I'm pretty excited about."

Sam leaned closer; eyes bright. "Tell me."

"Bioremediation. The Derjviks poisoned so much of our land and water, and let's be honest, humans were just as bad before the invasion. I have some test runs I plan to do here where the toxins aren't so overwhelming. If it works, we'll take it to the cities and the areas that are barely livable."

"Oh fantastic. I want to help if I can."

"I have plans for that too." Kjell stretched and helped himself to another cheese smeared cracker. "I'm taking it as a win that there are multi-country agreements coming out of the meeting to prohibit, or at least restrict, some of our worst pre-invasion bad habits like factory farming and single use plastics, just to name a few."

"It's a start, and I'm circling back to the landrace and heritage farming." Sam leaned forward to shoo his cat away from the cheese plate Makade was eyeing up. "Namid and I cooked up a little something while you and Aragon were down in the city."

Kjell narrowed his eyes, raising his teacup to his lips. Sam conspiring with his sister-in-law might bode evil. "Why does this worry me?"

"We're spending the weekend on the farm." Sam beamed like a kid at a birthday party, something Kjell hadn't experienced before coming here.

He sputtered his tea. "Are you kidding?"

"You sat through lectures on it. You need to *experience* it, lover-boy."

"I did. We went once. A goat screamed at me. I nearly wet myself."

Sam chuckled, deepening Kjell's annoyed glare. "I know. We're still laughing."

He set his tea aside. "And you somehow think I want to repeat this experience."

"You said it yourself. If we educate the people, climate-friendly, sustainable living will be more acceptable. Barring the last six months, your entire exposure to food consisted of protein bars and shakes those fucking aliens forced you to eat, and nothing in the city changed after they were gone. Most of those in the cities are still eating grey-brown goop. You're learning to fish and hunt and garden here. Let's see how you do with chickens, lambs, goats and horses."

"Horribly. That's how I'll do but…." Kjell trailed off, licking his lips nervously. "I'm interested in the natural dyeing techniques your sister-in-law was using and the whole spinning wool thing. Do you think she'd teach me?"

Sam took his hand. "She would be thrilled. And now that I have the highlights of the conference, I want to introduce you to some of the local wildlife and their mating rituals."

Kjell snorted. "That is the cheesiest line yet, much cheesier than those." He pointed to the goat milk spread. "And I've had that introduction. I'm ready for the advanced course."

"I hope you don't think that was any less cheesy." Sam stood and tugged Kjell up after him.

"No, we're completely embarrassing."

"Yep." He stood on tip toe and kissed Kjell. "Let's burn off some of that green energy of yours."

~

KJELL STUDIED Sam and Aragon fixing part of the fence. No one would doubt they were brothers. Both Ojibwe men about six feet tall with straight thick hair so black ravens would be jealous. Both wore it in a plait to mid back and both had coppery skin and cheekbones so high they invited kisses. Namid had done just that before slapping Aragon's flat butt and sending him off to work while she herded her three children as well as their dogs herded the sheep. Goats proved more resistant to herding, to cajoling, to anything resembling sense or sanity.

Contently watching Sam's strong body as he worked—even though they were nearly done—Kjell had no intentions of doing anything else, but Mikom, Sam's youngest nephew, caught hold of his hand and tugged. "Come see the babies!"

The babies proved to be goats a few months old, according to Namid. They regarded him with their slit-pupils, thinking evil thoughts, he had no doubt. All of them were brownish, but some had softer coats and others had something wrong with them.

Kjell pointed to the wrong ones. "What happened to them? They have no ears!"

Namid laughed and scooped one of the earless babies up. "These are American LaManchas. They have ears, see? Little gopher ones, but I'll grant you, they look earless. They are super sweet and they produce a lot of milk so we can make our cheese and yogurt. Go ahead, pet him. He won't bite."

Kjell was less sure, but he stroked the goat's head. It maa-ed at him and he jumped back. Mikom laughed.

"You're so big and he's so little." Mikom shoved Kjell's leg.

"No mocking, son." Namid tapped his head.

Kjell turned from them, spotting a different adult goat with pendulous ears and wicked horns curving back over its head. It was a pretty dark grey. "What's that one then?"

"She's an angora goat. You should see her when she's in wool."

"We have pictures!" Mikom blurted out.

"Speaking of that, I had something I wanted to-"

Something slammed into Kjell's knees taking him down before he could complete his thought. The cloven hooved bastard jumped on his back when he was on the ground and maa-ed straight in his ear to show him who had won this round. Hearing all the laughter, Kjell contemplated becoming one with the ground. Someone rescued him from his goaty overlord and he rolled into a sitting position. Naturally Sam and Aragon had finished fence work in time to see his downfall.

"A baby beat you up." Mikom giggled.

He made a face at him. "Didn't your mother just say no mocking?"

"Yeah, but that might deserve it." Namid fluffed her son's hair.

"Are we *sure* sustainably raising those horned beasts is great for the planet?" He stood up and rubbed his sore knee.

"No, but they are entertaining," Sam replied. "Are you done playing with them? Because Namid has a task for you?"

"Should I worry?" He dusted himself off and glared at his adorable would-be assassin.

"Nah. It'll be fine. Like I said, if you're going to go to conferences to help promote sustainable farming, you should have some skills. Has he asked you his big question yet, Namid?"

"No, he was too busy being defeated by a kid." She laughed and Kjell side-eyed her.

"I *was* interested in the natural dyeing process you use and learning to deal with wool, but if you're just going to mock me...."

"I made you a pie," she interjected, knowing his weakness.

"All is forgiven." Pie healed many wounds, especially the pies Sam's mother and Namid baked up.

"Hold that thought until you see this." Sam slapped Kjell's back lightly.

Aki, her eldest daughter, had a goat on a lead. The brown creature eyed him with criminal intent, Kjell had no doubt. Her swollen teats wobbled as Aki led her up onto a small stage. "Here you go, Mom."

"You can help if you want, Aki. We're teaching Kjell how to milk a goat."

"We're what now?" Kjell widened his eyes. "That sounds like an incredibly daft idea."

"Did you or did you not listen to my brother wax poetically about picking goats for the climate they're in and the idea of which are better milkers, fiber producers or meat?" Sam cocked up his eyebrows at him.

"I mostly listened to the talks on bioremediation and biofuel," Kjell replied, as if that could stave off the inevitable. He was going to have to prove his lack of fear here or get owned by a goat. He knew where his money was.

"It's easy." Namid pulled up a stool and sat by the goat. "Milly here is a calm doe. Yes, we do have milking machines, but again we're talking about keeping farms relatively small and more humane, so it does help to learn how to do this by hand. First." She beckoned to Aki who handed her a bucket. "You give a little squirt and have a look to make sure there's no blood. If there is, the doe has mastitis that requires treatment and rest." She made it seem easy, shooting a little stream into the bucket. She peered into it. "She's good. Just watch my hands for a minute to see how I do it and then we'll switch places."

Namid's hands fell into an easy rhythm working the goat's udder with seemingly no cause for concern on Milly's part. Was she relieved not to be carting around that much milk inside her?

"Aki!" a shout echoed in the air.

Namid sat back, hands on her knees as she turned to her daughter. "You better go see what your brother wants or he'll just keep hollering. Come on up here, Kjell, and I'll walk you through it."

He'd rather go see what Aki's brother wanted, but he obeyed. The stool was not at the best height for Kjell. At 6'7" a lot of things weren't at the best height for him. He tentatively touched Millie's furry side, her warmth sinking into his fingertips.

"You need to start up high on the teat and move your hand down with a bit of a circular motion." Namid milked the air.

Kjell worked his hands against Milly's warm udder, but nothing happened. "I don't think she likes me."

"Don't worry, it takes practice," Sam said. "You don't have the hand movement right."

"What? Start high, move down." He tried it again with the same result.

"No, watch. Use your forefinger and thumb and it's a circular motion. Come on, you can't tell me you haven't milked other things just like this." Namid demonstrated with a lascivious look.

"Namid!" Sam snorted.

Kjell flushed hot, resting his face against Milly's back. The redness of the blush always made the green in his skin go darker, like he was Christmas on legs. *This family!* "Yes," he muttered, getting fuzz against his lips. "I know that motion."

"Then let's pretend you're having a good night in and see what happens."

"Way to make it weird, Namid."

Sam wasn't going to stop laughing any time soon. And it was more weird thinking about milking like some kind of strange hand job but it worked. Milly didn't seem to mind, and he actually got some milk out of her before Namid took over and finished the job.

"See, you managed a goat without dying. Imagine that." Sam hugged him.

"Nearly died of embarrassment. This family…."

"We're the best," Namid said.

"You're something." Kjell snorted. "But it's nice. I don't remember my parents. I doubt anyone in the city does. I was taken away and modified with the chloroplasts before I was weaned."

Sam hugged him harder and Namid piled on.

"Then you need to come here more often and be part of this family," she said. "The kids could always use another uncle. They're still trying to find homes for all the kids in the Derjvik factory orphanages seven years out. I'm thinking of taking in one or two. I'd try to convince this one to adopt, but he's still breaking in a new partner." Namid patted Sam's shoulder.

"I think I'm doing a good job of it, but yes, not sure we're ready for a kid to be tossed into the mix," Sam said. "But if any of us here knows what those kids went through, it's Kjell."

"That's true. Hope and Tim have been talking about mixing a few adoptees into their hoard of kids. That should be…interesting. Okay, do I need to milk another goat or can we talk dyeing?"

"Let's do dyes. This should be right up your alley. A lot of that info was lost or at least hasn't yet been rediscovered, but what did make it through the invasion is really neat. It's all about the chemistry. Ph of the water, the temperature, the humidity all plays a role in what colors you can get, so you can start with the exact same flowers, the same mordant—that's the fixator—and water, but the time of year might change the color."

"That is interesting."

"Come on, let me show you my shed for dye prep. Sam's a big help in this actually."

Kjell eyed his partner. He hadn't known that. "Really?"

"My cranberries can be used for dyes," Sam said as they followed Namid.

She returned Milly to the pasture. "Cranberries give you the expected reds for the most part, and we have walnuts around here too that Sam collects. You'll get browns from that."

"Turns your skin brown too. I know. He had me help hull them."

"Different parts of a plant can give different colors. Dandelion roots are pink while the leaves and flowers give greens and yellows, and of course all of the plant is medicinal."

"Tastes it too." Kjell made a face.

"Ah, wait until you try some of Aragon's dandelion wine, bet you like that."

"I'm always willing to try."

Kjell sat entranced as Namid went through the various plants she had in-house and the way they changed based on the chemicals used in the water bath. She plopped a hunk of unprocessed wool into his hands so he could get a feel for it.

"I'm amazed at how many colors you can get with this."

"The natural colors are usually more muted than artificial, but I think we can learn to live with that rather than returning to dangerous polluting chemicals. Most of the natural dyes are coming from things we already eat so the danger is far more negligible." Namid shrugged. "It's fun to experiment with color. Wool's amphoteric, meaning it can take acidic and basic dyes so you have a wide palette of color. I can start you playing with that. Learning to spin and weave will come later."

"Sounds good. I like this." He hefted the wool. "It's so soft. Aragon had a bit in his talk about how fiber animals *must* be sheared, that it's harmful not to do so."

Namid nodded. "People apparently worried about that in the past, and it's better to point it out to the current generations so it doesn't become a fresh concern. I'll get you spinning and weaving before you know it. Sam won't be of much help though. He's all thumbs."

Sam snorted. "Just expose me."

"He got caught up in the spinning wheel once."

He wrinkled his nose at her. "And that's why we don't wear our long hair loose while spinning." He rubbed the back of Kjell's bare neck. "Not a problem here."

Kjell ran a hand over his short, very pale hair. "No, I toyed with letting it longer but it got annoying in the lab so off with it."

"Too bad, because your hair is fun to play with." Sam grinned.

"I'll keep that in mind. That said, I don't think a man who spun his own hair into the yarn skein should laugh at me for getting beaten up by a goat."

"A kid. You got taken out by a baby. On the other hand, I'm glad it wasn't the adult because you might be too bruised to have fun tonight."

Namid shot them an arched look. "Do I need to remind you there are young children in my house and to keep the noise level down?"

"Not sure how noisy you think we are, but consider us warned." Sam laughed. "She can show you how to spin later. Aragon wants to show us some of the landrace stuff he brought back from the conference, even if it's a bit late in the year to start those seeds. He has plans."

"At least the plants won't attack me, though I did tangle with the raspberry bushes."

"Blackberries are up next and wait until you see the gooseberry bushes. Those are thorny bastards," Sam promised him.

"Splendid." Could he slide out of gooseberry season? Maybe the lab would *really* need him then. Of course, he'd never let Sam fend on his own. He was going to bleed.

ARAGON AND NAMID had a spot of pure beauty on their farm. Kjell loved the gazebo-pier combo that overlooked a sizable pond. They assured him no one fished it and you could swim freely there without fear of hooks, like the kids and some of their friends were doing now. A few of the engineered biolumines-cent trees along with the glowing algae that Sam maintained along with the biofuel ones started to glow as the sun slipped from the sky. Namid assured him that the plants she had chosen for around the gazebo weren't just there for their beauty. Many of them were also supposed to repel biting insects. For his money, he was betting on the carbon dioxide traps to do more.

"You look relaxed," Sam said, sitting next to Kjell's lounger. Aragon and Namid sat to the other side of them.

"I am."

"I worried you might never learn to do that." Sam reached over and took Kjell's hand.

"Me too, truth be told." Gazing over the lake where the kids swam and splashed about playing with a floating ball, Kjell sighed. "I'm still not entirely comfortable with all this space and the sounds in the night, but I'm learning. When I went back to Madison, it felt suffocating and my anxiety rocketed through the roof. Everywhere I looked, I saw the Derjviks. Here…it's better."

"You have no idea how happy it makes me to hear that."

"That goes for all of us and next conference, Sam, you need to go to talk about your algae." Aragon stabbed a finger toward the lantern filled with the glowing stuff. "More people need to hear about this, but more importantly-"

"You know I don't like talking in front of large groups of people." Sam scowled.

"As I was saying, more importantly, your partner could use the support." Aragon inclined his head to Kjell. "Some of the talks got a little rough."

Sam turned startled eyes on Kjell. "You never said."

He sipped his wine—strawberry, not the dandelion as Namid had deemed it not ready yet—before setting the glass aside and answering. "I didn't want you to worry. A few of the talks I might have been better off not attending, but I thought I had insight that was relevant."

"There were some arguments about bioengineering things like our trees." Aragon swept a hand to the luminescent trees. "Or should we keep up the Derjvik processes for altering humans to be autotrophs by giving them chlorophyll, in order to not have to resort to big farms?"

When Sam's expression morphed into one of pure horror, Kjell said quickly, "I pointed out that yes, in theory the sun gives me enough energy to survive, but not necessarily thrive. Even when the Derjviks were here, I still required protein supplements and I still feel hungry. Humans are genetically designed to be omnivores and, without the correct balance, we fall ill. Sunlight alone isn't enough for us. We need an omnivorous or well-balanced vegetarian diet. I'm not so sure I made any impact, but I suppose if they want altered humans, then let them be the ones. There is a plan to restrict it to after the age of consent for the time being." He sucked in a ragged breath. "But it was hard. I don't remember it being done to me, and maybe I'd mind it less if it hadn't been done by *them*. All I know is it stirred up a lot of bad stuff."

"Why didn't you call me? I would have-"

He lifted Sam's hand to his lips and brushed them over his knuckles. "Come all the way down there? No, it's fine. I'm fine. I think we did make ourselves heard. Small sustainable farms, biofuels, working toward cleaning the soil air and water, natural dyes and no going back to single use plastics, no matter how easy that might be."

"I advocated for reestablishing corn, hemp, oat and bamboo fields where it won't overrun the natural ecosystem," Aragon put in. "Corn, hemp and bamboo polymers can be used to make things to eliminate the plastics, and oat is one of the more sustainable milk substitutes, even if it has far less protein."

"Now that the chaos left after the Derjviks has dissipated some, I think we're off to a good start," Kjell said. "And I was fine on my own, so don't worry about that, Sam. That said, I'd love it if you did come next time. You're doing amazing things to improve the carbon capture and carbon neutrality of your biofuels. People should hear about that from you as well as from others in my lab."

Sam nodded. "I'll come with you, promise."

"And if we don't mind, this is making me jittery. Can we talk about something else?" Kjell reached for his wine again.

"Sure, how about we talk about how Aki would like to start an apiary," Aragon said.

"I know next to nothing about bees," Kjell said.

"My niece will fill you in. We should also talk about how, before we leave the farm, you should get a swimming lesson in that pond," Sam said.

Kjell sighed. "I have been putting that off." He shouldn't. He often worked water's edge and would be even more so with the new bioremediation project. "Yes, we're doing that."

"I'll help," Namid said. "Samwise is *not* the most patient of instructors."

"I've noticed." Kjell snorted. "You should see the side eye I got when he taught me to cast a fishing line."

"You should also have seen how many times I nearly got a fishhook to the face." Sam demonstrated his masterful side eye. "I'm an excellent teacher."

"I didn't say you weren't. I said you were impatient. You'll be there. I can't haul your giant of a boyfriend out of the lake if he drowns."

"I feel safer already," Kjell muttered.

"Rethinking that comment about it being better here?" Sam cocked up an eyebrow.

Kjell gazed up at the night sky, not that he needed to think on the answer. "No. When I first came here, I found a home. When I came back, I realized I had found something I've never had before, a family."

Sam leaned over the arms of their loungers and kissed Kjell's cheek.

"You better keep him, Sam. He's sweeter than this wine," Namid laughed.

"He's staying," Sam said decisively.

Yes, he most definitely was.

Jana is Queen of the Geeks (her students voted her in) and her home and office are shrines to any number of comic book and manga heroes along with SF shows and movies too numerous to count. There is no coincidence the love of all things geeky has made its way into many of her stories. To this day, she's still disappointed she hasn't found a wardrobe to another realm, a superhero to take her flying among the clouds or a roguish star ship captain to run off to the stars with her.

Website: http://www.janadenardo.com
Facebook: https://www.facebook.com/jana.denardo/Twitter: https://twitter.com/JanaDenardo

YOU MIGHT ALSO LIKE...

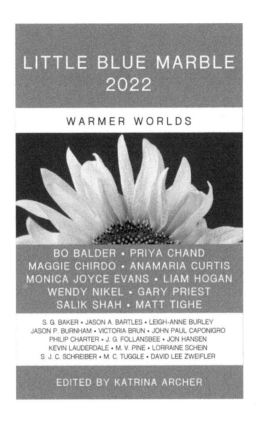

Little Blue Marble 2022: Warmer World

Ganache Media

https://littlebluemarble.ca/anthologies/little-blue-marble-2022/

2022: The last eight years have been the warmest on record.

Little Blue Marble's anthology of speculative climate fiction and poetry from an international slate of authors mourns and hopes in equal measure for the fate of our world and its ecosystems.

May these visions of the future inspire collective action before climate chaos becomes irreversible.

ABOUT OTHER WORLDS INK

Other Worlds Ink (OWI) is the brainchild of author J. Scott Coatsworth and his husband Mark D. Guzman. It's part publisher, part blog tour company, and part author support organization.

We publish the annual Queer Sci Fi flash fiction anthologies, many of Scott's books, and we're now branching out to other things, including this anthology.

We are dedicated to making the world better, now and in the future.

OTHER BOOKS FROM OWI

Queer Sci Fi Flash Fiction Anthologies

Ink | Clarity | Rise (Oct 2023)

———

Writers Save the World Anthologies

Fix the World | Save the World

———

J. Scott Coatsworth's Works

Liminal Sky: Ariadne Cycle

The Stark Divide | The Rising Tide | The Shoreless Sea

Liminal Sky: Redemption Cycle

Dropnauts

Liminal Sky: Tharassas Cycle

The Dragon Eater | The Gauntlet Runner (Sept 2023) | The Hencha Queen (Mar 2024) | The Death Bringer (Sept 2024) | Tales From Tharassas

Liminal Sky: Oberon Cycle

Skythane | Lander | Ithani

Other Sci Fi/Fantasy

Cailleadhama | Homecoming | The Autumn Lands | The Great North | The Last Run | Wonderland

Short Story Collections

Spells & Stardust | Tangents & Tachyons | Androids & Aliens

Contemporary/Magical Realism

Between the Lines | Flames | The River City Chronicles | Slow Thaw

99¢ Shorts

The Emp Test

Audiobooks

Cailleadhama | The Autumn Lands | The River City Chronicles | Dropnauts | Skythane | Lander (2023)

Printed in the USA
CPSIA information can be obtained
at www.ICGtesting.com
LVHW020742150923
758166LV00003B/93

9 781955 778534